Where Life Begins

Choosing Tomorrow, Book 1

Written by Diane Kann

Brought to you by Volans Galaxy Press

Published by Kannceptual Creations LLC

An imprint of Volans Galaxy Press

ISBN: 978-1-971356-42-6

Printed in the United States of America

First Edition, January 2026

Contents

Dedication

For every heart that has known both longing and hope. For the dreamers who believe in gentle love, in honest beginnings, and in the kind of connection that feels like coming home. For those who carry memories, mistakes, and hope all at once, and still dare to open their hearts again.

May this story remind you that some bonds are not broken by distance, some love grows stronger in silence, and some endings are only beginnings in disguise.

Always trust the quiet pull of your heart—and never stop believing in the beauty of choosing love.

CHAPTER ONE

The Arrival at Havenridge

The transport's hum faded, replaced by a profound, almost deafening silence. Mara Quinn stepped onto the polished ferro-concrete of Havenridge, her senses immediately recalibrating. The air, she noted, was unnaturally clean, scrubbed free of the grit and dust that had become an insidious part of existence in the fractured world beyond. It carried a faint, sterile scent, like a hospital ward scrubbed too thoroughly. Her gaze swept over the meticulously planned pathways, the clean, unadorned lines of the buildings that rose with an almost austere elegance. Everything here spoke of order, of precision, of a world painstakingly stitched back together from the unraveling threads of chaos. This was not merely a settlement; it was a statement, a defiant assertion of control against the overwhelming tide of environmental collapse.

She clutched the worn strap of her pack, the worn fabric a familiar, grounding sensation against her palm. Inside, not just her meager possessions, but the weight of everything she had lost. The ghosts of emerald fields, the echo of rain on parched earth, the phantom warmth of a sun unfiltered by smog – these were the specters she carried, the remnants of a life irrevocably altered. Havenridge, with its promise of predictability, its carefully curated environment, was her chosen sanctuary. Here, she hoped, the unpredictable nature of the outside world, the capricium of weather systems gone wild and resources suddenly scarce, would no longer penetrate. It was a shield, a bulwark against the volatility that had nearly consumed them all.

The inhabitants she observed moved with a quiet purpose. Their movements were economical, their interactions muted, almost hesitant. There was a pervasive lack of vibrant color, not just in their functional clothing, but in their very demeanor. Muted grays, soft blues, and earthy browns seemed to be the palette of Havenridge, mirroring the subdued emotional landscape. It was a society that had clearly prioritized survival above all else, where the boisterous laughter of a crowded marketplace or the spontaneous burst of song felt like relics from a forgotten age. This was not merely survival; it was a recalibration of what it meant to be human in a world that had demanded drastic revisions to its operating manual. The very efficiency of the place, its sterile beauty, underscored the value placed on function, on preservation, on a life stripped down to its bare, essential elements. It was a stark contrast to the messy, unpredictable exuberance of the life she had once known, and in that starkness, Mara found a peculiar, almost desperate comfort.

This was the price of safety, she reasoned, and it was a price she was willing to pay.

The architecture of Havenridge was a testament to human ingenuity, a monumental effort born from the desperate desire to impose order upon a world teetering on the precipice of entropy. Mara's initial days were spent absorbing the intricate details of its design, each element meticulously crafted to ensure the community's survival and, more importantly, its stability. Her assigned living quarters, a compact yet functional module, adhered to the same principles: clean lines, utilitarian furniture that served multiple purposes, and a complete absence of superfluous ornamentation. Even the communal spaces were designed with an almost clinical efficiency. The dining hall, for instance, featured long, communal tables arranged with precise spacing, fostering a sense of shared purpose without encouraging undue familiarity. Meals were served on a strict schedule, the nutrient-rich, synthesized sustenance a far cry from the varied, often uncertain fare of the outside.

For Mara, this was not a confinement, but a carefully constructed promise. It was the assurance that life could, indeed, be managed, that unpredictability could be mitigated, that safety was attainable through diligent adherence to a meticulously planned system. She found a quiet solace in the rhythmic pulse of the community: the gentle chime that signaled the transition between scheduled activities, the hum of the air filtration systems, the soft shuffle of feet on the pathways. Each rule, each defined task, each predictable interval, felt like a stone laid firmly upon the shifting sands of her past. These stones formed a foundation, a sturdy platform upon which she could begin to rebuild, brick by painstaking brick, the life that had been so brutally dismantled. The volatile unpredictability that had led to the world's current state seemed a distant, almost abstract concept within these controlled walls. Here, chaos was anathema, a word whispered in hushed tones, a cautionary tale told to children about the dangers of the world beyond their carefully constructed perimeter.

Her exploration of Havenridge continued, each discovery reinforcing the profound commitment to rigorous planning that permeated every aspect of the community. The hydroponic farms, bathed in the soft glow of artificial light, were paragons of efficiency, rows upon rows of nutrient-rich greens and vegetables cultivated with scientific precision. She marveled at the advanced recycling centers, humming with activity as waste was transformed into reusable resources, a closed-loop system designed to minimize any external dependence. The communal learning halls were hushed spaces where knowledge was imparted in structured modules, catering to the practical skills deemed essential for Havenridge's continued existence.

The inhabitants, while not unkind, maintained a distinct reserve. Their interactions were polite, functional, yet devoid of the spontaneous warmth that Mara remembered. There was a subtle, almost imperceptible distance in their eyes, a wariness that suggested a deep-seated understanding of shared fragility. It was a society that had consciously, deliberately, prioritized function over form, survival over the often messy, unpredictable joys of genuine human connection. Mara, however, viewed this as a necessary evolution, a pragmatic, albeit somber, response to existential threats. She embraced the anonymity it offered, the quiet invisibility that allowed her to recede into the background, to observe and learn without drawing undue attention. This, she believed, was the only path forward in a world that had taught her that visibility often meant vulnerability. The controlled environment was not a prison; it was a necessary adaptation, a calculated step towards a future where humanity might finally learn to coexist with a wounded planet, not by dominating it, but by meticulously managing its own existence within its recovering embrace.

Yet, despite the pervasive order, despite the deliberate insulation Havenridge provided, Mara could not entirely escape the phantom echoes of the life that had been lost. Fleeting images would surface without warning: the impossibly vibrant green of a sun-drenched meadow, the clean, sharp scent of pine needles after a spring rain, the cacophony of laughter and bartering from a bustling marketplace. These memories, sharp and poignant, would drift through her mind during quiet moments, often tinged with a profound, aching sadness. She tried to categorize them, to label them as ghosts, as artifacts of a past that had no place in the structured, pragmatic present of Havenridge. They were remnants of a life she had been forced to shed, a skin she had outgrown in her relentless pursuit of security.

But these fragments, these insistent whispers from another time, served as subtle, undeniable reminders of what 'living' had once meant. It wasn't just about breathing, about consuming resources, about maintaining a functional existence. It was about experiencing, about feeling, about the vibrant, messy tapestry of emotions and sensations that had made life not just survivable, but meaningful. The concept of living, in its fullest sense, was something she was slowly, tentatively beginning to distance herself from, acknowledging its beauty but also its inherent danger in a world that demanded such stringent control. The pursuit of security had become a consuming drive, an all-encompassing imperative that overshadowed the very essence of what it meant to truly be alive. The memories, therefore, were not just sorrowful reminders of loss; they were also, in their own quiet way, a nascent form of resistance, a subconscious plea from a part of herself that still yearned for the unmanaged, the untamed, the beautifully imperfect.

As Mara settled into the predictable rhythm of Havenridge, a subtle unease began to stir beneath the placid surface of her carefully constructed existence. It wasn't a disquiet born of external threats or internal turmoil, but a nascent awareness of an unspoken tension, a quiet undercurrent that permeated the community. The order was almost *too* perfect, the conformity a little too uniform. She started to notice the furtive glances exchanged between residents when someone deviated, however slightly, from the expected norms. A hushed conversation would abruptly cease when an authority figure, a designated 'Monitor' or a Council member, approached, leaving an awkward silence in its wake. These were not overt acts of rebellion, but subtle, almost instinctual reactions that hinted at a deeper, more pervasive control.

This undercurrent suggested that the price of their carefully constructed order, the meticulously maintained illusion of safety, might be higher than mere inconvenience or the sacrifice of spontaneous joy. It was a price that might involve the suppression of individual expression, the quiet stifling of dissent, the subtle erosion of personal autonomy. This realization, though still nascent, sparked a question in Mara's mind, a tiny seed of doubt planted in the fertile ground of her newfound security. Was this true safety, this perfectly managed existence, or was it merely a more sophisticated form of imprisonment? The sterile air of Havenridge, once a symbol of its protective strength, now felt perhaps a little too thin, a little too easily compromised, hinting at a fragility that lay not in the external environment, but within the very fabric of their controlled society. The silence, once a balm to her fractured spirit, now seemed to hold its breath, waiting for a ripple that might shatter its carefully maintained composure.

The Lure of Structure

Havenridge presented itself as an answer, a meticulously crafted antidote to the pervasive chaos that had become the defining characteristic of the world beyond its shimmering perimeter. Mara found herself drawn into its elegant, almost austere design, a stark departure from the haphazardness of her previous existence. Her assigned living module, a marvel of efficient engineering, boasted clean, unadorned lines and furniture that seamlessly transitioned between purposes – a table that folded into a wall, a seating unit that concealed storage. There was no wasted space, no extraneous detail, a design philosophy that extended to every corner of the settlement. Communal areas, like the vast dining hall, were designed to foster a sense of shared purpose without encouraging the kind of easy familiarity that could, in Mara's estimation, lead to unpredictable complications. Long, polished tables were spaced with an almost mathematical precision, encouraging a quiet camaraderie born of shared necessity rather than spontaneous affection. Meals, served at strictly appointed times, consisted of nutrient-dense, synthesized sustenance, a far cry from the often meager and unpredictable fare she had grown accustomed to scavenging.

For Mara, this was not a restriction; it was a profound, almost intoxicating, promise. It was the assurance that life, which had felt like a runaway train perpetually on the verge of derailment, could, in fact, be steered. Predictability, once a luxury she had long forgotten, was now the very bedrock of existence. Safety, a concept that had previously felt as elusive as clean air, was now a tangible, attainable goal, achievable through diligent adherence to a system designed for optimal survival. She discovered a quiet solace in the rhythmic pulse of Havenridge. The gentle, resonant chime that signaled the transition between scheduled activities – from work shifts in the hydroponic farms to communal learning sessions – became a comforting anchor. The constant, unobtrusive hum of the air filtration systems, a testament to their advanced environmental controls, was a lullaby of security. The soft, rhythmic shuffle of feet on the meticulously maintained pathways, each step measured and purposeful, all contributed to a symphony of order. Each rule, each defined task, each predictable interval, felt like a stone laid firmly upon the shifting, treacherous sands of her past. These stones, she believed, were forming a foundation, a sturdy platform upon which she could begin, brick by painstaking brick, to rebuild the life that had been so brutally dismantled by the capricities of the outside world. The volatile unpredictability that had led to the world's current state, the erratic weather patterns, the resource wars, the societal breakdowns, seemed like a distant, almost abstract concept within these controlled walls. Here, chaos was not merely undesirable; it was anathema, a word whispered in hushed tones, a cautionary tale reserved for children, a stark reminder of the dangers that lay beyond their carefully constructed, meticulously managed perimeter.

Her days settled into a pattern, a rhythm that mirrored the structured existence of Havenridge itself. Mornings began with the gentle chime, signaling the start of her assigned work shift. Today, it was the hydroponic farms, vast, cavernous spaces bathed in the soft, perpetual glow of full-spectrum grow lights. Rows upon rows of nutrient-rich greens and vegetables stretched out before her, each plant meticulously cultivated, its growth monitored by unseen sensors and sophisticated algorithms. She learned to calibrate the nutrient dispensers, to identify the subtle signs of nutrient deficiency or pest infestation, her hands moving with a growing efficiency that belied her initial apprehension. The work was not strenuous, but it was precise, demanding a level of focus that kept the ghosts of the past at bay. The air in the farm was humid and carried the faint, earthy scent of growing things, a welcome contrast to the sterile air of her living quarters. It was a controlled environment, of course, the humidity and temperature precisely regulated, but it felt alive, a vibrant testament to the human capacity to nurture life even in the most challenging of circumstances.

After her shift, there was the communal meal. She found a quiet spot at one of the long tables, observing the interactions around her. Conversations were muted, polite, and largely focused on the day's work or the scheduled activities. There were no boisterous outbursts, no lingering laughter that might disrupt the prevailing atmosphere of calm. The food, a creamy, protein-rich paste flavored with synthesized spices, was palatable and undeniably filling. It lacked the vibrant flavors and textures of real food – the crispness of a fresh apple, the tangy zest of a sun-ripened tomato – but it provided the essential nutrients her body craved, a testament to Havenridge's commitment to functional sustenance. She ate slowly, deliberately, allowing the quiet murmur of conversation and the gentle clinking of utensils to wash over her. It was in these moments, surrounded by the quiet hum of collective existence, that the promise of Havenridge felt most potent. This was a society that had learned from the mistakes of the past, a society that understood the fragility of life and had dedicated itself to its preservation through meticulous planning and unwavering discipline.

In the afternoons, Mara participated in the communal learning sessions. Today, the topic was advanced resource management, a crucial subject in a world where scarcity had driven so much conflict. The instructor, a woman named Elara with sharp eyes and an even sharper intellect, spoke with an almost reverent tone about the intricate systems that governed Havenridge's closed-loop resource economy. She explained the advanced recycling centers, where every scrap of waste was broken down and repurposed, minimizing the need for external input. She detailed the water purification systems, capable of transforming even the most contaminated sources into potable water, a precious commodity. Mara listened intently, absorbing the information, impressed by the sheer ingenuity and foresight that had gone into building this self-sustaining community. It was a stark contrast to the wasteful, consumerist culture of the past, a culture that had ultimately led to the environmental degradation that had brought them to this point. Havenridge was a living embodiment of a new philosophy, one that valued conservation, efficiency, and the collective good above all else.

The inhabitants themselves, while not unkind, maintained a distinct reserve. Their interactions were polite, functional, yet devoid of the spontaneous warmth that Mara remembered from her former life. There was a subtle, almost imperceptible distance in their eyes, a wariness that suggested a deep-seated understanding of shared fragility, a collective trauma that had bonded them in ways that went beyond superficial pleasantries. It was a society that had consciously, deliberately, prioritized function over form, survival over the often messy, unpredictable joys of genuine human connection. Mara, however, viewed this as a necessary evolution, a pragmatic, albeit somber, response to existential threats. She embraced the anonymity it offered, the quiet invisibility that allowed her to recede into the background, to observe and learn without drawing undue attention. This, she believed, was the only path forward in a world that had taught her that visibility often meant vulnerability. The controlled environment was not a prison; it was a necessary adaptation, a calculated step towards a future where humanity might finally learn to coexist with a wounded planet, not by dominating it, but by meticulously managing its own existence within its recovering embrace.

Yet, despite the pervasive order, despite the deliberate insulation Havenridge provided, Mara could not entirely escape the phantom echoes of the life that had been lost. Fleeting images would surface without warning, unbidden and potent. The impossibly vibrant green of a sun-drenched meadow, the clean, sharp scent of pine needles after a spring rain, the cacophony of laughter and bartering from a bustling marketplace – these memories, sharp and poignant, would drift through her mind during quiet moments, often tinged with a profound, aching sadness. She tried to categorize them, to label them as ghosts, as artifacts of a past that had no place in the structured, pragmatic present of Havenridge. They were remnants of a life she had been forced to shed, a skin she had outgrown in her relentless pursuit of security.

But these fragments, these insistent whispers from another time, served as subtle, undeniable reminders of what 'living' had once meant. It wasn't just about breathing, about consuming resources, about maintaining a functional existence. It was about experiencing, about feeling, about the vibrant, messy tapestry of emotions and sensations that had made life not just survivable, but meaningful. The concept of living, in its fullest sense, was something she was slowly, tentatively beginning to distance herself from, acknowledging its beauty but also its inherent danger in a world that demanded such stringent control. The pursuit of security had become a consuming drive, an all-encompassing imperative that overshadowed the very essence of what it meant to truly be alive. The memories, therefore, were not just sorrowful reminders of loss; they were also, in their own quiet way, a nascent form of resistance, a subconscious plea from a part of herself that still yearned for the unmanaged, the untamed, the beautifully imperfect.

As Mara settled deeper into the predictable rhythm of Havenridge, a subtle unease began to stir beneath the placid surface of her carefully constructed existence. It wasn't a disquiet born of external threats or internal turmoil, but a nascent awareness of an unspoken tension, a quiet undercurrent that seemed to permeate the very fabric of the community. The order was almost *too* perfect, the conformity a little too uniform, like a painting where every brushstroke was flawlessly applied but lacked a certain soul. She started to notice the furtive glances exchanged between residents when someone deviated, however slightly, from the expected norms. A hushed conversation would abruptly cease when an authority figure, a designated 'Monitor' or a Council member, approached, leaving an awkward, almost palpable silence in its wake. These were not overt acts of rebellion, not grand gestures of defiance, but subtle, almost instinctual reactions that hinted at a deeper, more pervasive form of control. It was as if the community operated under an unspoken agreement, a collective understanding that straying from the designated path was not merely discouraged, but inherently dangerous.

This undercurrent suggested that the price of their carefully constructed order, the meticulously maintained illusion of safety, might be higher than mere inconvenience or the sacrifice of spontaneous joy. It was a price that might involve the suppression of individual expression, the quiet stifling of dissent, the subtle erosion of personal autonomy. The very efficiency that had drawn her to Havenridge now seemed to have a sharper edge. The smooth, unblemished surfaces of the buildings, the meticulously curated green spaces, the predictable routines – they all began to feel less like deliberate design and more like a subtle, pervasive cage. This realization, though still nascent, sparked a question in Mara's mind, a tiny seed of doubt planted in the fertile ground of her newfound security. Was this true safety, this perfectly managed existence, or was it merely a more sophisticated form of imprisonment? The sterile air of Havenridge, once a symbol of its protective strength, now felt perhaps a little too thin, a little too easily compromised, hinting at a fragility that lay not in the external environment, but within the very fabric of their controlled society. The silence, once a balm to her fractured spirit, now seemed to hold its breath, waiting for a ripple, a tremor, a single, discordant note that might shatter its carefully maintained composure. She found herself constantly scanning the faces of the people around her, searching for any sign of genuine emotion beneath the placid surface, any flicker of rebellion or discontent, but she found only a carefully cultivated equanimity. It was a disquieting thought, the possibility that in escaping the chaos of the outside world, she might have unknowingly walked into a gilded cage, where freedom was merely an illusion, a carefully constructed narrative designed to keep them compliant. The lure of structure, she was beginning to understand, could be as seductive as it was restrictive.

The air within Havenridge was a constant, gentle caress, meticulously filtered and calibrated to an optimal seventy-two degrees Fahrenheit. Mara had found herself breathing it in deeply during her initial days, a stark contrast to the often acrid or dust-laden air she had grown accustomed to in the settlements and scavenged territories beyond the shimmering perimeter. This controlled atmosphere, she'd reasoned, was a fundamental component of the sanctuary's promise: a bulwark against the unpredictable environmental assaults that had plagued the rest of the world. The hydroponic farms, where she spent her allocated work shifts, were a testament to this commitment. Vast, cathedral-like spaces, they hummed with an almost reverent quiet, punctuated only by the soft whir of automated nutrient delivery systems and the rhythmic drip of purified water. Rows upon rows of verdant growth stretched out under the unblinking gaze of full-spectrum lights, a vibrant, almost defiant display of life cultivated against all odds. She learned the delicate art of calibrating the nutrient dispensers, her fingers, once accustomed to the rough texture of salvaged metal, now moved with a surprising dexterity over the smooth, responsive controls. She could identify, with growing confidence, the subtle yellowing of a leaf that signaled a deficiency, or the faint, almost imperceptible pattern of webbing that might indicate an early infestation. Each task, though seemingly mundane, was a step towards understanding the intricate machinery that sustained Havenridge, a tangible contribution to its enduring promise of survival. The faint, earthy aroma of growing things, though subtly different from the wild, untamed scents of the natural world, was a comforting presence, a reminder that life, in its most essential form, was still being nurtured here.

Beyond the farms, the recycling centers pulsed with a ceaseless, understated energy. They were the beating heart of Havenridge's closed-loop economy, a place where nothing was truly wasted. Mara had witnessed the process firsthand during a brief, mandatory orientation: hulking automatons, their metallic limbs moving with practiced efficiency, sorted and processed every discarded item, from the smallest food scrap to the worn-out components of aging machinery. Here, the concept of 'waste' was a relic of a bygone era, a symbol of the profligacy that had led to the world's current state. Each atom, each molecule, was meticulously reclaimed, broken down, and repurposed, a testament to a profound understanding of resource scarcity. The hum of the machinery was a constant, low thrum, a symphony of efficiency that spoke of a society that had learned, perhaps too late, the true value of every single element. It was a system designed not just for survival, but for sustainability, a long-term vision that prioritized the careful stewardship of limited resources. This was not merely about living; it was about enduring, about ensuring that the generations to come would inherit a world that could still support life, however carefully managed.

The communal learning halls, when not in use for work-related training, became spaces for broader enlightenment. Today, the topic was advanced ecological restoration, a subject that resonated deeply with Mara, given the scarred and wounded planet that lay beyond Havenridge's protective dome. The instructor, a woman named Lyra with kind eyes and a voice that carried a quiet authority, spoke of bio-engineered mosses designed to break down toxic residues, of airborne drones that seeded barren landscapes with resilient flora, and of sophisticated atmospheric scrubbers that worked in concert with natural processes to heal the ravaged skies. She illustrated her points with holographic projections that depicted once-desolate regions slowly, painstakingly, being coaxed back to life, a visual narrative of hope and resilience. Mara found herself leaning forward, captivated by the sheer ingenuity and the unwavering optimism that permeated Lyra's presentation. It was a stark counterpoint to the constant narratives of decay and collapse she had encountered in her previous life. Here, within the controlled environment of Havenridge, the focus was on rebuilding, on healing, on a conscious, deliberate effort to mend what had been broken. It was a powerful testament to humanity's capacity for adaptation and innovation, a belief that even in the face of overwhelming devastation, the will to survive, and even to thrive, could prevail.

The inhabitants of Havenridge, as Mara had observed, were a study in polite reserve. They moved through their days with a quiet grace, their interactions governed by a code of conduct that emphasized efficiency and mutual respect, but rarely ventured into the realm of genuine warmth. Greetings were brief, functional, often accompanied by a subtle nod of acknowledgment rather than an extended conversation. Mealtimes in the vast, meticulously organized dining hall were marked by a hushed murmur of polite discourse, the clinking of cutlery a soft counterpoint to the measured rhythm of their eating. There were no boisterous laughter, no spontaneous outbursts of joy, no lingering embraces that spoke of deep affection. It was a society that had, it seemed, deliberately pruned away the excesses of emotional expression, deeming them inefficient, perhaps even dangerous, in a world that demanded such stringent control. They were polite, certainly, and never overtly unkind, but there was an undeniable distance in their interactions, a subtle, almost imperceptible barrier that discouraged true intimacy. Their eyes, when they met hers, often held a flicker of recognition, a shared understanding of the precariousness of their existence, but rarely a spark of personal curiosity or genuine connection. It was as if they had collectively agreed to prioritize function over form, survival over the often messy, unpredictable, and time-consuming intricacies of deep human relationships.

Mara, however, did not view this as a failing. In fact, she saw it as a necessary evolution, a pragmatic, albeit somber, response to the existential threats that had forced humanity to seek refuge within these walls. The chaos, the violence, the sheer unpredictability of the world outside had taught her that vulnerability often lay in emotional entanglement, in the messy, untidy business of caring for and being cared for. Here, in Havenridge, she could finally shed that burden. The anonymity it offered was a balm to her fractured spirit, a shield that allowed her to observe, to learn, and to exist without the constant fear of exposure, of being targeted, of being hurt. She could blend into the meticulously ordered landscape, a shadow among shadows, her past a carefully guarded secret, her presence unremarkable. This, she believed, was the only path forward in a world that had taught her, through harsh and brutal lessons, that visibility often meant vulnerability. Havenridge, with its carefully cultivated order and its emphasis on function, was not a prison, but a necessary adaptation, a calculated step towards a future where humanity might finally learn to coexist with a wounded planet, not by dominating it, but by meticulously managing its own existence within its recovering embrace. The controlled environment was a deliberate choice, a conscious sacrifice of the ephemeral for the enduring.

The predictable rhythm of Havenridge, the carefully orchestrated flow of her days, had initially been a source of profound relief. It was the antithesis of the erratic, survival-driven existence she had endured for so long. The gentle chime that signaled the transition between scheduled activities – from her shifts in the hydroponic farms to the communal learning sessions, to the shared meals – was a comforting anchor in the swirling currents of her past. The constant, unobtrusive hum of the air filtration systems, a testament to their advanced environmental controls, was a lullaby of security, a promise that the air she breathed was clean and safe. The soft, rhythmic shuffle of feet on the meticulously maintained pathways, each step measured and purposeful, all contributed to a symphony of order that soothed her jangled nerves. Each rule, each defined task, each predictable interval, felt like a stone laid firmly upon the shifting, treacherous sands of her past. These stones, she believed, were forming a foundation, a sturdy platform upon which she could begin, brick by painstaking brick, to rebuild the life that had been so brutally dismantled by the capricities of the world beyond.

Yet, as days bled into weeks, and the initial novelty of sanctuary began to wear off, a subtle, almost imperceptible shift occurred within Mara. It was not a sudden epiphany, but a gradual dawning, a growing awareness of an unspoken tension that seemed to permeate the very fabric of the community. The order was, she began to notice, almost *too* perfect. The conformity was a little too uniform, like a meticulously crafted imitation that, upon closer inspection, lacked the subtle imperfections that made the original real. She found herself observing the fleeting, furtive glances exchanged between residents when someone deviated, however slightly, from the expected norms. A hushed conversation would abruptly cease, heads would snap up, and a palpable silence would descend the moment an authority figure, a designated 'Monitor' or a member of the ruling Council, approached. These were not overt acts of rebellion, not grand gestures of defiance, but subtle, almost instinctual reactions that hinted at a deeper, more pervasive form of control. It was as if the community operated under an unspoken agreement, a collective understanding that straying from the designated path was not merely discouraged, but inherently dangerous.

This undercurrent suggested that the price of their carefully constructed order, the meticulously maintained illusion of safety, might be higher than mere inconvenience or the sacrifice of spontaneous joy. It was a price that might involve the suppression of individual expression, the quiet stifling of dissent, the subtle erosion of personal autonomy. The very efficiency that had drawn her to Havenridge now seemed to possess a sharper edge. The smooth, unblemished surfaces of the buildings, the meticulously curated green spaces, the predictable routines – they all began to feel less like deliberate design and more like a subtle, pervasive cage. This realization, though still nascent, sparked a question in Mara's mind, a tiny seed of doubt planted in the fertile ground of her newfound security. Was this true safety, this perfectly managed existence, or was it merely a more sophisticated form of imprisonment? The sterile air of Havenridge, once a symbol of its protective strength, now felt perhaps a little too thin, a little too easily compromised, hinting at a fragility that lay not in the external environment, but within the very fabric of their controlled society. The silence, once a balm to her fractured spirit, now seemed to hold its breath, waiting for a ripple, a tremor, a single, discordant note that might shatter its carefully maintained composure. She found herself constantly scanning the faces of the people around her, searching for any sign of genuine emotion beneath the placid surface, any flicker of rebellion or discontent, but she found only a carefully cultivated equanimity. It was a disquieting thought, the possibility that in escaping the chaos of the outside world, she might have unknowingly walked into a gilded cage, where freedom was merely an illusion, a carefully constructed narrative designed to keep them compliant. The lure of structure, she was beginning to understand, could be as seductive as it was restrictive. It was a structure built not just on physical walls and advanced technology, but on the invisible architecture of social conformity and a carefully curated fear of the unknown. The very order that had promised solace now seemed to whisper a different kind of warning: that the absence of chaos did not automatically equate to the presence of freedom.

The sterile air of Havenridge, meticulously scrubbed and precisely tempered, had become Mara's new normal. It was a constant, silent testament to the sanctuary's promise: a world shielded from the harsh realities that had reshaped the planet. She had learned to appreciate its predictability, its absence of the acrid bite of pollutants or the gritty texture of pervasive dust. This controlled atmosphere was a fundamental component of the haven's design, a deliberate barrier against the environmental chaos that had driven humanity to seek refuge. Her days were structured around the hydroponic farms, vast, cathedral-like spaces where life was coaxed from nutrient solutions under the unwavering glow of full-spectrum lights. The rhythmic hum of automated systems and the soft drip of purified water formed a constant, almost meditative soundtrack. She found a quiet satisfaction in the work, calibrating nutrient dispensers, her fingers, once roughened by the demands of scavenging, now moved with an unexpected grace over the smooth controls. Identifying the subtle signs of nutrient deficiency or the faint whisper of an insect infestation became a small victory, a tangible contribution to the intricate machinery of survival. The faint, earthy aroma that filled the farms, though manufactured, was a comforting presence, a reminder that life, in its most basic form, was still being nurtured.

The recycling centers were another marvel of Havenridge's self-sufficiency, a testament to a society that had learned to wring every last drop of utility from its resources. Hulking automatons, efficient and tireless, sorted and processed every discarded item, transforming what would have been waste in the old world into raw materials for new beginnings. The concept of 'waste' was a historical footnote here, a symbol of the profligacy that had nearly undone them. The low thrum of the machinery was a constant, underlying pulse, a symphony of efficiency that spoke of a profound understanding of scarcity. It was a system built not just for survival, but for endurance, a long-term vision that prioritized the careful stewardship of limited resources.

In the communal learning halls, topics like advanced ecological restoration offered glimpses of a world slowly, painstakingly, being healed. Lyra, the instructor with kind eyes and a voice of quiet authority, spoke of bio-engineered mosses that consumed toxins, drones that seeded barren lands, and atmospheric scrubbers working in concert with nature. Holographic projections displayed scenes of desolate regions slowly regenerating, a visual narrative of hope that stood in stark contrast to the narratives of decay Mara had known. It was a powerful testament to humanity's capacity for adaptation, a belief that even in the face of overwhelming devastation, the will to survive and thrive could prevail.

The inhabitants of Havenridge moved with a polite reserve, their interactions governed by a code of conduct that emphasized efficiency and mutual respect. Greetings were brief, functional nods. Mealtimes in the dining hall were punctuated by a hushed murmur of polite discourse, the clinking of cutlery a soft counterpoint to measured eating. There was no boisterous laughter, no spontaneous joy, no lingering embraces. It was a society that seemed to have deliberately pruned away the excesses of emotional expression, deeming them inefficient, perhaps even dangerous. They were never unkind, but a subtle, almost imperceptible barrier discouraged true intimacy. Their eyes, when they met Mara's, often held a flicker of recognition, a shared understanding of their precarious existence, but rarely a spark of personal curiosity. It was as if they had collectively agreed to prioritize function over form, survival over the messy intricacies of deep human relationships.

Mara, however, didn't view this as a failing. She saw it as a necessary evolution, a pragmatic response to the existential threats that had driven them to seek refuge. The chaos, the violence, the unpredictability of the world outside had taught her that vulnerability often lay in emotional entanglement. Here, in Havenridge, she could shed that burden. The anonymity it offered was a balm to her fractured spirit, a shield that allowed her to observe, to learn, and to exist without the constant fear of exposure. She could blend into the meticulously ordered landscape, a shadow among shadows, her past a carefully guarded secret. Havenridge, with its carefully cultivated order, was not a prison, but a necessary adaptation, a calculated step towards a future where humanity might learn to coexist with a wounded planet not by dominating it, but by meticulously managing its own existence.

The predictable rhythm of Havenridge had initially been a source of profound relief, an antithesis to the erratic, survival-driven existence she had endured. The gentle chime that signaled transitions between activities, the constant, unobtrusive hum of the air filtration systems, the soft shuffle of feet on meticulously maintained pathways – it all contributed to a symphony of order that soothed her jangled nerves. Each rule, each defined task, each predictable interval felt like a stone laid firmly upon the shifting sands of her past, forming a foundation upon which she could begin to rebuild.

Yet, as days bled into weeks, a subtle shift occurred. The order, she began to notice, was almost *too* perfect. The conformity was a little too uniform, like a meticulously crafted imitation lacking the subtle imperfections of the real. She found herself observing fleeting, furtive glances exchanged when someone deviated, however slightly, from the expected norms. Conversations would cease abruptly, heads would snap up, and a palpable silence would descend the moment an authority figure approached. These were not overt acts of rebellion, but subtle, almost instinctual reactions that hinted at a deeper, more pervasive form of control. It was as if the community operated under an unspoken agreement that straying from the designated path was inherently dangerous. This undercurrent suggested that the price of their carefully constructed order might be higher than mere inconvenience. It was a price that might involve the suppression of individual expression, the quiet stifling of dissent, the subtle erosion of personal autonomy.

The very efficiency that had drawn her to Havenridge now seemed to possess a sharper edge. The smooth surfaces, the curated green spaces, the predictable routines – they all began to feel less like deliberate design and more like a subtle, pervasive cage. This realization, though nascent, sparked a question: Was this true safety, or merely a more sophisticated form of imprisonment? The sterile air, once a symbol of protective strength, now felt a little too thin, hinting at a fragility that lay not in the external environment, but within the very fabric of their controlled society.

The silence, once a balm, now seemed to hold its breath, waiting for a ripple, a tremor, a discordant note that might shatter its carefully maintained composure. She found herself scanning faces, searching for any sign of genuine emotion beneath the placid surface, but found only carefully cultivated equanimity. The thought was disquieting: in escaping the chaos of the outside world, had she unknowingly walked into a gilded cage, where freedom was an illusion?

The lure of structure, she was beginning to understand, could be as seductive as it was restrictive, built not just on walls and technology, but on the invisible architecture of social conformity and a curated fear of the unknown. The order that had promised solace now whispered a different warning: that the absence of chaos did not automatically equate to the presence of freedom.

One cycle, during a rare moment of unscheduled respite, Mara found herself by one of the vast observation windows that offered a controlled glimpse of the world beyond Havenridge's shimmering dome. The sky was a bruised, perpetual twilight, the landscape a tapestry of muted browns and grays, scarred and worn by centuries of ecological neglect. Yet, it was not the desolation that held her gaze, but the phantom landscapes that flickered at the edges of her vision. A sudden, inexplicable urge washed over her, a visceral longing that had nothing to do with the meticulously cultivated beauty of Havenridge's interior. She saw, with a clarity that stole her breath, a rolling expanse of emerald green, impossibly vibrant, stretching to a horizon so vast it felt infinite. It was a field, she knew, a place where the wind whispered secrets through tall grasses, a place where sunlight, unfiltered and warm, kissed the earth.

The scent of rain on dry soil, a scent she hadn't consciously recalled in years, bloomed in her memory, so potent it felt as if she could taste it on her tongue. It was the smell of life, raw and untamed, a stark contrast to the sterile, recycled air of her present. And then, the sound: a cascade of boisterous laughter, the joyful cacophony of a marketplace teeming with people, a vibrant symphony of voices raised in commerce and camaraderie. It was a sound so rich, so full of life, it made the quiet hum of Havenridge feel like a muffled echo. These were not mere memories; they were apparitions, spectral remnants of a life she had deliberately buried, artifacts of a past that had no place in the structured, predictable present she had so painstakingly built.

She recognized them for what they were – ghosts. They were the spectral echoes of a world that no longer existed, and perhaps, never truly existed as she remembered it. The fields, she suspected, were likely long gone, swallowed by the encroaching desolation. The rain, if it fell at all, was probably acidic, a corrosive tear from a wounded sky. And the marketplaces... well, the very idea of such vibrant, public gatherings felt like a dangerous anachronism in a world that had learned to fear proximity.

Yet, despite their spectral nature, these phantom images and scents served as subtle, insistent reminders of what 'living' once meant. It was a concept Mara was slowly, deliberately, beginning to distance herself from, a concept that seemed antithetical to the security she now pursued. To 'live' had once meant embracing the unpredictable, the messy, the vibrant chaos of existence. It had meant feeling the sun on her skin, breathing in the scent of the earth after a storm, sharing in the uninhibited joy of human connection. It had meant risk, and vulnerability, and an openness that Havenridge had taught her was a luxury she could no longer afford.

She acknowledged these remnants with a profound, almost aching sadness. They were the ghosts of a life she had lost, and in acknowledging them, she felt a pang of grief for the person she had been, the person who had once reveled in such simple, wild things. But then, the ingrained discipline of Havenridge asserted itself. She compartmentalized the feelings, pushing the images and scents to the back of her mind, labeling them as 'irrelevant data.' They were distractions, vestiges of a past that threatened to undermine the carefully constructed present. They were artifacts, nothing more, and artifacts belonged in museums, not in the living, breathing reality of Havenridge.

The logic was sound, almost undeniable. To dwell on what was lost was to invite the very instability she had escaped. The pursuit of security demanded a pruning of the past, a conscious effort to sever ties with the emotions and experiences that could weaken her resolve. Havenridge offered a meticulously crafted survival, a life devoid of the sharp edges of raw emotion, a life where danger was a theoretical construct rather than a tangible threat. This was the trade-off, the necessary sacrifice for enduring.

Still, as she turned away from the window, the phantom scent of rain lingered, a faint, almost imperceptible whisper against the sterile perfection of the air. The echo of laughter seemed to resonate in the quiet efficiency of the corridors. These ghosts, she realized, were not entirely banished. They were woven into the fabric of her being, subtle reminders of a concept called 'living' that Havenridge, for all its safety, could never truly replicate. They were the whispers of a life she had known, and perhaps, a life she might, in some distant, unimaginable future, rediscover.

For now, however, they were simply echoes, fading but persistent, a counterpoint to the controlled quietude of her sanctuary. She filed them away, these spectral remnants, acknowledging their existence but refusing to let them dictate her present. Havenridge was her present, her future, and the echoes of the outside, however poignant, were now just that – echoes. She breathed in the filtered air, a conscious act of acceptance, and turned towards the scheduled rhythm of her day, the ghost of a smile touching her lips. It was not a smile of joy, but a smile of profound, hard-won pragmatism. The world outside was a memory, and memory, she had learned, could be a dangerous thing to hold onto too tightly.

The meticulously calibrated environment of Havenridge, once a source of profound relief, was beginning to feel... different. Mara found herself noticing things she'd previously overlooked, small fissures in the polished veneer of their ordered existence. It wasn't a sudden revelation, more like a slow-blooming awareness, akin to the subtle unfurling of leaves on one of the hydroponic plants she tended. The predictable rhythms, the gentle chimes, the hushed efficiency—these were the very elements that had drawn her in, promising a sanctuary from the chaotic world outside. But now, an almost imperceptible dissonance hummed beneath the surface, a low frequency that vibrated just beyond the edge of conscious perception.

It manifested in the way conversations would falter and die the moment she entered a communal space, a collective inhale of stillness before the polite, measured discourse resumed. It was in the fleeting, almost imperceptible glances exchanged between individuals when someone, for the briefest of moments, strayed from the expected path. A misplaced step on a designated walkway, a slightly longer pause before a prescribed mealtime, a lingering gaze fixed on one of the observation windows a fraction too long—these minor deviations seemed to trigger a silent, communal recalibration, a subtle tightening of the reins. No one ever spoke of it, no disciplinary measures were visibly enacted, yet the effect was undeniable. It was as if the very air in Havenridge held a collective breath, waiting for any hint of anomaly to be swiftly, silently, corrected.

Mara's past had been a brutal education in survival, in reading the subtle cues of danger, the flicker of intent in a stranger's eyes, the tension in a hunched shoulder. These were the instincts she had tried to suppress, deeming them irrelevant in this haven of enforced tranquility. Yet, they were resurfacing, reawakening to the subtler, more insidious forms of control that seemed to permeate Havenridge. It wasn't the overt oppression of a dictator, but something far more pervasive: a societal conditioning so deeply ingrained that it bordered on instinct. The inhabitants, she realized, were not just following rules; they were *being* the rules, their movements and interactions choreographed to an invisible, unspoken score.

She recalled her initial assessment of their politeness, their reserve. Now, she saw it not as a chosen mode of conduct, but as a carefully maintained façade. Beneath the smooth surface of their interactions lay a network of subtle pressures, a collective policing that discouraged individuality as much as it abhorred waste. The efficiency she had admired now seemed to possess a sharper edge, the meticulous order a more claustrophobic quality. It was the quiet efficiency of a well-oiled machine that had no room for unexpected parts, no tolerance for friction.

One cycle, while working in the nutrient processing sector, she overheard a snippet of conversation that prickled her senses. Two technicians, their faces illuminated by the soft glow of their monitors, were discussing the latest atmospheric recalibration. Their voices were low, almost conspiratorial, and when Mara's footsteps approached, they abruptly ceased, their heads swiveling towards her with an unnerving synchronicity.

"Just... fine-tuning the CO2 scrubbers, Mara," one of them, a man named Silas, said, his voice a little too casual, his smile a touch too fixed.

"Everything's within optimal parameters," the other, Elara, added, her eyes darting back to her screen as if her attention had never wavered.

Mara nodded, a polite smile mirroring theirs. "Good to know. Efficiency is key." She moved on, the hum of the machinery suddenly sounding less like a testament to progress and more like a muffled heartbeat, its rhythm dictated by an unseen conductor. The ease with which they had shut down their conversation, the immediate assumption of her scrutiny, spoke volumes. They weren't just concerned with external threats; they were vigilant against internal deviations, against anything that might disrupt the delicate balance.

Later that cycle, during her assigned reflection period in the communal lounge, Mara observed a young woman, no older than herself, sketching in a small, worn notebook. The woman's brow was furrowed in concentration, her hand moving with an artist's fluidity. Mara, still processing the earlier encounter, found herself watching her, a flicker of curiosity stirring within her. The woman was drawing, not the functional schematics of hydroponic systems or the precise diagrams of recycling protocols, but something... organic. Swirls and lines that hinted at natural forms, a flower perhaps, or a bird. It was a private act, unobtrusive, yet Mara felt a prickle of unease. This was not a sanctioned activity. Personal expression, beyond the strictly utilitarian, seemed to be a luxury not readily afforded in Havenridge.

Suddenly, the soft chime indicating the end of reflection period echoed through the lounge. The young woman's head snapped up, her eyes wide with a fear that seemed disproportionate to the innocuous sound. With an almost frantic haste, she snapped her notebook shut, tucking it away beneath her tunic. Her movements were jerky, her face flushed. She avoided eye contact with anyone, her gaze fixed on the floor as she joined the stream of individuals filing out.

Mara's own heart gave a small, involuntary lurch. It was a visceral reaction, a phantom echo of her own past, of hiding, of fear. This wasn't just about rules; it was about the emotional toll of constant surveillance, the internalized pressure to conform to a point of absolute rigidity. The young woman's fear wasn't for a tangible punishment, but for something far more subtle: disapproval, ostracism, a disruption of the carefully maintained social equilibrium.

The realization settled upon Mara with a quiet, yet profound weight. Havenridge's promise of safety was undeniable. The external world, ravaged and unforgiving, was a stark counterpoint to the protected existence within the dome. But the price of that safety, she was beginning to understand, was not merely the relinquishing of certain freedoms, but the suppression of a fundamental aspect of human nature: the need for authentic expression, for individuality, for the messy, unpredictable, yet vital act of being truly oneself.

The question that had begun as a whisper, a faint disquiet, was now growing louder in the quiet corners of her mind: Was this true safety, or a more sophisticated, gilded cage? The efficiency that had once seemed so reassuring now felt like a subtle form of control, a velvet glove over an iron fist. The order that had promised solace now whispered a different warning: that the absence of chaos did not automatically equate to the presence of freedom. She was living in a perfectly managed ecosystem, where every element was accounted for, every deviation monitored. But what happened when the most unpredictable element of all—the human spirit—began to chafe against the constraints? The very air, so meticulously scrubbed and tempered, now seemed to hold its breath, as if anticipating a tremor, a discordant note that might shatter its carefully maintained composure.

The façade of placidity was beginning to crack, revealing an unseen undercurrent of tension, a silent struggle for something more than mere survival.

CHAPTER TWO

The Seeds of Disagreement

Mara found herself drawn to the edge of the hydroponic gardens, the gentle hum of the nutrient pumps a familiar lullaby. She ran a hand over the cool, smooth leaves of a synth-lettuce, its vibrant green a testament to Havenridge's meticulously controlled environment. For weeks, she had been meticulously adhering to the rhythms of this place, her past a carefully compartmentalized memory, her focus solely on the present, on survival. Yet, a subtle disquiet had begun to bloom within her, like a weed pushing through the perfectly manicured soil. It was the quiet understanding that safety, when stripped of all its messy, vibrant humanity, could feel a lot like confinement.

It was during one of her designated maintenance cycles in Sector Gamma, the air thick with the scent of processed algae and filtered water, that the usual predictability of her day fractured. She was calibrating the nutrient flow to a row of nutrient-rich kelp, her fingers deft and sure, when a voice, uncharacteristically resonant, cut through the ambient drone.

"Remarkable growth, wouldn't you say?"

Mara's head snapped up, her hand instinctively pausing its calibration. The voice was deep, carrying a warmth that was startlingly out of place in the sterile environment. Standing a few paces away, leaning against a support column with an ease that seemed to defy the rigid posture of most Havenridge residents, was a man. He wasn't like the others she'd encountered. His clothing, a simple, functional jumpsuit, seemed to hang on him with a certain relaxed grace, not the almost uniform stiffness she'd grown accustomed to. His eyes, a startling shade of hazel flecked with gold, met hers directly, devoid of the usual polite deference or carefully constructed neutrality. There was an intelligence in his gaze, a spark of something that felt both knowing and unburdened.

"The parameters are optimized," Mara replied, her voice betraying a slight tremor she immediately regretted. She tightened her grip on the calibration tool, forcing herself to meet his gaze. "It's a matter of precise resource allocation."

The man offered a slow, genuine smile, a gesture so uncommon here that it felt almost disarming. "Precision is certainly a hallmark of this place. But I find myself wondering," he took a step closer, his movements unhurried, "if there's more to it than just the numbers. Don't you ever just... marvel at it?"

Mara blinked, processing his words. Marvel? The concept felt alien, a relic from a life she had long since buried. "We are here to maintain systems, not to indulge in sentiment," she said, her tone sharper than she intended. She disliked the way his presence disrupted her carefully cultivated composure. He seemed to radiate a different kind of energy, one that was neither compliant nor deferential.

He chuckled, a low, pleasant sound. "And is there no room for appreciation in maintenance? Do the engineers who designed these systems not marvel at their own creations? Or is the appreciation deemed... inefficient?"

His question hung in the air, laced with a gentle, probing wit. Mara found herself momentarily at a loss for words. She was accustomed to directness, to information exchanged for function. This man, Eli, as she would later learn his name was, seemed to operate on a different frequency entirely. He didn't just ask questions; he seemed to excavate them, peeling back layers of unspoken assumptions.

"Efficiency is the cornerstone of survival," Mara stated, her voice firm, a practiced response. "Sentimentality can lead to errors. Errors can lead to... undesirable outcomes."

Eli's gaze softened, a hint of understanding flickering within it. He didn't challenge her directly, but there was a subtle shift in his posture, a slight inclination of his head that suggested he heard more than she was saying. "Undesirable outcomes," he echoed, the words tasting strange on his tongue. "Yes, I've seen enough of those in my time. But I've also seen the 'undesirable outcomes' that arise from the absence of something else. The absence of joy, of curiosity, of the simple act of *seeing* beyond the immediate function."

He gestured around them, not with a sweeping flourish, but with a quiet inclusivity. "Look at this kelp, Mara. Yes, it's providing nutrients. But it's also a testament to life's tenacity, its ability to thrive even in a controlled environment. It's a miracle of biological engineering, isn't it? A tiny green defiance against the void."

Mara's fingers tightened around the calibration tool. Miracle. Defiance. These were not words used in Sector Gamma. Here, life was a resource, meticulously managed. The kelp was a product, not a phenomenon. "It is a product of precise environmental controls and nutrient delivery systems," she corrected, her voice flat.

Eli's smile returned, a shade wider this time, as if he found her resistance amusing rather than frustrating. "And what a product it is. Tell me, in your experience, what is the most essential nutrient for this kelp?"

Mara hesitated for a fraction of a second. This was a knowledge test, a standard interaction. "Nitrogen, phosphorus, potassium, and trace elements, in carefully balanced concentrations."

"Of course," Eli nodded. "But what about the intangible ones? The ones that don't register on a sensor? What about hope?"

The word, delivered so casually, struck Mara with the force of a physical blow. Hope. It was a word she had systematically purged from her internal lexicon. It was a luxury, a dangerous indulgence that had cost her dearly in the past. Here, in

Havenridge, survival was a given, a meticulously engineered certainty. Hope was irrelevant.

"Hope is not a quantifiable metric for plant growth," she stated, her voice tight. She could feel her heart beating faster, a disquieting rhythm against the steady pulse of the machinery.

Eli's gaze held hers, steady and unblinking. There was no judgment in his eyes, only a quiet observation. "Perhaps not for the kelp. But for the people who tend it? For the people who depend on it? I've seen communities wither when hope is absent, even when their nutrient levels are perfectly balanced. They cease to strive, to innovate, to believe in a future beyond the next harvest."

He paused, his voice dropping slightly, becoming more intimate, more engaging. "My name is Eli, by the way. Eli Rowan." He extended a hand, his palm open, a gesture of introduction that felt refreshingly straightforward.

Mara looked at his outstretched hand, a silent debate raging within her. Accepting it meant acknowledging him, acknowledging this disruption. But the alternative, to refuse, felt churlish, and worse, it felt like a reinforcement of the very rigidity she was beginning to question. With a sigh she barely registered, she placed her hand in his. His grip was firm, warm, and surprisingly gentle. It was a simple handshake, yet it felt like a point of departure.

"Mara," she replied, her voice softer now.

"Mara," Eli repeated, his eyes crinkling at the corners. "It's a pleasure to meet you. You have a... unique perspective on things, for someone in Sector Gamma."

"I am efficient," Mara corrected, though the word felt hollow even to her own ears. The way he looked at her, the way he spoke, it was as if he saw the carefully constructed walls she had built around herself, and was subtly, persistently, chipping away at them.

"Efficiency is certainly valuable," Eli conceded, his gaze sweeping over the rows of kelp again. "But I also believe in the power of the unscheduled observation, the moment of genuine curiosity. It's in those moments, I think, that we truly learn. Not just about the systems we maintain, but about ourselves, and about the world we're trying to preserve."

He shifted his weight, his gaze now fixed on a small, almost imperceptible blemish on one of the kelp fronds. "This one," he pointed with a long finger, "it's showing a slight deficiency. Iron, I'd wager. See the paleness in the veins?"

Mara followed his gaze, her training kicking in. He was right. A faint yellowing was indeed developing along the vascular tissue. It was a minor issue, easily correctable, but one she hadn't yet flagged. She had been too focused on the overall system, on the broad strokes of maintenance.

"You have a keen eye, Eli," she admitted, a grudging respect stirring within her. It was unsettling, to be surpassed in her own domain, especially by someone who didn't appear to be part of the designated maintenance cadres.

"I spend a lot of time observing," he said, his tone casual, but his eyes held a depth that suggested more than just passive observation. "It's a habit I picked up before... well, before I found myself in a place like Havenridge. You learn to see the subtle shifts, the first whispers of discord, before they become the deafening roar of crisis."

He looked back at her, his gaze direct. "Havenridge offers a certain kind of safety, a precious commodity in these times. But safety, in its purest form, can be a very sterile thing. It's like a perfectly sterilized operating room. Essential for preventing infection, but hardly a place one would choose to live."

Mara felt a prickle of unease. His words resonated with the growing disquiet within her. He spoke of safety not as an absolute good, but as a compromise, a trade-off. And he seemed to suggest that Havenridge, with all its order and predictability, was sacrificing something vital in its pursuit of it.

"We are protected from the chaos outside," Mara said, her voice a little defensive. "That is its purpose."

"And it serves that purpose admirably," Eli agreed, his smile returning, gentler this time. "But protection from chaos doesn't automatically equate to living. It means we don't have to fight for survival, but that doesn't mean we should cease to *live*. There's a difference. A vast, significant difference."

He turned to leave, his movements fluid and unhurried. "Think about it, Mara. The kelp needs nitrogen, phosphorus, and potassium. But perhaps, in its own way, it also needs the sun's warmth, the rain's gentle touch, the unpredictable dance of life. And perhaps, we humans are no different."

He offered a final nod, a silent acknowledgment of their brief, yet strangely profound, encounter, and then he was gone, melting back into the controlled environment of Havenridge as if he had been a figment of her own restless imagination. Mara stood for a long moment, the calibration tool still in her hand, the hum of the nutrient pumps suddenly sounding a little less comforting, a little more like a cage. Eli Rowan. He had entered her carefully ordered world like a rogue element, a spark of untamed life that had ignited a flicker of something she thought long extinguished. He hadn't argued with her, hadn't challenged her beliefs directly. He had simply presented an alternative perspective, a gentle suggestion that perhaps safety wasn't the only currency worth valuing. And in doing so, he had sown a seed of doubt, a tiny, persistent weed pushing through the meticulously cultivated soil of her newfound peace. The encounter had been brief, polite, yet it felt like a turning point, a subtle but undeniable shift in the carefully calibrated atmosphere of her existence. She was safe, yes, but for the first time, the question lingered: safe for what?

The sterile air of Havenridge, once a symbol of salvation, now felt heavy with an unspoken truth. Eli's words, a gentle current against Mara's meticulously constructed dam of logic, had found a crack. He hadn't preached rebellion, nor had he dismissed the necessity of their sanctuary. Instead, he had articulated a philosophy that resonated with a dormant part of her soul, a part she had ruthlessly suppressed in her desperate bid for survival.

"Survival alone," Eli had mused, his gaze steady as he gestured towards the perfectly aligned rows of synth-crops, "is merely the act of persisting. It's breathing, but is it truly *living*?" He had spoken of the vibrant hues of a sunset, the infectious melody of a song, the warmth of a shared laugh – experiences that held no quantifiable nutritional value, no direct impact on the efficiency of the hydroponic systems, yet possessed an immeasurable weight in the human experience. "We've engineered out the variables, Mara," he had continued, his voice a low murmur that seemed to echo the subtle hum of the life support systems, "but in doing so, we've also engineered out the essence of what makes life, *life*."

Mara found herself replaying his words, not with the dismissive logic she usually employed, but with a nascent curiosity. She remembered the fleeting image he had painted of his past, a world where people gathered not for necessity, but for joy. He had described spontaneous music in public squares, shared meals where the focus was not merely sustenance but camaraderie, and the simple act of creating art for the sheer pleasure of it. These were not concepts that fit neatly into the sterile schematics of Havenridge. Here, every action was dictated by a protocol, every interaction measured for its utility.

Art, music, uninhibited laughter – these were inefficiencies, potential distractions from the paramount goal of maintaining the delicate balance that kept them alive.

"They call it the Philosophy of Thriving," Eli had explained, his eyes alight with a conviction that was both unsettling and deeply compelling. "It's the understanding that mere existence is a hollow victory if it's devoid of richness. It's the belief that our capacity for joy, for creativity, for deep, genuine connection – these aren't luxuries; they are fundamental needs. They are the very things that fuel our resilience, that give us the strength to face adversity, not just endure it."

Mara had always viewed resilience as a matter of internal fortitude, of rigorous self-discipline and adherence to protocols. She had believed that by eliminating emotional volatility, by suppressing the messy, unpredictable aspects of human nature, they had created a more robust, more sustainable society. Yet, Eli's words suggested a different paradigm. He argued that by striving for absolute control, they had inadvertently created a sterile environment that, while safe from external threats, was slowly suffocating the very spirit they sought to protect.

"Consider the children," he had said, his voice tinged with a gentle melancholy. "They are raised in an environment of perfect safety, their every need meticulously met. But what do they learn about navigating disappointment? About the thrill of discovery? About the messy, beautiful process of falling in love?

We are raising a generation that is safe, yes, but are we raising a generation that is truly alive?"

The question hung in the air, heavy with implication. Mara thought of the quiet children she occasionally saw in the communal areas, their games polite and orderly, their laughter muted. They were healthy, well-fed, educated according to the strict curriculum, but there was a certain hollowness in their eyes, a lack of the vibrant spark she dimly recalled from her own childhood, a childhood that, while fraught with hardship, had also been filled with spontaneous bursts of laughter, whispered secrets, and the fierce joy of discovery.

Eli's philosophy wasn't about abandoning safety; it was about redefining it. He proposed that true security lay not just in the absence of physical threat, but in the presence of emotional and spiritual well-being. He spoke of the importance of community, of shared purpose that extended beyond mere survival. "When people feel connected," he had explained, his gaze sweeping across the functional, impersonal architecture of Havenridge, "when they feel their contributions are valued not just for their efficiency, but for their humanity, they are more invested. They are more willing to protect what they have, not just out of fear of loss, but out of love for what they stand to gain."

He had painted a picture of a different kind of sanctuary, one where the hum of the life support systems was complemented by the murmur of conversation, where the glow of the hydroponic lights was augmented by the warmth of shared meals, and where the meticulous care of the crops was balanced by the nurturing of human relationships. It was a vision that seemed impossibly distant from the reality of Havenridge, a reality defined by strict routines and emotional restraint.

"We are essentially functioning like a highly advanced biological machine," Eli had continued, a hint of sadness in his voice. "Each component plays its role, perfectly calibrated. But machines, no matter how sophisticated, lack the spark. They lack the capacity for wonder, for empathy, for the illogical leaps of faith that drive innovation and inspire art. We are more than the sum of our biological functions, Mara. We are beings who crave meaning, who need to feel, to connect, to create."

Mara found herself wrestling with these ideas. Her entire existence had been dedicated to the pursuit of perfect order, to the elimination of all that was unpredictable and inefficient. Eli's philosophy suggested that this very pursuit was flawed, that in seeking to perfect the system, they had inadvertently stripped away the very things that made life worth preserving. He argued that the "messiness" of human emotion, the irrationality of passion, the vulnerability of connection – these were not weaknesses to be eradicated, but essential components of a truly thriving existence.

"Think of it like this," Eli had said, his tone patient and inviting. "A plant needs sunlight, water, and nutrients to survive. But what makes it truly beautiful? The way its leaves unfurl towards the light, the unique pattern of its veins, the way it sways in the breeze. These are the qualities that inspire awe, that bring joy. We are no different. We need the basic necessities, yes, but we *thrive* when we have the space to express our unique patterns, to sway in the breeze of our own emotions, to reach for the light of our own aspirations."

He had paused, allowing his words to sink in. "Havenridge has given us safety. And that is a profound gift. But we must ask ourselves, is safety the ultimate goal, or is it merely the foundation upon which we can build a life worth living? Are we merely surviving, or are we truly thriving?"

The question was a gentle prod, an invitation to introspection. Mara had spent so long focused on the *how* of survival, on the meticulous execution of protocols, that she had rarely stopped to consider the *why*. Why were they surviving? What was the ultimate purpose of this carefully managed existence? Eli's philosophy offered a compelling answer: to live, truly live, in all its messy, beautiful, unpredictable glory.

She had always prided herself on her detachment, her ability to make objective decisions based on data and logic. But Eli's words had introduced a new variable into her calculations – the intangible, yet undeniably powerful, force of human spirit. He hadn't dismissed the importance of their controlled environment, but he had argued that it was not an end in itself. It was a means to an end, and that end should be a life rich with experience, connection, and meaning, not just the mere absence of death.

"We are not just cells in a petri dish, Mara," Eli had concluded, his voice soft but firm. "We are human beings. And human beings are meant to feel, to dream, to connect. To suppress those fundamental aspects of our nature in the name of perfect safety is to create a gilded cage, where we may be protected from harm, but we are also denied the very essence of what makes us alive."

His words lingered in the sterile air, a counterpoint to the rhythmic hum of the machinery. They were a challenge, not to the integrity of Havenridge, but to the prevailing interpretation of its purpose. He had planted a seed of doubt, a question that Mara could no longer ignore: was the sterile safety they had achieved worth the sacrifice of their humanity? And if not, what would it take to cultivate a life that was not just sustainable, but truly vibrant? The Philosophy of Thriving, a concept previously alien and perhaps even frivolous, now seemed to hold a profound, and perhaps even necessary, truth. It spoke of a future where survival was not the only imperative, but a springboard for something more – a future where humanity, in all its complexity, could truly flourish.

The scent of damp earth and the faint, sweet perfume of the hydroponic orchids filled the air, a stark contrast to the sterile efficiency Mara usually associated with such environments. She stood amidst the precisely manicured rows of nutrient-rich synth-crops, the emerald leaves catching the soft, artificial light. Each plant was positioned at an exact angle, every stem supported with the same meticulous care. This was her domain, a testament to the power of order, a living monument to the principles that had saved them. Eli, on the other hand, seemed to draw energy from the very disorder he embodied, his presence a vibrant splash of color against the controlled verdancy.

"Spontaneity, Eli," Mara began, her voice carefully modulated, devoid of the tremor she felt threatening to surface. "You speak of it as if it were a virtue, a lost art to be rediscovered. But I remember what spontaneity looks like when it's unchecked. I remember the hunger, the fear, the sheer, unadulterated chaos that drove us here." She gestured broadly, encompassing not just the verdant sanctuary but the unseen, broken world beyond their shielded walls. "The world outside was not destroyed by a lack of vibrant sunsets or impromptu music. It was consumed by recklessness, by a failure to plan, by a species that prioritized fleeting desires over long-term survival."

Her gaze swept over the glowing tubes nurturing the crops, the precise flow of water and nutrients meticulously monitored by an invisible network of sensors. "This," she said, her voice gaining a steely edge, "is not a gilded cage. This is salvation. This is the result of rigorous discipline, of understanding that every variable must be accounted for, every risk mitigated. We survived because we learned to impose order on the chaos that threatened to swallow us whole."

She turned to face him, her expression earnest, the conviction in her eyes unwavering. "You speak of thriving, of living vibrantly. But what does that mean when the very ground beneath our feet can crumble? What does it mean to 'feel' deeply when that feeling can lead to irrational decisions, to dangerous distractions? My childhood was not a sterile wasteland; it was a brutal lesson. I saw families torn apart by impulsivity, communities fractured by unchecked passions, entire cities reduced to rubble by the inability to prioritize collective well-being over individual whims."

Mara walked a few steps, her boots treading lightly on the synthetic soil. "The children you mentioned," she continued, her tone softening slightly, but the core of her argument remaining firm, "they are safe. They are educated. They are provided for. Is it so terrible that their games are orderly, their laughter perhaps a little less boisterous than what you recall? This is not about suppressing joy; it's about ensuring its survival. It's about building a future where such joy can exist without being immediately extinguished by the very forces that made it a luxury in the first place."

She paused, letting her words hang in the humid air. "Your 'Philosophy of Thriving' sounds beautiful, Eli, like a song sung in a world that has forgotten how to listen. But a song cannot feed us. A sunset cannot shield us from radiation. And a spontaneous burst of creativity cannot rebuild a broken infrastructure. We are here because we understood these truths. We built Havenridge because we recognized that survival demands pragmatism, not poetry. It demands a relentless commitment to control, to efficiency, to the unglamorous, often tedious, work of maintaining balance."

Eli remained silent, his gaze fixed on her, his expression unreadable. The orchids seemed to pulse with an inner light, their delicate petals a testament to the very principles Mara championed – careful cultivation, controlled environments, meticulous attention to detail. Yet, he saw not just the order, but the life, the delicate beauty that order could foster.

"You equate spontaneity with recklessness," Mara pressed on, her voice a low hum that seemed to vibrate with the underlying systems of Havenridge. "You see my adherence to protocol as a suppression of the human spirit. But I see it as the scaffolding that allows the human spirit to endure. I see it as the responsible act of ensuring that the vibrant life you so cherish has a stable foundation upon which to stand. What happens when the 'swaying in the breeze' you spoke of becomes a violent storm? What happens when the 'unique patterns' of human nature lead to conflict, to resource depletion, to the very self-destruction we fled?"

She stepped closer, her voice now tinged with a plea, a desperate attempt to make him understand the depth of her conviction, forged in the crucible of a world teetering on the brink. "My memories are not of a past that was lost to a lack of spontaneity. They are of a past that was lost to a surfeit of it. A past where every whim was indulged, every impulse acted upon, until there was nothing left to indulge or act upon. We are not machines, Eli, but we are also not gods. We are fragile beings, and our fragility demands that we build strong walls, that we establish clear boundaries, that we understand the profound responsibility that comes with freedom. And sometimes, that responsibility means choosing order over the siren song of unfettered expression."

She gestured towards a particularly robust vine, its leaves perfectly formed, its tendrils reaching out with predictable intent. "This vine thrives not because it was left to its own devices, but because it was guided, nurtured, and protected. It reached its full potential within the parameters set for it. We, too, are capable of reaching our full potential, but only if we understand and respect those parameters. The chaos you admire is the very force that would unravel this vine, that would leave it choked by weeds, starved of light, and ultimately, withered and dead. Is that the 'thriving' you envision for us?"

Mara looked around the garden, the meticulous arrangement of plants, the precise irrigation systems, the filtered air, all designed to create an environment where life could flourish safely. "We have created a haven from the storm, Eli. We have built a sanctuary where the variables that led to our destruction have been eliminated. And yes, perhaps in doing so, we have removed some of the jagged edges, some of the raw, unpredictable intensity that characterized the old world. But we have also removed the potential for self-inflicted wounds. We have chosen a life of measured existence, of predictable growth, of guaranteed continuation. And in my eyes, that is not a sacrifice; it is the ultimate victory."

She met his gaze directly, her own unwavering. "The Philosophy of Thriving suggests that we are more than just our biological functions. And I agree. We are beings with aspirations, with the capacity for love and connection. But those aspirations are best pursued from a place of stability. That connection is most profound when it is not threatened by the unpredictable whims of those we are connected to. Your vision of a vibrant life is one I can appreciate intellectually, but my experience has taught me that such vibrancy is a luxury we can only afford to explore once the fundamental necessity of survival has been unequivocally secured. And that, Eli, requires order. Unwavering, absolute, and unyielding order."

The hum of the Council chamber had been a low thrum of agreement, a rare symphony of consensus that both soothed and unsettled Mara. She sat on the polished synth-wood bench, her hands clasped tightly in her lap, the smooth surface cool against her skin. The air, scrubbed clean and recycled, carried the faint scent of ozone and something vaguely floral, a testament to Havenridge's constant pursuit of environmental equilibrium. Around the polished, oval table sat the members of the Council, their faces etched with the gravity of their responsibilities, their eyes reflecting the soft, ambient light. Elder Maeve, her silver hair pulled back in its customary severe bun, had just delivered the verdict.

"And so," Elder Maeve's voice, though gentle, carried an unmistakable authority, "it has been decided. The arboretum project will proceed, and its oversight will be a shared responsibility." A collective sigh, a barely perceptible exhalation of breath, rippled through the chamber. Mara felt a prickle of apprehension, a familiar tightening in her chest. Shared responsibility. It sounded so benign, so equitable. But she knew, with a certainty that settled like a stone in her gut, what it truly meant. It meant Eli.

"Mara," Elder Maeve's gaze found hers, her expression laced with a blend of hope and caution, "your expertise in resource management and sustainable cultivation is unparalleled. Your understanding of ecological systems, of how to coax life from even the most challenging substrates, is precisely what this project needs. You will be responsible for the foundational planning, the allocation of resources, and ensuring the long-term viability of the revitalized section."

Mara inclined her head, a polite, measured acknowledgment. This was within her purview, a natural extension of her work in the hydroponic farms and the climate-controlled biodomes. She could already envision the detailed schematics, the nutrient dispersal matrices, the carefully calculated light spectrum adjustments. It would be a testament to precision, a flawless execution of established protocols.

Then, Elder Maeve turned her attention to Eli, who stood leaning against the far wall, his usual relaxed posture a stark contrast to the formal setting. A small, almost imperceptible smile played on his lips, an expression Mara found unnervingly ambiguous.

"Eli," Elder Maeve continued, her voice softening slightly, a concession to his less conventional nature, "your... unique perspective on organic growth, on the integration of natural aesthetics, and your intuitive understanding of living systems are equally vital. You will be responsible for the creative vision, for introducing elements of natural diversity, and for fostering an environment that encourages organic, rather than purely engineered, growth. Your role will be to ensure that the arboretum doesn't just survive, but truly *thrives*."

Mara's jaw tightened almost imperceptibly.

Thrives. The word, so loaded with Eli's philosophy, hung in the air like a challenge. She understood the Council's intention, of course. They saw the friction between her meticulous pragmatism and Eli's flamboyant idealism. They saw the potential for him to inject a much-needed spark, a connection to the wilder, more beautiful aspects of life that her methods sometimes seemed to sterilize. And they saw her as the steady hand, the anchor to prevent his creative impulses from veering into the dangerous territory of unchecked spontaneity. It was a delicate balancing act, and she suspected she would be the one doing most of the balancing.

"This arboretum," Elder Maeve went on, gesturing with a slender, aged hand, "is more than just a collection of plants. It is a symbol of our past, a living repository of what was lost, and a promise of what can be rebuilt. The section we have designated for revitalization has been dormant for years, a forgotten corner that has become overgrown with hardy, untamed growth, but lacks the structured beauty and diversity that our ancestors cherished in such spaces. It requires both rigorous restoration and imaginative re-creation."

Mara's mind was already cataloging the tasks. Soil analysis, pest control protocols, selection of genetically stable heirloom species, establishment of a tiered irrigation system, integration of atmospheric scrubbers to manage any lingering toxins, and the meticulous planning of growth patterns to maximize sunlight exposure and minimize resource drain. She could see the digital blueprints forming in her mind, each line a commitment to order, each calculation a step towards guaranteed success.

Eli, meanwhile, had straightened from his casual stance, his eyes now sparkling with an uncharacteristic intensity. He walked towards the table, his movements fluid and unhurried. "A forgotten corner," he mused, his voice a low rumble that seemed to draw the attention of everyone in the room. "Perhaps it has not been forgotten, Elder. Perhaps it has simply been allowed to *be*. To find its own way. To reclaim itself." He glanced at Mara, a subtle challenge in his gaze. "And I believe it holds the potential for more than just structured beauty. It can be a place where life finds unexpected avenues, where the very act of living is celebrated in its most authentic, untamed form."

Mara felt a familiar surge of protectiveness, a visceral urge to defend the principles she held dear. "Authenticity, Eli, is a dangerous abstraction when it leads to uncontrolled proliferation, to invasive species overwhelming native ones, to a lack of resources that leads to decay. My focus will be on creating an environment that is not only sustainable but resilient. A system designed to withstand external pressures, to ensure that the life within it has every advantage, every precisely calibrated condition for optimal growth."

Elder Maeve observed them both, her expression unreadable. "Precisely," she interjected, her voice cutting through the nascent tension. "And that is why this collaboration is so crucial. Mara will lay the groundwork, the secure foundation. Eli, you will paint the canvas, bringing color and vibrant life to that structure. The goal is not to create a sterile, engineered garden, nor is it to allow a chaotic, unsustainable wildness to take root. The goal is to find the perfect synthesis, a harmonious integration of order and organic freedom. A testament to Havenridge's ability to learn from the past and build a future that embraces both reason and beauty."

Mara knew, with a certainty that bordered on resignation, that this project would be a crucible. It would force her into close proximity with Eli, with his disarming charm and his infuriatingly optimistic worldview. She would have to explain her protocols, justify her careful calculations, and witness his often-unconventional approaches firsthand. It would be a constant negotiation, a dance on the edge of their opposing philosophies.

She pictured the section of the arboretum Elder Maeve referred to. It was a less-developed area, situated on the periphery of the main cultivated zones. Years ago, it had been intended as an experimental ground for introducing more diverse flora, but the project had been curtailed due to resource reallocation during a particularly challenging phase of Havenridge's development. Now, it was a tangle of hardy, almost stubborn, growth – resilient weeds, thickets of self-seeded shrubs, and a handful of hardy trees that had managed to push their way through the reclaimed earth. It was a testament to nature's tenacity, but it lacked the curated elegance of the biodomes or the meticulously ordered rows of the synth-crop farms. It was, in many ways, a mirror of the very chaos that had threatened to consume their ancestors, yet it also possessed a raw, undeniable beauty.

"The designated zone," Mara stated, her voice regaining its measured tone, "is approximately two hectares. It currently exhibits a species diversity of approximately seventy percent invasive or self-colonizing flora, with a nutrient depletion rate in the upper soil strata that requires significant remediation. My initial proposal includes a phased approach: decontamination and soil enrichment, followed by the establishment of a controlled microclimate using atmospheric regulators, and then the introduction of a curated selection of genetically stable, low-resource-demand species. We will prioritize plants that offer demonstrable benefits, such as air purification, aesthetic value, and potential for sustainable biomass generation. My team will prepare a full environmental impact assessment and resource allocation proposal within the standard cycle."

Eli's response was immediate, his eyes alight with a spark she couldn't quite decipher – was it amusement, challenge, or something else entirely? "And my contribution," he said, stepping forward with an easy grace, "will be to ensure that this controlled microclimate doesn't feel like a prison for the life it contains. I will work to integrate natural patterns of growth, to create spaces where the wind can whisper through the leaves, where sunlight can dapple the ground in shifting mosaics. I want to foster an environment where the plants feel not just *maintained*, but truly *alive*. Where the very act of their existence is a celebration. We will introduce species known for their resilience, yes, but also for their unique beauty, for their unpredictable blossoming, for the way they interact with each other and their surroundings in ways that even the most advanced algorithms can't fully predict."

Mara felt a familiar prickle of unease. Unpredictable blossoming. Interactions that couldn't be fully predicted. These were the very concepts she worked so hard to mitigate, to control, to bring within the realm of quantifiable outcomes. Yet, she also saw the appeal. The idea of a space that wasn't just a perfectly engineered garden, but a living, breathing ecosystem that held its own surprises, its own moments of unexpected delight.

"We will need to establish clear boundaries," Mara stated, her voice firm, unwavering. "Protocols for managing any emergent invasive tendencies, for ensuring that the aesthetic appeal does not compromise the ecological stability. We cannot afford to repeat the mistakes of the past, Eli. Unchecked growth, unchecked passion, led to ruin. My plan ensures predictability, resilience, and sustainability. It is the only responsible path forward."

Eli met her gaze, his own steady and surprisingly gentle. "And my approach," he replied, his voice a low, even tone, "will ensure that life, in its most vibrant and inspiring form, has the space to flourish. We are not simply tasked with survival, Mara. We are tasked with living. With creating a future that is not just safe, but also beautiful. I believe that true resilience comes not just from rigid control, but from the ability of life to adapt, to find new pathways, to surprise us with its enduring capacity for beauty. This arboretum will be a testament to that truth."

The Council exchanged glances, their faces a mixture of hope and concern. Elder Maeve nodded slowly. "Then it is settled," she announced, her voice resonating with a quiet authority. "Mara, Eli, you will begin your work immediately. The arboretum awaits. May your collaboration bring forth a new blossoming for Havenridge, one that honors both our past and our future."

As Mara rose from the bench, the weight of the task settled upon her. It was more than just a project; it was a test. A test of her principles, of her ability to compromise, and of her capacity to find common ground with someone who saw the world so differently. She glanced at Eli, who was already sketching in a small, worn notebook, his brow furrowed in concentration, a faint smile gracing his lips. The seeds of disagreement had been sown, but perhaps, just perhaps, within the fertile ground of this shared endeavor, something new, something unexpected, could also begin to grow.

The designated zone, a sprawling two-hectare expanse on the less-trafficked edge of Havenridge, was a forgotten tapestry of nature's determined reclamation. Hardy weeds, their roots tenacious, pushed through the cracked earth, interspersed with dense thickets of self-seeded shrubs that had woven a seemingly impenetrable green curtain. A handful of hardy trees, stoic sentinels against the passage of time, had managed to assert their presence, their branches reaching towards the filtered sunlight. This was Mara's canvas, and her initial approach was one of methodical assessment, akin to a surgeon preparing for a complex procedure. Her mind, a highly calibrated instrument, immediately began to process the data.

The soil, she noted, was depleted, its upper strata leached of essential nutrients by years of unchecked growth and lack of intervention. Its composition would require rigorous analysis, a deep dive into its mineral content, its pH balance, its microbial population – or lack thereof. Her team, already anticipating her directives, would be equipped with portable soil scanners, their data streams feeding directly into her central planning nexus.

She envisioned a phased approach, a carefully choreographed sequence of events designed to bring order to this nascent chaos. Phase one: decontamination and soil enrichment. This would involve a multi-pronged strategy, beginning with the removal of any residual toxins that might have seeped into the earth over the decades, followed by the introduction of carefully formulated nutrient blends, bio-engineered to restore fertility without overwhelming the delicate ecosystem that was beginning to reassert itself.

Phase two: establishing a controlled microclimate. This was where the atmospheric regulators would come into play, finely tuned instruments designed to modulate temperature, humidity, and light exposure, creating an environment that was both protective and conducive to growth. It was a necessary intervention, she reasoned, a shield against the unpredictable environmental fluctuations that could so easily derail even the most robust of species. And then, phase three: the introduction of a curated selection of plants. Not just any plants, but those that were genetically stable, with low resource demands, and that offered demonstrable benefits – air purification, aesthetic appeal, and the potential for sustainable biomass generation. Each selection would be a calculated decision, a piece of a larger, intricate puzzle. Her team would be preparing a comprehensive environmental impact assessment and a detailed resource allocation proposal, adhering strictly to the standard operational cycle. Precision, predictability, and sustainability were her guiding principles, the bedrock upon which this arboretum would be built.

Eli, however, moved through this same space with an entirely different rhythm. Where Mara saw data points and protocols, he saw stories, histories written in the language of roots and leaves. He walked the perimeter not with a scanner, but with a quiet reverence, his boots crunching softly on the fallen leaves. His eyes, a shade of mossy green, scanned the existing growth, not to catalog it for removal, but to understand its resilience, its inherent wisdom. He would crouch, his fingers gently sifting through the soil, feeling its texture, its moisture content, not with the intention of remediation, but of communion. He'd trace the gnarled branches of an ancient-looking shrub, murmuring to himself, a low, almost inaudible stream of observations.

"Look at this one," he'd say, his voice carrying a melodic resonance, even when speaking to himself. "Managed to find its own water source, even in this dry spell. Remarkable tenacity." He wasn't concerned with its species classification or its potential invasiveness, but with its will to survive, its elegant adaptation to scarcity. He'd identify a cluster of wildflowers, their vibrant colors a stark contrast to the muted greens and browns, and smile. "These little ones," he'd muse, "they know something we've forgotten. They know how to bloom, even when the world tells them not to."

His approach was less about imposing a predetermined structure and more about coaxing forth the latent potential that already existed. He'd point to a natural clearing, an area where the sunlight dappled the ground in a way that seemed almost intentional, and envision it as a gathering space for the flora, a place where they could interact and thrive in a way that felt organic and unforced. He was drawn to the existing contours of the land, the gentle slopes, the natural depressions where water might collect, seeing them not as challenges to be overcome with engineering, but as opportunities to be embraced.

Their initial days working side-by-side were a testament to their contrasting methodologies, a silent ballet of divergent philosophies. Mara would arrive each morning with her datapad, a crisp, digital blueprint of her planned interventions already loaded. She'd meticulously mark out grids, designate zones for soil testing, and schedule precise watering times, each droplet accounted for, each nutrient infusion carefully calculated. Her voice, when she spoke, was clipped and efficient, issuing clear directives to her team. "Quadrant Gamma requires immediate ph-balance recalibration. Allocate two-point-five liters of nutrient solution C-7 to each designated plot. Monitor atmospheric humidity levels for optimal germination."

Eli, on the other hand, would often be found already at work, seemingly absorbed in a world of his own making. He'd be gently clearing away encroaching vines from a struggling sapling, his movements slow and deliberate, or examining the intricate patterns of moss that had claimed a weathered rock. He rarely consulted schematics, his understanding of the landscape seemingly intuitive, guided by an inner compass that navigated the subtle energies of the earth. When Mara approached him, her datapad projecting a complex irrigation schematic, he'd nod, his eyes still focused on the delicate unfurling of a fern. "Yes, yes, the water will find its way," he'd say, his tone placid, almost dismissive of the need for such intricate planning. "Nature has her own ways of distributing her gifts."

This lack of direct engagement, this polite but firm divergence in their approaches, began to create a subtle friction, a tension that hummed beneath the surface of their shared endeavor. Mara found it both frustrating and, she had to admit, oddly intriguing. She'd watch Eli, his brow furrowed in concentration as he studied a patch of wildflowers, his hands stained with earth, and feel a flicker of something akin to envy. There was a freedom in his method, a surrender to the organic flow of life that was utterly alien to her own carefully constructed existence. Yet, her ingrained sense of responsibility, her deeply held belief in the necessity of order and control, would always pull her back.

One afternoon, Mara was overseeing the installation of a series of soil enrichment modules, each one precisely calibrated to deliver a specific blend of minerals. Her team worked with silent efficiency, their movements synchronized, their tools humming softly. Eli, meanwhile, had found a fallen log, half-rotted and covered in a vibrant ecosystem of fungi and moss. He sat on it, a small sketchbook open on his lap, his charcoal pencil dancing across the page.

"Mara," he called out, his voice cutting through the low hum of machinery, "have you observed the mycorrhizal networks in this area? They're quite extensive, supporting a surprising diversity of fungal life. It would be a shame to disrupt them unnecessarily."

Mara paused, her hand hovering over a control panel. She consulted her datapad. "The network analysis indicates a moderate presence," she replied, her voice carefully neutral. "However, the soil composition in this sector is suboptimal for the introduction of our primary cultivated species. The modules are designed to improve the substrate density and nutrient availability within a controlled radius, ensuring a higher success rate for germination."

Eli smiled, a slow, gentle unfolding of his lips. "But what if the existing network offers a benefit we haven't accounted for? What if these fungi are already preparing the soil, in their own way, for what is to come? Sometimes, the best approach is to work *with* what is already there, rather than imposing our will upon it."

Mara felt a familiar tightness in her chest. "My approach guarantees a successful outcome, Eli. It minimizes risk and ensures the long-term viability of the arboretum. We cannot afford to gamble with the resources and the future of Havenridge." She gestured towards the modules. "These are not arbitrary impositions. They are the result of extensive research and predictive modeling. They represent the most efficient and responsible path forward."

He stood then, brushing a speck of dirt from his sleeve. He walked towards the modules, his gaze not on the machinery, but on the small, hardy plants that were already beginning to sprout in the uncultivated edges of the zone. "Efficiency is a valuable tool, Mara," he conceded, his voice soft. "But it is not the only measure of success. Sometimes, the most beautiful discoveries are made when we allow ourselves to deviate from the plan, to embrace the unexpected." He knelt beside a cluster of tiny, star-shaped blue flowers. "These, for instance," he said, pointing. "They are not on any of your planting lists, are they? Yet, they have found their way here, blooming with such quiet determination. They add a touch of magic, don't you think?"

Mara looked at the flowers, their delicate petals a surprising splash of color against the muted earth. They were indeed beautiful, and she couldn't deny the simple, unengineered charm they possessed. But her mind immediately began to calculate. Were they native? Were they invasive? What were their resource requirements? "They are an anomaly," she stated, her voice firm. "We will assess their impact, but our priority must remain the successful cultivation of the designated species."

Eli sighed, a sound so subtle it was almost imperceptible. He didn't argue, didn't push. Instead, he returned to his log, his gaze once again drawn to the intricate patterns of the fungi. It was in these small moments, these unspoken exchanges, that the true nature of their collaboration, and the unspoken disagreements that underscored it, became most apparent. Mara, the architect of order, meticulously constructing a future based on reason and control. Eli, the poet of nature, seeking to unearth the inherent beauty and resilience that already existed, urging for a gentler, more intuitive approach. The arboretum, meant to be a symbol of unity, was rapidly becoming a silent battleground of their opposing worldviews, each ripple of disagreement a testament to the vibrant, and at times tumultuous, pulse of life itself.

The days bled into weeks, and the arboretum began to transform, albeit under two vastly different visions. Mara's side of the project progressed with the predictable, steady rhythm of a well-oiled machine. The soil enrichment modules hummed with quiet efficiency, their steady output of nutrients a visible balm to the depleted earth. Designated planting zones, marked by precise laser lines, awaited their carefully selected inhabitants. Her team, clad in sterile white environmental suits, moved with military precision, adhering to strict decontamination protocols and timing each action to the nanosecond. Mara herself was a constant presence, her datapad a digital extension of her will, her eyes scanning holographic projections of soil composition, atmospheric readings, and growth projections. She had overseen the installation of a sophisticated irrigation system, a network of subsurface pipes and micro-emitters, each programmed to deliver the exact amount of water to each designated plant at the optimal time of day, ensuring no drop was wasted, no root left thirsty or waterlogged. She had meticulously cataloged every seed, every sapling, its genetic lineage, its expected growth trajectory, its projected resource consumption. It was a symphony of scientific precision, a testament to her unwavering commitment to order.

Eli's contributions, however, were far more subtle, less about grand interventions and more about gentle guidance. He spent his time observing, sketching, and, when Mara wasn't looking, subtly encouraging the existing flora. He'd gently clear away invasive weeds from around a particularly stubborn patch of wild heather, not to eradicate it, but to give it space to breathe. He'd identify areas where natural drainage seemed to be occurring, and subtly redirect minor water flows from Mara's irrigation system towards these points, creating small, naturally flourishing pockets of moisture. He'd talk to the plants, his voice a low murmur, as if sharing secrets with an old friend. "You're doing so well," he'd whisper to a cluster of resilient wildflowers pushing through a crack in a weathered stone. "Just a little more sunlight, a little more space, and you'll be magnificent."

Mara observed these subtle interventions with a mixture of exasperation and a grudging admiration. She knew, intellectually, that Eli's methods were not aligned with her own, that they introduced an element of unpredictability into her carefully constructed system. Yet, she couldn't deny that the areas he "tended" seemed to possess a certain vitality, a natural beauty that her own meticulously planned sections, while perfectly executed, sometimes lacked. She'd watch him kneeling amongst a patch of native grasses, his fingers tracing the delicate blades, and feel a pang of something she couldn't quite name – curiosity, perhaps, or a fleeting sense of longing for that unburdened connection to the natural world.

One crisp morning, Mara was overseeing the delicate process of transplanting a genetically stable strain of heirloom apple saplings. Each sapling, no older than a year, had been nurtured in a sterile laboratory environment, its root system meticulously pruned and treated. Her team worked with the utmost care, their gloved hands ensuring minimal disturbance to the fragile life they were about to introduce to its new home.

"The soil in Sector Delta is now at optimal moisture saturation," Mara announced, her voice crisp and clear as she reviewed her datapad. "The nutrient readings are within the established parameters. Begin the transplant sequence in T-minus thirty seconds."

Just as the countdown reached T-minus ten, Eli appeared, a small, woven basket slung over his shoulder. He moved with his characteristic unhurried grace, his eyes scanning the area. He approached Mara, a gentle smile playing on his lips. "Mara," he began, his voice a soft counterpoint to the whirring of the automated equipment, "I've found something rather special near the eastern ridge. A colony of a particular species of orchid, one I haven't seen flowering in Havenridge for decades. They're quite tenacious, finding a foothold in the most unlikely places."

Mara's brow furrowed. "Orchids?" she repeated, her gaze flicking from her datapad to Eli. "Are they on the approved species list? Their propagation can be notoriously difficult, and their resource requirements can be unpredictable."

"They are not on the list," Eli admitted, his smile unwavering. "But their resilience is extraordinary. And their beauty... it's a testament to the wild spirit that still thrives, even in the forgotten corners." He gestured towards the saplings. "These are wonderful, Mara, truly. But I believe this arboretum needs more than just perfectly cultivated specimens. It needs moments of surprise, of unexpected joy. These orchids, they would bring that."

Mara felt a familiar surge of internal resistance. "Eli, we have a plan. A carefully considered, rigorously researched plan. Introducing unlisted species, especially one as potentially demanding as an orchid, could jeopardize the entire project. We have protocols for a reason. We have to ensure the sustainability and ecological balance of this space."

He met her gaze, his green eyes soft but firm. "And I believe that true sustainability lies not just in control, but in adaptability. In allowing life to find its own paths. These orchids have survived, Mara, without our intervention. They are a living demonstration of nature's ingenuity. Perhaps, instead of removing them, we could learn from them. Perhaps we could find a way to integrate them, to allow their unique beauty to enhance, rather than detract from, our vision."

He reached into his basket and gently produced a small, intricately patterned bloom, its petals a delicate shade of violet. "See?" he murmured, holding it out to her. "Is this not a wonder?"

Mara looked at the orchid, its fragile beauty a stark contrast to the robust, engineered saplings. She felt a strange conflict within her. Her logical mind, her ingrained training, screamed caution. The protocols, the risk assessments, the potential for unforeseen consequences – they were all flashing red alerts in her internal system. But her eyes, drawn to the delicate symmetry of the petals, the subtle iridescence, couldn't entirely dismiss the simple, undeniable allure of the bloom. It was a whisper of something wild, something untamed, something that her meticulously ordered world struggled to encompass. The first ripples of disagreement, subtle yet significant, were beginning to spread, not just through the soil of the arboretum, but through the very foundations of their collaboration.

CHAPTER THREE

Weeding the Past

Mara's workspace within Havenridge was a testament to her disciplined approach to life. It was a sanctuary of order, a stark contrast to the unpredictable wildness she was attempting to tame in the arboretum. Here, within the sterile, climate-controlled confines of her laboratory and planning center, every tool had its designated spot, every datapad was charged and updated, and every document was filed with meticulous precision. Sunlight, filtered through smart glass that adjusted its opacity based on the time of day and ambient light levels, cast a soft, even glow across her meticulously organized desk. The air was clean, recycled, and subtly perfumed with a neutral, unobtrusive scent designed to promote focus.

She spent hours poring over digital schematics, her fingers gliding across the holographic displays that projected intricate three-dimensional models of the arboretum's planned layout. Planting schedules were not mere lists; they were complex algorithms, factoring in soil composition, light exposure, predicted rainfall patterns (however minimal in this controlled environment), and the specific genetic predispositions of each plant species. She cross-referenced historical agricultural data with the latest bio-engineering reports, ensuring that every seed, every sapling, was allocated precisely the conditions it needed to not just survive, but to thrive. Her research delved into the most obscure botanical journals, seeking out any scrap of information that could optimize her efforts. She studied the micronutrient requirements of rare mosses and the optimal humidity levels for the delicate ferns that were slated for the shaded, northern slopes of the arboretum.

Her datapad was a constant companion, its smooth surface cool against her palm. It held the sum total of her project – the initial soil analysis reports, the atmospheric regulator calibration logs, the genetic sequencing of every approved plant specimen, and the detailed resource allocation projections. She updated her progress logs with an almost ritualistic cadence, each entry a precise record of actions taken and data collected. There were no ambiguities, no estimations, only facts and carefully calculated projections. If a particular strain of drought-resistant grass showed a slightly lower-than-expected germination rate in its initial test plots, Mara would immediately initiate a secondary analysis, cross-referencing atmospheric humidity logs with the nutrient delivery schedule for that specific sector. She believed that every deviation, every anomaly, was simply a puzzle piece waiting to be correctly placed, a problem solvable through rigorous analysis and precise intervention.

The outside world, with its capricious weather, its unpredictable pests, and its general disregard for logical progression, was a constant source of low-level anxiety for Mara. It was a reminder of the inherent chaos that threatened to unravel even the most carefully constructed systems. Her work in the arboretum, her dedication to creating a controlled, predictable environment, was more than just a project; it was a personal mission. It was an attempt to impose order on a world that had, for her, often felt overwhelmingly capricious. This meticulous organization, this unwavering adherence to protocols, was her shield. It was her way of ensuring that within this specific two-hectare expanse, the unpredictable would be minimized, the variables controlled, and the outcome, as far as humanly possible, guaranteed.

She had a dedicated section within Havenridge's central complex, a room that mirrored her workspace in its absolute order. Here, rows of sterilized tools were neatly arranged in custom-fitted drawers. Planting trays, each labeled with a specific seed lot number and planting date, were stacked with military precision. She even had a small, high-resolution scanner dedicated solely to analyzing soil samples, its output directly feeding into her central database. Each day began with a review of her projected tasks, a mental checklist that would guide her through the hours. She would analyze the atmospheric regulator readings from the previous night, adjust the humidity levels in the propagation domes by fractions of a percent, and confirm the nutrient slurry mix for the morning's scheduled delivery to the soil enrichment modules.

"Morning, Mara," a cheerful voice chirped, breaking her concentration. It was Dr. Jian Li, a plant geneticist who worked in a neighboring lab. He stood in the doorway, holding a steaming mug. "Making good progress on the arboretum schematics?"

Mara looked up, a small, almost imperceptible softening in her expression. "Good morning, Jian. Yes, the models are running within projected parameters. I'm just finalizing the nutrient deployment strategy for Sector Gamma. The soil analysis indicates a slight deficiency in magnesium, so I'm adjusting the C-7 blend accordingly." She gestured to a holographic display that shimmered with complex data streams.

Jian peered at the projection, his eyes widening slightly. "That's incredibly detailed, Mara. Most people would just rely on the automated sensors to handle that."

"Automation is only as good as its programming," Mara replied, her tone matter-of-fact. "And its programming is based on data. My data. I prefer to have direct oversight. It minimizes the potential for error." She tapped a section of the display. "The historical rainfall data for this region, even with the atmospheric regulators, suggests a potential for minor desiccation in the southern hemisphere planting zones if we don't account for micro-climates created by the topographical shifts."

Jian nodded slowly, a thoughtful expression on his face. "It's fascinating, the level of control you're exerting. I admire your dedication to precision." He took a sip of his mug. "You know, sometimes I find that nature itself has a way of surprising us, even in the most controlled environments. Like that little patch of hardy wildflowers that managed to sprout near the ventilation shaft last week. Didn't seem to be on any of your planting lists."

Mara's gaze briefly flickered towards a different section of her datapad, where a small, almost dismissive note was logged about "unidentified flora presence, Sector Alpha, requiring assessment." She didn't voice her thoughts, choosing instead to focus on the immediate task. "Wildflowers are charming, Jian, but our objective is the establishment of a sustainable, multi-functional arboretum. That requires a curated selection, not random proliferation. The protocols are in place to ensure the success of that objective."

"Of course, of course," Jian said quickly, sensing a subtle shift in her demeanor. "Just an observation. Keep up the good work, Mara. I'll let you get back to it." He offered another smile and retreated, leaving Mara alone with her data and her meticulously planned future.

She returned her attention to the schematics, her focus absolute. The arboretum was more than just a collection of plants; it was a meticulously engineered ecosystem, a testament to human ingenuity and foresight. It was a deliberate counterpoint to the unpredictable, the chaotic, the wild. And in its perfect order, in its predictable progression, Mara found a profound sense of peace, a quiet reassurance that some things, at least, could be controlled. The hum of the environmental controls, the soft glow of the holographic displays, the precise click of her stylus on the datapad – these were the sounds and sensations of a world she understood, a world she could shape, a world that, unlike so many others, would bend to her will.

Her current focus was the soil enrichment modules, the heart of her revitalization efforts. She had spent weeks designing their placement, their operational cycles, and the precise nutrient blends they would dispense. Each module was a marvel of bio-engineering, equipped with sensors that continuously monitored soil pH, moisture content, and microbial activity, feeding data back to her central nexus. The plan was to deploy them in a phased approach, starting with the most depleted sectors and gradually expanding coverage. Mara had calculated the optimal spacing to ensure complete saturation of nutrient dispersal without creating an over-concentration that could shock the nascent ecosystem.

"Initiating deployment sequence for Soil Enrichment Modules, Sector Alpha," she murmured, her voice resonating slightly in the quiet room. Her fingers danced across the datapad, activating the automated deployment drones. She watched on a separate screen as the small, specialized machines lifted off from their charging stations, their metallic bodies glinting under the filtered sunlight. They moved with an uncanny grace, navigating the terrain of the arboretum with pre-programmed precision, their articulated arms carefully positioning each module into its designated spot.

Mara meticulously reviewed the sensor readings as each module was placed. The data flooded her screen – temperature, humidity, mineral content, organic matter percentage. She cross-referenced each data point against her projected parameters, her brow furrowed in concentration. A slight variance in the moisture reading from Module A-7 caught her attention. "Hmm," she mused, zooming in on the data. "Slightly higher than expected. A localized subterranean water pocket, perhaps? Or an anomaly in the sensor calibration?" She initiated a secondary diagnostic on the module and cross-referenced it with topographical scans of the area. "Minor discrepancy," she concluded after a few moments. "Within acceptable tolerances. It may even prove beneficial for initial root establishment." She made a note to monitor the sector more closely, but the flow of her work was not significantly interrupted.

The nutrient delivery system was equally complex. Mara had designed a series of bio-available compounds, each tailored to the specific needs of the soil and the intended plant species. There were blends rich in nitrogen and phosphorus for robust growth, others with a higher potassium content to strengthen cellular walls, and specialized formulations to encourage beneficial microbial colonization. She had even incorporated trace elements, such as iron and zinc, in carefully calibrated micro-doses, recognizing their crucial role in plant metabolism, even in minute quantities. The system was designed to release these nutrients gradually, mimicking the slow, steady decomposition of organic matter that would occur in a mature, healthy ecosystem. This gradual release was key, she believed, to preventing nutrient burn and ensuring that the soil's microbial community, which her team was working to re-establish, had time to adapt and thrive.

"Commencing nutrient infusion, Sector Alpha," she announced, her voice steady. She watched as the nutrient slurry, a viscous, earthy-brown liquid, began to flow through the subsurface pipes, guided by the intricate network of her design. The system was programmed to deliver a precise volume to each module, ensuring that every square meter of designated soil received the same carefully calculated dose. She monitored the flow rate, the pressure, and the chemical composition of the infusion in real-time, ready to make micro-adjustments should any deviations occur.

Her workspace within Havenridge was a stark contrast to the raw, untamed earth she was working to transform. It was a space of pure intellect, where the messiness of the natural world was reduced to data points and algorithms. Every tool, every piece of equipment, was impeccably clean and perfectly maintained. Her datapad, a sleek, obsidian rectangle, was her primary interface with the project, a window into the arboretum's past, present, and meticulously planned future. She would spend hours in this sterile sanctuary, surrounded by the quiet hum of climate control systems and the soft glow of holographic projections. Here, she could retreat from the unpredictable elements that constantly threatened to derail her efforts.

She was currently immersed in refining the planting schedule for the arboretum's western quadrant. This section was slated to become a showcase for genetically stable, low-resource-demand species – hardy grasses, resilient succulents, and a selection of drought-tolerant shrubs that had been engineered to thrive even in arid conditions. Mara consulted her research, her fingers flying across the datapad, adjusting projected growth rates based on the latest atmospheric data. She factored in the optimal light cycles, the precise watering schedules, and the estimated nutrient uptake for each species. Every action was deliberate, every decision informed by a wealth of data and a commitment to efficiency.

Her workspace was an extension of her mind: orderly, precise, and ruthlessly logical. Tools were arranged by function and size, from the smallest precision tweezers to the larger soil sampling augers, all gleaming under the soft, consistent light. Planting trays, each meticulously labeled and dated, were stacked in sterile bays, ready for their carefully selected occupants. She had even devised a system for her digital files, a complex hierarchy of folders and subfolders, ensuring that any piece of data, from a single soil pH reading to a comprehensive genetic profile of a plant species, could be retrieved in seconds. This unwavering dedication to organization was more than just a personal preference; it was a fundamental aspect of her methodology, a necessary shield against the inherent unpredictability of the natural world.

The arboretum project, for Mara, was an exercise in control. It was about taking a chaotic, neglected space and imposing upon it a system of order, a blueprint for success. She believed that by meticulously planning every step, by controlling every variable, she could guarantee the revival of this forgotten land. Her focus was on the tangible, the measurable, the predictable. She would spend hours analyzing soil composition reports, cross-referencing atmospheric regulator data with predicted growth patterns, and calculating the precise nutrient ratios needed for optimal plant health.

One afternoon, while poring over the latest soil analysis reports for Sector Delta, a minor anomaly pinged on her screen. The magnesium levels, while within the acceptable range for most plants, were slightly lower than her projected ideal for the heirloom apple saplings scheduled for that area. "A deviation," she murmured to herself, her brow furrowing slightly. She immediately accessed the nutrient blend formulas, her fingers tapping rapidly on the datapad. She adjusted the C-7 nutrient solution, increasing the magnesium concentration by 0.03%. "This should compensate," she stated, making a mental note to recalibrate the nutrient delivery schedule for that specific sector. This wasn't an oversight; it was a fine-tuning, a constant process of optimization.

Her research was exhaustive. She delved into obscure botanical texts, seeking out any information that could inform her approach. She studied the historical records of the region, looking for clues about its past flora and its resilience. She even consulted with specialists in plant genetics and soil science, ensuring that her plans were based on the most current and reliable scientific understanding. Every decision, from the type of irrigation emitters to be used to the precise depth at which seeds should be planted, was backed by extensive research and careful consideration.

Her workspace was a physical manifestation of this commitment to control. It was a climate-controlled environment within Havenridge, meticulously organized and sterile. Every tool, every piece of equipment, had its designated place. Her datapad, a constant extension of her will, displayed real-time data streams from the arboretum's sensors, holographic projections of planting grids, and detailed growth projections. She found a deep sense of comfort in this order, in this ability to manage and predict. It was a stark contrast to the unpredictable nature of the outside world, and a necessary buffer against the inherent chaos that could so easily undermine even the most well-intentioned efforts. This methodical approach, she firmly believed, was the key to the arboretum's eventual success.

Eli's approach to the arboretum was a symphony of gentle observation, a stark counterpoint to Mara's meticulously orchestrated scientific endeavor. Where she saw data points and algorithms, he saw life unfolding, a vibrant tapestry woven with threads of resilience and quiet persistence. His days were not dictated by the cool, sterile hum of climate-controlled labs, but by the dappled sunlight filtering through the leaves, the whisper of the wind, and the subtle shifts in the earth beneath his bare feet. He moved through the arboretum with a reverence that bordered on the spiritual, his worn leather satchel slung over his shoulder, filled not with datapad chargers and nutrient analysis kits, but with sketchpads, charcoal sticks, and small, carefully preserved seed packets.

He would often find himself drawn to the untamed corners, the spaces that Mara's meticulous plans had yet to fully encompass. It was here, amidst the tenacious weeds and the hardy, uninvited blooms, that Eli found his inspiration. He would sit for hours, his back against the rough bark of an ancient oak, or crouch low beside a patch of stubborn clover, his charcoal dancing across the page. His sketches were not sterile botanical illustrations, meticulously detailing every vein and petal. Instead, they captured the essence of growth, the character of each plant, the way it reached for the sun, the determined spread of its roots, the subtle resilience etched into its very being. He'd trace the gnarled patterns of a weed's stem, marveling at its ability to find purchase in the most unforgiving soil. He'd sketch the elegant arc of a wild vine, noting how it had adapted to climb and intertwine with whatever support it could find.

"Well now, aren't you a determined little thing?" he'd murmur, his voice a low rumble, as he sketched a cluster of dandelions pushing through a crack in a forgotten pathway. He wasn't speaking to himself, but to the plant, as if engaging in a quiet conversation. "Found a good spot, didn't you? Plenty of sun, and a bit of a shelter from the wind. Smart." He'd smile, a genuine, unforced expression that crinkled the corners of his eyes. These were not mere observations; they were acknowledgments, a recognition of the inherent will to survive that pulsed through every living organism.

His hands, calloused and earth-stained, were surprisingly gentle as he touched the leaves, feeling their texture, their temperature, their subtle vibrations. He learned their stories through touch, through scent, through the way they responded to the slightest breeze. He would often speak to them, his words a soft cadence that seemed to blend seamlessly with the natural sounds of the arboretum. "Good morning," he'd whisper to a patch of moss clinging to a damp stone. "Keeping that corner nice and cool, are you? You're doing a fine job." To a struggling sapling, he might offer encouragement, "Don't you worry, little one. The sun will find you. Just keep reaching."

Mara's approach was about imposing order, about sculpting the environment to fit her specifications. Eli's was about listening, about understanding, and then about weaving himself into the existing narrative. He saw the existing flora not as an obstacle to be cleared, but as a foundation, a testament to what could thrive in this specific place, given time and the right encouragement.

He understood that nature had its own inherent wisdom, its own time-tested strategies for survival. His role, as he saw it, was not to dictate, but to facilitate.

"You've got some real fighters here," he'd remark to himself, examining a patch of resilient ground cover that had managed to survive despite the initial clearing efforts. "Proven themselves already. Why would we try to replace them with something weaker?" He'd carefully collect seeds from these hardy specimens, tucking them into small, labeled envelopes in his satchel. These were not exotic imports, engineered for specific traits. These were the unsung heroes of the arboretum, the plants that had already demonstrated their ability to adapt and endure the unique microclimate of Havenridge.

He was particularly drawn to the wild grasses, the tenacious wildflowers, and the unassuming shrubs that seemed to thrive on neglect. He believed that these native or naturalized species held the key to the arboretum's long-term success. They were inherently adapted to the local soil, the prevailing weather patterns, and the established insect and microbial populations. Introducing them was not about filling empty spaces; it was about reinforcing the ecosystem, about strengthening its natural defenses and promoting its inherent biodiversity.

One afternoon, while Mara was meticulously calibrating the atmospheric regulators for the arid zone, Eli was engrossed in a different kind of calibration. He was observing a small swarm of native bees diligently visiting a patch of wild thyme that had established itself near a crumbling section of the arboretum's outer wall. He'd noticed the bees weeks ago, and had since made a point of ensuring that area remained undisturbed.

"Look at you go," he'd said, his voice soft, watching their busy movements. "Busy as always. You know where to find the good stuff, don't you?" He'd pull out his sketchpad, capturing the delicate dance between bee and bloom, the intricate relationship that sustained both. He believed that introducing these native pollinators was as crucial as any engineered plant species. They were an integral part of the arboretum's future, vital for the reproduction of many of the plants he intended to cultivate, and for the overall health of the ecosystem.

He'd carefully collect small samples of the pollen that clung to the bees' legs, not for genetic analysis, but to understand the range of plants they were visiting. He'd compare this with the wild flora he was identifying, building a mental map of the existing pollinator network. This information, he knew, would be invaluable when he began to introduce his own carefully selected seed strains. He wanted to ensure that the new plants would complement, rather than compete with, the existing ecological web.

His interactions with the plants were far more intimate than Mara's data-driven approach. He would gently prune away dead or diseased branches, not with sterile surgical instruments, but with a keen eye and a steady hand, always observing how the plant responded. He'd remove invasive species, yes, but he did so with a careful consideration, trying to understand why they had become so dominant, and whether any of their beneficial properties could be preserved or harnessed.

"You're a bit too enthusiastic, aren't you?" he might say to a particularly aggressive vine, as he carefully redirected its growth. "You'll choke out your neighbors if you're not careful. Let's find you a nice, sturdy trellis instead." He'd then look for a suitable structure, perhaps an old, weathered fence post or a dead tree that needed to be preserved for its ecological value, and gently guide the vine's tendrils towards it.

Eli's philosophy was rooted in the belief that nature possessed an innate ability to heal and regenerate, provided it was given the space and the right conditions. He wasn't trying to force the arboretum into a predetermined mold. He was seeking to coax it back to life, to nurture its natural tendencies. This meant embracing a degree of unpredictability, a willingness to let go of absolute control.

He would often spend time simply sitting in quiet contemplation, observing the subtle shifts in the environment. He'd notice the way the light changed throughout the day, the patterns of the clouds, the subtle rustling of leaves that indicated a change in wind direction. He believed that these seemingly insignificant details held a wealth of information, clues that could guide his efforts far more effectively than any complex algorithm.

"The air feels different today," he'd remark, sniffing the breeze. "Moister. The rain's not far off. Better make sure those young ferns are well-watered before it arrives, so they don't get washed out." He'd then gather his watering can, not to follow a pre-programmed schedule, but to respond to the immediate needs of the plants, guided by his intuitive understanding of their environment.

He had a particular affinity for the smaller, often overlooked elements of the ecosystem. He'd spend time examining the complex network of fungi growing on decaying logs, recognizing their vital role in decomposition and nutrient cycling. He'd observe the busy work of earthworms, their tireless efforts aerating the soil and enriching it with their castings. He saw these as essential collaborators, partners in the grand project of creating a thriving arboretum.

"You're doing good work down there," he'd say, gently prodding the soil with a stick. "Keeping things healthy. This soil is rich because of you." He'd often leave small offerings of decaying organic matter, like fallen leaves or compost scraps, in areas where he knew these microscopic engineers were at work, ensuring their continued productivity.

When it came to introducing new plant species, Eli's approach was cautious and deliberate. He favored hardy, wild strains that had demonstrated their resilience to environmental shifts and their ability to thrive with minimal intervention. These were not the genetically modified marvels that Mara might select for their specific traits, but species that had naturally evolved to withstand the challenges of the local climate. He would scout for these plants in nearby wildlands, carefully collecting seeds or cuttings, always ensuring he took only a small portion, leaving the parent plant healthy and undisturbed.

"These little guys have seen it all," he'd explain, holding up a handful of seeds from a tough, native wildflower. "Drought, wind, frost – they've weathered it. They know how to survive here. They'll make a good backbone for our planting." He wasn't interested in creating a pristine, manicured garden. He was aiming for a robust, self-sustaining ecosystem that could weather future uncertainties.

His methods were less about dominance and more about co-existence. He saw himself not as a controller of nature, but as a steward, a facilitator of its inherent processes. He believed that by working *with* the environment, rather than *against* it, he could achieve a more sustainable and ultimately more beautiful outcome. This meant embracing the unexpected, the spontaneous, the wildness that Mara sought to tame.

"You can't force a flower to bloom before its time," he'd muse, watching a sapling that was slow to show new growth. "You can only give it the best conditions, and then trust that it will do what it's meant to do, when it's ready." He was patient, his trust in the natural world unwavering. This patience, this willingness to allow for the inherent unpredictability of growth, was perhaps the most significant difference between his approach and Mara's.

He would often find himself working in areas that Mara had deemed less critical, or had yet to address in her detailed plans. These were the forgotten corners, the overgrown patches, the spaces where nature had already begun to reclaim its territory. He'd spend his time there, gently clearing away choking brambles, creating small clearings for sunlight, and preparing the soil with compost and organic matter, all while sketching the existing flora, noting its resilience and adaptability.

"See this?" he'd say to himself, pointing to a patch of tenacious ground ivy that had spread across a large area. "It's tenacious. It holds the soil together. Maybe we don't need to rip it all out. Maybe we can find a way for it to coexist, or at least use its strengths." He'd then investigate methods of integration, perhaps encouraging more light to reach its surface, or introducing companion plants that could benefit from its ground-covering properties.

His approach was a form of deep listening. He was attuned to the subtle language of the plants, the soil, the air. He could sense when a plant was stressed, when it needed more water, or when it was thriving. This intuition, honed over years of observation and practice, was his most valuable tool. It allowed him to respond to the immediate needs of the arboretum in a way that no amount of data could fully replicate.

"You're thirsty, aren't you?" he'd murmur to a wilting rose bush, its petals starting to droop. He'd then fetch his watering can, its metal surface cool against his skin, and gently water the roots, his movements slow and deliberate. He wouldn't overwater, of course. He'd watch the soil, feeling its moisture with his fingertips, ensuring he gave it just enough, but no more.

He was also acutely aware of the interconnectedness of the arboretum's ecosystem. He understood that every element, from the smallest microbe in the soil to the tallest tree, played a role in the overall health of the environment. His interventions were always guided by this holistic perspective, ensuring that his actions would benefit the entire system, not just individual plants.

"We need the fungi to break down the dead wood," he'd explain, as he deliberately left a decaying log in place, rather than removing it. "And we need the insects to pollinate the flowers. Everything has its purpose. We just need to make sure we're not disrupting the balance." He saw himself as a guardian of this balance, a protector of the delicate web of life that was slowly but surely taking root within the arboretum.

His conversations with the plants, while seemingly whimsical, were a way of deepening his understanding and connection. By articulating his observations, by posing questions, he was actively engaging with the living world around him. It was a form of active meditation, a way of grounding himself in the present moment and fostering a sense of mutual respect between himself and the arboretum.

"How are you feeling today, little oak?" he might ask, placing a hand on the rough bark of a young oak sapling. "A bit crowded perhaps? That vine is growing quite vigorously. I'll see if I can give you a bit more breathing room." He'd then carefully prune the vine, not to eliminate it, but to create a healthier balance for both plants.

Eli's workspace, unlike Mara's sterile sanctuary, was a comfortable, sun-drenched corner of a rustic shed on the arboretum's periphery. It was filled with the scent of drying herbs, damp earth, and aged paper. His sketchbooks were piled high, their pages filled with detailed observations of plant growth, insect activity, and soil conditions. Small bags of seeds, meticulously labeled with species names and collection dates, were organized in wooden crates. Tools were not gleaming and sterile, but well-used and familiar, their handles smooth from years of handling. A faint dusting of soil often settled on his workbench, a constant reminder of his connection to the land.

He was a believer in nature's inherent resilience. While Mara relied on sophisticated technology and precise calculations, Eli trusted the fundamental drive of life to persist. He introduced hardy, wild strains that had proven their ability to withstand environmental shifts, believing that nature's own adaptability was the ultimate key to long-term success. He didn't aim to conquer the wild, but to harmonize with it, to foster a co-existence that would benefit both the arboretum and the wider ecosystem. He saw his role as that of a gentle guide, encouraging growth rather than dictating it, fostering a natural unfolding rather than enforcing a rigid design. His methods were less about dominance and more about a profound respect for the intricate, often unpredictable, processes of life itself.

Mara's gaze swept over the data streams projected onto the transparent screen before her. Efficiency metrics, nutrient absorption rates, atmospheric humidity deviations – a constant, quantifiable hum of information that painted a picture of the arboretum's progress. It was a picture she meticulously curated, every pixel, every data point, a testament to her rigorous planning. Then, her eyes drifted to a live feed from Sector Gamma, a section of the arboretum she had designated for preliminary soil conditioning and native species introduction. Eli was there, a smudge of dirt on his cheek, his hands submerged in a patch of what looked suspiciously like... weeds.

A sigh escaped her, barely audible above the soft whir of the climate control systems. He was supposed to be focusing on the designated plots, the ones prepped with optimal nutrient profiles and carefully calibrated soil pH. Instead, he was engaging in what she could only describe as a botanical excavation, gently unearthing what appeared to be a tenacious network of dandelion roots.

"Eli," she began, her voice cutting through the ambient quiet of the control center, her tone carefully modulated to convey polite inquiry rather than exasperation. She had learned that direct confrontation was rarely as effective as a well-placed, almost disbelieving question. "What are you doing in Sector Gamma? That area is scheduled for the initial planting of the modified

Lycopersicon variants this cycle. Are you... performing an unscheduled clearing?"

Eli looked up, a sun-warmed smile creasing his face. He held up a clump of soil and roots, a few stubborn yellow flowers still clinging to the green stems. "Mara! Good to see you. Unscheduled clearing? Not exactly. I'm having a chat with these little fellows." He gestured to the dandelions. "They've worked hard to establish themselves here, you know. Found good drainage, plenty of sun. Tough little survivors, really."

Mara blinked, the data streams momentarily blurring. "Survivors? Eli, they are invasive weeds. They compete for resources, disrupt soil structure, and can overwhelm desirable species. Our projections clearly indicate their removal is a prerequisite for successful

Lycopersicon establishment." Her voice remained calm, but a subtle tension tightened her jaw. "They are an anomaly in the plan. An inefficiency."

He chuckled, a low, rumbling sound that seemed to vibrate with an entirely different frequency than her own calculated responses. "Inefficiency, you say? I see resilience. I see a natural indicator of what this soil can sustain. And honestly, Mara, 'invasive' is such a harsh word. They're just trying to make a living, like everything else." He carefully placed the dandelions into a canvas bag, not in the waste receptacle, but in a separate section. "Besides," he added, his eyes twinkling, "these seeds are packed with nutrients. And the roots, when processed, can be quite useful. Wouldn't want to waste that, would we?"

Mara's internal diagnostics registered a spike in her stress hormones. "Waste is precisely what I am trying to avoid, Eli. We have a finite timeline, and a very specific set of outcomes to achieve. Every deviation from the meticulously calculated parameters introduces an unacceptable risk. These 'tough little survivors,' as you call them,

are the risk. They are unscripted variables in an equation that demands precision." She tapped a finger against the screen, highlighting a projection of optimal growth curves for the engineered tomatoes. "These curves are dependent on predictable conditions. Unpredictable elements, like... dandelions, threaten the entire trajectory."

He walked over to a young, struggling sapling near the edge of the plot, its leaves a pale, sickly green. He knelt beside it, his fingers brushing away a cluster of what Mara's system identified as *Convolvulus arvensis*, a particularly aggressive bindweed. "And what about this one, Mara? Is this an acceptable variable? It's not a weed in your definition, I suppose, but it's certainly not thriving. It's being choked out. These *Convolvulus* are stealing its light, its moisture. So, are we going to rip out the bindweed, or are we going to help the sapling push through?" He looked up at her, his expression earnest. "My approach is to understand *why* the bindweed is thriving, and *why* the sapling is struggling, and then find a way for them to coexist, or at least for the sapling to gain the advantage it deserves. Your approach, if I understand correctly, is to eradicate the bindweed, regardless of the collateral damage to the soil ecosystem, and hope the sapling magically flourishes in its absence."

Mara felt a prickle of defensiveness. "My approach is to create the optimal environment for the sapling's success. Eradicating competing species is a necessary step in that process. It's about resource allocation. The bindweed is a wasteful drain. Removing it redirects those resources – water, nutrients, sunlight – directly to the target species. It's logical. It's efficient."

"Efficient," Eli echoed, his voice a soft murmur that seemed to carry the weight of countless seasons. "But is it understanding? You see a weed, I see a plant that has found a niche. You see competition, I see an interaction. You want to remove the competitor. I want to understand the dynamic. Perhaps the bindweed is stabilizing loose soil, preventing erosion. Perhaps its deep roots are drawing up nutrients from lower strata that the sapling can't reach. Perhaps its presence indicates a specific microbial imbalance that we should address, rather than just cutting down the plant that's telling us about it."

He stood up, dusting off his hands. "My worry, Mara, is that in your relentless pursuit of efficiency, in your desire to control every variable, you risk sterilizing the very life you're trying to cultivate. Nature is not a sterile laboratory. It's messy, it's dynamic, it's full of surprises. And those surprises, those 'inefficiencies,' are often where true strength and resilience are born."

Mara watched him move through the sector, his movements fluid and unhurried, in stark contrast to her own precise, almost surgical, approach. He would pause to examine a patch of moss growing on a rock, or to observe a line of ants marching purposefully across a fallen log. He wasn't just planting; he was observing, conversing, *feeling* the pulse of the arboretum. It was an approach that seemed to defy the very principles of controlled growth that were the bedrock of her work.

"But Eli," she countered, her voice tinged with a frustration she was struggling to contain, "that 'messiness' is precisely what we're trying to mitigate. Havenridge was a damaged ecosystem. We are not merely cultivating; we are restoring. And restoration, by its very definition, requires a structured, deliberate intervention to correct imbalances. We can't afford to wait for nature to 'figure it out' at its own pace. The environmental shifts are accelerating. We need results. We need plants that are optimized for survival in a post-collapse world, not just a thriving patch of dandelions."

"And what do you think makes a plant optimized for survival, Mara?" Eli asked, his gaze meeting hers across the rows of meticulously prepared soil. "Is it the genetic modifications you've painstakingly engineered? Or is it the inherent toughness, the adaptability, the ability to find a way, no matter the conditions, that nature has instilled over millennia? These plants that have survived the 'unscripted' chaos of the outside world – they carry that wisdom within them. My goal is to nurture that wisdom, to integrate it, not to pave over it with a layer of sterile, engineered perfection."

He gestured to a small, vibrant cluster of wildflowers, a mix of blues and yellows, that had somehow sprung up between the designated planting beds. Mara's system flagged them as non-native, opportunistic bloomers. "See those? They weren't in the planting schedule. But look at them. They're drawing in pollinators. They're enriching the soil with nitrogen. They're adding color, and beauty, and life. Your algorithms might see them as an anomaly, an inefficiency. I see them as a gift. A sign that even in this controlled environment, life finds a way, and it's often far more resourceful than we give it credit for."

"A gift that could potentially cross-pollinate with our sensitive *Lycopersicon* strains," Mara stated, her tone hardening. "Introducing uncontrolled variables into a controlled genetic experiment is... irresponsible, Eli. We have engineered these plants for specific resilience traits. Unforeseen cross-pollination could dilute those traits, or worse, introduce unforeseen vulnerabilities. The risk is too great. We need to maintain a sterile buffer zone around the experimental plots."

Eli sighed, a sound of genuine disappointment. "Sterile buffer zone. Of course. Because nothing that isn't precisely cataloged and controlled is allowed to exist. So, we rip out the wildflowers, we eradicate the dandelions, we spray anything that dares to sprout without our permission. And what happens when a blight strikes, Mara? Or when a sudden, unexpected frost hits? Will your perfectly sterile, perfectly controlled *Lycopersicon* variants have the innate resilience to cope? Or will they crumble because they've never known anything but perfect conditions, never had to fight for survival, never learned to adapt from the 'weeds' around them?"

He walked towards her, his hands clasped behind his back, his presence a calming counterpoint to her own restless energy. "My methods might seem slow, Mara. They might seem inefficient. But they are about collaboration. They are about learning from what already exists. They are about building a system that can *learn* and *adapt*, not just follow a pre-programmed directive. When I work with the soil, I'm not just amending it; I'm listening to it. When I observe a plant, I'm not just cataloging it; I'm understanding its story. And the story of this place, Mara, is one of incredible tenacity. It's a story that your algorithms can't quite capture, a narrative that your sterile protocols can't account for."

Mara felt a flicker of something akin to recognition, a subtle resonance with his words that she quickly suppressed. His perspective was so fundamentally at odds with her own, so driven by an intuitive, almost spiritual, connection to the living world, that it felt alien. Yet, she couldn't entirely dismiss the conviction in his voice, the quiet certainty in his eyes. It was a different kind of intelligence, one that operated on a spectrum she hadn't quite learned to measure.

"But that intuition, Eli," she said, her voice softening almost imperceptibly, "can be fallible. It can be influenced by sentimentality, by a romanticized view of nature. My methods are based on empirical data, on repeatable results, on a scientific understanding of biological processes. They are designed to eliminate guesswork, to ensure the highest probability of success."

"And yet," Eli replied, a gentle smile returning to his lips, "your 'empirical data' doesn't account for the sheer will to live, does it? It can't quantify the resilience of a seed that waits for decades for the right conditions, or the stubborn persistence of a root that finds its way through solid rock. Those are not sentimental notions, Mara. They are fundamental forces of life. My work is about acknowledging those forces, about working *with* them, not trying to suppress them in the name of an idealized, sterile outcome. Your approach is about building a fortress against nature. Mine is about becoming part of its ecosystem, about learning its language."

He picked up a smooth, grey stone from the path, turning it over in his hand. "This stone, for instance. Your system might log it as an inert obstacle, something to be removed if it impedes planting. I see it as a microhabitat. It retains moisture, it provides shelter for insects, it's a anchor for moss and lichen. It's part of the soil's history, and its present. To remove it, without understanding its role, is to lose a piece of the puzzle."

Mara watched him, a strange duality unfolding within her. Her logical mind screamed that he was being inefficient, reckless, jeopardizing the entire project with his whimsical approach. But another part of her, a quieter, more curious part, was captivated by the depth of his connection to the arboretum, by the way he seemed to converse with the very earth beneath his feet. His methods were chaotic, unpredictable, and deeply rooted in a philosophy she could barely grasp. Yet, as she observed him gently coaxing a struggling vine onto a support structure, his movements imbued with a profound respect, she couldn't deny a nascent fascination. He wasn't just planting trees; he was weaving himself into the arboretum's narrative, allowing its own stories to guide his hand. This fundamental difference in their philosophies, she realized with a growing, unsettling awareness, was not just a professional disagreement. It was a chasm that, surprisingly, seemed to be drawing her gaze, and her attention, ever more intently towards him.

The hum of the atmospheric processors was a constant, a low thrum that usually soothed Mara's analytical mind. Today, it felt like a monotonous drone, amplifying the unease that had settled in her stomach since her conversation with Eli. She stood on the observation platform overlooking Sector Delta, a sprawling expanse of what had once been dense, uncontrolled growth. The automated clearing drones had done their work, leaving behind swathes of disturbed earth punctuated by the stubborn persistence of life. It was a scene that, to her, represented the raw material of her carefully constructed future, a chaotic canvas awaiting her precise brushstrokes. Yet, Eli's words echoed, a persistent counter-melody to the drone of the machines: "The story of this place is one of incredible tenacity."

She descended to the main concourse, her boots clicking on the recycled composite flooring. Eli was already there, a smudge of dark soil adorning his cheek, a faint scent of damp earth clinging to him. He was kneeling beside a cluster of what Mara's internal botanical database identified as *Rumex acetosella*, commonly known as sheep's sorrel. The small, heart-shaped leaves, tinged with a deep, almost defiant green, had pushed through a thick mat of decaying leaf litter, their presence a testament to their successful, uninvited colonization.

"Good morning, Mara," Eli greeted, his voice warm, unperturbed by the slight frost in the air that still clung to the edges of the sector. He carefully cupped his hands around the sorrel, as if shielding it from an unseen threat. "Look at this. Persistent little things, aren't they? They've managed to find their footing even after the drones went through."

Mara approached, her gaze sweeping over the area. The sorrel was indeed thriving, its tenacious root system likely anchoring it firmly against the mechanical intrusion. "They are an example of opportunistic growth, Eli. They exploit the disruption. We'll need to ensure they are fully eradicated before the next planting cycle. Their seeds can remain viable for years, posing a long-term threat to the stability of the newly established ecosystem." Her tone was factual, devoid of emotion, but the internal conflict gnawed at her. Eli's perspective was undeniably... different.

Eli carefully loosened the soil around the base of the sorrel with a small trowel, not to uproot it, but to examine its structure. "Threat? Or a sign? They're telling us that this soil, even after years of neglect, has a capacity to support life. These aren't delicate hothouse blooms, Mara. These are survivors. They've navigated drought, frost, probably nutrient deficiencies, and still, they flourish." He gestured to the intricate network of fine, red roots he had exposed. "This root system isn't just anchoring the plant; it's aerating the soil, breaking down organic matter. It's contributing to the very structure we need for our engineered crops."

"But at what cost?" Mara countered, her voice carefully measured. "They compete for water, for nutrients. Our *Solanum lycopersicum* variants are optimized for specific nutrient absorption profiles. Introducing competition, even for beneficial compounds, dilutes their efficacy. We have precise nutritional requirements for optimal growth and yield. Uncontrolled variables, like these wild plants, introduce unacceptable risk to our projected timelines and resource allocation." She tapped a stylus against her forearm-mounted display, bringing up a holographic projection of a perfectly cultivated tomato plant, its form idealized, its growth curve a smooth, upward trajectory. "This is the outcome we are working towards. This is the future we are building. It's about controlled progression, not embracing... wildness."

Eli looked up, his eyes, the color of warm earth, meeting hers. "Wildness is where resilience is forged, Mara. These plants have evolved without our intervention. They've faced challenges we can only simulate in our labs. Their genetic makeup is a library of survival strategies. By eradicating them, we're not just removing competition; we're discarding invaluable data. We're silencing voices that have whispered secrets of adaptation for centuries." He gently unearthed a particularly stubborn clump of sorrel, revealing a small, almost iridescent beetle clinging to its roots. "See? This beetle has found a home here. Its life is intertwined with this plant. We remove the plant, we disrupt its world. It's a ripple effect, and we're only just beginning to understand how interconnected everything is."

He then moved a few meters away, towards a patch of ground that seemed slightly more compacted, less disturbed by the drones. Here, a low-growing, almost silvery-leaved plant had taken root. Mara's database identified it as *Plantago lanceolata*, or ribwort plantain. It was nondescript, unglamorous, yet it had managed to establish itself firmly in the less-than-ideal conditions.

"And this," Eli continued, his voice softening with a quiet reverence, "this plantain. It's been used for centuries in traditional medicine, for its anti-inflammatory and wound-healing properties. Its roots help to break up compacted soil, making it easier for other plants to establish. It's a pioneer species, Mara, preparing the ground for others. It doesn't demand much, but it gives a great deal back to the soil." He gently ran a calloused thumb over a broad, ribbed leaf. "Your engineered crops might be more productive in ideal conditions, but this little fellow can thrive in conditions that would wither them. It's a different kind of strength, a quiet, enduring fortitude."

Mara felt a familiar tightness in her chest. "Enduring fortitude is precisely what we are engineering into our crops, Eli. We are not trying to replicate nature's haphazard process; we are attempting to surpass it. We have the knowledge, the technology, to create plants that are not only resilient but also optimized for specific roles in our rebuilding efforts. These wild species are beautiful in their own way, I grant you, but they are also unpredictable. And in a world that demands predictability, that demands efficiency, unpredictability is a luxury we cannot afford."

"But what if predictability is an illusion?" Eli countered, his gaze earnest. "What if true resilience lies not in the absence of unpredictability, but in the ability to adapt *to* it? These plants have survived the Collapse, Mara. They've weathered the environmental upheaval, the years of neglect, the harsh realities that followed. They are living proof that life, in its most fundamental form, is inherently adaptable. They haven't waited for us to engineer them for survival; they've simply *been* surviving. They've found ways to persist, to reproduce, to continue their lineage against all odds." He carefully dug around the base of the plantain, revealing a network of surprisingly deep taproots. "These roots are reaching for water, for nutrients, far deeper than your engineered tomatoes will initially be able to. They are making the soil more accessible, more hospitable, for the very crops you want to cultivate."

He stood up, brushing dirt from his knees. "When I look at these plants, I don't see weeds that need to be eradicated. I see teachers. I see living laboratories that have been conducting trials for decades, centuries even, proving what works, what endures. Your approach is to clear the slate, to impose a new order. My approach is to learn from the existing order, to understand its inherent strengths, and to integrate them into our efforts. It's about collaboration, not conquest."

Mara watched him, her analytical mind grappling with the intuitive logic of his observations. She understood the scientific principles of soil health, of nutrient cycling, of plant competition. But Eli spoke of these things with a depth of understanding that transcended mere data points. He saw the interconnectedness, the inherent value in every living organism, regardless of its utility to human design.

"But Eli," she said, her voice a little softer than intended, "the Collapse was a catastrophic event. The ecosystem was severely damaged. We are not simply tending to a healthy environment; we are actively engaged in restoration. Restoration requires careful, targeted intervention. We cannot afford to let opportunistic species dictate the pace or the composition of our rebuilding efforts. Our engineered crops are designed for specific functions – food production, atmospheric regeneration, bio-remediation. These functions are critical for our survival, for establishing a stable civilization. We need to prioritize those engineered solutions."

Eli nodded slowly, his expression thoughtful. "I understand the urgency, Mara, I truly do. But I worry that in our rush to engineer a perfect solution, we might overlook the perfection that already exists. These resilient plants, they are not just survivors; they are evidence of nature's inherent capacity for renewal. They hold genetic secrets that could be invaluable. Perhaps they possess natural resistance to diseases that plague our engineered strains. Perhaps their root systems can break down toxins in the soil that our crops cannot tolerate. By dismissing them as 'weeds,' we are closing ourselves off to potentially vital allies in our restoration efforts."

He knelt again, this time by a patch of ground where a cluster of tiny, vibrant blue flowers had pushed through. Mara's system identified them as *Myosotis sylvatica*, common forget-me-nots. They were delicate, almost ethereal, and certainly not part of any planned planting.

"Look at these," Eli whispered, as if afraid to disturb them. "They're not aggressive. They're not taking over. They're simply... being. And in their being, they attract pollinators. They add a touch of beauty, a reminder of what we're fighting to reclaim. They might not have a designated role in your spreadsheets, Mara, but they have a role in the ecosystem. They are a part of the tapestry, and every thread, no matter how small, is important."

Mara's gaze followed his, her eyes tracing the delicate petals. The forget-me-nots were indeed lovely, a stark contrast to the utilitarian greens and browns of the operational sectors. For a fleeting moment, her carefully constructed logical framework wavered. She remembered the stark, sterile landscapes of her childhood, before the Collapse, before the constant, pervasive struggle for resources. Beauty, in that world, had been a luxury, a distant memory.

"Beauty doesn't feed us, Eli," she said, the sharpness returning to her voice, though it felt less convincing now. "It doesn't regenerate the atmosphere. It's a non-essential variable in the equation of survival."

"But it's what makes survival worth fighting for," Eli replied, his voice gentle but firm. "What is the point of a perfectly engineered, perfectly efficient world if it lacks the very things that make life meaningful? These plants, these 'weeds,' they represent a different kind of efficiency – the efficiency of life itself. They have found ways to thrive with minimal input, to contribute to their environment, to endure. We can learn from them, Mara. We can integrate their inherent resilience into our engineered solutions, creating crops that are not only robust but also deeply connected to the natural systems we are trying to re-establish."

He stood, his movements fluid and unhurried. "Think of it this way, Mara. Your engineered crops are like finely tuned machines. They perform their functions flawlessly, but they are dependent on a constant supply of precisely calibrated energy and maintenance. These wild plants, on the other hand, are like hardy, self-sufficient organisms. They find their own sustenance, they adapt to changing conditions, they regenerate themselves. Wouldn't it be more sustainable, more secure, to build our future by learning from these natural exemplars, by weaving their inherent tenacity into the fabric of our engineered systems?"

He walked towards a particularly overgrown corner of the sector, where a gnarled, tenacious vine had woven itself around a decaying metal structure, its leaves a deep, rich green. Mara's system flagged it as *Hedera helix*, English ivy, a species known for its aggressive growth and ability to outcompete other plants.

"This ivy," Eli said, his voice filled with a surprising admiration. "It's choked out everything else around it, hasn't it? In your view, it's a parasitic menace. But look closer. Its roots are stabilizing this ancient structure, preventing it from collapsing further. Its dense foliage provides shelter for small animals. It's a micro-ecosystem unto itself. And its leaves... they're packed with chlorophyll, constantly working to convert sunlight into energy, into oxygen. It's a highly efficient photosynthetic machine, wouldn't you say?"

Mara's analytical gaze scanned the ivy, her internal algorithms processing its dense biomass, its high rate of transpiration, its potential for uncontrolled spread. Her programming screamed 'eradicate.' But Eli's words, his almost reverent tone, were beginning to chip away at her certainty.

"Its efficiency comes at the expense of other species, Eli," she stated, her voice still firm, but with a hint of something else – curiosity, perhaps, or a dawning, uncomfortable awareness. "It's a zero-sum game. It wins, everything else loses."

"Or perhaps," Eli countered, his eyes reflecting the muted sunlight filtering through the canopy, "it's a lesson in resource management. It has learned to access what it needs, to maximize its growth in a challenging environment. If we can understand *how* it does that, Mara, perhaps we can adapt those strategies for our own crops. Instead of viewing it as an enemy, what if we viewed it as a mentor? What if we could engineer our plants to have some of its robust root systems, its efficient photosynthesis, its ability to thrive on marginal land, without its aggressive, all-consuming nature?"

He gently touched a thick, woody stem of the ivy. "The Collapse taught us that we cannot simply impose our will on nature. We are part of it. And the more we try to isolate ourselves from it, the more vulnerable we become. These plants, these weeds, they are not flaws in our system. They are indicators. They are lessons waiting to be learned. They are the embodiment of resilience, a quality we desperately need to cultivate, both in our crops and in ourselves."

Mara remained silent for a long moment, her gaze fixed on the ivy, then drifting to the sorrel, the plantain, the forget-me-nots. They were, undeniably, survivors. They had endured a world far harsher than anything her meticulously controlled arboretum could replicate. They represented a raw, untamed strength, a testament to the indomitable will of life. Her meticulously planned future, built on the foundation of engineered perfection, suddenly felt... incomplete. It lacked the hard-won wisdom, the deep-seated adaptability, that these seemingly insignificant plants embodied.

"So," Mara said, her voice barely a whisper, the analytical facade cracking, "you're suggesting we... study them? Integrate their traits?"

Eli turned to her, a hopeful smile gracing his lips. "Exactly, Mara. Not eradication, but observation. Not conquest, but collaboration. We can learn so much from these resilient pioneers. They are not just weeds; they are the architects of their own survival. And in understanding their strategies, we might just find the key to building a truly resilient future, a future that can weather any storm, not by conquering nature, but by learning to live in harmony with it." He extended a hand, his palm facing upwards, as if offering a new perspective. "They are unearthing a resilience that we, in our quest for control, have almost forgotten how to see."

Mara looked at his outstretched hand, then back at the thriving, defiant plants. A slow, unfamiliar warmth spread through her. It wasn't the cold, calculated logic of her algorithms, but something deeper, something akin to hope. Perhaps, just perhaps, Eli was right. Perhaps the true path to restoration wasn't paved with sterile perfection, but with the messy, resilient, and ultimately beautiful, strength of life itself. The data streams on her display still hummed with projected outcomes, but for the first time, Mara found herself looking beyond the numbers, towards the quiet wisdom of the wild.

Mara's internal chronometer registered the subtle shift in ambient light as the sun began its descent, casting long, distorted shadows across the arboretum. The low hum of the life support systems, a constant companion to her existence, seemed to fade into the background, replaced by the gentle rustle of synthesized foliage and the distant whirring of maintenance drones. She had been cataloging nutrient levels in Sector Gamma, a painstaking process of data collection and analysis, when Eli's voice, a melodic counterpoint to the mechanical symphony, had cut through her concentration. He had found something.

"Mara, you need to see this," he had called, his tone laced with an excitement that was both infectious and, to her, slightly bewildering. Eli's excitement often stemmed from phenomena she had already classified and dismissed as predictable biological responses. Yet, his persistence was a force of nature in itself, and she had reluctantly set aside her datapad, the sterile glow of its screen momentarily forgotten.

She found him near the far western perimeter of Sector Gamma, a region deliberately left less manicured, a buffer zone designed to mimic the transitional ecotones that had once existed before the Collapse. It was a place where the engineered perfection of her planned ecosystems met the untamed resilience of the reclaimed environment. Eli was kneeling, his focus intently fixed on a patch of ground that was, by all her calculations, unsuitable for significant botanical growth. The soil here was thin, compacted, and received only dappled sunlight, filtered through the dense canopy of the engineered forest.

"What is it, Eli?" she asked, her voice betraying none of the curiosity that was, despite her best efforts, beginning to stir within her. She approached cautiously, her boots making barely a sound on the soft, mulchy earth.

Eli looked up, his face illuminated by the soft, golden light. A genuine smile played on his lips, a rare sight that always managed to disarm her analytical defenses. He gestured with a dirt-stained finger towards a tangle of growth that, at first glance, appeared to be little more than a collection of hardy weeds, similar to the sorrel and plantain she had encountered earlier. But as Mara's enhanced vision scanned the area, her internal database cross-referenced with Eli's gestural indication, a subtle difference emerged.

Clinging to the rough bark of a nearby stabilizing structure, a structure she had planned for gradual demolition, was a vine. It wasn't the aggressive, all-consuming ivy she had encountered before. This vine was different. Its tendrils, slender and delicate, had found purchase in the most improbable of places, weaving their way through crevices and cracks, seemingly defying the very laws of structural integrity that governed her engineered world. What truly captured her attention, however, were its flowers.

Small, star-shaped, and a vibrant, almost impossibly deep shade of amethyst, they bloomed in clusters, pushing forth from amidst the dense, leathery leaves. The color was unlike anything she had encountered in her controlled cultivation. It was a shade that spoke of an ancient, untamed beauty, a pigment forged not in a laboratory but by the raw alchemy of nature. The flowers seemed to glow with an inner light, their delicate petals unfurling with a silent tenacity, a testament to their struggle for existence.

"It's... a vine," Mara stated, her voice carefully neutral, her mind already attempting to categorize and assess. "What is its designation?"

Eli chuckled, a warm, resonant sound. "Designation? I don't have a designation for it. I've never seen anything like it. It's not in any of the pre-Collapse botanical archives I have access to. It's as if it just... appeared." He gently traced a tendril with his fingertip. "Look at how it grows, Mara. It's not aggressively seeking sunlight. It's thriving in the shade, finding its own unique niche. And these flowers... they're breathtaking."

Mara knelt beside him, her usual reserve momentarily forgotten. She reached out, her gloved finger hovering just above one of the blossoms. The velvety texture, the intricate pattern of veins on each petal, the subtle, sweet fragrance that now reached her nostrils – it was all so unexpected. Her datapad remained unconsulted, her analytical processes momentarily superseded by a purely sensory experience. This plant, this defiant splash of color in the shadowed corners of their world, was undeniably beautiful.

"It's adapting," she murmured, the word feeling inadequate to describe the phenomenon before her. "It's found a way to exist where conditions are suboptimal. The nutrient content of the soil here is minimal, the light exposure is limited, and yet..." She trailed off, unable to articulate the profound sense of wonder that was beginning to bloom within her, mirroring the flowers at her feet.

Eli's gaze met hers, and for the first time, she saw not just a fellow scientist, but someone who understood the inherent poetry of existence, even in its most unexpected forms. "It's not just adapting, Mara. It's flourishing. It's creating its own beauty, its own purpose, independent of our plans. This vine, these flowers, they are a living defiance of the bleakness we've so carefully tried to engineer away."

He carefully nudged aside a fallen leaf, revealing more of the vine's root system. It was a marvel of biological engineering, a network of fine, fibrous roots that had spread through the compacted soil, seeking out every available micro-nutrient, every minuscule pocket of moisture. "Look at its roots," Eli continued, his voice hushed with awe. "They're not just anchoring it; they're breaking down the compacted soil, aerating it, making it more hospitable for other life forms. It's doing the work of a pioneer species, but with an elegance we rarely see."

Mara's analytical mind, though momentarily subdued, began to reassert itself. "The genetic makeup of this species is unknown. Its reproductive cycle, its potential for spread, its interaction with the established engineered flora – all of it is a significant unknown variable. It could pose a risk."

"Or," Eli countered softly, his eyes still fixed on the flowers, "it could be a solution. A source of inspiration. Imagine if we could understand how it thrives in such adverse conditions. Imagine if we could engineer our crops to possess even a fraction of its resilience, its ability to find beauty and sustenance where we see only barrenness." He picked up a fallen bloom, its petals still vibrant, and held it out to her. "This isn't a risk, Mara. It's a gift. A reminder that life, in its purest form, is an act of relentless, exquisite creation."

Mara hesitated for a moment, then slowly reached out and took the flower. It was cool and delicate in her palm, its color a stark contrast to the muted tones of her uniform. The vibrant purple seemed to thrum with a life force that her datapad could never quantify. She looked from the flower to Eli, and in that shared moment, surrounded by the quiet hum of their artificial world, a fragile bridge seemed to form between their disparate philosophies.

The vine, with its impossibly purple blooms, was a tangible embodiment of everything Eli believed in: the inherent strength of nature, the beauty of imperfection, the boundless capacity of life to endure and even to thrive against all odds. For Mara, it was a challenge to her meticulously constructed worldview, a living testament to the limitations of even the most advanced engineering when confronted with the raw, untamed power of the natural world.

"It's... remarkable," she conceded, the word carrying more weight than she had intended. The analytical part of her brain was still buzzing with questions, with the need to classify, to understand, to control. But another part of her, a part she rarely acknowledged, was captivated. She saw not a threat, but a marvel. Not a weed to be eradicated, but a miracle to be studied.

Eli smiled, a genuine, unburdened smile that reached his eyes. "Remarkable, yes. And it's here, in our carefully curated arboretum, a place designed to showcase our ability to control and replicate nature. It's a humbling thought, isn't it? That even in our most controlled environments, nature finds a way to surprise us, to remind us of its own inherent power and beauty."

He stood, offering Mara a hand to help her up. As she rose, her gaze swept over the area once more. The vine seemed to weave a tapestry of defiance, its amethyst blooms a beacon of hope in the subdued light. It wasn't just a plant; it was a symbol. A symbol of resilience, of beauty found in adversity, of the enduring spirit of life.

"We'll need to analyze its genetic structure, of course," Mara said, her voice regaining some of its customary precision, though the edge of wonder remained. "And determine its compatibility with our existing cultivars."

"And while we do that," Eli added, his gaze still lingering on the vine, "we can simply appreciate it. We can learn from its quiet strength. We can allow it to remind us that even in a world striving for engineered perfection, there is still room for the wild, for the unexpected, for the breathtaking beauty of nature's own design."

He gestured to the vine, its tendrils snaking through the shadows, its blooms a vibrant testament to life's persistent spirit. "This, Mara," he said, his voice soft, yet filled with an undeniable conviction, "is what hope looks like."

Mara looked at the vine, then at Eli, and for the first time, she truly saw the shared ground between them. It wasn't in the sterile precision of her algorithms, nor in the untamed wilderness of his philosophy. It was here, in this unexpected bloom of amethyst, a silent testament to the enduring power and beauty of life itself, a beauty that transcended even the most carefully constructed systems. The divide between them, vast and seemingly insurmountable, had, in this moment, been bridged by a single, resilient vine. The shared discovery was not just of a plant, but of a possibility – a possibility for understanding, for collaboration, and perhaps, for a future that embraced both the engineered and the wild. The air between them, once charged with unspoken disagreement, now held a quiet sense of shared wonder, a recognition of a natural marvel that had managed to bloom, quite literally, in the space between their worlds. It was a moment of quiet communion, a silent acknowledgment that even in their divergent paths, they could both find profound meaning in the persistent, beautiful spirit of life.

CHAPTER FOUR

The Language of Growth

Mara's fingers danced across the holographic interface of her datapad, each keystroke a precise, deliberate action. The ambient light of the arboretum, calibrated to mimic the soft glow of late afternoon, cast a warm hue over the holographic projections of her data streams. She was in her element, a conductor orchestrating a symphony of biological information. Each entry was a testament to her dedication, a meticulously crafted record of the arboretum's ongoing evolution. She began with the general parameters, the foundational elements that governed the entire ecosystem.

"Observation Log, Cycle 74.3. Primary environmental stability indicators nominal," she dictated, her voice a calm, measured cadence that resonated with quiet authority within the cavernous space. "Atmospheric composition remains within optimal ranges: Oxygen 20.98%, Nitrogen 78.01%, Argon 0.93%, trace gases negligible. Internal temperature maintained at 22.4 degrees Celsius, humidity at 55%." She paused, her gaze sweeping over the verdant expanse. The air, carefully recycled and purified, carried the faint, earthy scent of living plants, a fragrance that, to Mara, was the smell of controlled success.

Her focus then narrowed, delving into the specifics of the soil. This was the bedrock, the foundation upon which all life in the arboretum depended. She had sampled and analyzed numerous plots throughout Sector Gamma, the sector where Eli's unexpected discovery had occurred. The data from these samples formed a complex mosaic, a testament to the varied conditions within even this carefully managed zone. "Soil analysis, Sector Gamma, subsection Delta-7: pH reading averaged 6.8, indicating a slightly acidic to neutral balance, conducive to a broad spectrum of botanical life. Organic matter content at 12.7%, with nitrogen levels at 0.15%, phosphorus at 0.08%, and potassium at 0.12%. Trace mineral profiles within established parameters." She scrolled through the data, her eyes scanning the readouts with an practiced ease. Each number, each percentage, represented a deliberate choice, a calculated risk assessed and managed.

She moved on to the light exposure, a critical factor in photosynthesis and overall plant health. The arboretum's lighting system was a marvel of engineering, capable of precisely mimicking the diurnal and seasonal cycles of pre-Collapse Earth. Yet, even with such advanced technology, natural variations within the environment could influence the microclimates. "Light intensity readings, Delta-7: average diurnal exposure recorded at 12.7 kilolux, with peak photosynthetic photon flux density reaching 450 micromoles per square meter per second. Variations noted due to canopy density and reflective surfaces, with localized dips to 8.2 kilolux in shaded undergrowth areas." She made a mental note to cross-reference these readings with the growth rates of the flora in those specific sub-sections. Every deviation, however small, was a data point to be understood.

Water intake was another crucial metric. The arboretum's closed-loop water recycling system was designed for maximum efficiency, but precise delivery to each plant was paramount. "Hydration levels, Delta-7: average water uptake per plant cycle, estimated at 150 milliliters. Soil moisture content consistently maintained between 40-60% saturation. No instances of over- or under-watering detected in monitored plots." She was meticulous, leaving no room for ambiguity. For Mara, clarity in data was the first step towards control, and control was the key to survival.

Then came the growth rates, the tangible indicators of success. This was where the true effectiveness of her management strategies became evident. She meticulously recorded the progress of each designated species, comparing current growth against projected models. "Growth rate analysis, Delta-7: *Artemisia annua* cultivars exhibiting average stem elongation of 2.3 centimeters per cycle, with leaf biomass increase at 0.15 grams per cycle. *Salvia officinalis* specimens showing robust root development and an average flowering initiation period of 8.7 cycles. Overall growth trends within 98.7% of projected models." She prided herself on these numbers, on the predictability and reliability they represented. It was a testament to her understanding of biological systems, to her ability to translate complex scientific principles into tangible, observable results.

Her digital log, a vast repository of information stretching back to the early days of Havenridge, was more than just a record; it was a narrative. It told the story of their persistence, of their unwavering commitment to rebuilding a sustainable future from the ashes of the past. Each entry was a chapter, each data point a sentence, building a comprehensive chronicle of their efforts. She believed that by understanding the past, by meticulously documenting the present, they could chart a course for a more secure future.

She paused, her gaze drifting towards the western perimeter of Sector Gamma. The area Eli had drawn her attention to, the seemingly barren patch of compacted soil, was a stark contrast to the lushness surrounding it. Her analytical mind, even as it diligently logged the expected data, couldn't entirely dismiss the anomaly. She had already run the standard environmental scans on that specific micro-location. The readings were as she expected: low nutrient content, suboptimal light, limited water retention. By all scientific metrics, it was an area designated for minimal impact, perhaps even eventual reclamation for structural purposes.

Yet, the vine persisted. Its vibrant, amethyst blooms were a splash of audacious color against the muted greens and browns of the engineered foliage. The scientific part of her brain acknowledged the plant's remarkable resilience, its ability to thrive in conditions that would be detrimental to most other species. It was an anomaly, an outlier in her carefully constructed datasets. She had already initiated a preliminary genetic sequencing on a small sample she had discreetly collected. The initial results were inconclusive, pointing to a genetic lineage that was either highly divergent or entirely novel.

"Further analysis required for novel flora specimen observed in Delta-7, coordinate G-14," she dictated, her voice retaining its professional detachment, though a subtle undertone of intrigue now colored her words. "Preliminary environmental conditions recorded as: soil pH 7.2, organic matter content 3.1%, nitrogen 0.05%, phosphorus 0.03%, potassium 0.04%. Light exposure averaging 5.8 kilolux. Soil moisture content fluctuating between 20-35%. These readings fall outside optimal parameters for sustained vegetative growth of known species." She paused, the datapad's holographic display shimmering as she added the cross-referenced data. "Despite these suboptimal conditions, the specimen exhibits active flowering and vegetative propagation. This anomaly warrants further investigation."

She continued her logging, her fingers moving with practiced efficiency, detailing the hydration systems, the atmospheric regulators, the nutrient delivery schedules for the sectors she had been assigned to survey. Her mind, however, kept returning to the amethyst blooms. They were a silent challenge to her carefully ordered world, a living embodiment of the unpredictable, the wild, the untamed. Her protocols dictated that such anomalies be thoroughly investigated, assessed for potential risks, and, if necessary, eradicated to maintain the integrity of the engineered ecosystem. But a small, persistent voice within her, a voice she had long suppressed, whispered a different possibility.

This was not just a data point; it was a phenomenon. It was proof that even in their meticulously controlled environment, life found a way to surprise, to adapt, to create its own beauty. The vine wasn't just surviving; it was flourishing, its tendrils reaching out, its blooms unfurling with a silent, defiant grace. She cross-referenced the growth patterns of the engineered flora in the adjacent plots, noting the subtle differences in their response to environmental stressors. The *Artemisia annua*, typically robust, showed a slight decrease in leaf vitality in areas with lower light penetration. The *Salvia officinalis*, while healthy, displayed a less vigorous flowering cycle compared to its counterparts in more favorable conditions.

The vine, however, seemed indifferent to these subtle struggles. It had found its niche, its own unique path to sustenance and reproduction. Its root system, as Eli had pointed out, was a marvel of adaptation, not just anchoring the plant but actively breaking down the compacted soil, enriching it with its own biological processes. This was not merely survival; it was an active contribution to the environment, a subtle redefinition of its parameters.

Mara initiated a new sub-protocol, a dedicated section within her log for the undocumented species. She began with a comprehensive environmental profile of its immediate surroundings, meticulously documenting the soil composition, light spectrum and intensity, humidity levels, and air circulation patterns within a five-meter radius of its location. She even included a detailed analysis of the insect and microbial life present in that specific microclimate, noting the presence of certain beneficial fungi that seemed to have colonized the vine's root structure.

"Environmental profile, Specimen X, coordinate G-14, Delta-7: Soil composition characterized by low organic matter and limited nutrient availability. Ambient light levels below optimal photosynthetic thresholds for most known flora. Water retention capacity of substrate minimal." She continued, her voice a steady stream of information, her mind working at an accelerated pace. "However, microbial analysis of the rhizosphere reveals a high concentration of mycorrhizal fungi, species designation pending, exhibiting symbiotic relationships with Specimen X's root structures. This fungal network may be instrumental in nutrient acquisition and water transport under suboptimal conditions."

She then moved on to the plant's morphological characteristics, describing its vine-like growth habit, the texture and color of its leaves, and the distinctive shape and hue of its flowers. She noted the delicate nature of the tendrils, their ability to adhere to rough surfaces, and the remarkable flexibility of their structure. The amethyst blooms were the most striking feature, their color an intense, almost luminous shade that defied easy categorization. She ran spectral analysis on the pigment, her datapad displaying a complex graph of light absorption and reflection. "Floral pigmentation analysis: Spectrographic data indicates a unique pigment profile, with peak absorption in the blue-violet spectrum and significant reflection in the purple range. This pigment may possess properties beyond aesthetic appeal, potentially related to UV protection or insect attraction."

Her datapad's internal chronometer signaled the approaching end of her designated observation period for the day. Yet, she found herself lingering, her gaze drawn back to the vine. It was more than just a scientific curiosity; it was a symbol of something she had almost forgotten existed: the sheer, unadulterated power of life. Her world was built on logic, on predictable outcomes, on the careful management of resources. But this vine, this defiant splash of amethyst, was a reminder that nature, in its infinite complexity, would always hold a few secrets, a few surprises.

She made one final entry before deactivating her holographic interface, her words a quiet testament to a shift in her perspective, a subtle acknowledgment of the intangible. "Overall assessment: Specimen X represents a significant biological anomaly within Sector Gamma. Its ability to thrive under adverse conditions, coupled with its unique genetic makeup and pigment profile, suggests a high degree of adaptability and resilience. Further long-term monitoring and analysis are recommended, not only to assess potential risks but also to explore potential benefits and applications. The continued existence and propagation of this specimen may offer invaluable insights into ecological resilience and the broader principles of sustainable growth."

As she rose, her boots sinking slightly into the soft earth, she cast one last look at the vine. Its amethyst blooms seemed to shimmer in the fading light, a silent promise of continued growth, of enduring beauty. It was a whisper of wildness in their ordered world, a seed of hope planted in the heart of their engineered sanctuary. The data she had collected was invaluable, a testament to her rigorous scientific approach. But the unspoken understanding, the nascent appreciation for the sheer tenacity of life, was something that couldn't be logged, something that transcended the cold, hard facts. It was a feeling, a recognition, a quiet awe that settled deep within her, a feeling that, perhaps, was the most important observation of all.

Eli's boots crunched softly on the gravel path, a sound so different from Mara's precise, almost silent steps on the arboretum floor. Where Mara saw data streams and environmental parameters, Eli saw life, vibrant and pulsating with an energy that hummed beneath the surface of observation. He didn't carry a datapad, not for this. His tools were his senses, honed by a lifetime spent in communion with the soil and the sky, long before the sterile embrace of Havenridge. He would often stand at the edge of a newly planted sector, not to scan nutrient levels or measure light saturation, but to simply *be*. To breathe in the mingled scents of damp earth and nascent leaves, to feel the subtle vibrations of roots pushing deeper into the soil, to listen to the whisper of wind through the engineered canopy.

He would run his fingers through the soil, not for a precise pH reading, but for the texture, the moisture, the very *feel* of it. Was it heavy and cloying, suggesting overwatering and poor drainage? Or was it light and crumbly, indicative of good aeration and the promise of healthy root growth? His touch was a form of communication, a silent dialogue with the earth. He would close his eyes, letting his fingertips trace the contours of the soil, sensing the faint warmth radiating from it, the subtle coolness that hinted at hidden moisture. He could discern the difference between soil that was merely damp and soil that was alive, teeming with the unseen microorganisms that were the true architects of fertility.

The plants themselves were his most eloquent teachers. He didn't need spectral analysis to understand the distress of a wilting leaf. He could see the subtle droop, the slight discoloration, the way the edges curled inward, not as a data anomaly, but as a plea. He would approach a struggling sapling, not with a nutrient injector, but with a gentle touch, his palm laid flat against its stem. He would feel for the faint thrum of its life force, the hesitant pulse that spoke of its struggle. Sometimes, it was a matter of light. Not the measured lux readings Mara meticulously logged, but the *quality* of the light.

Was it too harsh, scorching the delicate leaves? Or too dim, starving the plant of the energy it craved? He would observe how the leaves angled themselves, their subtle shifts like tiny sun-seeking compasses, revealing their thirst for illumination.

His approach to the amethyst vine, the anomaly Mara had documented, was a prime example of this intuitive understanding. While Mara analyzed its genetic makeup and documented its improbable survival against all odds, Eli simply sat beside it. He didn't prod or poke. He just observed. He watched the way the tendrils reached out, not with the desperate, clinging grasp of a plant in distress, but with a confident, exploratory exploration of its surroundings. He noticed how the amethyst blooms, so striking to Mara's analytical eye, seemed to hold a quiet energy, a subtle luminescence that wasn't just pigment, but a reflection of its inner vitality.

He would reach out, his fingers hovering just above the vibrant petals, feeling the faint, almost imperceptible warmth they radiated. He could sense, not the exact temperature, but the *health* of the bloom, its fullness of life. He saw how the dew drops clung to its leaves, not as a measure of humidity, but as tiny jewels reflecting the plant's inherent beauty. He noticed the way the leaves, a deep, almost iridescent green, unfurled with a supple grace, each one catching the ambient light in a unique way. He would trace the delicate veins that crisscrossed their surface, not to map their vascular system, but to appreciate their intricate artistry.

Eli believed that plants communicated through a silent, complex language, a symphony of subtle cues that transcended the limitations of scientific measurement. It was a language of growth, of resilience, of quiet determination. The rustling of leaves in the wind wasn't just air movement; it was a song, a sigh, a murmur of contentment or a whisper of unease. The unfurling of a new bud wasn't just a biological process; it was a declaration, a promise of future beauty. The deep, resonant hum he sometimes felt emanating from mature trees wasn't just the flow of sap; it was the song of centuries, a testament to their enduring strength.

He remembered, as a child, his grandmother's small garden. It was a chaotic riot of color and scent, untamed and unmanaged by any scientific metrics. Yet, everything thrived. His grandmother would spend hours there, not with tools and readings, but with her hands in the dirt, her voice a gentle murmur to the plants. She would explain to him that the tomatoes looked "thirsty," not because the soil moisture was below a certain percentage, but because their leaves had lost their perky vitality. The roses needed "more sun," not because the light levels were insufficient for photosynthesis, but because their buds were reluctant to open. She spoke of the plants' "moods," of their "preferences," of their "desires." At the time, Eli had taken it as a child's fanciful interpretation, but as he grew, he began to understand that there was a profound truth in her words.

This intuitive understanding extended to the soil itself. Eli would kneel, scooping a handful into his palm. He would feel its coolness, its weight, its texture. He could tell if it was tired, depleted of its life-giving nutrients, or if it was rich and full of potential. He could sense the presence of beneficial microbes, the tiny architects of decomposition and nutrient cycling, not by analyzing their DNA, but by feeling the vibrant, subtle energy they imparted to the earth. He would often rub a bit of soil between his fingers, noticing how it clung or crumbled, how it released its scent. A rich, loamy smell spoke of health and abundance, while a sour, stagnant odor was a clear warning sign.

He would watch the way water was absorbed. Did it sink in quickly, indicating good drainage? Or did it pool on the surface, a sign of compacted earth and poor aeration? He could feel, with his hands, the subtle differences in soil moisture, not by reading a sensor, but by the way the earth yielded to his touch, the way it clung to his skin. He understood that plants didn't just need water; they needed the *right kind* of moisture, delivered in the *right way*, and his hands could often tell him if these conditions were being met.

When he approached the amethyst vine, he approached it as a fellow inhabitant of this world, not as a scientist dissecting a specimen. He could feel its deep roots anchoring themselves, not just into the compacted soil of that specific patch, but drawing sustenance from a wider, more complex network beneath. He sensed a vibrant energy, a quiet confidence that pulsed from its core. It wasn't struggling; it was thriving, its growth a testament to an inherent strength that transcended the limitations of its immediate environment.

He noticed the subtle interplay of light and shadow on its leaves. The engineered arboretum provided a controlled spectrum, but the vine seemed to absorb and refract this light in its own unique way. Its leaves weren't just passively receiving photons; they were actively interacting with the light, their surfaces shimmering with an almost iridescent quality. He could feel the subtle warmth radiating from them, a sign of efficient photosynthesis, even in what Mara's readings suggested were suboptimal light conditions. It was as if the vine had its own internal compass, guiding it towards the most beneficial light, regardless of the external parameters.

The amethyst blooms themselves were a source of endless fascination for Eli. He didn't need to analyze their pigment. He could see the depth of their color, the way it seemed to absorb and hold the light, giving them a luminous glow. He sensed a unique energy emanating from them, a subtle vibration that spoke of their purpose, their role in the vine's life cycle. He could almost feel the draw for pollinators, the silent invitation broadcast through their radiant hue. He imagined the insects, drawn by this unspoken language, their own intricate dance of life intertwined with the vine's existence.

Eli's empathy for the plant world was not a learned skill; it was an innate connection. He could sense, with a surprising accuracy, when a plant was stressed, when it was flourishing, when it was simply existing. It was a form of biological telepathy, a deep, resonant understanding that bypassed rational thought and went straight to the heart of the matter. He could feel the quiet joy of a plant basking in the sun, the gentle sigh of a tree releasing its leaves in autumn, the determined push of a seedling breaking through the soil. These weren't anthropomorphisms; they were his genuine perceptions of the plant's state of being.

He recalled an instance from his youth, when a sudden frost had threatened his grandmother's prized orchids. While others rushed to cover them with tarps, his grandmother had simply sat with them, her hands gently stroking their leaves, her voice a low, soothing hum. Eli had felt it too, a subtle shift in the plants' energy, a dimming of their vibrant pulse. It was as if they were drawing inwards, conserving their life force in response to his grandmother's calm presence. The next morning, miraculously, the orchids had shown far less damage than any of the covered plants. It was not a scientific explanation, but it was an undeniable truth he had witnessed.

This intuitive understanding allowed him to anticipate needs before they became critical. He wouldn't wait for a plant to show signs of wilting before watering; he would sense its subtle thirst, the faint drawing-in of its leaves, the almost imperceptible dimming of its vitality. He wouldn't wait for a nutrient deficiency to manifest as yellowing leaves; he would feel the plant's subtle hunger, its quiet yearning for replenishment. His hands, his senses, were his diagnostic tools, far more nuanced and responsive than any sensor array.

When Mara had first shown him the data on the amethyst vine, he had nodded, acknowledging the scientific rigor of her analysis. But his own internal response was different. He felt no surprise at its resilience, only a quiet affirmation of the inherent power of life. He saw not an anomaly to be studied and potentially controlled, but a testament to nature's boundless creativity and adaptability. He felt a sense of kinship with this plant, a recognition of its quiet defiance, its ability to carve out its own existence against all odds.

He believed that the engineered environment of Havenridge, while necessary for survival, had inadvertently stifled this deeper language of growth. The constant monitoring, the precise calibration, the eradication of any deviation from the norm – it all created a sterile silence, a void where the natural symphony of life should have been. The plants were surviving, yes, but were they truly thriving? Were they expressing their full potential, their inherent wildness? Eli suspected not.

He would often walk through the arboretum, his hands trailing lightly over the leaves of the engineered flora. He could feel their contentment, their compliance with the established parameters. But he also sensed a certain... uniformity. A lack of the vibrant, unpredictable individuality that characterized wild growth. It was like listening to a perfectly tuned orchestra playing a technically flawless but soulless rendition of a masterpiece.

The amethyst vine, however, was different. It was a wild melody in a meticulously composed symphony. It sang its own song, with its own rhythm and its own unique timbre. Eli felt a profound sense of respect for it, a recognition of its untamed spirit. He saw in its persistence not a deviation from the norm, but a redefinition of it. It was teaching them, he believed, a new language, a language of adaptation, of resilience, of finding life in the most unlikely of places.

He would spend time observing the soil around the vine, not with a trowel and sample bag, but with his hands. He could feel the subtle changes occurring beneath the surface, the way the vine's roots were interacting with the compacted earth, breaking it down, enriching it. He sensed a gentle aeration, a slow but steady process of improvement. It was as if the vine was not just surviving in its environment, but actively transforming it, making it more hospitable for itself and, perhaps, for other life forms yet to emerge.

His gaze would linger on the amethyst blooms, not to categorize their spectral properties, but to appreciate their inherent beauty and their function. He could feel the subtle vibrations they emitted, a silent call to the pollinators that were still a rarity in the controlled environment of Havenridge. He imagined the intricate dance of life that would unfold around them, a miniature ecosystem blossoming in the heart of their engineered sanctuary.

Eli's connection to the natural world was a testament to a different kind of intelligence, one that operated not on algorithms and data points, but on empathy and instinct. It was a language of growth that spoke not in numbers, but in the silent poetry of existence. He understood that true understanding came not just from observing and measuring, but from feeling and connecting. And in the vibrant hues of the amethyst vine, he saw a profound lesson, a reminder that life, in its most essential form, would always find a way to bloom, to adapt, and to sing its own magnificent song, even in the most unexpected of soils. His presence by the vine was not one of scientific inquiry, but of silent communion, a shared moment of existence between two beings connected by the fundamental, unspoken language of life itself. He felt the sun on his face, the earth beneath his knees, and the quiet hum of the vine a comforting presence, a living testament to the power of nature's enduring spirit.

The arboretum, once a sterile battleground of competing methodologies, began to subtly reconfigure itself into a shared space, a silent classroom where Mara and Eli found themselves engaged in a profound, unspoken dialogue. It was a language woven from shared observation, a delicate exchange that transcended the sterile pronouncements of data streams and the guttural affirmations of instinct. Mara, accustomed to the crisp certainty of her readouts, found herself increasingly attuned to the subtle shifts in Eli's demeanor, the almost imperceptible flickers of his expression that spoke volumes.

She began to notice the way his shoulders would relax, a subtle unclenching of tension, when he stood before a thriving sector, his gaze soft and appreciative. It wasn't the data confirming optimal growth metrics that pleased him; it was something more visceral, a visual affirmation that resonated with his deep connection to the living world. Conversely, a slight furrow in his brow, the almost imperceptible tightening around his eyes, would signal his concern long before any wilting leaf or stunted growth appeared on her scanners. He would often pause, his head tilted slightly, as if listening to a whispered secret the plants were sharing, a signal that his intuition had picked up on a nascent issue that her instruments, for the moment, had not. This silent communication, this reading of Eli's body language, became a new layer of data for Mara, one she found herself both fascinated by and increasingly reliant upon.

Eli, for his part, began to see the invaluable foresight embedded within Mara's meticulous data collection. He had initially dismissed her constant scanning and detailed logging as a superfluous, even intrusive, layer of analysis. Yet, he couldn't deny the evidence. Her predictions of nutrient deficiencies, based on spectral analysis of leaf pigmentation, often preceded any visible signs of distress. Her humidity and temperature logs, meticulously recorded at precise intervals, allowed them to anticipate environmental shifts that could impact the delicate balance of the arboretum, providing a crucial buffer against unforeseen challenges. He began to recognize that her data-driven approach wasn't just about measurement; it was about prediction, a powerful tool that could prevent problems before they even had a chance to manifest. He found himself adjusting his own intuitive assessments based on her projected outcomes, a subtle integration of their disparate approaches.

Their professional disagreements, once sharp and often charged with unspoken frustration, began to mellow. The sharp edges of their clashes softened, replaced by a growing, if still largely unspoken, mutual respect. Mara observed how Eli's touch, his almost reverent interaction with the plants, often revealed subtle issues that her sensors couldn't detect, a delicate touch that could soothe a stressed sapling or encourage a reluctant bloom. She saw the wisdom in his patience, the profound understanding that some processes could not be hurried, that nature had its own rhythm, its own timetable. She started to appreciate that his seemingly abstract connection to the plants was, in fact, a highly sophisticated form of observation, a deep empathy that allowed him to perceive nuances she often missed.

Eli, in turn, began to acknowledge the undeniable utility of Mara's precision. He saw how her early warnings, based on the complex algorithms she employed, had saved countless specimens from the brink of collapse. He recognized that his intuitive understanding, while powerful, was inherently reactive, whereas her approach was proactive. She offered a layer of foresight, a scientific scaffolding that reinforced the fragile structure of their engineered ecosystem. He began to see her spreadsheets not as sterile collections of numbers, but as a testament to her dedication, her unwavering commitment to the preservation of life, albeit through a different lens.

There were moments, quiet interludes amidst the hum of the climate control systems and the gentle rustle of engineered leaves, where this unspoken dialogue became particularly poignant. Mara would be meticulously charting the growth rate of a particular hybrid rose, her brow furrowed in concentration. Eli might be nearby, his hands gently cupping a struggling seedling, his gaze fixed on its delicate structure. A slight nod from Eli, a subtle almost imperceptible softening of his expression, would be Mara's cue that the seedling was responding positively to his ministrations, that his gentle encouragement was proving effective. She would then cross-reference this visual confirmation with her own data, noting the correlation, a quiet affirmation of their complementary skills.

Conversely, a sharp intake of breath from Mara, a quick glance at her datapad with a worried frown, would signal to Eli that a parameter was trending in a concerning direction. He would then approach the affected area, his movements unhurried, his senses already attuned to the subtle cues that her instruments were relaying. He would run his hands over the leaves, feel the texture of the soil, his intuitive assessment running parallel to her data-driven diagnosis. He might then suggest a slight adjustment to the watering schedule, or the introduction of a specific organic compound he felt would be beneficial, actions that were informed by his innate understanding but guided by the foresight her data provided.

The amethyst vine, the enigmatic anomaly that had initially brought them into such stark professional contrast, became a focal point for this evolving dynamic. Mara continued her rigorous analysis, documenting its unique cellular structure, its improbable resilience in the face of environmental stressors. But now, she also found herself watching Eli's interactions with it. She observed the way he would sit beside it for extended periods, not taking notes, not scanning, but simply *being*. She saw the subtle arc of his back, the relaxed posture that spoke of a profound connection. When the vine bloomed prolifically, she noted how Eli's eyes would light up, a genuine joy radiating from him that was more expressive than any graph.

Eli, in turn, understood Mara's quiet dedication. He saw the late nights she spent poring over her data, the meticulous way she charted every fluctuation. He recognized that her drive wasn't for control, but for understanding, for the desire to unravel the complex mechanisms of life. He began to see the beauty in her logical framework, the elegant structure she built with her numbers. He acknowledged that while he felt the life force of a plant, she could quantify its health, providing a tangible, verifiable measure of its vitality.

One crisp morning, as the artificial dawn painted the arboretum in hues of rose and gold, Mara noticed Eli standing by a section of meticulously cultivated bioluminescent moss. His head was bowed, his posture radiating a quiet contemplation. She approached, her datapad in hand, ready to log the ambient light levels and humidity readings. But as she drew closer, she saw that Eli wasn't looking at his own readings. He was observing the moss itself, his fingers hovering inches above its softly glowing surface. There was a subtle tension in his shoulders, a slight grimace.

"Something wrong?" Mara asked, her voice softer than usual.

Eli looked up, a flicker of surprise in his eyes, as if he hadn't expected her to approach. "It's... hesitant," he said, his voice a low murmur. "The luminescence is there, but it's not as vibrant as it should be. It feels... subdued."

Mara immediately brought up the moss's data profile. "Readings are nominal," she stated, a hint of her usual defensiveness creeping in. "Light output is within the expected parameters. Humidity and temperature are stable."

Eli walked closer, his gaze sweeping over the glowing carpet. "Nominal doesn't mean optimal," he replied, his tone gentle but firm. He reached out, his fingertips brushing lightly against the velvety surface. "It feels... dry, deep down. Not on the surface, but beneath. Like it's holding back."

Mara frowned, her scientific mind struggling to reconcile his sensory input with her objective data. She checked the sub-surface moisture sensors. "Those readings are also within range," she reported.

Eli closed his eyes for a moment, as if concentrating. "It's not a lack of water, not in the way the sensors read it," he insisted. "It's more like... a hesitation to draw it up. A reluctance." He then looked at her, his gaze direct. "Did you notice any changes in the nutrient feed cycle yesterday? Any minor adjustments?"

Mara's brow furrowed as she scrolled back through the recent logs. "There was a minor recalibration of the nitrogen levels," she admitted. "Just a fractional adjustment, supposed to prevent potential over-saturation."

Eli's eyes widened slightly. "Nitrogen," he mused, "can sometimes inhibit bioluminescence if not perfectly balanced with other micronutrients. It can make the glow... shy." He then looked at the moss again, a subtle understanding dawning on his face. "It's not dying. It's just... holding back its light. Afraid of overexposing itself, perhaps, because of that imbalance."

Mara stared at the data, then at Eli, a new understanding dawning within her. His intuitive assessment, that subtle sense of hesitation he'd perceived, had pointed to a specific cause that her objective readings had merely registered as a minor fluctuation. Her data had provided the framework, but his lived experience, his deep understanding of plant physiology, had provided the crucial insight.

"So," she began, a hesitant curiosity coloring her voice, "if we slightly adjust the potassium levels, to counterbalance the nitrogen... do you think that would encourage it?"

Eli smiled, a genuine, warm smile that transformed his face. "I think," he said, his voice filled with a quiet optimism, "that we might just see a bit more of its true radiance."

As Mara began to input the new parameters, a sense of quiet accord settled between them. It wasn't a victory for one over the other, but a shared moment of collaborative success, a testament to the unspoken language they were both learning to speak, a language where data and intuition wove together to foster growth, not just in the plants, but in their own understanding of each other. The arboretum, in its silent, verdant expanse, had become more than just a research facility; it had become their shared sanctuary, a place where the language of growth was spoken not just by the flora, but by the evolving bond between two dedicated souls.

The seeds of this understanding were sown in countless small moments. Mara would find herself unconsciously mirroring Eli's posture when examining a particularly robust specimen, a subtle shift from her usual analytical stance to one of quiet appreciation. She'd catch herself looking for his nod of approval, his almost imperceptible sigh of contentment, before fully trusting her own data. It was as if his emotional resonance with the plants was acting as a kind of somatic barometer for her, a confirmation that her readings were not just numerically accurate, but ecologically sound.

Conversely, Eli began to anticipate Mara's data-driven inquiries. When he felt a plant was exhibiting unusual behavior, he would make a mental note to alert her to specific environmental factors that might be at play. He wouldn't just say "it seems off." He would offer observations that could be quantified. "This vine's leaves are curling inwards," he might say, "and I've noticed a subtle shift in the ambient temperature around it, a slight dip." This provided Mara with a more targeted starting point for her analysis, allowing her to hone in on potential causes with greater efficiency.

Their conversations, while still often brief and functional, started to carry a different weight. The terse exchanges about nutrient ratios and light spectrums began to be interspersed with more collaborative brainstorming sessions. Mara might present a complex problem, a peculiar set of readings indicating a stress response in a particular species. Instead of simply offering solutions based on her established protocols, she would turn to Eli. "What are you feeling from it?" she'd ask, her voice open and curious.

He would then spend time with the plant, his hands tracing its leaves, his body language conveying a deep connection. He might report back with insights that were initially abstract. "It feels... conflicted," he'd say. "Like it's being pulled in two directions. There's a desire to grow upwards, but also a deep-seated need to anchor itself more firmly."

Mara would then translate his observations into tangible hypotheses. "Conflicted," she'd muse, tapping her stylus against her chin. "Could that be related to the uneven distribution of root-stimulating hormones in the substrate? Or perhaps a slight variance in the substrate density, leading to uneven anchoring opportunities?" This interplay, this translation of sensory input into scientific inquiry, was a profound evolution from their initial adversarial dynamic.

The amethyst vine continued to be a silent, vibrant testament to their burgeoning synergy. Mara's latest reports detailed its astonishing rate of cellular regeneration, a phenomenon that defied conventional biological understanding. But alongside the hard data, she also noted Eli's consistent presence. She saw how his calm demeanor seemed to soothe the plant, how his gentle touch appeared to encourage its resilience. And Eli, in turn, observed how Mara's relentless pursuit of understanding was slowly, meticulously, revealing the vine's secrets, not by dissecting its life force, but by documenting its intricate dance with its environment.

One afternoon, as a soft, diffused light filtered through the arboretum's canopy, Mara found herself watching Eli as he examined a sapling that had been struggling for weeks. He wasn't touching it, but stood a respectful distance away, his gaze intense, his entire being focused on the young plant. She could sense the quiet urgency in his posture, the deep concern emanating from him.

"What do you think?" she finally asked, her voice barely a whisper.

Eli let out a slow breath. "It's fighting," he said, his voice resonating with an almost palpable empathy. "But it's tired. It's been fighting for so long, trying to overcome... something. Something it can't quite identify." He paused, then looked at

Mara, his eyes holding a quiet plea. "Is there anything in the soil composition that might be... subtly toxic? Something we might have overlooked in the initial analyses?"

Mara's fingers flew across her datapad, pulling up the detailed soil analysis for that specific sector. She scrolled through the complex array of elements, the micronutrients, the organic compounds. Her brow furrowed. "Everything is within accepted parameters," she reported, then hesitated. "However... there was a trace amount of a residual contaminant detected during the last full spectrum scan. It was deemed negligible, below any threshold for concern. A byproduct of the old soil synthesis process, we believe."

Eli's gaze sharpened. "Negligible," he repeated slowly, his eyes fixed on the struggling sapling. "But perhaps not to a plant that is already under stress. Perhaps that 'negligible' amount is the tipping point." He looked back at Mara, a newfound respect in his eyes. "Can we... can we try to neutralize it? Introduce a chelating agent?"

Mara, for the first time, didn't immediately launch into a discussion of protocol or risk assessment. Instead, she nodded, a small, decisive movement. "We can. I'll need to run a simulation first, of course, to ensure no adverse reactions..." She trailed off, realizing that even in her scientific caution, there was an underlying trust in Eli's intuitive leap. Her data had identified the presence of the contaminant; his senses had told them it was the problem. Together, they had moved from mere observation to active intervention.

The silence that followed was not an empty one. It was filled with the unspoken acknowledgment of their shared purpose, their complementary strengths. Mara, the scientist who saw the world in quantifiable data, and Eli, the empath who felt the pulse of life itself, were slowly, surely, learning to speak the same language. It was the language of growth, of nurture, of a shared hope for the burgeoning life within the arboretum, and in the fragile ecosystem of their own evolving partnership. The unspoken dialogue had begun, and in its quiet hum, Mara and Eli were finding not just a way to understand the plants, but a way to understand each other. Their work was no longer just a task; it was becoming a conversation, a testament to the power of collaboration, a quiet symphony played out in the vibrant, ever-growing heart of the arboretum.

The air, usually a balmy, controlled caress, turned sharp and biting overnight. Mara woke to the shrill alarm of a temperature anomaly, a stark red alert flashing across her datapad. An unseasonal frost, an aggressive rogue wave of cold air that had bypassed the outer atmospheric regulators, was creeping into the arboretum. Her trained eyes immediately scanned the projected impact zones, her mind racing through contingency plans. Her gaze landed on a particular sector, a small, sheltered alcove where a cluster of newly grafted saplings were undergoing their most vulnerable stage of acclimation. Among them, a single specimen, a delicate hybrid engineered for its bioluminescent properties and its unusual affinity for arid conditions, was directly in the path of the encroaching freeze.

Mara moved with practiced efficiency, her movements economical and precise. She pulled on her insulated jumpsuit, the familiar hum of its internal heating a comforting presence against the sudden chill seeping into her quarters. Within minutes, she was navigating the hushed corridors of the arboretum, the ambient glow of the flora casting long, dancing shadows. Arriving at the sapling's location, she saw that the frost's tendrils were already beginning to lace the delicate leaves, turning their vibrant emerald hue to a sickly, translucent white. Her immediate, ingrained response was to deploy the emergency protective sheeting. The fabric, a multi-layered composite designed to trap heat and repel frost, was standard protocol for such an event. She reached for the stored rolls, her fingers already anticipating the familiar texture.

"Mara, wait."

Eli's voice, soft but firm, cut through the sterile quiet. He stood a few paces away, his expression one of deep concern, but not panic. He gestured not towards the sheeting, but towards a group of mature, exceptionally hardy succulents that stood a meter or so beyond the sapling. These plants, with their thick, waxy leaves and deep root systems, were naturally resistant to extreme temperature fluctuations.

"We don't need to smother it," he said, his gaze flicking between the sapling and the succulents. "We can use them."

Mara paused, her hand hovering over the sheeting. "Use them how?" she asked, a hint of her ingrained skepticism in her tone. The concept of using other plants as a shield, rather than a direct protective barrier, felt... unconventional. Her protocols were clear, direct, and scientifically validated.

Eli walked closer, his movements unhurried, his hands held slightly open as if to emphasize his non-confrontational approach. "Look at the windbreak they provide," he explained, his voice low and measured. "And their density. If we carefully reposition a few of the larger ones, we can create a natural microclimate around the sapling. It will shield it from the direct frost, while still allowing for the minimal airflow it needs to prevent condensation buildup that could be even more damaging."

Mara's gaze followed his, her mind whirring. She ran a quick simulation in her head. The succulents were robust, their foliage dense. Their proximity to the sapling was already providing a slight buffer. Repositioning them would indeed create a more effective thermal barrier. It was an ingenious solution, born not from a database of emergency procedures, but from an intimate understanding of the arboretum's living architecture. It was... adaptive.

Her protocols were designed for predictability, for scenarios where deviations were minimal and risks calculable. But the arboretum, as they were discovering daily, was anything but predictable. Nature, even in its engineered form, possessed an inherent capacity for the unexpected. Eli, with his deep, almost primal connection to the flora, seemed to intuitively grasp this fluidity.

"But... the sheeting is proven," Mara countered, the ingrained logic of her training still tugging at her. "It's guaranteed to maintain a specific temperature range. This... this is less precise."

Eli offered a small, encouraging smile. "Precision isn't always about control, Mara. Sometimes, it's about understanding the system well enough to work *with* its natural tendencies. The sheeting would trap heat, yes, but it also traps moisture and restricts airflow entirely. This method, using the succulents, leverages their own resilience. It allows the sapling to experience a slightly less extreme, but still protected, environment. It's about adaptation, not just insulation."

He knelt beside the sapling, his fingers brushing against its frost-kissed leaves with a tenderness that Mara was beginning to recognize as a profound form of scientific inquiry. "See how the frost is already clinging to these outer leaves?" he murmured, his voice laced with concern. "The sheeting would seal that in. Here," he gestured to the succulents, "we can redirect the coldest air *around* it, not directly onto it. The larger plants will absorb the initial chill, and radiate a slightly warmer, more stable pocket of air."

Mara watched him. She saw the logic in his words, the elegance of a solution that utilized existing resources, that respected the natural interactions within the ecosystem. It was a stark contrast to her own approach, which often involved introducing external elements to correct or compensate for perceived deficiencies. Her mind, accustomed to dissecting problems into discrete variables, was slowly expanding to encompass a more holistic perspective. Eli wasn't just seeing a problem; he was seeing a system, a complex web of interconnected life, and he was finding a way to mend it by enhancing its inherent strengths.

Without another word, Mara retracted her hand from the sheeting and moved towards the mature succulents. Eli, with a grateful nod, began to carefully guide the branches of the closest ones, angling them to create the desired shield. Together, they worked in a silent, synchronized dance, their movements guided by a shared purpose, a mutual respect that had blossomed in the fertile ground of their collaboration. Mara's initial hesitation was giving way to a cautious curiosity, a willingness to explore an alternative that defied her established comfort zone.

They moved a total of three large succulents, their thick, fleshy leaves forming a dense, overlapping barrier around the fragile sapling. The frosty air, now prevented from directly assaulting the young plant, seemed to swirl and eddy around the protective ring of larger flora. Mara activated her internal scanners, her datapad displaying a real-time thermal map of the microclimate they had created. The temperature directly around the sapling remained a few degrees warmer than the surrounding air, and crucially, the humidity levels were within acceptable parameters.

It wasn't the perfectly controlled environment of the sheeting, but it was a far cry from the lethal direct exposure.

They stayed there for nearly an hour, monitoring the situation, as the frost continued its assault on the arboretum. Mara observed Eli's posture, the subtle tension in his shoulders slowly easing as the temperature stabilized around the sapling. She noted how he would occasionally reach out, not to touch, but to feel the subtle currents of air, his senses tuned to the nuances of their improvised shelter.

As the artificial dawn began to break, painting the arboretum in hues of soft lavender and rose, the frost began to recede. The alarm on Mara's datapad finally silenced, replaced by a steady green indicator of normalized temperatures. She turned her attention back to the sapling. The protective sheeting lay unused, a testament to a protocol bypassed. The succulents stood sentinel, their leaves slightly dusted with frost but otherwise unharmed. And the sapling... the sapling was still alive.

She knelt beside it, her gaze sweeping over its leaves. The translucent white sheen was slowly receding, revealing the underlying green. A few of the most exposed leaves bore the unmistakable signs of frost damage, a slight wilting, a darkening of the edges. But the core of the plant, the tender new growth, was vibrant and intact. It had survived. It had adapted, not through artificial intervention, but through the subtle, intelligent application of its own biological resilience, amplified by the ingenuity of its caretakers.

Mara looked at Eli, a sense of quiet awe settling within her. This was more than just a successful rescue; it was a revelation. Her protocols, meticulously crafted and thoroughly tested, were invaluable. They provided a solid foundation of knowledge, a safety net against predictable threats. But they were, by their very nature, rigid. They were designed for a world that behaved according to established parameters.

Eli, on the other hand, operated on a different frequency. He understood the inherent variability of life, the capacity for growth and adaptation that lay dormant within every organism. He saw the arboretum not as a collection of specimens to be managed, but as a dynamic, interconnected ecosystem. His solutions were fluid, responsive, and often, more elegant.

"It's... it's remarkable," Mara admitted, her voice hushed. She ran her scanner over the sapling again, the data confirming its survival and the minimal damage. "The sheeting would have worked, but this..." She gestured to the succulents, their sturdy forms a testament to their resilience. "This feels... more natural. More respectful of the plant's own capabilities."

Eli smiled, a genuine, open expression that reached his eyes. "Nature is always finding a way, Mara. We just need to learn to listen. Sometimes, the best intervention is the one that allows the system to heal itself." He looked at her, his gaze steady and encouraging. "Your protocols are essential. They provide the framework. But there's always room for... improvisation. For adapting the solution to the specific needs of the moment, and the organism."

The memory of the sheeting, lying unused, felt like a discarded constraint. The image of the hardy succulents standing guard, their living forms creating a protective shield, was imprinted in her mind. It was a tangible demonstration, a practical lesson in adaptation that her data logs could never fully capture. It was one thing to read about resilience; it was another to witness it, to be a part of creating it.

Later that day, as the arboretum hummed with its usual quiet energy, Mara found herself reviewing the frost incident report. She meticulously documented the temperature fluctuations, the deployment of the succulent microclimate, and the sapling's response. But as she typed, her focus kept drifting from the cold, hard data to the warmth of the lesson she had learned. She realized that her pursuit of scientific accuracy, while vital, had sometimes led her to overlook the potential of organic solutions, the power of working *with* nature rather than simply imposing order upon it.

Eli's approach, she understood, was not about abandoning science, but about enriching it with a deeper understanding of biological processes. It was about recognizing that even in a meticulously controlled environment, the principles of natural selection and adaptation still held sway. The frost had been a crisis, a challenge that had threatened to derail weeks of careful work. But in its wake, it had left something far more valuable: a profound lesson in the art of adaptation, a lesson that Mara, the scientist, was finally beginning to truly comprehend. She looked at the data logs for the sapling, the lines and numbers that charted its survival. But in her mind's eye, she saw not just the graphs, but the living testament to a different kind of growth – one that was flexible, responsive, and deeply in tune with the pulse of life itself. The arboretum, she realized, was not just a laboratory; it was a classroom, and Eli, with his quiet wisdom, was proving to be an exceptional teacher. The rigid walls of her own scientific dogma had begun to soften, allowing for a more expansive, a more compassionate, understanding of what it truly meant to nurture life.

The frost incident had been a watershed moment, not just for the sapling, but for Mara's entire understanding of success. The sterile, quantifiable metrics that had once defined her work – survival rates, growth speed, resource efficiency – suddenly felt insufficient. They were crucial, of course, the bedrock upon which any horticultural endeavor was built. But they failed to capture the essence of what was happening within the arboretum, and more importantly, what was blooming between her and Eli.

She found herself spending more time simply observing, allowing the subtle rhythms of the arboretum to imprint themselves upon her. It wasn't just about diagnosing problems or implementing solutions anymore. It was about witnessing the intricate dance of life, the delicate balance of competition and cooperation, the quiet triumph of a vine finding its way to sunlight, or the unexpected burst of color from a cross-pollination that had occurred without any direct intervention. These were the moments that Eli seemed to intuitively understand, the ones he pointed out with a quiet reverence that had begun to infect her own perspective.

One afternoon, while tending to a patch of newly introduced ground cover, Mara noticed Eli spending an unusual amount of time near a cluster of indigenous mosses. They were hardy, their role in the ecosystem well-documented, yet he seemed captivated. She joined him, her initial instinct to scan for any signs of distress or unusual growth patterns.

"They're not doing much, are they?" she commented, referring to the unassuming, verdant carpet. "From a pure growth perspective, they're rather slow."

Eli smiled, a knowing glint in his eyes. "They're not about rapid growth, Mara. They're about endurance. Look closer." He gestured with a gentle finger towards a section where the moss had begun to spread, not in a uniform patch, but weaving its way around the base of a small, struggling sapling. "See how it's holding the moisture in the soil for it? And how its dense structure is providing a small barrier against wind erosion? It's not actively 'growing' in the way a flowering plant does, but it's actively *supporting*."

Mara leaned in, her analytical mind re-calibrating. She saw it then – the subtle, almost imperceptible ways the moss was contributing. It was a form of success that didn't involve a dramatic spike on a graph, but a steady, quiet provision. It was the success of quiet stewardship, of contributing to the overall health and stability of the environment without demanding attention. This was a far cry from the efficiency models she had always relied on, which prioritized observable, measurable output.

"So, success isn't always about the individual plant's peak performance," she mused aloud, the realization settling in. "It's about the collective health, the support system it provides for others."

"Exactly," Eli affirmed, his gaze sweeping across the arboretum, taking in the sprawling network of interdependence. "It's about the harmony. When the ecosystem thrives, the individual plants will ultimately thrive too, but in a way that's sustainable, that's *integrated*."

This new understanding began to permeate every aspect of their work. They started to measure success not just by the survival of a single specimen, but by the resilience of the entire sector. They looked for signs of emergent properties, of unexpected beauty that arose from the interactions between different species. The bioluminescent hybrid that had survived the frost, for example, was now being observed not just for its light-producing capabilities, but for the way its soft glow seemed to attract specific pollinators to nearby night-blooming flowers. This wasn't a planned outcome; it was a serendipitous synergy, a beautiful emergent property of their careful cultivation.

"It's like... like a living painting," Mara found herself saying one evening, as they sat overlooking the arboretum under the soft glow of the engineered constellations. The air was filled with the gentle hum of the climate control systems, but it was punctuated by the chirps of nocturnal insects and the faint rustle of leaves. "We set out the canvas, we prepare the pigments, but the true art happens in the way the colors bleed into each other, the way the textures interact."

Eli chuckled, a warm, resonant sound. "That's a beautiful way to put it, Mara. And we are the artists, but also, in a way, the observers. We provide the conditions, but we must also allow for the unexpected strokes, the unplanned flourishes."

The idea of "unplanned flourishes" was a foreign concept to Mara's rigorously structured mind. Her training had emphasized predictability, control, the minimization of variables. But Eli's perspective invited chaos, not as a destructive force, but as a catalyst for creation. He spoke of "controlled wildness," a concept that initially sounded contradictory but, as Mara observed its application, began to make perfect sense. It was about creating environments with enough inherent structure to be stable, but with enough freedom to allow for natural processes to unfold.

They began to document these emergent beauties, not as anomalies to be corrected, but as valuable data points illustrating the arboretum's evolving narrative. A particular type of flowering vine, known for its aggressive growth, had been carefully managed to prevent it from overwhelming more delicate species. However, Mara and Eli noticed that where it had been allowed to spread slightly beyond its designated area, it had created a dense, shaded microclimate that was perfectly suited for a rare, shade-loving fern that had previously struggled.

"So, its 'aggressive' nature, when given a slight degree of controlled freedom, actually became its strength," Mara noted, recording the observation. "It wasn't a failure of containment; it was a misinterpretation of its optimal function."

Eli nodded, adding his own observations. "And notice how the vine's tendrils have intertwined with the fern's fronds? They're not competing for resources; they're creating a mutually beneficial structure. A beautiful, unplanned architectural innovation."

Their definition of success had expanded beyond mere survival and efficiency to encompass concepts like ecological integrity, biodiversity, and aesthetic value. The arboretum was no longer just a collection of individual projects; it was a single, living entity, and its health was a holistic measure. The resilience they cultivated in the plants was now mirrored in their own partnership. They learned to adapt to each other's strengths and weaknesses, to find solutions that honored both their scientific rigor and his intuitive understanding of living systems.

This redefined success also extended to their relationship. Mara, who had always viewed emotional connection as a potentially distracting variable, found herself embracing the unexpected emotional landscape that had opened up with Eli. Their shared experiences, their debates, their moments of quiet understanding – these were not distractions from their work, but integral components of a richer, more fulfilling existence. She began to see their developing relationship as another kind of ecosystem, one that thrived on open communication, mutual respect, and the shared cultivation of something beautiful and enduring.

The thought struck her one evening as she watched Eli meticulously tie up a climbing rose, his movements practiced and gentle. His success wasn't just in the scientific accuracy of his knots, but in the care he was imparting to the plant, the quiet joy it seemed to bring him. Her own success, she realized, was no longer solely defined by the quantifiable achievements she could list on a report. It was also in the warmth she felt when he smiled at her, in the quiet comfort of his presence, in the shared vision they were building together.

"You know," she said, breaking the comfortable silence, "I used to think success was all about measurable outcomes. Proof. Data. But lately... I'm not so sure."

Eli looked up from the rose, his brow furrowed slightly in thought. "What's changed?"

Mara gestured vaguely around them, encompassing the softly glowing plants, the gentle hum of life, and the shared space between them. "Everything, I think. It's about the quiet strength of things that endure, not just the flash of things that thrive quickly. It's about the beauty that emerges when things are allowed to be themselves, to connect in their own ways. And it's about... finding joy in the process, not just the final result."

He met her gaze, a slow smile spreading across his face. "That sounds like a pretty good definition of success to me, Mara. Perhaps even a better one."

The arboretum, in its burgeoning complexity, was mirroring the blossoming of their own understanding. They were learning to see success not as a destination, but as a journey, an ongoing process of growth and adaptation, of nurturing not just plants, but also the unexpected beauty that arose from connection and shared purpose. The quantifiable metrics still mattered, but they were now part of a larger, more profound tapestry, woven with threads of resilience, harmony, and the quiet, enduring strength of life itself. And in this expanded vision, Mara found a deeper, more sustainable kind of fulfillment, a sense of purpose that resonated far beyond the sterile confines of data and efficiency. She was learning to appreciate the art of growth, in all its myriad, wonderful forms.

CHAPTER FIVE

Whispers of Control

The Havenridge Council, a name whispered with a mixture of reverence and an almost unconscious acceptance, was the silent architect of their present reality. They were the custodians of the 'Great Accord,' the foundational document that had guided their community from the ashes of the collapse, charting a course through the treacherous waters of rebuilding. Their pronouncements, delivered with the weight of undeniable necessity, were rarely challenged. They spoke of resource allocation, population management, and environmental stewardship with a tone that brooked no dissent, framing each directive as a critical bulwark against the chaos that still lurked at the edges of their existence.

Mara, however, had begun to feel a subtle disquiet, a prickle of unease that started as a faint hum beneath the surface of her daily life and was gradually growing into a more insistent thrum. It wasn't that the Council's directives were inherently wrong, or that their stated aims were anything less than noble. The preservation of Havenridge, the fragile ecosystem they had painstakingly nurtured, the delicate social fabric they had woven – these were all paramount. But in the meticulous, almost ritualistic way these directives were issued, she detected a certain inflexibility, a deeply ingrained resistance to deviation.

She saw it in the way new proposals, even those born from her own evolving understanding of the arboretum's needs, were met with polite but firm redirection back to established protocols. When she suggested a trial expansion of the bioluminescent flora, citing the unexpected pollinator attraction data, the response was a reiteration of the strict zoning regulations designed to prevent uncontrolled spread. "The Accord outlines specific zones for bio-luminescence cultivation," the official reply had stated, devoid of any acknowledgment of her findings, "deviations require a comprehensive risk assessment that has not been conducted for this proposed alteration."

It felt less like considered wisdom and more like dogma, a set of commandments etched in stone rather than adaptable guidelines for a living, evolving community. The spirit of innovation, the very drive that had allowed them to survive the initial collapse and then thrive, seemed to be slowly calcified by an unwavering adherence to the past. The Accord was their salvation, yes, but was it also becoming their cage?

Eli, with his innate sensitivity to the subtle energies of the natural world, seemed to pick up on her growing apprehension. One evening, as they surveyed a new section of the arboretum that was struggling with an unusual fungal blight, Mara voiced her frustrations. "It's like they expect the world to adhere to the original blueprint, Eli. We have this blight, and my immediate thought is to adapt our containment strategies, perhaps even introduce a new fungal strain that could outcompete it. But the Council's response would be to refer to the approved pest management protocols, which are frankly, insufficient for this particular threat."

Eli leaned against a sturdy oak sapling, its leaves still tinged with the early hues of autumn. "The Accord was designed for a world that was *being built* from scratch, Mara. It was about establishing order where there was none. It's a magnificent piece of work, a testament to their foresight. But the world didn't stop evolving just because Havenridge was founded." He paused, his gaze sweeping across the arboretum, taking in the vibrant, complex tapestry of life that was constantly in flux. "And we, as its caretakers, must evolve with it."

"But how do we encourage that evolution when the very structure of our governance resists it?" Mara pressed, the frustration evident in her voice. "When every new challenge is met with a 'refer to section 7, sub-paragraph C' kind of response? It feels like they're prioritizing the preservation of the *plan* over the preservation of the *life* it was meant to protect."

Eli's expression was thoughtful. "Perhaps they see the plan as the only true path to preservation. They lived through the collapse, Mara. They saw what happens when systems fail, when order breaks down. For them, the Accord isn't just a document; it's a shield. And they're terrified of any chink in that armor."

This insight, while understandable, only amplified Mara's concern. The fear of the past, she realized, was breeding a fear of the future, a resistance to adaptation that could prove far more dangerous than any uncontrolled bloom or invasive species. The Council's mandate, once a beacon of hope and stability, was beginning to cast a long, shadow of stagnation.

She started to notice it in other areas, too. The agricultural sector, for instance, was still strictly adhering to the crop rotation schedules established years ago, even though Mara's own arboretum research had demonstrated the potential benefits of intercropping and companion planting for soil health and pest resistance. When the farmers proposed minor adjustments to accommodate a particularly promising new hybrid grain, they were met with a stern reminder of the established agricultural charter. The efficiency of their current methods, painstakingly documented and approved, was held up as the gold standard, discouraging any exploration of potentially more resilient, albeit less predictable, alternatives.

It was a subtle form of control, not overtly tyrannical, but pervasive. The Council's influence wasn't a heavy hand, but an invisible current, guiding every decision, shaping every outcome. Their authority stemmed from the deep-seated respect they commanded as the founders, the survivors who had charted their course. But this respect had, over time, calcified into an almost unquestioning deference, a passive acceptance of their pronouncements as immutable truths.

Mara found herself having hushed conversations with Eli, dissecting the Council's edicts, searching for the logic, and often finding only adherence to precedent. "It's like they're so focused on preventing a recurrence of the past that they're blind to the present," she'd confide. "We are no longer in the immediate aftermath of the collapse. We have a stable ecosystem, we have resources, we have knowledge. We can afford to be more... exploratory. More adaptive."

Eli would listen, his quiet presence a comforting anchor. "You're seeing the arboretum as a dynamic entity, Mara. They see Havenridge as a system that needs constant, meticulous management to prevent collapse. Their perspective is rooted in the immediate post-collapse era, a time of extreme scarcity and vulnerability. They are, in their own way, still fighting that war."

This explanation resonated. The Council members, many of whom bore the visible scars of the collapse, were driven by a profound need for security, for predictability. Their mandates were not born of malice, but of a deep-seated fear of chaos. However, Mara argued, an environment that was too rigidly controlled, too resistant to change, would eventually become brittle. True resilience, as she was learning from her plants, came not from rigid defense, but from adaptability, from the ability to bend without breaking, to integrate new elements and find strength in diversity.

She began to subtly push back, not through open defiance, but through persistent data collection and well-reasoned proposals. When a new pest threatened the fruit orchards, she didn't just present the problem; she presented multiple solutions, including one that involved the controlled introduction of a predator insect not currently on the approved list. The Council's initial response was, as expected, a referral to the existing pest management protocol. But Mara countered with detailed reports on the predator's ecological niche, its expected impact on the local ecosystem, and projections of its long-term efficacy compared to the current, less effective treatments.

"The data suggests that Protocol 12B, while effective against common pests, is insufficient for the *Xylos* beetle," she explained during a community forum, her voice steady and clear. "My proposal for the *Coccinella septempunctata* offers a more sustainable, long-term solution, with a projected reduction in crop loss by an additional 15% within two growing seasons. I've also included simulations demonstrating its minimal impact on beneficial insect populations."

There were murmurs in the audience, a mix of curiosity and ingrained deference. The Council members, seated at the front, exchanged glances. Elder Thorne, a man whose stern demeanor was as much a part of Havenridge as its carefully cultivated flora, finally spoke. "The Council values your diligence, Mara. However, Protocol 12B is our established procedure. Introducing non-native species, even beneficial ones, carries inherent risks. The Accord prioritizes stability."

"But Elder Thorne," Mara countered, her gaze unwavering, "isn't the ultimate goal of stability to ensure continued growth and prosperity? If our current methods are insufficient to protect our crops, are we not then undermining the very stability the Accord seeks to preserve? This beetle is a direct threat to our food supply, a threat that Protocol 12B, by its own limitations, cannot fully address."

Her words hung in the air, a quiet challenge to the unquestioned authority. She saw a flicker of something in Elder Thorne's eyes – not anger, but a sort of troubled contemplation. It was a small victory, a tiny crack in the edifice of dogma. The decision wasn't immediately made, but for the first time, a Council directive wasn't simply accepted without a second thought.

The arboretum became her testing ground, a microcosm where she could explore these ideas of controlled adaptation. She began to document the subtle ways the ecosystem was naturally evolving, the emergent properties that arose from unexpected interactions. She found that a particular variety of fast-growing vine, when allowed a limited degree of unchecked expansion, created a denser canopy that fostered the growth of a rare, shade-loving fern that had previously struggled. This wasn't a deviation from the plan; it was an observation of a new, beneficial synergy. She meticulously recorded the data, the soil moisture levels, the light penetration, the fern's improved health metrics.

Her reports to the Council became not just requests for approval, but presentations of emergent ecological phenomena. She framed them as opportunities, not deviations. "The 'aggressive' growth of *Vitis volubilis* in Sector Gamma," she'd write, "while initially a concern for containment, has inadvertently created an ideal microclimate for *Asplenium scolopendrium*, a species vital for soil stabilization in shaded areas. This natural adaptation presents a more efficient and cost-effective method for cultivating *Asplenium* than our current artificial shading systems."

Eli supported her efforts, often providing his own observations that lent further weight to her findings. He would point out how certain plant communities, left to their own devices within designated zones, were developing unique symbiotic relationships, creating a natural resilience that surpassed anything that could be engineered. "It's the wildness within the order," he'd say, his eyes alight with passion. "It's where the true strength of Havenridge lies, in the intelligent chaos that the Accord, in its effort to control everything, might inadvertently stifle."

The Council, while still cautious, was beginning to respond, albeit slowly. The sheer volume of Mara's data, the undeniable evidence of ecological benefits, was starting to wear down their rigid adherence to protocol. They authorized small, controlled trials, allowing her to expand the *Vitis volubilis* slightly in a designated area, to introduce a limited number of *Coccinella septempunctata* into a specific orchard. Each successful trial chipped away at the perception of risk, replacing it with a dawning understanding of adaptive potential.

Mara realized that her struggle wasn't against the Council itself, but against a deeply ingrained fear of the unknown, a fear born from the very trauma they had all endured. Their mandates were not a cage built of malice, but a fortress built of necessity and past suffering. Her role, as she saw it, was not to dismantle the fortress, but to show them that its walls could be reinforced and expanded, not by adding more stone, but by incorporating new, living materials, by allowing for controlled growth and adaptation.

She began to focus her arguments not just on efficiency or ecological benefit, but on the concept of long-term resilience. "The Accord ensures our survival *today*," she explained to a concerned Elder Thorne, during one of their increasingly frequent, albeit still formal, exchanges. "But true resilience, the kind that will see Havenridge thrive for generations, requires us to embrace adaptability. It requires us to learn from the natural world, to understand that stability doesn't mean stagnation, but rather the capacity to change and evolve in response to new challenges."

She spoke of the sapling that had survived the frost, not just as an anomaly, but as a testament to inherent resilience. She spoke of the moss that provided silent support, not just as a botanical curiosity, but as a model for understated, yet crucial, contribution. She was weaving a narrative, a new understanding of success that extended beyond the quantifiable metrics of the Accord, a narrative that encompassed the emergent beauty, the quiet strength, and the vital importance of adaptability.

The Council's mandate, she understood, was to protect Havenridge. But the true protection, she was coming to believe, lay not in rigid control, but in fostering an environment where life, in all its unpredictable, beautiful complexity, could continue to flourish. Her work in the arboretum was not just about cultivating plants; it was about cultivating a new way of thinking, a new understanding of what it meant to be truly resilient in a world that was constantly, irrevocably, changing. The whispers of control were still there, but now, they were being met with a growing chorus of whispers about adaptation, about potential, about the enduring power of life to find its own way, to bloom even in the most unexpected of circumstances. And Mara, with Eli by her side, was determined to amplify that chorus until it could no longer be ignored. The arboretum was not just a sanctuary; it was a testament to a different kind of success, one that the Council, in their wisdom and their fear, was slowly beginning to recognize.

The illusion of freedom in Havenridge was a delicate tapestry, woven with threads of purpose and woven with the expectation of compliance. Each resident, from the youngest sapling tender to the oldest bio-engineer, was assigned a role, a function that slotted seamlessly into the intricate machinery of their community. This was not a dictatorial decree, but rather a guiding hand, an assurance that one's talents would be utilized for the collective good, that their contribution would be meaningful. And for Mara, at least for a long time, this structured existence had been a source of profound comfort. After the chaos of the collapse, the certainty of belonging, of having a defined purpose within the Havenridge framework, had been a balm to her restless spirit. The Council's pronouncements, though often delivered with an air of absolute authority, felt less like commands and more like the gentle, experienced instructions of a seasoned gardener guiding a fragile plant. They were the architects of this ordered world, and their blueprint, the Great Accord, was the very soil from which Havenridge had sprung.

Yet, a disquiet had begun to stir within her, a subtle awareness that the roots of her contentment were perhaps entwined with something less organic, something more... managed. It wasn't that she wished for the anarchy of the past. Far from it. The very existence of Havenridge was a testament to the necessity of order. But she was beginning to see the subtle edges of that order, the way it gently, almost imperceptibly, nudged individuals back onto the designated paths. It was in the way a suggestion for an unconventional crop rotation was met with a polite but firm redirection to the established agricultural charter, the way a proposed alteration to a building's facade, however aesthetically pleasing, was politely but firmly rejected on grounds of architectural uniformity. These weren't harsh rebukes, but rather a series of soft, insistent pressures, like a shepherd guiding a straying lamb back to the flock, not with force, but with a patient, unwavering presence.

She found herself observing Eli, his quiet contemplations, his subtle questioning of the established norms, and seeing them through a new lens. He didn't rebel, not in any overt way. His challenges were like the slow erosion of a riverbank, a gentle persistence that gradually reshaped the landscape. When he questioned the rationale behind a particular water-rationing schedule, citing his observations of the arboretum's unique microclimates and the potential for more efficient, localized irrigation, his concerns were listened to, acknowledged, and then gently reframed within the existing parameters of the Accord. The response was always framed in terms of necessity, of precedent, of the established protocols that had, after all, kept them safe. "Eli," Elder Thorne had once explained, his voice a low rumble of seasoned wisdom, "your insights into the arboretum are invaluable. However, the current water allocation is designed for equitable distribution across all sectors, ensuring no single area depletes resources vital to another. Deviations, even seemingly minor ones, could have unforeseen ripple effects. The Accord anticipates these complexities."

Mara understood the logic, the deep-seated need for a system that functioned without unpredictable variables. But Eli's quiet persistence chipped away at her own ingrained acceptance. He wasn't trying to dismantle the system; he was trying to understand its inherent limitations, to find the spaces where a different kind of growth, a more nuanced approach, might be possible. And in his gentle dissent, Mara began to see a reflection of her own burgeoning doubts. She, too, had begun to feel the invisible reins of control, the subtle guidance that steered them away from the unpredictable and towards the assured.

It was the arboretum, her sanctuary, that had become the focal point of this awakening. Her work with the plants, her intimate understanding of their need for adaptation, for a certain degree of freedom to explore and evolve, had begun to inform her perception of Havenridge itself. She saw how her own proposals, born from rigorous observation and a desire to innovate, were invariably met with a gentle redirection back to established protocols. When she'd identified the potential for a new, more resilient strain of nutrient-rich moss to thrive in the shaded undergrowth, a strain that could supplement their existing food sources and improve soil quality, the Council's response had been to commend her initiative while reminding her of the strict zoning regulations for edible flora. "The introduction of novel food sources requires extensive testing and Council approval, Mara," the official communication had stated, politely but firmly. "Our current moss cultivation is well within established parameters for safety and yield. Any new introductions must follow the stringent evaluation process outlined in Appendix G of the Accord."

The implication was clear: her findings, while perhaps scientifically interesting, did not align with the established order, the proven path. It wasn't that her ideas were dismissed outright, but rather that they were carefully contained, absorbed into the existing framework without truly challenging it. It was like presenting a rare, exotic seed to a meticulously manicured garden and being told that it simply didn't fit the established aesthetic. The seed might be viable, even beautiful, but its very existence outside the planned design was deemed a disruption.

This subtle enforcement of conformity extended beyond her own work. She saw it in the carefully curated social interactions, the encouragement of communal activities that reinforced shared values and societal norms. Even leisure time was, in a way, structured. There were designated recreational areas, organized group activities, and a pervasive cultural emphasis on productive engagement. Spontaneous gatherings, while not forbidden, were rare. The prevailing sentiment was that time was a precious resource, to be utilized for the betterment of oneself and the community. To simply *be*, without a tangible objective, was viewed with a sort of polite bewilderment, as if one had forgotten the fundamental purpose of existence.

Mara found herself caught in a peculiar dichotomy. She cherished the stability Havenridge offered, the absence of the desperate scramble for survival that had plagued the generations before. She was grateful for the security, for the knowledge that her needs would be met, her contribution valued. Yet, a yearning had begun to bloom within her, a quiet rebellion against the subtle homogenization of spirit that seemed to be an inherent byproduct of their perfect order. She saw the potential for a richer, more vibrant existence, one that embraced the unpredictable beauty of emergent complexity, the spontaneous flourishing that arose not from meticulous planning, but from a certain degree of freedom to explore the unknown.

She began to notice the nuances in Eli's approach. He wasn't an outsider, nor was he a vocal dissenter. Instead, he was a keen observer, a quiet questioner who nudged at the edges of the established narrative. He would ask subtle questions during community forums, not to challenge, but to illuminate. "If the nutrient cycles in the northern quadrant are showing a consistent surplus," he might ask, his voice calm and measured, "could we not consider reallocating some of that excess to the southern agricultural plots without compromising the integrity of the northern ecosystem?" These questions, framed in terms of optimization and efficiency, were difficult to dismiss. They spoke to the spirit of improvement, a tenet deeply ingrained in Havenridge's ethos. Yet, even these carefully worded inquiries were often met with a reiteration of the existing protocols, the "why" behind them already deemed settled, unchallengeable.

Mara realized that the Council's control wasn't exercised through overt coercion, but through an ingrained system of expectations and gentle redirection. It was a system that rewarded compliance and subtly discouraged deviation. The "freedom" they enjoyed was the freedom to perform their designated roles with excellence, to contribute within the predefined boundaries. It was the freedom of a perfectly cultivated bonsai tree, beautifully shaped and meticulously maintained, but whose growth was ultimately dictated by the gardener's shears.

She began to see how her own initial comfort with Havenridge's structure had been a reflection of her own deep-seated need for order after the trauma of the collapse. The Council's mandates had provided a clear path, a defined purpose, a sense of agency within a controlled environment. But now, as she witnessed Eli's quiet pursuit of deeper understanding and observed the subtle ways Havenridge guided its residents, she began to question if this carefully constructed order was, in fact, a cage, albeit a gilded one. The illusion of freedom was powerful, seductive even, but it was an illusion nonetheless. And the whispers of control, once a comforting lullaby of security, were beginning to sound like the rustling of bars.

This realization wasn't a sudden epiphany, but a gradual dawning, like the slow unfurling of a new leaf. It was a recognition that the very systems designed to ensure their survival and prosperity might also be subtly stifling their potential for true growth, for a more expansive and vibrant future. The Great Accord, once a symbol of their salvation, was beginning to feel like a beautifully constructed straitjacket, designed to keep them safe, but also to keep them from reaching their full, untamed potential. She found herself having hushed conversations with Eli, their discussions now tinged with a shared understanding of this subtle constraint. "It's like we're living in a garden that's been perfectly pruned for centuries," she'd muse, her gaze drifting towards the carefully delineated rows of flora outside her window. "Everything is in its place, beautiful and ordered. But what if, somewhere in the untouched wilderness beyond the walls, there are plants that could heal us, that could feed us in ways we haven't even imagined?"

Eli would nod, his eyes reflecting a similar contemplation. "The Council's intention is never malicious, Mara. They believe they are protecting us, preserving the delicate balance they fought so hard to create. They experienced the unbridled chaos, the devastation of unchecked growth. Their fear of repetition is a powerful motivator. But sometimes, in their effort to prevent disaster, they inadvertently prevent discovery."

Mara understood this fear. She saw it etched on the faces of the elders during Council meetings, the residual echoes of hardship and loss. Their dedication was unquestionable, their commitment to Havenridge absolute. But their perspective, rooted in the immediate aftermath of the collapse, seemed to struggle to encompass the possibility of a future that required more than just rigorous adherence to established safety protocols. They saw resilience as a static state, a carefully maintained equilibrium, rather than a dynamic process of adaptation and change.

She began to notice how this ingrained caution manifested in everyday life. When a new artistic endeavor emerged, something that didn't quite fit the established aesthetic guidelines for communal art installations, it was gently discouraged, reframed as perhaps better suited for private expression. When a group of younger residents proposed a less structured approach to their educational modules, suggesting more free-form exploration and less regimented curriculum, their proposal was met with polite, but firm, reaffirmation of the proven educational framework. The underlying message, delivered not with an iron fist but with a velvet glove, was that deviation was a risk, and risk was the enemy of stability.

Mara felt a growing internal conflict. She was a product of this system, and a beneficiary of its order. She had found her purpose within its framework, her skills honed and valued. But Eli's quiet questioning, coupled with her own observations in the arboretum, had awakened a new desire: the desire for a freedom that wasn't just about performing a role, but about the possibility of *becoming* something new, something unplanned. It was the freedom to explore, to experiment, to risk failure in the pursuit of discovery.

She realized that the illusion of freedom was most potent when it was invisible, when the constraints were so subtly woven into the fabric of daily life that they were no longer perceived as restrictions, but as natural inclinations. The residents of Havenridge were free to pursue their assigned vocations, to contribute to the community, to live peaceful, ordered lives. But the freedom to stray from the path, to explore the uncharted territories of thought and action, was a freedom that was, in effect, highly managed. And in this subtle, pervasive control, Mara began to see a quiet danger, a potential for stagnation that could, ironically, make Havenridge more vulnerable in the long run, not less. The perfect garden, after all, could become sterile if it was never allowed to experience the wild, unpredictable bloom of something new.

Eli's resistance was not a thunderclap, but a persistent hum, an undercurrent beneath the polished surface of Havenridge's order. It was woven into the very fabric of his interactions, a quiet testament to a spirit that refused to be entirely molded. He didn't shout from the rooftops, nor did he openly defy the Council. Instead, his dissent manifested in thoughtful inquiries, in carefully worded suggestions that probed the edges of established protocols, and in a gentle, almost imperceptible encouragement of independent thought amongst his peers. He was a quiet revolutionary, armed not with weapons, but with reason and a profound respect for the human capacity for original thought.

He saw the Great Accord not as immutable law, but as a living document, one that, like any living thing, might require thoughtful adjustment to thrive. When the water allocation system was discussed during a community forum, a system designed for absolute equity but which, in Eli's estimation, was inefficient in certain microclimates, he didn't present a grand, disruptive proposal. Instead, he posed a series of questions, each one a carefully placed pebble in the smooth surface of consensus. "Elder Thorne," he might begin, his voice carrying a tone of genuine curiosity, "I've observed that the eastern arboretum, due to its unique soil composition and prevailing winds, consistently retains moisture for significantly longer periods than the western sector. Given this data, could we explore the feasibility of a slightly adjusted irrigation schedule for the east, perhaps redirecting a small surplus during the monsoon season to areas experiencing more rapid evaporation, without compromising the overall equitable distribution mandate?" His questions were always framed within the existing paradigm, seeking not to dismantle, but to optimize, to refine. He understood that to propose radical change was to invite immediate dismissal; to offer incremental improvements, rooted in observable data, was to open a crack in the door of possibility.

Mara watched these exchanges with a growing fascination, and a prickle of unease. Eli's approach was so elegantly subtle, so perfectly aligned with the principles Havenridge itself espoused – efficiency, optimization, the pursuit of the greater good. Yet, the Council's responses, while always polite, often skirted the core of his suggestions. They would commend his diligence, acknowledge the accuracy of his observations, and then reiterate the fundamental necessity of the current system. "Eli," Elder Thorne might respond, his voice a low, steady rumble, "your dedication to understanding our hydrological systems is commendable. However, the current allocation schedule was established through extensive modeling, designed to account for every variable and ensure absolute fairness. Any deviation, however small, could introduce unforeseen complications. The Accord prioritizes stability, a proven model that has served us well. We must not risk what we have for the allure of a theoretical improvement." The underlying message was clear: the system was designed for safety, and safety demanded predictability. Innovation, unless it could be proven not to disrupt that predictability, was a dangerous indulgence.

Eli's influence, however, was not confined to the formal forums. He possessed a remarkable ability to foster a sense of individual value in others, a quiet cultivation of self-worth that ran counter to the homogenizing forces of collective identity. He'd spend time with the younger tenders in the hydroponics bays, not just instructing them on optimal nutrient levels, but asking about their dreams, their ideas, the things that sparked their own curiosity. "Anya," he might say, his gaze thoughtful as he observed her meticulously tending a row of leafy greens, "you have a particular knack for coaxing the best growth from these Solanum varieties. Have you ever considered experimenting with different light spectrums? I recall reading some fascinating, albeit unverified, theories about how certain wavelengths might impact flavor profiles." He wouldn't provide answers, only more questions, planting seeds of independent inquiry. He encouraged them to record their own observations, to develop their own hypotheses, to see their work not merely as a function, but as an opportunity for personal discovery.

This subtle encouragement of individuality was a silent rebellion against the pervasive narrative that the collective good was the ultimate measure of success. While Havenridge celebrated contributions to the community, it did so within a framework that often obscured the unique motivations and personal growth of the individuals contributing. Eli, by contrast, seemed to celebrate the *process* of discovery, the internal journey of learning and exploration, as much as the outward result. He understood that true resilience wasn't just about enduring hardship; it was about cultivating a robust inner life, a capacity for critical thinking and creative problem-solving that could adapt to any unforeseen challenge.

Mara found herself increasingly drawn to Eli's perspective. Her work in the arboretum, her intimate understanding of the delicate balance between order and chaos in the natural world, resonated deeply with his quiet philosophy. She saw how even the most carefully planned ecosystem benefited from unexpected mutations, from the resilience that arose from diversity, not uniformity. The Council's approach, while rooted in a genuine desire to protect Havenridge, felt increasingly like an attempt to freeze time, to create a perfect, unchanging tableau that, in its very rigidity, might become brittle.

One evening, as they shared a communal meal in the brightly lit refectory, Eli leaned closer to Mara, his voice a low murmur that was easily lost in the general hum of conversation. "I've been reviewing the historical logs for the atmospheric processors," he said, his eyes scanning the room as if ensuring their privacy. "The current efficiency ratings are high, undoubtedly. But I've noticed a slight but consistent degradation in filtration capacity over the past five cycles, particularly in the sub-filters designed to capture particulate matter from the outer atmospheric layers.

My preliminary analysis suggests that a more aggressive, albeit short-term, backflush cycle, coupled with a more frequent replacement of these specific sub-filters, could potentially extend the overall lifespan of the primary filtration units by a significant margin."

Mara listened, her mind racing. This was not a minor adjustment; it was a proposal that touched upon a critical piece of Havenridge's infrastructure, something directly related to their survival. The implication was that the current maintenance schedule, dictated by the Accord, might be suboptimal, leading to a premature aging of vital equipment. "And the Council?" she asked, her voice barely a whisper. "How did they respond to this observation?"

Eli offered a small, almost imperceptible shrug. "They acknowledged the data. They reminded me that the current protocols are based on extensive research conducted during the early years, research that established the current replacement schedule as the most cost-effective and reliable method to ensure continuous operation. They suggested that any deviation would require extensive re-evaluation, a process that could disrupt the current allocation of resources for maintenance crews." He paused, his gaze meeting hers, a flicker of something akin to disappointment in his eyes. "The Accord, Mara. It's a powerful anchor. It holds us steady, but it also prevents us from drifting into uncharted waters, even when those waters might hold the key to a safer harbor."

His quiet defiance was a constant, gentle reminder of what was at stake. It wasn't just about the physical security of Havenridge; it was about the preservation of the human spirit's most vital attribute: its capacity for independent thought and action. He believed that true survival, in the long run, was not solely dependent on robust walls and efficient resource management. It required a population that could think critically, adapt creatively, and question when necessary. To stifle that, even with the best intentions, was to invite a different kind of decay, a slow erosion of the very ingenuity that had allowed them to build Havenridge in the first place.

Mara found herself reflecting on her own proposals, the ones that had been gently redirected. The new moss strain, the ideas for optimizing the arboretum's irrigation – they weren't wild, unscientific notions. They were born from deep observation, from a desire to improve, to innovate. But the system, designed for stability, had a way of absorbing such proposals without truly embracing them. They were acknowledged, filed away, and then gently steered back towards the established, proven path. It was like trying to introduce a wild, untamed flower into a perfectly manicured rose garden; it might be beautiful, even beneficial, but it didn't fit the established design.

Eli, however, seemed to understand that true strength lay not in an unchanging perfection, but in the capacity for adaptation. His resistance was a testament to this belief. He didn't seek to overthrow the Council or dismantle the Accord. Instead, he worked from within, using their own principles of logic and efficiency as a tool to gently pry open the tightly shut doors of convention. He was a sculptor of thought, patiently chipping away at the stone of ingrained dogma, revealing the more nuanced form that lay beneath.

He also had a way of subtly encouraging this same spirit in others, often without them even realizing it. He would engage individuals in conversations that nudged them towards their own insights. He might ask a resident working on the fabrication of solar arrays about their personal experiences with energy efficiency, prompting them to consider how their daily habits might be further optimized, beyond the mandated guidelines. He would listen with genuine interest to their responses, validating their perspectives, and then offer a gentle, often hypothetical, question that encouraged further exploration. "It's fascinating, Jian," he might say, after Jian had described his personal efforts to minimize energy consumption at his domicile, "that you've found such success with that particular low-draw lighting system. I wonder if the principles behind its design could be applied to the communal lighting grids in sectors three and four, perhaps with some minor modifications?" He wasn't directing; he was inviting, subtly planting the seeds of self-directed inquiry.

Mara saw this ripple effect in the quiet conversations she overheard, in the slightly more engaged questions that some of her colleagues were beginning to pose during project debriefs. It was as if Eli's quiet insistence on the value of individual perspective was slowly, almost imperceptibly, shifting the collective consciousness. He was a living embodiment of the idea that true resilience wasn't just about having a strong defense, but about fostering a population that was intellectually agile, unafraid to question, and capable of generating novel solutions.

His resistance, then, was not a threat to Havenridge's stability, but a necessary counterpoint to its rigid adherence to established order. It was the quiet hum that prevented the symphony of their society from becoming monotonous. And for Mara, who was beginning to feel the subtle constraints of their meticulously crafted world, Eli's quiet defiance was not just inspiring; it was a vital reminder that the human spirit, like the most resilient of plants, needed not just sustenance and shelter, but also the freedom to grow, to adapt, and to reach for the sun in its own unique way. His quiet resistance was, in essence, a testament to the enduring power of hope, the unwavering belief that even within the most controlled environment, the capacity for individual thought and the pursuit of knowledge could not be entirely extinguished. It was a beacon, a silent whisper in the carefully orchestrated order, that reminded her that true survival wasn't merely about existing, but about thriving, about the continuous, and sometimes messy, process of becoming.

Mara had always been a creature of order. Her life in the arboretum was a testament to this inherent inclination. Every leaf was cataloged, every bloom meticulously documented, every dewdrop accounted for in her meticulous hydrological calculations. She found solace in the predictable cycles of growth and decay, in the quiet hum of systems designed for balance and efficiency. Havenridge, with its carefully planned sectors, its regulated resources, and its overarching Great Accord, was the embodiment of that order. It was a sanctuary, built on the ashes of a chaotic past, and she believed, with every fiber of her being, in the wisdom of its foundations. The Council, with their measured pronouncements and their unwavering commitment to stability, were the guardians of that sanctuary. Their intentions, she knew, were pure: to protect, to provide, to ensure the survival of their community.

Yet, Eli's presence, like a persistent vine subtly weaving its way through the perfectly ordered trellises of her mind, was beginning to disrupt that carefully cultivated peace. He spoke of lived experience, of the unquantifiable nuances that existed beyond the cold logic of data and protocol. He challenged the very notion of a perfect, static system, suggesting that true resilience lay not in rigid adherence to the past, but in the dynamic capacity to adapt and evolve. His quiet arguments, framed in carefully chosen words and backed by an almost unsettlingly calm demeanor, began to chip away at the unshakeable edifice of her conviction.

She remembered a recent discussion in the communal hydroponics bay. A young tender, Anya, had been experimenting with a new nutrient blend, a deviation from the standard formula. The results were promising – a subtle but noticeable increase in the vibrancy of the Solanum plants, a richer hue to their leaves. When Anya presented her findings, Elder Thorne had listened with his characteristic patience, his gaze steady. "Anya," he'd said, his voice resonating with the weight of authority, "your dedication to optimizing growth is commendable. However, the current nutrient composition has been validated over decades, ensuring consistent yield and nutritional profiles for our community. While your observations are interesting, the Accord mandates adherence to established protocols for the safety and well-being of all." Anya had nodded, her shoulders slumping almost imperceptibly, and the opportunity for further inquiry, for genuine innovation, had dissolved back into the sterile efficiency of the approved formula.

Eli, who had been observing from a nearby station, had approached Anya later. Mara had been pruning a nearby section of lumina-vines, her movements silent, her senses attuned to the subtle shifts in the environment, and she'd overheard their exchange. "Anya," Eli had murmured, his voice a gentle counterpoint to the whirring of the nutrient pumps, "you noticed a difference in the Solanum's color, yes? Did you also perceive any difference in the aroma, or perhaps the texture of the leaves when you handled them?" Anya had hesitated, then admitted, "The aroma seemed... richer. And they felt a little more supple." Eli's eyes had lit up, not with a triumphant 'I told you so,' but with a quiet spark of shared discovery. "Fascinating," he'd said. "The Accord, of course, prioritizes quantifiable outcomes. But sometimes, the most profound changes are those that touch our senses, that speak to a deeper, less tangible aspect of life. Perhaps, next cycle, you could keep a private journal, noting these subtle sensory details alongside the official metrics. It's valuable data, even if it doesn't fit neatly into the current reporting structures."

Mara had felt a jolt, a disquieting resonance. Eli wasn't dismissing the Accord; he was suggesting a way to honor its spirit while acknowledging the limitations of its scope. He was validating Anya's observations, validating the very human impulse to perceive and appreciate the world beyond mere numbers. It was this subtle validation of the lived experience that was so compelling, and so unsettling.

Her own work in the arboretum had always been guided by a deep respect for the natural world's inherent complexity. She understood that life was not a static equation, but a fluid, ever-changing process. She had witnessed, firsthand, the surprising resilience of certain hardy species that thrived in seemingly inhospitable conditions, their existence a testament to adaptation rather than rigid design. She'd also seen how attempts to impose too much control could stifle growth, leading to a fragile uniformity that was easily disrupted. There was a particular section of the arboretum, a carefully cultivated biome designed to mimic a pre-Accord desert landscape, where the slightest fluctuation in humidity or temperature could lead to a cascade of wilting. The plants there, bred for perfect adherence to the simulated environment, lacked the inherent adaptability of their wild ancestors.

And so, Eli's perspective struck a chord deep within her. He was not advocating for chaos, but for a more nuanced understanding of order, one that embraced the unpredictable beauty of life. He saw the Accord not as an impenetrable fortress, but as a framework, one that could be strengthened by allowing for intelligent adaptation, not just unyielding adherence.

The conflict, however, was not a raging storm within her, but a quiet, persistent undercurrent. She believed in the safety Havenridge provided. She remembered the stories of the Collapse, of the desperate scramble for resources, the breakdown of societal structures. Havenridge was the antithesis of that, a carefully constructed bastion against such horrors. The Council's vigilance, their emphasis on established protocols, were the very bulwarks that protected them. To question that, to suggest that perhaps their meticulous order was, in some subtle way, stifling them, felt like a betrayal of that safety.

She found herself replaying a conversation she'd had with Eli just days ago, amidst the gentle rustling of the bio-luminescent fungi in Sector Gamma. He had been explaining his ongoing research into the atmospheric processors, a topic of vital importance to their enclosed ecosystem. "The readings indicate a consistent, albeit small, decline in the efficiency of the tertiary particulate filters," he'd stated, his voice low and even. "My projections suggest that if this trend continues, we could see a significant impact on the lifespan of the primary filtration units within the next ten cycles. A minor adjustment to the backflush sequence, perhaps an increase in the frequency of replacement for these specific sub-filters, could mitigate this degradation without impacting the overall resource allocation."

Mara had listened, her mind already processing the implications. This wasn't a theoretical musing; it was a practical, data-driven observation that directly addressed a critical system. But her immediate thought, almost instinctual, was the Council's likely response. "And the Council, Eli?" she'd asked, her voice tinged with a familiar apprehension. "How did they receive this information?"

He'd offered a faint smile, a gesture that held both understanding and a touch of weariness. "They acknowledged the data, of course. Elder Thorne reminded me, as he often does, that the current maintenance schedule is a product of extensive modeling, designed for maximum reliability and cost-effectiveness. He suggested that any deviation would require a full review, a process that could divert resources from other essential maintenance tasks. The Accord, Mara, is a powerful shield. But sometimes, it feels as though it's so tightly held, it obscures our view of the horizon."

His words hung in the air, heavy with unspoken meaning. She understood the logic of the Accord, the paramount importance of stability. But she also felt a growing unease. Was the price of this absolute stability a subtle erosion of their capacity to innovate, to adapt? Was the shield that protected them also blinding them to potential threats, or even to opportunities for growth?

She found herself comparing Eli's approach to her own past attempts to introduce new ideas. The proposal for the drought-resistant moss strain, for instance. She had painstakingly gathered data on its germination rates in controlled arid simulations, its minimal water requirements, its ability to stabilize soil. The Council had acknowledged the data, praised her diligence, and then suggested that the existing hydro-absorbent polymers were sufficient, their performance proven and integrated into the established irrigation protocols. Her moss strain, though potentially beneficial, had been deemed an unnecessary variable, a deviation from the known and the reliable. It was as if Havenridge, in its pursuit of perfection, was unwilling to accommodate the wild, untamed beauty and resilience that often arose from unexpected places.

The conflict within Mara was not about choosing sides. It was about reconciling two fundamental aspects of her own nature: her deep-seated need for order and security, and a burgeoning, almost defiant, appreciation for the vital, messy, unpredictable essence of life that Eli so effortlessly championed. She respected the Council's vision, the immense effort that had gone into creating Havenridge. But Eli's gentle insistence on the value of individual observation, of lived experience, was like a persistent whisper in her ear, reminding her that true survival might require more than just meticulous planning. It might require the courage to embrace the unknown, to trust in the inherent adaptability of both nature and humanity.

She looked at her hands, calloused from years of tending to the arboretum. They were the hands of someone who understood growth, who understood that change, even when challenging, was often the catalyst for something stronger, something more vibrant. Eli's quiet rebellion wasn't a rejection of Havenridge; it was an argument for its evolution, a plea for it to embrace the very qualities that made life, in all its glorious imperfection, worth protecting. And Mara, caught between the comfort of the known and the magnetic pull of the unknown, found herself increasingly drawn to the quiet wisdom of his dissent. The safety she had always sought might, in fact, be at odds with the very richness of existence she was beginning to crave. The meticulously constructed order of Havenridge, while providing a vital shield, also threatened to become a gilded cage, limiting not just her choices, but the very spirit of what it meant to be alive. This was the quiet war within her, a struggle between the ingrained desire for security and the nascent longing for a life that was not just lived, but truly experienced, in all its glorious, unpredictable complexity.

The arboretum was more than just a collection of carefully curated flora; it was a living laboratory, a testament to Havenridge's commitment to ecological restoration. For Mara, it had always been a sanctuary, a place where the intricate dance of life unfolded with a predictable, comforting rhythm. Each species, from the drought-resistant succulents of the arid biome to the ethereal glow of the lumina-fungi, had its designated place, its needs meticulously charted and provided for. This order, this controlled environment, was the bedrock of her belief in Havenridge's philosophy of survival. The Great Accord, with its emphasis on regulation and adherence to proven protocols, was, in her mind, the ultimate safeguard against the chaos that had nearly extinguished humanity.

Eli, however, saw the arboretum with different eyes. He recognized the order, the meticulous planning, but he also perceived the subtle limitations, the unintended consequences of such stringent control. His approach, born from a deep understanding of systems and a relentless curiosity, was one of gentle perturbation, of exploring the edges of what was known. He didn't advocate for dismantling the established order, but for understanding its vulnerabilities, for finding the spaces where innovation could breathe.

Their recent collaboration on the rare 'Sunpetal' orchid had become a quiet nexus of their contrasting philosophies. The orchid, a delicate bloom once believed extinct, was notoriously temperamental. Its survival in the arboretum had been a triumph of Mara's horticultural expertise, a careful replication of its ancestral environment, complete with precisely regulated light cycles, nutrient delivery, and atmospheric composition. Yet, despite her best efforts, the orchids had remained stubbornly infertile, their beauty a solitary, unfulfilled promise.

"The soil pH is within optimal parameters," Mara had stated, her brow furrowed as she examined the readings from the sensor array embedded in the ceramic pot. "The nutrient solution is identical to the one documented in the original research logs. And the humidity levels are maintained within a two-tenth of a percent variance." She ran a gloved finger along the velvety petal, a gesture of almost maternal concern. "They thrive, yet they do not propagate. It's as if they are preserved, but not truly alive."

Eli had been observing from a nearby workbench, meticulously calibrating a micro-drone designed for atmospheric sampling. He'd paused, his attention drawn to Mara's quiet frustration. "The recorded data tells one story, Mara," he'd said, his voice a low hum against the ambient hum of the arboretum's life support. "But perhaps the orchids are speaking a different language, one that doesn't translate directly into our current metrics."

He had approached the orchids, not with the sterile precision of a technician, but with a contemplative grace. He'd knelt, his gaze level with the delicate blossoms. "The logs mention sunlight, yes? But what kind of sunlight? Was it the direct, unfiltered glare of an open sky, or the dappled light that filters through a canopy? Our simulated sun provides a consistent lumen output, a precise spectrum. But nature, even in its most protected forms, is rarely so... uniform."

Mara had watched him, a flicker of intrigue stirring beneath her ingrained adherence to protocol. Eli's questions were unconventional, bordering on the poetic. But there was an undeniable logic to them. The original research logs, dating back to the pre-Collapse era, were fragmented, relying on observational data that was often subjective.

"The original habitat was described as a 'sun-dappled glade'," Mara conceded, recalling the dusty archives. "But 'sun-dappled' can encompass a wide range of variations."

Eli had nodded, a faint smile touching his lips. "Exactly. And our 'precise' simulation, while safe, might be missing the very essence of that dappled variability. What if," he'd continued, his voice dropping conspiratorially, "we introduced a controlled, intermittent interruption of the primary light source? Not a blackout, but a brief, naturalistic dimming, perhaps mimicking the passage of a cloud. A subtle shift in intensity and duration, not just a reduction in overall output."

Mara's initial reaction was one of instinctive resistance. Deviation from established parameters was precisely what the Accord sought to prevent. It introduced uncertainty, a variable that could, in theory, lead to catastrophic failure. Yet, Eli's hypothesis was rooted in an understanding of biological adaptation, a concept that Mara, despite her structured approach, deeply respected. She had seen how life, in its rawest form, found ways to persist, to change, to overcome even the most formidable obstacles.

"It's a significant deviation, Eli," she'd cautioned, her voice tight. "The risk of shock to the plant's photosynthetic processes... it could be detrimental."

"Or," Eli had countered gently, "it could be the catalyst it needs. Think of it as introducing a controlled stressor, one that mimics the challenges its ancestors faced. Sometimes, it is through adaptation to environmental fluctuations that organisms develop reproductive resilience." He'd then proposed a phased introduction, beginning with minute variations and meticulously monitoring the orchids' responses.

Hesitantly, Mara had agreed. It was a leap of faith, a step beyond the sterile certainty of her meticulously crafted environment. They spent the next several cycles refining the new light protocol. Eli's technical skill ensured the dimming was precise and repeatable, while Mara's horticultural expertise guided the intensity and duration of the disruptions, always attuned to the subtle physiological cues of the orchids.

The initial results were almost imperceptible. A slight deepening of the green in the leaves, a fractionally increased turgor in the stems. Then, one morning, Mara arrived to find it. A tiny, delicate bud, nestled amongst the foliage, promising a new bloom. And within weeks, not one, but three more had appeared. The Sunpetal orchids, once stubbornly infertile, were showing signs of successful pollination.

The success wasn't a loud, triumphant declaration, but a quiet, profound affirmation. It was a demonstration, tangible and undeniable, that their seemingly disparate approaches could, in fact, converge. Mara's structured planning provided the necessary foundation, the controlled environment that prevented outright collapse. Eli's adaptive flexibility, his willingness to explore the nuances, had unlocked the potential that rigid adherence had kept dormant.

"It's not about abandoning order, Mara," Eli had explained one evening, as they cataloged the new blooms. The arboretum was bathed in the soft, artificial twilight, the air rich with the scent of damp earth and exotic blossoms. "It's about understanding that true sustainability, in nature and in us, isn't about achieving a static state of perfection. It's about the capacity to adapt, to respond to change, to find resilience not in rigidity, but in intelligent flexibility."

He gestured towards a patch of hardy, ground-covering flora that had begun to creep into a less manicured corner of the arboretum, a zone Mara had initially planned to replant. "Look at this," he'd said. "It's not what we intended, but it's thriving. It's filling a niche, stabilizing the soil. We could rip it out, maintain our original design. Or, we could study it. Understand why it's growing there, what benefits it might offer. Perhaps it can be integrated, not as a planned element, but as a natural evolution."

Mara had looked at the creeping vines, their tenacity a silent testament to life's persistent urge to flourish. She'd always viewed such intrusions as imperfections, deviations from the intended design. But Eli saw them as opportunities, as whispers of a more dynamic, self-correcting system.

This realization began to shift her perspective on Havenridge itself. The Great Accord, with its stringent regulations and its emphasis on preventing any deviation from established protocols, felt less like a fortress of safety and more like a meticulously constructed enclosure. It protected them from the storms of the past, but was it also preventing them from experiencing the full spectrum of life, from developing the adaptive resilience that true survival demanded?

She found herself observing the Council meetings with a new lens. Elder Thorne, a man whose wisdom was as deep as the roots of the oldest arboreal specimens, spoke with unwavering authority about maintaining the established order. He cited historical precedents, the statistical evidence of past successes, the unassailable logic of their carefully constructed systems. His pronouncements, once a source of comfort and reassurance, now seemed to carry a subtle undertone of fear – a fear of the unknown, a fear of anything that deviated from the path already charted.

During a discussion about resource allocation for a new atmospheric filtration unit, Eli had presented data suggesting a slight modification to the standard purification cycle. He argued that a subtle shift in the ionic balance, while requiring a marginal increase in energy consumption, would significantly extend the lifespan of the primary filtration membranes, thereby saving resources in the long run.

Elder Thorne had listened, his expression unreadable. "Eli," he'd said, his voice resonating with the gravitas of years of leadership, "your analytical skills are, as always, commendable. However, the current cycle has been proven effective and predictable for over two decades. The Accord mandates adherence to validated systems. Any deviation, however seemingly minor, introduces an unacceptable level of risk. We cannot afford to gamble with our atmospheric integrity."

The other Council members had nodded in agreement, their faces reflecting a shared commitment to the established order. Mara, seated amongst them, felt a familiar knot of apprehension tighten in her stomach. She understood the Council's reasoning; the stakes were incredibly high. But she also saw the missed opportunity. Eli's proposal wasn't a reckless gamble; it was a data-driven optimization, a proactive measure to enhance long-term efficiency. It was a concept that, in the arboretum, had yielded positive results.

"But Elder Thorne," Mara had interjected, her voice softer than she intended, "the Sunpetal orchids... their propagation was achieved through a controlled deviation from our established protocols. We introduced a variability that mimicked natural adaptation, and the results were... quite remarkable."

A ripple of surprise went through the Council. Elder Thorne turned his gaze towards Mara, his eyes sharp and questioning.

"Mara, the arboretum is a controlled ecosystem, designed for specific research. Havenridge is a community. The variables we manage here are of a fundamentally different nature. The Accord is not a suggestion; it is a blueprint for survival. And that blueprint prioritizes stability above all else."

The unspoken message was clear: the arboretum was a safe space for experimentation, but Havenridge was a different matter. The lessons learned within its controlled walls could not be directly extrapolated to the complex, interconnected systems of their entire community. Yet, Mara couldn't shake the feeling that they were missing a crucial point. The resilience of life, whether in a delicate orchid or in a thriving community, wasn't solely about maintaining a perfect, static state. It was about the ability to bend without breaking, to adapt and evolve in the face of inevitable change.

Later, as she walked through the arboretum, the scent of damp earth and blooming flowers filling her senses, Mara reflected on the Council's discourse. They spoke of survival as if it were a matter of holding the line, of defending against threats. But what if survival also required growth, adaptation, and the courage to embrace the unpredictable? The arboretum, once a symbol of her belief in rigid order, was slowly transforming in her mind. It was becoming a testament to a different kind of strength – the strength of balance, of integrating the meticulously planned with the intelligently emergent. It was a microcosm, indeed, of the larger challenge facing Havenridge: to find a way to live, not just to survive, in a world that demanded both structure and adaptability, both control and freedom. The lessons of the arboretum, she realized, were far more profound than she had initially understood. They were lessons in the very nature of life itself, and the true meaning of resilience.

CHAPTER SIX

Seasons of Change

The first whispers of autumn arrived not with a dramatic gust, but with a subtle shift in the quality of light. The relentless, high-summer sun softened, casting longer shadows across Havenridge's meticulously planned plazas and verdant common areas. Mara noticed it first in the arboretum, a place where she spent a significant portion of her days overseeing the intricate balance of life. The air, once thick with the cloying sweetness of late-blooming flowers, began to carry a sharper, cleaner scent, tinged with the dry, earthy aroma of decaying leaves. Sunlight, filtering through the canopy of genetically resilient oaks and maples, took on a warmer, more golden hue, painting the usually vibrant greens with strokes of amber and russet. It was a predictable transition, meticulously accounted for in Havenridge's annual cycle. Every community member understood the rhythm: summer's bounty would yield to autumn's preparation, which would then give way to winter's dormancy, and finally, the hopeful reawakening of spring.

For Mara, this seasonal shift was less about aesthetic appreciation and more about strategic planning. Her mind, ever attuned to the practicalities of resource management and community welfare, immediately began to catalog the implications. The gardens, usually bursting with nutrient-rich produce, would soon enter their less productive phase. This meant a heightened focus on harvesting, preserving, and recalibrating nutrient distribution for the months ahead. The carefully cultivated flora, designed to maximize yield and resilience, would still require monitoring, but their energy would now be directed inward, conserving for survival rather than outward growth. She observed the changing leaves with a detached fascination, admiring the artistry of nature, but her thoughts were already a few steps ahead, calculating the increased energy demands for heating communal spaces, the need for increased insulation checks in residential units, and the logistical challenges of stockpiling provisions. The beauty of the autumnal palette was a gentle reminder of the work that lay ahead, a beautiful, yet urgent, call to action.

She walked through the arboretum, her sensible boots crunching softly on fallen leaves that had already begun to carpet the pathways. The 'Crimson Cascade' vine, a cultivar specifically engineered for its vibrant autumn display, was living up to its name, its tendrils dripping with fiery red foliage. Nearby, the 'Golden Orb' ornamental gourds, their harvest already secured, lay in neat rows in a designated staging area, awaiting processing and storage. Mara paused beside a bed of 'Everbloom' asters, their resilient purple petals still bravely facing the encroaching chill. She ran a gloved hand over a velvety leaf, the coolness seeping through the material. These plants, like so many others in Havenridge, were a testament to human ingenuity, designed to thrive in a post-Collapse world. But even the most resilient life forms followed the earth's ancient rhythms.

"They're holding on longer this year," a voice remarked from beside her. Mara turned to see Eli, leaning against a sturdy oak, his hands tucked into the pockets of his well-worn utility vest. He gestured towards the asters with a slight tilt of his head. "The atmospheric regulators seem to be doing their job, keeping the microclimate just temperate enough."

Mara nodded, her gaze returning to the asters. "The models predicted a slightly warmer early autumn. We're within acceptable variance. The nutrient feeds are adjusted accordingly to support prolonged flowering. It's all in the schedule." She tapped a stylus against a data slate she carried, its screen displaying a complex web of environmental readings and resource projections. "The real concern is the water reclamation. With less rainfall predicted, we'll need to ensure the reserves are managed even more judiciously."

Eli pushed himself off the tree, his movements fluid and unhurried. He approached the asters, not with Mara's data-driven assessment, but with a more observational curiosity. He knelt, his eyes tracing the intricate patterns of the leaves, the delicate structure of the petals. "It's more than just the temperature, though, isn't it? There's a certain... robustness to them this year. Almost as if they're anticipating something."

Mara allowed herself a small, almost imperceptible sigh. Eli's tendency to anthropomorphize the natural world, while often charming, could sometimes distract from the core operational realities. "They are designed to be robust, Eli. That's the point of Havenridge's horticultural protocols. Resilience through genetic engineering and controlled environments."

"But is it just engineering, Mara?" he countered softly, his gaze still fixed on the asters. "Or is it also about connection? You mentioned the nutrient feeds, the controlled atmosphere. But what about the subtle energy exchange? The way the roots communicate beneath the soil, the way they respond to the changing light, even the almost imperceptible shifts in atmospheric pressure?" He looked up at her, his eyes alight with a familiar spark of intellectual curiosity. "We meticulously control every measurable variable, but sometimes, I wonder if we're missing the intangible ones."

Mara found herself momentarily stalled. The 'intangible' was not a metric she typically dealt with. Her domain was the quantifiable: pH levels, lumen output, nutrient concentrations, harvest yields. Yet, she couldn't entirely dismiss Eli's perspective. The Sunpetal orchid incident had taught her that. There were aspects of life, even within their carefully managed systems, that defied simple classification. "Those are... less quantifiable factors, Eli," she said, her tone even. "While I appreciate the… poetic consideration, our primary focus must remain on the data that ensures our survival. Resource allocation, caloric intake projections, energy expenditure for the winter months – these are the variables that demand our immediate attention."

Eli straightened, a faint smile playing on his lips. He understood her focus; it was her strength, the very reason she was so effective. But he also saw the potential limitations of such a rigidly defined worldview. "And that data is crucial, Mara, I don't dispute that. But perhaps," he continued, his voice gentle, "understanding the 'intangible' can inform the data. Perhaps knowing *why* the asters are thriving, beyond just the adjusted nutrient feeds, could lead to even more efficient resource management in the future. For instance, if we could somehow replicate that 'robustness' in other crops, even those less genetically modified, wouldn't that be an even greater victory for our resourcefulness?"

He gestured around them at the arboretum. "Look at this place. It's a marvel of control and precision. But it's also a vibrant, living ecosystem. And ecosystems, by their very nature, are complex, interconnected webs of influence. We've managed to recreate the perfect conditions for a thousand species, but are we truly understanding the symphony, or just the individual notes?"

Mara remained silent for a moment, her gaze sweeping across the arboretum. She saw the ordered rows, the clearly labeled specimens, the neatly integrated sensor arrays. She saw the result of years of meticulous planning and execution. But as Eli spoke, she began to see it through a slightly different lens. She noticed the way the smaller, hardier ground cover plants, ones not explicitly part of her planting schematics, were weaving their way between the larger, more cultivated specimens, their roots subtly stabilizing the soil. She saw how a colony of beneficial insects, whose presence had been noted but not actively encouraged, were diligently tending to the rose bushes, keeping aphids in check. These were not deviations to be corrected; they were emergent behaviors, natural processes that were contributing to the overall health of the arboretum.

"The protocols are designed to prevent unpredictable outcomes," she stated, the ingrained conviction in her voice unwavering. "Unpredictability is the enemy of survival."

"And yet," Eli countered, his voice soft but persistent, "isn't adaptation the greatest form of survival? The ability to change, to respond to unforeseen challenges, to find new pathways when the old ones are blocked? The Accord, for all its merits, prioritizes stability. And stability is important, of course. But what happens when stability itself becomes a cage, preventing us from evolving?"

He paused, letting his words settle. The crisp autumn air seemed to hold its breath, the gentle rustling of leaves the only sound. "Think about the Sunpetal orchids again. Your precise controls created the perfect environment, but it was the introduction of a controlled *deviation* – a naturalistic variability in the light – that unlocked their reproductive potential. It wasn't chaos; it was a carefully managed embrace of unpredictability."

Mara felt a familiar tug-of-war within her. Her training, her experience, her very identity as a guardian of Havenridge's safety, screamed adherence to the established order. The Great Accord was the bedrock of their security, the shield that had protected them from the devastating chaos of the Collapse. But Eli's words resonated with a truth she had begun to glimpse, a truth reflected in the quiet resilience of the arboretum itself. The world outside their meticulously constructed Havenridge was not static. It was a dynamic, ever-changing entity. To survive, truly survive, perhaps they needed to cultivate not just resilience against change, but resilience *through* change.

She looked at Eli, at the earnestness in his eyes, the genuine belief in his words. He wasn't advocating for recklessness; he was advocating for a deeper understanding, a more nuanced approach to life itself. He was suggesting that perhaps their carefully constructed walls, while protective, also limited their capacity for growth and adaptation.

"The Council would never agree to such a... philosophical shift in our approach," Mara stated, her voice laced with a hint of weariness. "Elder Thorne's adherence to the Accord is absolute. Any suggestion of deviating from established protocols, especially regarding resource management or environmental controls, would be met with immediate dismissal."

"I understand that," Eli replied, his tone sympathetic. "But dialogue begins somewhere, doesn't it? And perhaps, in observing the subtle victories, the emergent successes within places like this arboretum, we can build a case. A case for the idea that true sustainability isn't about maintaining a perfect, unchanging state, but about fostering the capacity for dynamic adaptation. It's about understanding that the most robust systems are not the most rigid, but the most flexible."

He gestured to a cluster of late-blooming wildflowers that had begun to naturalize in a less manicured corner of the arboretum, a space Mara had flagged for future replanting with more "productive" specimens. "Look at them. They weren't planted, they weren't scheduled, but they're thriving. They're adding to the biodiversity, stabilizing the soil, providing a food source for pollinators. They're an unplanned contribution to the system. And instead of seeing them as an anomaly to be eradicated, we could see them as an opportunity. An opportunity to learn, to integrate, to evolve."

Mara followed his gaze. The wildflowers, a vibrant splash of yellow and purple against the muted greens and browns of early autumn, were indeed beautiful. They represented an uncontrolled element, a deviation from the intended design. Yet, they were undeniably thriving, contributing to the overall health of their surroundings in ways that her meticulously planned plantings sometimes struggled to achieve. The idea of embracing these natural intrusions, of studying them rather than eradicating them, felt both foreign and strangely... hopeful.

"It's a paradigm shift," she murmured, more to herself than to Eli. The very concept felt like a tremor beneath the foundations of her carefully constructed worldview.

"Perhaps it is," Eli agreed, his voice gentle. "But isn't it time for one? The world outside Havenridge is a testament to the fact that life always finds a way, that adaptation is the ultimate currency. If we are to truly thrive, not just survive, we must learn to embrace that same adaptive spirit. We must find the balance between order and organic evolution, between the certainty of our plans and the emergent beauty of the unexpected."

He met her gaze, his expression sincere. "The autumn's arrival is a reminder, Mara. A reminder that change is inevitable, and that within change lies both challenge and opportunity. Our task isn't to prevent the seasons from turning, but to learn how to flourish within them, to harness their power, to adapt our strategies to their inevitable rhythm."

Mara looked around the arboretum, the golden light of the declining sun illuminating the scene. She saw the meticulously managed flora, a testament to her own dedication and the scientific rigor of Havenridge. But now, she also saw the subtle tendrils of emergent life, the quiet resilience of nature's unscripted narratives, and she felt a new sense of possibility unfurling within her, as delicate and as potent as a nascent autumn bloom. The approaching winter, once a symbol of impending hardship to be endured, began to feel less like a threat and more like a period of necessary introspection, a time to recalibrate and to prepare not just for survival, but for a more adaptive, a more resilient future. The beauty of autumn was no longer just a visual spectacle; it was a profound lesson, a gentle yet insistent invitation to evolve.

Eli moved through the arboretum with a different rhythm than Mara, a more fluid, unhurried gait that seemed to mirror the gentle descent of the season. Where Mara saw tasks and projections, Eli saw a profound narrative unfolding. He knelt beside a fallen maple, its broad leaves a tapestry of crimson, gold, and burnt sienna. He didn't just see decaying organic matter; he saw the culmination of a year's vibrant growth, a necessary shedding that prepared the tree for what was to come. He carefully collected a few of the most intact leaves, their veining intricate and beautiful, and tucked them into a small satchel he carried.

He then turned his attention to the base of a towering oak, its acorns scattered like tiny, well-armored jewels on the damp earth. Eli gathered a handful, feeling the satisfying weight of them, the promise of future forests contained within their sturdy shells. These were not mere resources to be cataloged and managed; they were seeds of continuity, embodiments of the enduring power of nature. He saw the forest floor, usually a vibrant green in the height of summer, now becoming a rich mosaic of fallen foliage. This wasn't decay to be cleaned and eradicated; it was a blanket of life, slowly returning its borrowed nutrients to the soil, a silent act of generosity that nourished the very ground that sustained them.

"It's a kind of surrender, isn't it?" Eli murmured, his voice barely disturbing the quiet hum of the arboretum. He held up an acorn, turning it in his palm. "The trees, the plants, they don't fight the change. They embrace it. They let go of what they no longer need to make space for new life."

He continued his gentle exploration, his eyes missing nothing. He noted the delicate, almost transparent wings of a dragonfly, its summer flight now a memory, clinging to a dying stalk of a herbaceous plant. He observed the intricate patterns of frost that were beginning to etch themselves onto the surfaces of leaves, a subtle artistry that spoke of the encroaching cold. Each observation was a reinforcement of his belief in the inherent wisdom of natural cycles, a wisdom he felt Havenridge, in its relentless pursuit of control, often overlooked.

Havenridge was a marvel of engineering, a testament to human ingenuity and a bulwark against the chaotic remnants of the Collapse. Its meticulously managed environments, its climate-controlled domes, its precisely calibrated nutrient delivery systems—all were designed to create a stable, predictable existence. But stability, Eli mused, could also be a form of stagnation. Perpetual summer, perpetual abundance, perpetual control—it was a carefully constructed illusion that denied the fundamental truth of existence: that life is a ceaseless process of change, of ebb and flow, of birth, growth, decay, and rebirth.

He walked past a bed of 'Sunpetal' orchids, their blooms a vibrant testament to Mara's precise care and the advanced atmospheric regulators. They were thriving, undeniably so. But Eli remembered the brief, almost magical period a few cycles ago when a slight, accidental fluctuation in the light spectrum had triggered an unexpected surge in their reproductive capacity. It had been a deviation, a momentary lapse in perfect control, yet it had yielded a remarkable result. Mara had swiftly corrected the anomaly, her focus on restoring the established equilibrium. But Eli had seen it as a glimpse into a deeper truth: that sometimes, the most profound growth occurred not in the absence of disruption, but in the gentle embrace of it.

"We strive for perfection, for an unchanging ideal," Eli said, his voice a soft counterpoint to the rustling leaves. "But the natural world thrives on imperfection, on adaptation. The forest doesn't mourn the falling leaves; it welcomes them as nourishment. The seed doesn't fear the darkness of the soil; it understands it as the necessary precursor to growth."

He stopped by a cluster of 'Frostkissed' berries, their deep blue hue intensified by the cooler air. They were small, hardy fruits, engineered for resilience, but Eli found himself drawn to their unassuming beauty. They weren't the plump, succulent fruits of summer, but they held a concentrated sweetness, a testament to survival and adaptation. He tasted one, its tartness a welcome jolt. This was the flavor of resilience, he thought, the taste of a life that understood how to weather hardship and emerge stronger.

"Mara sees the autumn as a challenge to overcome," he continued, more to himself than to anyone else present. "A period of reduced productivity that requires increased vigilance and resource management. And she's right, of course. Those are vital considerations. But she doesn't always see the inherent beauty in the transition itself. The quiet dignity of the shedding, the promise of renewal held within the dormant seed, the intricate artistry of the frost on a dying leaf. It's all part of the same magnificent cycle."

Eli believed that Havenridge's obsession with eliminating all forms of 'waste' and 'inefficiency' was, in itself, a form of waste. The fallen leaves, the withered stalks, the scattered seeds—these were not discarded remnants but essential components of a larger, self-sustaining system. By meticulously cleaning, sterilizing, and re-purposing everything, they were, in a way, severing themselves from that natural generosity. They were becoming too self-contained, too isolated from the planet's own regenerative processes.

He picked up a fallen twig, its bark textured and worn. He imagined the countless storms it had weathered, the slow growth it had undergone to reach its full potential, and the eventual surrender back to the earth. It was a miniature history, a testament to the enduring power of natural forces. Havenridge had built its defenses against the unpredictable forces of nature, and rightly so. But in doing so, had they also built walls around their own capacity for organic growth, for intuitive understanding?

"We've engineered life to fit our needs, to conform to our schedules," Eli mused, looking up at the sky, where the clouds were beginning to gather, hinting at the coming rains. "But life has its own intelligence, its own wisdom. It knows when to grow, when to rest, when to let go. We try to impose our will upon it, to freeze it in a perpetual state of summer bounty. But the seasons always turn, and in that turning, there is a profound lesson."

He thought of the concept of "entropy" as explained in their physics classes—the tendency of systems to move towards disorder. Havenridge fought entropy with every fiber of its being, striving for perfect order. But Eli suspected that true strength, true resilience, lay not in resisting entropy, but in understanding its role within the larger cycle. Decay was not an end; it was a transformation. Dormancy was not death; it was a period of profound internal work.

"Perhaps," Eli said, his voice growing a little stronger, "our greatest achievement won't be in controlling nature, but in learning to dance with it. To understand its rhythms, to anticipate its shifts, and to find strength not in rigidity, but in adaptability. The arboretum, even with all its engineered perfection, is still a living system. And living systems are always evolving, always responding. We just need to learn to listen to the whispers of that evolution."

He carefully placed the leaves and acorns into his satchel, his movements reverent. These were not just samples for later study; they were tangible reminders of the world's enduring beauty and its tireless capacity for renewal. He saw the arboretum not as a sterile laboratory, but as a sacred space, a place where the wisdom of the earth was on full display. The fading light, the crisp air, the scent of damp earth and decaying leaves—it was all part of a grand, ongoing creation, and Eli felt a profound sense of peace in being a part of it, a quiet observer in the grand theater of the seasons. He was ready for whatever the turning of the year would bring, not with fear, but with an open heart and a deep appreciation for the wisdom that lay in surrender and rebirth.

The air in the arboretum had taken on a new crispness, a subtle but distinct chill that spoke of the approaching winter. Sunlight, once a bold declaration of warmth, now slanted through the skeletal branches of trees in softer, more diffused rays. It was during these twilight weeks of autumn, as the vibrant hues of fall began to deepen into the muted earth tones of dormancy, that Mara and Eli found themselves working side-by-side with a rhythm that had gradually, almost imperceptibly, taken root between them. The frantic urgency of spring planting and the relentless productivity of summer had given way to a more measured, reflective pace. Their collaboration, once a series of carefully coordinated tasks, had evolved into something far more organic, a silent choreography of shared purpose.

Mara, ever the pragmatist, moved with a focused intensity, her eyes scanning the rows of hardy vegetables that had defied the encroaching frost. Her gloved hands worked with practiced efficiency, plucking plump, late-season tomatoes that still clung stubbornly to their vines, their skins a deep, burnished red. Beside her, Eli moved with a gentler, more deliberate touch, his attention caught by the intricate patterns of frost that silvered the broad leaves of kale and the sturdy stalks of chard. He would often pause, not to delay their progress, but to admire the way the dying light caught the crystalline formations, transforming what others might see as mere signs of decay into ephemeral works of art.

"These Brussels sprouts are surprisingly robust this year," Mara commented, her voice carrying a note of satisfaction as she carefully snapped a cluster of compact, leafy buds from a stalk. She dropped them into the large woven basket they were filling, the gentle thud echoing in the quiet expanse of the arboretum. "I was worried about the fluctuating temperatures, but the nutrient sequencing seems to have held them steady."

Eli nodded, his own hands now gathering a handful of hardy, dark green leaves. "The earth is generous when we give it what it needs, even as the days grow shorter," he said, his gaze sweeping across the rows of resilient crops. He ran a thumb over the slightly rough surface of a kale leaf, appreciating its texture, the promise of sustenance it held. "It's a different kind of generosity than summer's bounty, isn't it? More concentrated, more about endurance than explosion."

Mara paused, a half-plucked carrot suspended in her hand. She looked at Eli, a flicker of a smile playing on her lips. There had been a time, not so long ago, when such observations from him might have been met with a slightly impatient redirection back to the task at hand. But now, she found a quiet pleasure in his perspective. It didn't derail their work; it enriched it, adding a layer of contemplation to their practical endeavors. "Endurance," she echoed softly, turning the word over in her mind. "Yes, that feels right. It's about making the most of what we have, ensuring there's enough to see us through."

Their shared task was the final harvest, a crucial undertaking that would provide the essential provisions for the community during the long, lean months of winter. The air was filled with the earthy scent of disturbed soil, the faint sweetness of ripening roots, and the subtle perfume of late-blooming herbs. They moved through the arboretum like two halves of a whole, their movements synchronized by an unspoken understanding. When Mara reached for a tool, Eli often already had it within her reach. When Eli paused to carefully untangle a vine, Mara would quietly continue filling the basket, giving him the space he needed.

They gathered sturdy root vegetables – carrots with their vibrant orange cores, parsnips with their creamy flesh, and potatoes dug from the yielding earth, still dusted with the rich soil that had nurtured them. There were late-blooming herbs too, their fragrant leaves and stems gathered with care before the first hard frost claimed them entirely. Eli, with his keen eye for detail, found a patch of hardy, late-season berries, their skins a deep, jewel-like purple, their flavor intensified by the cooler air. He carefully harvested them, his movements precise, ensuring that each berry was handled with respect.

"These are 'Frostjewels'," he explained, holding out a small cluster to Mara. "Developed for their resilience. They can withstand quite a bit of cold. The sweetness is incredible, a real surprise after the first frost hits them."

Mara accepted a few, popping one into her mouth. A small gasp of delight escaped her. The burst of tart sweetness was indeed a revelation, a potent reminder of the vibrant life that still pulsed beneath the surface of the world, even as it prepared for its winter slumber. "You're right," she said, her eyes widening slightly. "It's like a tiny explosion of summer. How do you always find these things?"

Eli shrugged, a gentle smile playing on his lips. "I suppose I'm looking for them," he admitted. "You're focused on the bounty, on the quantifiable yield. I'm... I'm looking for the stories. The resilience. The quiet victories."

He picked up a knobbly potato, its skin earthy and firm. He felt the weight of it in his hand, the promise of warmth and nourishment it represented. "Think of all this," he said, gesturing around them with a sweep of his arm, encompassing the rows of harvested crops and the remaining plants that would soon be covered for protection. "It's not just food, Mara. It's a testament. A testament to the season, to the earth, and to our ability to work with them."

Mara considered his words as she continued to sort through the harvested vegetables, her practiced hands ensuring only the best were set aside for preservation. She recognized the truth in what he said. They weren't just gathering provisions; they were participating in a fundamental human ritual, one that had been practiced for millennia. It was a connection to the past, a preparation for the future, and a grounding in the present moment.

"It's a good feeling," she conceded, her voice softer than usual. "Knowing that we've done our best to prepare. That there will be food on the tables, warmth in the hearths."

Eli met her gaze, and in the quiet space between them, something shifted. It was more than just professional respect, though that was certainly present. It was a nascent personal connection, forged in the shared purpose of their labor, in the comfortable silence that now punctuated their work, and in the occasional shared glance that spoke volumes. They had moved beyond the sterile efficiency of engineered systems and into the more nuanced territory of shared humanity.

As they worked, a familiar melody, almost a hum, drifted from Eli's lips. It was a simple, wordless tune, ancient and soothing.

Mara found herself unconsciously falling into sync with its rhythm, her movements becoming more fluid, more relaxed. Laughter, light and spontaneous, would bubble up when one of them unearthed a particularly gnarled carrot or when a sudden gust of wind sent a flurry of dry leaves spiraling around them. These moments, small and fleeting, wove themselves into the fabric of their collaboration, strengthening the unspoken bond that was growing between them.

Later, as the basket overflowed with their harvest, they began the meticulous process of preparation. Mara, with her innate understanding of preservation techniques, directed the cleaning and sorting of the vegetables. Eli, meanwhile, carefully arranged bundles of herbs to be hung and dried, his touch surprisingly delicate as he tied them with twine. They worked in tandem, anticipating each other's needs, their movements efficient and purposeful.

"We'll need to start the dehydrators soon for these herbs," Mara said, her brow furrowed in concentration as she examined a bunch of dried thyme. "And the root vegetables need to be stored in the cool, dark cellar. Have you checked the humidity levels down there?"

"I checked this morning," Eli replied, his voice calm. He was carefully brushing the soil from a basket of potatoes. "They're stable. The temperature is holding steady at just above freezing, which is perfect for them. I've also set aside a small section for the frost-kissed berries. We can try some experimental preservation methods with those."

Mara looked up, a spark of curiosity in her eyes. "Experimental? What did you have in mind?"

Eli's smile was a little wider now, a genuine warmth radiating from him. "I was thinking of a light sugar syrup, perhaps with a hint of spice. To capture that intense flavor without overpowering it. A sort of sweet-tart jewel, ready to be enjoyed on a cold winter's night."

Mara found herself smiling back, a genuine, unreserved smile. This was the Eli she was beginning to understand – not just the meticulous observer, but the one who saw potential, who found beauty in the unexpected, and who approached even the most practical tasks with a sense of wonder. This collaboration, this shared harvest, was more than just a job. It was a testament to their shared commitment to the community, and to the quiet, burgeoning connection that was growing between them, as resilient and as sweet as the last berries of the season. The basket was full, the task nearing completion, but the sense of shared accomplishment, and the unspoken promise of future collaborations, felt even fuller.

The crisp air, once a harbinger of change, now carried the bite of early frost, a stark reminder that the arboretum's vibrant life would soon retreat beneath a blanket of white. Mara, her mind already charting the course for the coming months, found herself poring over schematics, her desk a landscape of blueprints and environmental sensor data. Her initial strategy for the arboretum's winter defense was, in true Mara fashion, a symphony of technological precision. She envisioned a network of retractable thermal blankets, woven from advanced, self-repairing polymers, designed to unfurl automatically at predetermined temperature drops. Integrated micro-heating elements, powered by the arboretum's geothermal grid, would create localized warm zones, safeguarding the most sensitive specimens from the brutal chill.

"The thermal efficiency of these new membranes is exceptional," she explained to Eli, gesturing at a complex diagram spread across her screen. "We can maintain optimal temperatures for the delicate flora with a fraction of the energy consumption of older systems. And the automated deployment means we don't have to be here, physically covering everything, every single time the mercury dips." She traced a line on the screen. "This zone here, for the epiphytic orchids, will have a slightly higher temperature regulation, as they're the most susceptible to frost damage. The system is designed to learn and adapt, adjusting heat output based on real-time atmospheric pressure and wind velocity data."

Eli, who had been quietly observing, his gaze drawn to the intricate interplay of lines and labels, finally spoke. His voice was soft, yet it carried a weight of consideration. "It's certainly thorough, Mara. A very... engineered solution." He paused, letting the slight nuance in his tone hang in the air. "But what about the earth itself? What about allowing nature to participate in its own defense?"

Mara turned from her screen, her brow furrowed slightly. "Nature is precisely what we're trying to protect it from, Eli. Winter is a force. A brutal, unforgiving force. We need robust measures, not... passive hoping."

"Not hoping," Eli corrected gently, "but working *with* the natural cycles. I've been observing the patterns of the soil. Even in this weather, there's still microbial activity, a slow respiration. If we encourage a denser growth of hardy ground cover, species that naturally thrive in these conditions and can withstand frost, it would create a significant insulating layer. Think of it like a natural blanket, but one that's alive, that's constantly adapting." He walked over to a window, looking out at the arboretum grounds, now a tapestry of faded greens and browns. "And the windbreaks. We have a few scattered, but a more deliberate planting of resilient trees, species known for their density and ability to break the force of the wind, could create a microclimate within the arboretum itself, reducing the overall strain on the heating systems and the thermal covers."

Mara listened, her initial skepticism slowly giving way to a flicker of interest. She respected Eli's deep connection to the arboreal world, his uncanny ability to 'read' the needs of the plants and the soil. His suggestions, while seemingly less direct than her technological approach, often held a profound wisdom. "Ground cover," she mused, tapping a stylus against her chin.

"You're suggesting something like creeping thyme or hardy sedums? They can be quite invasive, though. We'd need to carefully select species that won't outcompete the established flora."

"Exactly," Eli affirmed, his eyes alight with the prospect. "We'd choose native, low-growing varieties that are known for their dense root systems, which also help with soil stability. And for the windbreaks, I was thinking of a mix of fast-growing conifers and deciduous trees with a naturally dense branching structure. Species like the Siberian Elm or the 'Ironwood' variety of birch. They're incredibly tough, low-maintenance, and their layered branches would diffuse the wind effectively without creating shadow issues for the plants beneath."

He picked up a fallen leaf, its edges already beginning to curl and brown. "Imagine this arboretum not just as a collection of plants housed within a protective shell, but as a self-sustaining ecosystem, where every element contributes to its resilience. The ground cover insulates, the windbreaks deflect, and the technological systems act as a final, crucial safeguard. It's a layered defense, Mara, a true collaboration between engineered solutions and natural processes."

Mara walked over to stand beside him, her gaze following his out to the grounds. She could visualize it – the low-lying carpets of greenery, the sturdy, wind-sculpting trees forming natural barriers. It wasn't about abandoning her advanced systems, but about augmenting them, making them more efficient, more holistic. "A layered defense," she repeated, the phrase resonating with her. Her mind, always seeking optimization, began to see the synergistic potential.

"So, we integrate your organic windbreaks with the existing perimeter fencing," she said, her voice now carrying a new energy. "We'd need to ensure the planting locations don't interfere with subterranean irrigation lines, and map out their growth patterns over the next five years to prevent any structural compromise. And for the ground cover, we could use the automated soil nutrient dispersers to seed the chosen species in the spring, once the primary frost risk has passed, ensuring they establish quickly before the following winter."

Eli smiled, a genuine, open smile that softened the lines around his eyes. "That sounds like a plan, Mara. A very good plan." He looked at her, a silent acknowledgment of their shared vision passing between them. "It's a different approach, perhaps, than what you initially envisioned, but I believe it will create a more robust, more adaptable arboretum. One that can weather not just a single winter, but many, by learning to live in harmony with the seasons, rather than fighting them."

The days that followed were a testament to their evolving collaboration. Mara, while still meticulously refining the technological aspects of the winter defense – calibrating the thermal blankets, optimizing the geothermal energy distribution, and programming the environmental sensors for peak performance – also began to incorporate Eli's organic strategies into the overarching plan. She found herself drawn to the elegance of his approach, the way it spoke to a deeper understanding of ecological balance.

Her digital models began to incorporate the projected density of the ground cover, simulating its insulating effect and how it would reduce the required heat output from the micro-elements. She ran simulations on wind dispersal patterns, factoring in the planned placement of the new windbreak trees, and adjusted the thermal blanket deployment algorithms to account for the reduced wind chill. It was a fascinating challenge, merging the precision of data-driven engineering with the inherent variability of natural systems.

Eli, meanwhile, was busy with the practicalities of his suggestions. He spent hours with the arboretum's extensive seed bank, meticulously selecting the most resilient and appropriate native ground cover species. He consulted historical records, cross-referencing with ecological surveys, to identify the optimal locations for the windbreak trees, ensuring they would provide maximum protection without impacting the sunlight reaching the more sensitive specimens. He even designed specialized, biodegradable planting tubes that would slowly release nutrients, aiding the young trees' establishment while minimizing any immediate nutrient drain on the surrounding soil.

"These 'Frost's Kiss' sedums are remarkable," Eli remarked one afternoon, holding up a small, hardy plant with fleshy, grey-green leaves. "They can survive temperatures well below freezing, and their dense, creeping habit forms an almost impenetrable mat. It will hold moisture in the soil and protect the root systems from frost heave." He explained how the succulent nature of the leaves helped them retain water, allowing them to survive dry spells even in the coldest months.

Mara, reviewing his selections on her tablet, nodded thoughtfully. "The water retention aspect is key. It will also help prevent soil erosion from any late-season rains or early thaws. We can program the irrigation system to provide minimal supplementary watering only when the soil moisture sensors indicate extreme dryness, which should be rare with this species."

The process of selecting and situating the windbreak trees was equally involved. Eli would mark out the intended locations with biodegradable stakes, meticulously ensuring each spot offered optimal sun exposure and sufficient root space. He'd explain his reasoning for each choice, detailing the specific characteristics of each tree species – their bark texture, branching density, and tolerance to different soil types.

"This Siberian Elm," he'd say, pointing to a designated spot, "has a naturally fissured bark that creates pockets of trapped air, further disrupting wind flow. Its growth is vigorous but manageable, and it's exceptionally drought-tolerant once established. We'll plant them in staggered rows, about ten meters apart, to create a substantial barrier without creating an impenetrable wall that might trap moisture and promote fungal growth."

Mara, accompanying him on these excursions, found herself increasingly drawn into the tactile, organic nature of his work. She'd run her fingers over the rough bark of a sapling, feel the surprising weight of a bag of specialized compost, and breathe in the earthy scent of newly turned soil. It was a welcome contrast to the sterile precision of her usual tasks.

One blustery afternoon, as they stood assessing a potential windbreak site, a particularly strong gust of wind whipped through the arboretum, sending a flurry of dry leaves skittering across the ground. Mara instinctively pulled her scarf tighter, a shiver running down her spine. Eli, however, seemed unfazed, his gaze fixed on the swaying branches of a distant, mature oak.

"See how that oak already deflects the worst of it?" he observed. "It's a natural windbreak, albeit an unmanaged one. Our planted trees will create a more uniform and effective shield." He turned to her, a slight smile on his face. "It's about working with the forces of nature, Mara, not against them. Making them our allies."

Mara nodded, a genuine appreciation dawning on her. She had always seen nature as something to be controlled, to be optimized through scientific intervention. But Eli showed her a different perspective – one of partnership, of understanding and utilizing natural processes to achieve a greater, more sustainable resilience.

The compromise they forged was a testament to their growing synergy. Mara's sophisticated thermal regulation systems would still be the primary defense against extreme cold snaps, ensuring the survival of the most delicate species. But Eli's ground cover would act as a vital insulating layer, reducing the energy demand on the heating systems and protecting the soil from drastic temperature fluctuations. The windbreak trees, strategically planted, would further mitigate the impact of harsh winds, creating a more stable microclimate and reducing the risk of frost damage caused by wind chill.

It was a truly integrated approach, a blend of cutting-edge technology and ancient ecological wisdom. Mara's algorithms began to factor in the windbreak's predicted efficiency and the ground cover's thermal resistance, leading to a more refined and energy-conscious deployment of the thermal blankets. Eli, in turn, worked with Mara's team to ensure the planting schedules and techniques were compatible with the arboretum's existing infrastructure, from irrigation to soil monitoring.

As winter's approach became undeniable, the arboretum began to transform. The first seeds of hardy ground cover were sown in carefully prepared beds, promising a lush, resilient carpet for the coming months. Saplings of Siberian Elm and 'Ironwood' birch were carefully planted along the arboretum's perimeter, their young branches already reaching towards the sky with determined strength. The thermal blankets were tested, their smooth, advanced polymer skins unfurling and retracting with silent efficiency, ready to be deployed at a moment's notice.

Mara stood on an overlook, her tablet in hand, reviewing the progress of the winter preparations. The vastness of the arboretum, once a symbol of spring's vibrant rebirth, now held a quiet anticipation of winter's slumber. She saw the integrated network of protective measures – the sleek, modern technology interspersed with the nascent greenery of the ground cover and the sturdy promise of the young trees.

Eli joined her, his presence a quiet counterpoint to the hum of the environmental controls. He followed her gaze, a satisfied expression on his face. "It's beautiful, isn't it?" he said softly. "Not just the plants, but the way we've worked together to prepare them. It's a testament to what we can achieve when we combine our different strengths."

Mara met his gaze, a warmth spreading through her that had little to do with the ambient temperature. "It is," she agreed, her voice filled with a newfound sincerity. "It's more than just a defense system, Eli. It's a promise. A promise that this place, this vital ecosystem, will endure. That we've done everything we can to ensure its survival, by understanding and respecting its inherent strengths."

The arboretum, poised on the cusp of winter, felt different. It was no longer just a site of scientific cultivation, but a living entity, a community of flora supported by a dual strategy of human ingenuity and natural resilience. The collaborative efforts of Mara and Eli had woven a complex tapestry of protection, a testament to their shared vision and the enduring power of nature, even in the face of the harshest season. It was a defense forged not just of technology and plant life, but of understanding, compromise, and the quiet, growing strength of their partnership.

The arboretum hummed with a low, contented energy. Winter's embrace was tightening its grip on the world outside, but within the geodesic domes and the meticulously planned outdoor zones, a vibrant resilience pulsed. Mara, however, found her attention increasingly drawn away from the complex algorithms governing the thermal regulation and the nutrient dispersal systems. It was the quiet hum of Eli's presence that now occupied her thoughts, a subtler, more persistent resonance.

Their work together on the winter defense strategy had forged an unexpected rhythm, a dance of contrasting disciplines that had, against all odds, found a harmonious cadence. What began as a necessity, a pooling of expertise to protect the arboretum from the encroaching chill, had blossomed into something far more profound. The shared challenges, the late nights poring over schematics and soil samples, the debates that dissolved into mutual understanding, had chipped away at the carefully constructed walls Mara had built around herself.

It started, perhaps, with the shared meals. Initially, they were pragmatic – quick, refueling stops in the arboretum's compact communal kitchen, usually punctuated by discussions of windbreak efficacy or ground cover growth rates. But as the days grew shorter, and the biting wind drove everyone indoors, these impromptu breaks became longer, more languid. Eli would often bring simple, wholesome fare he'd prepared himself – hearty stews simmering with root vegetables, freshly baked bread that filled the air with an irresistible aroma. Mara, accustomed to the sterile efficiency of synthesized nutrient pastes, found herself savoring the comforting, earthy flavors, the tangible evidence of someone's care.

One evening, as a particularly fierce squall rattled the greenhouse panes, they found themselves sharing a bowl of Eli's lentil soup. The usual arboretum chatter had faded, replaced by the soft clinking of spoons against ceramic and the distant roar of the wind. Mara, usually so focused on the data streams and system readouts, found her gaze drifting to Eli. He was leaning back slightly, his eyes closed for a moment, a faint, contented smile gracing his lips as he savored a spoonful of soup. There was a quiet strength in his stillness, a groundedness that she envied and, increasingly, found herself drawn to.

"This is... good, Eli," she said, the words feeling a little clumsy, inadequate to express the warmth that bloomed in her chest. "Really good."

He opened his eyes, his smile widening, a genuine crinkle appearing at the corners. "Thank you, Mara. It's an old family recipe. My grandmother used to make it on nights just like this. Said it was the best way to chase away the winter blues." He paused, his gaze softening. "Do you have recipes that bring back memories for you?"

Mara blinked, surprised by the personal turn of the conversation. Her memories were often tied to data logs, to diagnostic reports, to the sterile environments of her past. "Not really," she admitted, her voice softer than she intended. "My childhood was... more focused on efficiency. Less on nostalgia."

Eli didn't press, but his gaze held a flicker of understanding, a silent acknowledgment of her carefully guarded past. Instead, he offered a gentle anecdote about his own grandmother, a woman who, he said, could coax anything to grow, not just plants, but smiles and laughter too. He spoke of her hands, always dusted with soil, and her infectious optimism, even when facing hardship. Mara listened, captivated. It was a glimpse into a world so different from her own, a world of simple joys and deep connections, a world she hadn't realized she'd been missing.

Their conversations began to expand, weaving a delicate tapestry of shared moments and burgeoning intimacy. They talked about their childhoods, not in the sterile exchange of biographical data, but in the storytelling fashion Eli favored. He recounted tales of climbing trees that seemed as tall as mountains, of scraped knees and the triumphant feeling of nurturing a wilting seedling back to life. Mara, in turn, found herself sharing hesitant fragments of her own story – the relentless pursuit of knowledge, the isolation that came with her drive, the quiet ache of a childhood spent more in laboratories than in sunlight.

She discovered Eli's deep-seated love for the natural world wasn't just a professional interest; it was a fundamental part of his being. He spoke of the interconnectedness of all living things with a reverence that stirred something within her. He had a way of seeing the beauty in the smallest details – the intricate patterns on a fallen leaf, the resilience of a single blade of grass pushing through a crack in the pavement, the silent communication between trees through their root systems. He saw life where Mara had primarily seen data points and biological processes.

One crisp afternoon, they were inspecting the young windbreak saplings, their slender forms still fragile against the sharp bite of the wind. Eli paused, his hand resting gently on the bark of a young Siberian Elm. "You know," he said, his voice thoughtful, "I used to spend hours in forests like this when I was a kid. Just... listening. The trees have a language, if you're quiet enough to hear it. They speak of resilience, of adaptation, of the slow, patient work of growth."

Mara stood beside him, the wind tugging at her hair. She tried to listen, to hear the whispers Eli spoke of. She heard the rustle of dry leaves, the creak of branches, the distant sigh of the wind. But beneath it all, she felt a nascent stirring, a new awareness. "I've always seen them as... components," she admitted, her voice barely above a whisper. "Part of an engineered system. I never thought of them as... speaking."

Eli turned to her, his eyes warm and encouraging. "They are components, yes, but they are also individuals. Each with its own story, its own struggles, its own quiet triumphs. Just like us." He held her gaze for a moment, and Mara felt a strange sensation, as if a long-dormant part of her was slowly awakening.

As the days continued to shorten, and the arboretum's inhabitants retreated into their cozy, climate-controlled environments, Mara and Eli found themselves seeking each other's company with increasing frequency. The urgency of the winter preparations had lessened, replaced by a comfortable routine. They'd often find themselves in the same spaces, their work overlapping organically. Mara might be calibrating a thermal sensor near a row of Eli's newly planted ground cover, or Eli might be tending to the soil around the base of a sapling that Mara's system was carefully monitoring for moisture levels.

Their conversations, once strictly professional, now drifted with an easy grace. They spoke of their hopes, their fears, the dreams they held close to their hearts. Eli spoke of a future where humanity lived in greater harmony with the planet, where technology served to enhance nature's resilience, not to dominate it. He spoke of wanting to see the arboretum flourish, not just as a research facility, but as a sanctuary, a place where people could reconnect with the natural world.

Mara, in turn, found herself sharing ambitions she hadn't voiced to anyone before. She spoke of her desire to create systems that weren't just efficient, but that fostered life, that healed damaged ecosystems. She confessed her quiet longing for a sense of belonging, a feeling that her work, her very existence, had a deeper purpose beyond mere scientific advancement.

One evening, as they stood by a large panoramic window, watching the snow begin to fall in soft, silent flakes, Eli spoke. "You know, Mara," he began, his voice quiet, "when I first met you, I saw you as incredibly intelligent, incredibly driven. Brilliant, of course. But also… a little formidable. Like a perfectly engineered machine." He turned to her, a gentle smile playing on his lips. "I'm glad I was wrong."

Mara's breath hitched. She felt a blush creep up her neck, a warmth that had nothing to do with the ambient temperature of the dome. "And I," she replied, her voice a little husky, "thought you were just a gentle gardener. Someone who talked to plants." She met his gaze, a hint of a playful smile returning to her lips. "I'm glad I was wrong too."

In that moment, surrounded by the quiet beauty of the falling snow and the gentle hum of the arboretum's life support systems, Mara felt a profound shift within herself. The carefully constructed walls she had maintained for so long, the defenses she had painstakingly built against vulnerability, were beginning to crumble. It wasn't a dramatic collapse, but a slow, steady erosion, worn away by the persistent, genuine warmth of Eli's presence, his unwavering kindness, and the quiet, undeniable comfort of their shared company. She found herself anticipating their meetings, not just for the sake of the arboretum's well-being, but for the simple, profound joy of being with him. The sterile efficiency of her world was slowly, beautifully, being infused with a new kind of warmth, a gentle bloom of affection she hadn't realized was possible.

CHAPTER SEVEN

Winter's Stillness, Deeper Roots

The snow arrived not with a dramatic flourish, but as a slow, insistent dusting that gradually softened the sharp, angular lines of Havenridge. The stark efficiency of the community's design, usually a source of quiet pride and a testament to human ingenuity in a challenging world, became subtly muted, almost dreamlike. Each falling flake, a tiny, perfect crystal, seemed to absorb sound, muffling the already subdued hum of life support systems and the distant whir of automated maintenance units. The filtered air, always precisely regulated, now carried a sterile chill, a reminder of the external world's unforgiving embrace, a world that Havenridge had meticulously designed itself to withstand.

Inside the communal domes and residential modules, the rhythm of life shifted. The crisp, clear days of autumn, filled with the energetic preparations for winter, gave way to a more regimented existence. Outdoor patrols were shortened, their frequency dictated by the escalating sub-zero temperatures and the ever-present threat of atmospheric anomalies. Work, for many, transitioned indoors. The hydroponic bays, usually a riot of controlled greenery, became a central hub for resource management, with residents meticulously checking nutrient levels, calibrating light cycles, and overseeing the careful rationing of harvested produce. The fabrication workshops, once echoing with the clatter of construction and repair, now hummed with the quieter, more focused work of crafting replacement parts, mending insulation, and preparing essential supplies.

This enforced stillness, this drawing inward, amplified the internal landscapes of Havenridge's inhabitants. The quiet was no longer an absence of noise, but a palpable presence, a vast, echoing space that invited – or perhaps compelled – introspection. Conversations, once quick and task-oriented, now often drifted into more personal territories. The shared meals, already a cornerstone of community bonding, took on a new significance. The communal dining hall, bathed in the soft, artificial glow of the overhead lights, became a sanctuary from the encroaching darkness and cold. Faces, usually animated by the exchange of ideas and collaborative problem-solving, now held a deeper thoughtfulness, a certain quietude.

For Mara, this winter stillness was a double-edged sword. On one hand, the reduced external demands on her expertise, the shift from large-scale environmental control to the more granular management of indoor systems, afforded her a certain peace. Her focus narrowed, allowing her to delve deeper into the intricate workings of the arboretum's more delicate flora, ensuring they survived the lean months with minimal stress. She found a quiet satisfaction in the intricate dance of light and nutrient, in the subtle adjustments that coaxed life from dormancy. Yet, the pervasive stillness also amplified the quiet resonance of Eli's presence in her life. The shared moments, once a welcome distraction, now felt like an essential anchor in the quiet sea of her existence.

She found herself observing him more, not with the analytical gaze of a scientist assessing a specimen, but with a growing, almost tender curiosity. Eli moved through the hushed corridors and softly lit domes with a quiet grace that seemed to mirror the season. He still carried the scent of earth and growing things, a comforting contrast to the sterile air of Havenridge. His interactions with others were marked by a gentle patience, a genuine warmth that seemed to radiate outwards, a small, steady flame against the encroaching chill. He would pause to speak with elderly residents, his voice a low murmur, his hands often resting lightly on their shoulders, offering a silent reassurance. He'd share a knowing smile with the younger children, who, confined indoors, often displayed a restless energy that mirrored the trapped, wild creatures of the outside world.

One afternoon, Mara found herself in the arboretum's temperate zone, meticulously checking the humidity levels for a collection of rare orchids. The air here was thick with the scent of damp earth and exotic blossoms, a pocket of vibrant life pushing back against the winter's austerity. Eli entered, carrying a small, carefully wrapped package. He approached her, his boots making soft thuds on the mossy ground.

"Mara," he said, his voice a low, warm rumble that cut through the gentle dripping of condensation. "I found something that reminded me of you."

She turned, a faint smile gracing her lips. Her heart gave a familiar, pleasant lurch. "Oh? And what might that be?"

He carefully unwrapped the package, revealing a small, intricately carved wooden bird. Its wings were poised as if for flight, its tiny eye etched with surprising detail. It was fashioned from a dark, polished wood, smooth and cool to the touch.

"It's a wren," he explained, holding it out to her. "I found it tucked away in an old storage crate. It must have been made by one of the original settlers. They used to carve these. Said it brought good luck, a reminder of the wild things that lived beyond our walls before... well, before." He looked at her, his gaze direct and thoughtful. "When I saw it, I thought of how you tend to these delicate things, how you listen to their needs. There's a quiet strength in that, Mara. A careful, determined nurturing."

Mara took the wooden bird, her fingers tracing the smooth contours. It felt surprisingly substantial in her palm. She had always felt more comfortable with data streams and biological analyses, with the quantifiable certainties of her work. Yet, this small, imperfect carving, imbued with the echoes of a forgotten past, resonated with her in a way that complex algorithms rarely did.

"It's beautiful, Eli," she said, her voice softer than she intended. "Thank you."

He smiled, a genuine, open expression that always seemed to illuminate his face. "You're welcome. I just... I see the care you put into everything, Mara. Even the smallest detail. It's not just about efficiency for you, is it?"

The question hung in the air, laced with an understanding that went beyond the surface. Mara looked from the wooden bird in her hand to Eli's steady gaze. For so long, she had operated under the assumption that efficiency

was the ultimate goal, the sole metric of success. Her drive had been fueled by a relentless pursuit of perfection, of optimization, a desire to create systems that were flawless, unassailable. But Eli saw something else, something deeper. He saw the intention behind the actions, the nascent flicker of something that yearned for more than mere functionality.

"I... I don't know anymore, Eli," she admitted, the words feeling both liberating and terrifying. "Perhaps not. Perhaps I've been so focused on the mechanisms that I've forgotten the purpose."

He reached out, his hand gently covering hers, the wooden bird still nestled between their palms. His touch was warm, grounding. "The purpose is life, Mara. Always has been. These walls, these systems – they're all designed to protect and nurture life. And you, with your incredible mind, you are a part of that nurturing."

His words were a balm, a gentle reframing of her entire existence. In the sterile, controlled environment of Havenridge, where every aspect of life was meticulously managed, the wildness represented by the wren, the memory of what lay beyond, felt like a precious, almost forbidden concept. Yet, Eli, the keeper of the living world within their walls, embraced it. He didn't just manage life; he seemed to understand its intrinsic value, its inherent beauty, its unyielding resilience.

As the days bled into weeks, the snow continued to fall, a constant, silent presence outside the reinforced transparisteel windows. The world beyond Havenridge dissolved into a soft, white canvas, blurring the boundaries between sky and earth. Inside, the community settled into its winter routine, a carefully choreographed dance of resource management, indoor labor, and communal life. The stillness was profound, a deep, resonant quiet that permeated every dome, every corridor, every habitation unit. It was a stillness that, for some, felt comforting, a predictable rhythm in an unpredictable world. For others, it was a gilded cage, the comfort of order threatening to morph into a subtle suffocation.

Mara found herself seeking out Eli with a quiet regularity. Their encounters, initially dictated by shared projects, now felt more like intentional acts of seeking connection. She'd find him tending to the indoor gardens, his brow furrowed in concentration as he examined a wilting leaf, or sharing a hushed conversation with a group of children gathered to learn about seed propagation. He moved with a natural ease, a quiet authority that stemmed not from command, but from a deep understanding and respect for the living world he tended.

One evening, a communal gathering was held in the central dome. The mood was subdued, a mix of forced cheerfulness and quiet reflection. A holographic display showcased highlights from the past year – successful harvests, completed construction projects, the birth of a new generation within the community. It was a testament to their resilience, their ability to thrive even in the harshest of environments. Yet, as Mara watched the flickering images, a sense of disconnect settled over her. The achievements felt abstract, the numbers and statistics a pale imitation of the vibrant, messy, unpredictable reality of life.

Eli found her standing near the edge of the gathering, her gaze distant. He sat beside her, his presence a quiet comfort.

"It's a lot to take in, isn't it?" he murmured, his voice barely audible above the low murmur of conversation. "All the work, all the progress. Sometimes, it feels like we're just cataloging our survival."

Mara turned to him, her eyes reflecting the soft light of the holographic projections. "I feel... detached, Eli. Like I'm observing a simulation of life, not truly living it. The efficiency is so absolute, it leaves no room for… for the unexpected. For the beauty in imperfection."

He nodded slowly. "That's the challenge, isn't it? To maintain the order, the safety, without stifling the very essence of what we're trying to preserve. The wildness. The spirit." He gestured towards the display, which now showed a particularly robust growth spurt in the arboretum's fruit-bearing trees. "Those fruits," he said, his voice taking on a softer tone, "they aren't just sustenance. They're a promise. A promise of sweetness, of something beyond mere survival. They're a small rebellion against the sterile."

Mara felt a warmth spread through her chest, a response to his words, to his way of seeing the world. He saw the poetry in their meticulously planned existence, the quiet defiance in a single bloom, the profound significance in a perfectly ripe fruit. He saw her, too, not as a collection of algorithms and data points, but as someone capable of appreciating those things.

"You have a remarkable gift, Eli," she said, her voice filled with a sincerity that surprised even herself. "To see the life, the spirit, in everything."

He met her gaze, his eyes holding a gentle depth. "And you, Mara," he replied, his voice low, "you have the power to create the conditions for that life to flourish. You build the foundations, you manage the resources, you ensure the survival. Without that, there would be no seeds to sow, no blossoms to admire. We are… complementary."

The word hung in the air between them, simple yet profound. Complementary. Not opposing, not separate, but intrinsically linked, each necessary for the other's purpose. In the stillness of the winter, surrounded by the quiet hum of a community held in delicate balance, Mara felt a new root taking hold within her. It wasn't the stark, unyielding root of pure logic or solitary ambition. It was something softer, more yielding, nourished by shared understanding and the quiet promise of connection. The snow continued to fall, a silent, white shroud over the outside world, but within the heart of Havenridge, a different kind of stillness was settling, a stillness that felt less like an absence and more like a fertile ground for something new to grow. The regimented life, the conserved resources, the introspective quiet – all of it was setting the stage, not for a dwindling, but for a deeper, more profound flourishing.

The vast expanse of the arboretum lay hushed beneath its winter shroud. The intricate network of windbreaks, erected with painstaking precision, stood like silent sentinels against the biting winds that scoured the barren landscape outside Havenridge. Snow, a thick, downy blanket, concealed the intricate structures of the greenhouse domes, smoothing their sharp edges into soft, rolling mounds. It was a scene of profound dormancy, a world held in suspended animation, waiting for the distant promise of spring. Mara and Eli stood at the edge of the primary access tunnel, the thick, insulated door sealed tight behind them, a symbol of the barrier between the fragile life within and the unforgiving world without. The air that seeped from the ventilation grates was cool, carrying the faint, earthy scent of dormant soil and the ghost of blooming flowers, a subtle reminder of the life that slumbered just beyond their sight.

"It's... quiet," Mara murmured, her voice barely disturbing the profound stillness. She pulled her thermal cloak tighter, the manufactured warmth a stark contrast to the primal cold that this landscape represented. Even within the carefully controlled environment of Havenridge, the sheer scale of the arboretum, even in its dormant state, held a certain awe-inspiring power. It was a testament to their collective will, a fragile bastion of life carved out of an inhospitable planet.

Eli nodded, his gaze sweeping across the snow-covered terrain. He carried no tools, no diagnostic equipment. This visit was not about work, not about tending to immediate needs. It was about observation, about bearing witness to the culmination of their efforts. "It's the kind of quiet that hums with potential," he said, his voice a low resonance that seemed to blend with the hushed atmosphere. "Every seed, every root, every branch is holding its breath, conserving its energy. Waiting."

"Waiting," Mara echoed, the word taking on a weight she hadn't anticipated. She thought of the countless hours spent meticulously planning the arboretum's winter protocols. The selection of hardy, cold-tolerant species, the intricate irrigation systems designed to deliver precisely measured amounts of moisture without freezing, the carefully calibrated nutrient reserves that would sustain the plants through the long months of darkness. It was a monumental undertaking, a symphony of science and instinct.

"We did well with the windbreaks this year," Eli observed, pointing to a section where the angled panels seemed to have seamlessly integrated with the natural contours of the land. "The simulations predicted significant drift in this sector, but the revised angle held. Less snow accumulation means less structural stress when the thaw comes, and less manual clearing for the initial patrols."

Mara felt a familiar surge of professional pride, quickly followed by a softer, more personal satisfaction. "The thermal regulators in Dome C also maintained their target temperatures within a tenth of a degree, even during that unexpected atmospheric pressure drop last week. I was tracking the data remotely, of course, but seeing the integrity of the system firsthand... it's reassuring." She gestured towards a series of subtle vents integrated into the snow-covered mounds. "And the subsurface insulation seems to be performing beyond expectations. The heat loss is minimal."

"Your meticulous planning, Mara," Eli said, his gaze meeting hers, a warmth in his eyes that had nothing to do with the regulated temperature. "It's why this place can rest. You built a fortress around its dreams."

The compliment, delivered with such genuine sincerity, sent a small tremor through her. She had always viewed her work as a series of challenges to be overcome, problems to be solved. The arboretum was a complex system, and her role was to ensure its optimal function. But Eli's phrasing – "fortress around its dreams" – painted a different picture. It spoke of protection, of nurturing, of allowing something fragile and beautiful to exist and grow, shielded from harm. It was a perspective that resonated deeply with the quiet stirrings she'd been experiencing in the introspective silence of winter.

"And your understanding of the plants themselves, Eli," she countered, her voice soft. "Knowing their individual needs, their natural cycles of dormancy. That's what allowed us to design systems that truly support them, rather than simply imposing our will upon them. The nutrient delivery schedule for the root systems, for instance – it's based on their projected metabolic rates during stasis. Your input was invaluable."

He offered a small, self-deprecating smile. "I just listen to what they're telling me. Or rather, what they're *not* telling me. The absence of growth, the slowing of sap, the subtle shifts in leaf color even before dormancy sets in. It's all communication, if you know how to read it." He kicked gently at a snowdrift, sending a cascade of white powder down its slope. "They're like a different kind of people, aren't they? They have their own rhythms, their own needs, their own quiet resilience."

Mara watched him, a growing sense of wonder at his ability to connect with the living world on such an intuitive level. She understood the science, the biology, the intricate dance of molecules and energy. But Eli seemed to grasp something more, something that transcended the purely empirical. He saw the spirit within the biology, the inherent drive to live that pulsed even in the deepest slumber.

"It's a powerful symbiosis we've created here," she mused, tracing a pattern in the frost that had gathered on the inside of the tunnel entrance. "The technology to shield and sustain, and the understanding of life to guide its preservation. It's... more than just survival. It's a commitment to continuity."

"Exactly," Eli agreed, his voice filled with a quiet passion. "And that continuity is what gives us hope. When we look at this dormant landscape, we're not just seeing a lack of life. We're seeing the promise of it. Each seed is a future forest. Each hibernating root is a potential bloom. It's a reminder that even in the deepest stillness, life finds a way."

His words settled over Mara like a warm blanket, chasing away the lingering chill of the external world. She had always been driven by the logic of preservation, the necessity of maintaining Havenridge for future generations. But Eli's perspective added a layer of profound optimism, a belief in the inherent tenacity of life itself. The dormant arboretum, a stark testament to their engineering prowess, was also, as he saw it, a vibrant repository of potential, a silent testament to the enduring power of nature.

They stood in comfortable silence for a long moment, the only sound the faint, almost imperceptible hum of the life support systems deep within the earth. The snow-covered landscape stretched out before them, a canvas of white and muted grays, broken only by the stark lines of the windbreaks. It was a scene of stark beauty, a testament to the harsh realities of their existence, yet infused with an undeniable sense of peace.

"You know," Eli said, his gaze still fixed on the dormant expanse, "it's in these quiet moments, when everything is still, that you can really see the true strength of things. The underlying structure, the resilience. It's like... like us, I suppose."

Mara turned to him, her heart giving a gentle, unexpected leap. The unspoken had been present between them for weeks, a subtle undercurrent beneath their professional interactions, a shared glance that lingered a moment too long, a comfortable silence that spoke volumes. Now, in the hushed stillness of the arboretum, it seemed to surface, tentative yet undeniably present.

"Us?" she prompted, her voice barely a whisper.

He finally turned to face her, his eyes reflecting the soft, filtered light that permeated the entrance tunnel. "Yeah, us. You and me. We've been working together, building something. And this winter, while the arboretum sleeps, I feel like... like something else is growing. Quietly. Beneath the surface." He hesitated, then added, "Like those roots. Waiting for the right conditions to really take hold."

Mara's breath hitched. He had articulated the very feeling that had been blossoming within her, a quiet, persistent hope that had taken root in the sterile soil of her controlled existence. The shared purpose, the mutual respect, the intellectual connection – it had all coalesced into something more, something that felt both terrifying and exhilarating.

"I... I feel it too, Eli," she admitted, the words feeling fragile, precious. "It's like... a different kind of planning. A different kind of strategy."

He offered a gentle smile, a smile that reached his eyes and crinkled the corners. "A strategy for growth," he said, his voice a warm rumble that seemed to chase away the last vestiges of the external cold. "And for hoping."

He took a step closer, and Mara found herself meeting him halfway. The snow-covered landscape, the dormant plants, the silent windbreaks – they all faded into the background. In this quiet space, cradled by the sleeping heart of the arboretum, a new kind of seed was being sown, a promise of life, of connection, of a future that stretched beyond mere survival, into the fertile ground of shared hope and burgeoning affection. The stillness was no longer an absence, but a profound presence, a sanctuary for beginnings.

The chill of the arboretum's entrance tunnel still clung to Mara's skin, a stark reminder of the vast, dormant world outside. But the air within the communal living quarters of Havenridge was warmer, filled with the gentle hum of the internal heating systems and the soft glow of ambient lighting. It was here, in the shared spaces designed for respite and connection, that

Mara and Eli found themselves gravitating towards each other, their conversations evolving beyond the pragmatic necessities of their shared existence. The sterile efficiency of their previous encounters had begun to soften, yielding to a more profound and intimate dialogue.

They were sitting by one of the communal hearths, a marvel of salvaged technology meticulously maintained by Eli and his team. It wasn't a roaring blaze of crackling wood, a luxury long lost to their world, but a carefully controlled emission of radiant heat, designed to mimic the comforting warmth of a traditional fire. The soft orange glow cast dancing shadows on the polished ferro-concrete walls, creating an atmosphere of cozy intimacy that felt almost incongruous with the stark realities of their lives. Mara held a mug of synthetically brewed herbal tea, its warmth seeping into her chilled hands, while Eli nursed a similar beverage, his gaze thoughtful as he watched the subtle play of light on the hearth's surface.

"It's funny," Eli began, his voice a low murmur that was easily absorbed by the quiet ambiance. "I was thinking about the ancient forests today. The ones we only see in the archives, in holographic reconstructions. The sheer scale of them... the complexity of the ecosystems. It's breathtaking." He paused, a wistful expression on his face. "Imagine being able to walk beneath trees that have stood for centuries, millennia even. Feeling the earth beneath your feet, not filtered through layers of insulation and environmental controls. Just... raw, untamed life."

Mara found herself drawn into his reverie. She had always approached the natural world through the lens of data and protocols, of scientific understanding and technological intervention. The arboretum, her life's work, was a testament to that. But Eli's perspective was different. He spoke of nature with a reverence, a deep-seated connection that spoke of something more than just scientific curiosity. "I've seen some of the older simulations," she replied, her voice soft. "The ones that tried to recreate the primeval rainforests. The humidity, the constant drone of insects, the scent of damp earth and decaying vegetation... it was almost overwhelming, even in the digital space."

"Exactly," Eli agreed, turning his gaze to her, his eyes reflecting the warm glow of the hearth. "It's that overwhelming sense of life, isn't it? The feeling of being a small part of something immense and ancient. It makes you feel... grounded. Connected. We're so disconnected now, Mara. Everything is curated, controlled. Even the air we breathe, the water we drink, the food we eat – it's all a product of our technology. We've built these incredible systems to keep us alive, but sometimes I wonder if we've forgotten what it truly means to be alive."

His words resonated deeply with Mara. She understood the necessity of their carefully constructed world, the systems that kept the fragile ember of humanity alive. But there were moments, often in the quiet hours of the night, when the sheer weight of their isolation, the constant vigilance required for survival, pressed down on her. She had sought refuge in Havenridge, burying herself in the demanding work of maintaining life, hoping to outrun the ghosts of her past. But Eli's quiet introspection was slowly, gently, beginning to draw those ghosts into the light.

"I remember...," Mara began, her voice hesitant. She rarely spoke of her life before Havenridge, the memories too painful, too raw. But there was a safety in Eli's presence, a quiet understanding that encouraged her to unfurl, however tentatively. "I remember a small garden I had, back home. It wasn't anything grand, just a patch of earth behind our hab-unit. But I used to grow tomatoes. And strawberries. Simple things. But the taste of those strawberries, warm from the sun... it was..." She trailed off, searching for the words.

Eli's gaze was steady, encouraging. "Precious," he supplied softly. "It's the simple things, isn't it? The things we took for granted. The taste of fresh fruit, the smell of rain on dry earth, the warmth of the sun on your skin without a suit to filter it. We have life here, Mara, a remarkable feat of human ingenuity. But do we have... joy? Do we have those moments of simple, unadulterated pleasure?"

Mara nodded, a lump forming in her throat. "We have survival," she said, her voice barely a whisper. "And for a long time, that was enough. It had to be enough. The loss... it was so profound. The thought of creating anything, of nurturing anything, felt like a betrayal. It was easier to focus on the systems, the protocols, the absolute necessity of keeping things running. To keep the lights on, so to speak."

"Loss is a heavy burden," Eli said, his tone gentle. He reached out, his fingers brushing hers for a fleeting moment on the rim of her mug. The simple gesture sent a surprising warmth through her, a connection that bypassed the intellectual and settled directly into her heart. "But even in the deepest winter, Mara, life finds a way to persist. The roots are still there, beneath the frozen earth, waiting for the thaw. And perhaps," he continued, his gaze meeting hers, a hopeful glint in his eyes, "perhaps we can begin to cultivate those roots again. For ourselves. For each other."

He spoke of the ancient forests with a storyteller's passion, his words painting vivid pictures in Mara's mind. He described the intricate mycorrhizal networks, the symbiotic relationship between fungi and tree roots, allowing for the exchange of nutrients and information across vast distances. "It's like a hidden internet," he explained, a smile playing on his lips. "A vast, underground communication system that connects everything. The trees 'talk' to each other, warning of danger, sharing resources. It's a level of interconnectedness we can barely comprehend."

Mara listened, fascinated. Her own understanding of plant life was rooted in genetics, in controlled environments, in optimizing growth cycles. Eli's perspective was more organic, more holistic. He saw the forest not as a collection of individual specimens, but as a single, breathing entity. "It's a beautiful metaphor," she mused. "For us, perhaps. We're so isolated, so individualistic in our survival. But maybe we're capable of building our own kind of network. Our own shared understanding."

"I believe we are," Eli said, his voice firm with conviction. "It starts with these conversations, doesn't it? With sharing what's beneath the surface. You spoke of your garden, Mara. That's a piece of your past, a part of who you are that you've kept hidden. It's like a seed, waiting to be planted in fertile ground."

Mara felt a blush creep up her neck. She hadn't realized she had revealed so much, but Eli's quiet empathy had a way of disarming her defenses. "It was a long time ago," she said, her gaze drifting back to the hearth. "Before... before everything changed. We lived in a small community, not like Havenridge. More... exposed. We relied on our own resources. My father was a botanist, and he taught me everything he knew about growing things. It was a simple life, but it was good. It felt real."

She spoke of the challenges they faced, the constant struggle against the elements, the unpredictable nature of their food supply. She recalled the devastating drought that had wiped out their crops one season, the gnawing hunger that had followed, the fear that had permeated their community. "It made us resilient," she admitted, "but it also made us wary. Trust was a luxury we couldn't always afford. Every decision had to be calculated, every risk weighed. The idea of... of nurturing something, of allowing oneself to hope for something more, felt dangerous."

Eli listened intently, his hand resting on hers, a silent anchor. "That fear is understandable," he said, his voice laced with empathy. "When survival is the only goal, hope can feel like a vulnerability. But it's also what keeps us going, isn't it? The flicker of possibility, the belief that things can be better. Your father, he must have instilled in you a deep love for growing things, even in the face of such adversity."

"He did," Mara confirmed, a faint smile gracing her lips. "He always said that plants were the ultimate optimists. They always reach for the light, no matter how dark it gets. Even when they're broken, they find a way to sprout anew. I used to think he was just being poetic. Now... now I think he understood something fundamental about life that I was too young to grasp."

"And perhaps you're beginning to grasp it now," Eli said gently. He squeezed her hand, a silent reassurance. "We are, both of us, survivors. We've built this refuge, this arboretum, as a testament to our will to endure. But enduring isn't the same as living. And I think, Mara, that we're both ready to start truly living again."

He spoke of his own past, of the nomadic life he had led with his family in the early years after the Collapse. They had been part of a small, mobile community, constantly moving, seeking out pockets of arable land, always on the run from the harsh realities of the ravaged planet. He described the stark beauty of the untamed landscapes they had traversed, the thrill of discovery, but also the constant underlying tension, the knowledge that their existence was precarious.

"There was a particular region," he recalled, his eyes distant, "a vast, rolling steppe. The sky was an unbroken expanse of blue, and the wind carried the scent of wild grasses and distant, unseen flowers. We'd set up temporary camps there, and I'd spend hours just observing. The way the insects navigated the currents, the resilience of the wildflowers pushing through the dry soil. It was a harsh beauty, but it was also incredibly vital."

He explained how he had started to collect seeds, not for any immediate purpose, but simply out of a deep-seated instinct to preserve. He would carry them in small, carefully sealed pouches, a silent hope that one day, they might find a place where they could truly flourish. "It was a foolish endeavor, perhaps," he admitted with a wry smile. "Given the state of the world. But it felt like an act of faith. A small defiance against the overwhelming sense of loss."

"It wasn't foolish at all," Mara said, her voice filled with a newfound warmth. "It was incredibly brave. To hold onto that hope, that belief in the potential of life, in the face of such despair. That's what you bring to the arboretum, Eli. Not just the scientific understanding, but that deep, unyielding optimism. That faith in the future."

He met her gaze, his expression softening. "And you, Mara," he replied. "You bring the structure. The meticulous planning, the unwavering dedication that makes that faith possible. You build the fortress that allows the seeds to germinate, that protects them until they're strong enough to face the world. We complement each other. We always have."

The admission hung in the air between them, a tangible acknowledgment of the growing connection that had been blossoming between them for weeks. It had started subtly, with shared glances across the communal mess hall, with lingering conversations in the quiet corridors of the arboretum. Now, in the warm glow of the hearth, with the distant hum of Havenridge's life support systems a constant, reassuring presence, it had taken on a new dimension.

"I... I think you're right," Mara murmured, her voice a little shaky. She looked down at her hands, clasped around the warm mug, her heart beating a little faster. "I've always been so focused on the 'how.' How to keep things alive, how to maintain the systems. But you've shown me the 'why.' The reason for it all."

Eli reached out again, his fingers gently tracing the back of her hand. This time, he didn't pull away. The touch was electric, sending a ripple of warmth through her entire body. "The 'why' is the hope, Mara," he said, his voice a low, resonant whisper. "The belief that there's more to life than just survival. That there's beauty, and connection, and the promise of growth. And I think... I think we're ready to let that hope take root. Together."

The firelight flickered, casting a warm, intimate glow around them. The world outside, with its frozen stillness and its unforgiving winds, felt a million miles away. Here, by the hearth, surrounded by the quiet hum of life and the unspoken promises of their shared future, a new chapter was beginning. It was a chapter written not in data logs and scientific protocols, but in hushed conversations, in shared memories, and in the quiet, persistent blooming of hope, deep within the heart of Havenridge. The stillness of winter was giving way, not to the boisterous chaos of spring, but to the slow, deliberate, and deeply resonant growth of something new, something precious, something that felt undeniably like love.

Eli watched the embers in the communal hearth glow, a muted echo of the fires that once burned freely in the open world. The warmth that radiated from it was a carefully managed effluence, much like the systems governing Havenridge itself. He turned to Mara, who was tracing the rim of her mug, her brow furrowed in thought. The conversation had shifted, as it often did between them, from the immediate comforts of their present to the broader implications of their existence.

"You know," Eli began, his voice a low, reflective hum, "I was reading through some historical data logs this morning. Specifically, the records from the Great Famine of '78. Before the widespread adoption of enclosed agricultural systems, of course. They were entirely dependent on external weather patterns, their crops susceptible to blight, to frost, to drought. When one of those factors hit, especially if it was prolonged, the entire system collapsed. Entire regions starved."

Mara stirred, her gaze lifting from her mug. The mention of past failures always piqued her interest, a counterpoint to the successes she'd meticulously cultivated within the arboretum. "We learned from those failures," she stated, her tone matter-of-fact. "That's why Havenridge, and systems like it, are designed with such robust environmental controls. Redundancy. Fail-safes. We don't leave anything to chance anymore."

Eli offered a gentle smile, one that didn't quite reach his eyes. "And that's a marvel, Mara, truly. Your work with the arboretum is a testament to that. But I was thinking about the *nature* of those past failures. It wasn't just a single crop failing. It was the entire *approach* that was brittle. They built their entire existence around a set of assumptions about the world, and when those assumptions were proven wrong, everything crumbled. They didn't have the capacity to adapt, not quickly enough."

He leaned forward slightly, his gaze earnest. "Imagine a network of ancient trees," he continued, drawing a parallel to their earlier discussion. "The interconnectedness is vital, as we've talked about. But what if a new, aggressive fungal blight emerges that the established network has no defense against? If the trees are too rigidly connected, too reliant on the old ways of sharing nutrients and information, the blight could spread like wildfire, taking down the entire forest. True resilience, I think, lies not just in having strong roots, but in the ability to regrow, to adapt the root system, to find new ways to connect or even to isolate the infected parts before they compromise the whole."

Mara considered his words, the data points of her own experience warring with the philosophical implications he presented. She'd seen the devastating impact of inflexibility firsthand, not in a grand historical famine, but in the desperate, often futile, attempts of smaller communities to replicate old-world farming techniques in a drastically altered climate. They had clung to methods that were no longer viable, their rigid adherence to tradition a death knell.

"The arboretum itself is an example of adaptation, isn't it?" she ventured, her voice a little softer. "When the nutrient paste formulations for the Xylosian algae began to degrade at an accelerated rate, due to unforeseen atmospheric particulate contamination, we didn't just try to reinforce the old paste. We had to entirely re-engineer the synthesis process, factoring in those contaminants. It was a complete overhaul, not just a tweak."

"Exactly!" Eli's eyes lit up, a genuine warmth finally surfacing. "And that was a significant challenge, one that required immense ingenuity and flexibility from your team. But it was a *controlled* adaptation, within a largely controlled environment. What about the bigger picture? What if a new pathogen emerged that could bypass the arboretum's bio-filters? Or if the power grid, the very lifeblood of Havenridge, suffered a catastrophic, unrecoverable failure? Our current systems are designed to prevent such catastrophic failures, of course. But history teaches us that the unthinkable can, and does, happen."

He paused, letting the weight of his words settle. "The early settlements after the Collapse, they tried to recreate entire cities, to build back exactly as they were. They focused on replicating infrastructure, on rebuilding the old world. Many of them failed spectacularly. They were too rigid. They spent all their resources rebuilding what was lost, instead of investing in entirely new ways of living, ways that were better suited to the new reality. They were so focused on preventing *any* change that they became incapable of surviving it when it inevitably came."

Mara found herself nodding slowly. She understood the impulse. The desire for familiarity, for the safety of the known. Her own life before Havenridge had been a testament to that clinging to the past, even when it was a source of pain. The idea of deliberately embracing change, of fostering a capacity for adaptation rather than simply preventing failure, felt both foreign and, strangely, compelling.

"You're suggesting that our focus on absolute control, while necessary for survival, might also be a hidden weakness?" she asked, articulating the core of his argument.

"I'm suggesting that perhaps true resilience isn't about building an impenetrable fortress," Eli replied, "but about cultivating a garden that can flourish even when the external conditions shift unexpectedly. It's about building systems – and people – with the inherent capacity to learn, to evolve, to change course when necessary. It's about recognizing that rigidity, even in the name of safety, can ultimately lead to a more profound kind of failure."

He picked up a smooth, grey stone from the hearth's edge, turning it over in his fingers. "Think about the nomadic tribes, the ones who survived the early decades of the Collapse by remaining mobile, by constantly adapting their routes, their resource gathering, their social structures to the changing environment. They didn't have the luxury of enclosed biodomes or perpetual energy sources. Their strength was in their adaptability, their willingness to let go of what wasn't working and embrace what was. They were like water, finding its own path, wearing down obstacles through persistence and flexibility."

Mara traced the intricate patterns on her mug, the synthetic ceramic cool against her fingertips. Her work was built on the foundation of preventing such nomadic struggles, of providing a stable, predictable environment where life could be nurtured and sustained indefinitely. The idea of embracing unpredictability, even as a source of strength, was a significant departure from her core operational philosophy.

"But the risks..." she began, the ingrained caution surfacing. "The potential for catastrophic loss. The arboretum is a controlled ecosystem. We have meticulously cataloged every species, understood its needs, its tolerances. We've eliminated variables to ensure optimal growth. Introducing unpredictability, even in the name of resilience, feels... irresponsible."

"And I agree, to a point," Eli conceded. "The arboretum is a triumph of controlled adaptation. But what about beyond its walls? What about the human element, Mara? We are not as predictable as a Xylosian algae culture. Our capacity for innovation, for creative problem-solving, is our greatest asset. But it's an asset that thrives on... well, on a certain degree of freedom to explore, to experiment, even to fail in smaller, contained ways. If we over-engineer our lives to the point where there is no room for error, no space for emergent solutions, are we not diminishing our own resilience as a species?"

He looked at her, his gaze steady. "You spoke of your father, and his belief in plants as optimists. They always reach for the light. But what if the light source shifts? What if an overhang casts a shadow? A truly resilient plant doesn't just stay put, hoping the sun will return. It might send out new shoots, seeking the light from a different angle. It *adapts* its growth pattern. We, as humans, have that same capacity, but it needs to be nurtured, not suppressed by an overwhelming focus on preventing any deviation from the expected path."

Mara thought of the early days of Havenridge, the desperate scramble to establish basic life support. Failure then would have meant extinction. The rigid protocols, the unyielding adherence to established procedures, had been the only way to survive. But now, decades later, with the arboretum thriving and the systems stable, perhaps... perhaps there was room for a different kind of thinking.

"You believe we've become too rigid," she stated, her voice quiet.

"I believe we've become very good at *preventing* problems," Eli corrected gently. "And that's crucial. But preventing problems isn't the same as cultivating the ability to *handle* problems when they inevitably arise. It's like building a perfect, unbreakable shield. It might protect you from the first blow, but if the attack changes, if it finds a new way around or through the shield, you're left defenseless. A warrior who can deflect, who can adapt their stance, who can use their opponent's momentum against them – that warrior is far more resilient."

He gestured around the communal area, the softly lit space designed for comfort and interaction. "This is a step, isn't it? Fostering connection, encouraging dialogue, creating a space where different perspectives can be shared. It's a way of building that adaptability into our social fabric. But it needs to extend beyond these walls, into the very way we conceive of our systems, our work, our future."

Mara felt a familiar tension in her shoulders, the subtle tightening that always accompanied a challenge to her fundamental beliefs. Yet, there was a part of her, a growing part, that resonated with Eli's words. She had seen the extraordinary resilience of life in the arboretum, how a single mutation could lead to a stronger, more adaptable strain, how a new symbiotic relationship could unlock unforeseen benefits. She had, in a way, been cultivating adaptation all along, just within carefully defined parameters.

"The challenge," she mused aloud, "is to foster that capacity for adaptation without compromising the essential stability that keeps us alive. How do you allow for change without inviting chaos?"

Eli smiled, a genuine, hopeful smile this time. "That, Mara," he said, his voice soft, "is the most important question we can ask. And I believe the answer lies not in rigid protocols, but in fostering a culture of informed curiosity, of continuous learning, and of deep trust. Trust in our ability to face challenges, not by simply preventing them, but by meeting them with intelligence, creativity, and a willingness to evolve. It's about cultivating the roots, as we said, but also nurturing the branches that can reach for new light, even when the old sources falter."

He reached out, his fingers brushing hers as he gestured towards the hearth. "These fires, they are a symbol of our control. But the real warmth, the real life, comes from the energy source that fuels them, and the systems that distribute that energy. We maintain those systems with incredible diligence. But perhaps we can also begin to think about how to make the *system itself* more adaptable, more responsive to the unexpected. Perhaps we can begin to cultivate a different kind of strength, one that is less about impenetrable defense and more about fluid resilience."

Mara looked from Eli to the hearth, then out towards the reinforced viewport showing the stark, unchanging white of the winter landscape. The stillness outside was absolute, a vast emptiness that mirrored the fragility of their existence. Yet, here, within Havenridge, within the arboretum, and in the quiet conversations with Eli, she felt a stirring of something new. A recognition that true strength might not lie in an unyielding adherence to the status quo, but in the courage to adapt, to learn, and to grow, even in the deepest stillness. The seeds of a different kind of resilience were beginning to take root, not just in the soil of the arboretum, but in the very soil of her own beliefs.

The conversation had shifted, as it always did between them, from the grand pronouncements of resilience to the quieter, more personal landscapes of their inner lives. The communal hearth, a carefully regulated source of warmth, cast a gentle glow on Mara's face, highlighting the subtle anxieties that often flickered beneath her composed exterior. Eli, sensing the shift, softened his gaze, the intellectual sparring of moments before giving way to a shared quiet.

"You spoke of the arboretum, of its meticulous design, its controlled environment," Eli began, his voice a low murmur that seemed to absorb the ambient hum of Havenridge. "And I understand, truly, the immense effort and ingenuity that goes into creating such a sanctuary. But sometimes, when I look at it, I also see... a cage, however gilded." He paused, letting the word hang in the air. "A cage built to protect, yes, but a cage nonetheless. And I wonder, Mara, what happens to the spirit when it's confined, even for its own good?"

Mara stirred, her fingers tightening almost imperceptibly around the worn ceramic of her mug. The word 'cage' resonated with a disquieting familiarity, a faint echo of the suffocating limitations she had felt before Havenridge, before her own carefully constructed walls had been breached. "It's not a cage, Eli," she said, her voice steadier than she felt. "It's a haven. It's where life can thrive, where we can ensure its continuation, free from the whims of a world that has proven itself too volatile, too unforgiving. I've dedicated my life to building that safety. To ensuring that what we have, what we've managed to preserve, isn't lost. The thought of losing that... of everything I've worked for crumbling, of the carefully balanced ecosystem collapsing..." Her voice trailed off, the unspoken fear a palpable presence between them. "That is my greatest fear, Eli. Not a hypothetical failure of a system, but the absolute, irreversible loss of what we have painstakingly created. The chaos that would follow. The emptiness."

Eli nodded slowly, his eyes reflecting the flickering embers. "I understand that fear, Mara. I do. The instinct to protect what we've built, to shield it from any harm, is deeply ingrained. It's what has allowed us to survive this long. But my fear is... different. Or perhaps it's the flip side of yours. You fear the loss of what you've built, the chaos that would ensue. I fear that in our relentless pursuit of order, in our desperate attempt to control every variable, we might inadvertently extinguish the very spark of what makes us human. The spark of curiosity, of spontaneity, of the messy, beautiful, unpredictable essence of life."

He leaned forward, his gaze earnest, searching. "Think about it, Mara. We engineer every aspect of our lives, from the air we breathe to the food we eat, to the very patterns of our social interactions. We have eliminated risk, but in doing so, have we also eliminated growth? Have we created a society so optimized for survival that it has forgotten how to truly live? My fear is that we are so focused on preventing the potential for suffering, for failure, that we are also preventing the potential for true joy, for profound connection, for the unexpected leaps of innovation that arise from venturing into the unknown."

Mara looked down at her hands, the intricate network of faint scars on her palms a testament to years of working with delicate specimens, of countless small cuts and abrasions that had healed, leaving only faint reminders. Each scar was a story, a moment of intense focus, of a near miss, of a successful grafting or propagation. They were tangible evidence of her effort, her dedication. But Eli's words planted a seed of a different kind of unease. Were there other scars, less visible, that were forming from this constant vigilance, this unending effort to maintain control?

"I see the value in what you're saying, Eli," she admitted, her voice softer now, tinged with a vulnerability she rarely allowed to surface. "I've seen it in the arboretum. The most vibrant, resilient plants are often those that have had to adapt to less-than-ideal conditions. They develop deeper roots, stronger defenses, a more ingenious way of utilizing resources. But that adaptation often comes from struggle, from facing adversity. And I confess, I've worked so hard to shield us from that adversity." She met his gaze, a quiet confession passing between them. "The truth is, Eli, I'm afraid of that struggle. I'm afraid of the vulnerability that comes with it. When I think about the possibility of something going wrong, of Havenridge failing, it's not just a systemic collapse I envision. It's the personal failure. The thought that I, with all my knowledge and dedication, couldn't protect us, couldn't safeguard what matters most... it's a terrifying prospect."

Eli reached out, his hand hovering for a moment before gently covering hers where it rested on the table. His touch was warm, reassuring, a silent acknowledgment of her confession. "And that is a deeply human fear, Mara. The fear of inadequacy, of failing those who depend on us. It's a fear I share, though perhaps in a different context." He squeezed her hand gently. "My fear isn't about a failure of infrastructure, but a failure of spirit. I worry that in eliminating all friction, all challenge, we are creating a generation that is ill-equipped to handle the inevitable complexities of existence. That by shielding them from hardship, we are also shielding them from the lessons that hardship teaches. The lessons of resilience, yes, but also of empathy, of compassion, of the profound understanding that comes from shared struggle."

He withdrew his hand, gesturing towards the viewport that showed the stark, moonlit expanse of the frozen landscape. "Out there," he continued, his voice laced with a wistful melancholy, "life is a constant negotiation, a fierce, unyielding dance of survival. It's brutal, yes, but it's also incredibly pure. There's a rawness to it, a directness, that I think we've lost in here. We've traded that raw honesty for comfort, for predictability. And while I wouldn't wish the harshness of that world upon us, I worry that we've also traded away something vital. The capacity for genuine courage, for profound self-discovery, for the kind of resilience that is forged in the crucible of genuine adversity."

Mara leaned back in her chair, a knot of conflicting emotions tightening in her chest. She had always prided herself on her pragmatism, on her ability to assess risks and implement solutions. But Eli's words were not about risk assessment; they were about the fundamental nature of human experience. He spoke of a loss that was far more insidious than a system failure, a diminishment of the very essence of who they were.

"So, you're saying that our safety, our security, has come at a cost?" she asked, her voice barely a whisper. "That by eliminating the external threats, we've created internal ones? The threat of stagnation, of complacency, of... a kind of spiritual atrophy?"

"Precisely," Eli affirmed, his gaze steady. "I fear that Havenridge, in its perfection, has become a gilded cage for the human spirit.

We are protected, we are sustained, but are we truly thriving? Are we pushing ourselves, are we learning, are we evolving in ways that truly matter? Or are we simply existing, in a state of comfortable inertia? My fear is that we are so busy ensuring the survival of our bodies that we are neglecting the needs of our souls."

He paused, a thoughtful expression crossing his face. "You spoke of your father and his belief in plants as optimists. They always reach for the light. But what if the light source shifts? What if an overhang casts a shadow? A truly resilient plant doesn't just stay put, hoping the sun will return. It might send out new shoots, seeking the light from a different angle. It *adapts* its growth pattern. We, as humans, have that same capacity, but it needs to be nurtured, not suppressed by an overwhelming focus on preventing any deviation from the expected path."

Mara considered his words, the imagery of the reaching plant taking root in her mind. She had witnessed it countless times in the arboretum, the silent, determined striving of life. She had always seen it as a testament to the efficacy of her controlled environment, ensuring the optimal conditions for that growth. But what if the environment itself was the inhibitor? What if the very perfection she had cultivated was preventing a deeper, more meaningful kind of growth?

"I've always viewed resilience as the ability to withstand and recover from adversity," she admitted, a rare note of uncertainty in her voice. "To bounce back. But you're suggesting that perhaps true resilience is also about the ability to *seek* new growth, to adapt proactively, even in the absence of immediate threat. To thrive not just *despite* challenges, but perhaps even *because* of them."

"Exactly," Eli said, a warmth entering his eyes. "It's about cultivating a capacity for growth, not just a capacity for survival. And that capacity flourishes in an environment that allows for exploration, for experimentation, for the occasional misstep. It thrives on freedom, on choice, on the inherent human drive to discover and to create. My fear, Mara, is that in our pursuit of absolute safety, we have inadvertently stifled that drive."

He looked around the softly lit communal area, the space designed for comfort and interaction. "This is a step, isn't it? Fostering connection, encouraging dialogue, creating a space where different perspectives can be shared. It's a way of building that adaptability into our social fabric. But it needs to extend beyond these walls, into the very way we conceive of our systems, our work, our future. We need to create spaces where it's not just permissible, but encouraged, to question, to explore, to even fail in small, controlled ways, so that we learn and adapt."

Mara found herself nodding, a surprising sense of recognition blooming within her. She had always believed that her meticulous control of the arboretum was the highest form of care. But now, listening to Eli, she began to see that true care might also involve trusting in the inherent strength and adaptability of the living things she nurtured, and by extension, of humanity itself.

"So, my fear is the tangible loss of everything," she articulated, her voice gaining a quiet strength. "The collapse of our carefully constructed world. And your fear is the intangible loss of our very humanity, our spirit, our capacity for growth and discovery. We are both afraid of a form of extinction, aren't we? Yours is a slow fading, mine is a sudden, violent end."

Eli smiled, a gentle, understanding smile that reached his eyes. "Perhaps, Mara," he said softly. "And perhaps, in acknowledging these shared vulnerabilities, we can find a way to build something stronger. Something that honors both the need for safety and the necessity of growth. Something that doesn't just preserve life, but truly allows it to flourish, in all its messy, unpredictable, beautiful complexity." He picked up a smooth, grey stone from the hearth's edge, turning it over in his fingers. "Think about it, Mara. The most enduring ecosystems are not those that are perfectly static, but those that are dynamic, that are constantly adapting, integrating new elements, evolving. We have the capacity for that same kind of dynamic resilience. We just need to cultivate it, to allow it room to breathe, to grow."

Mara looked at Eli, at the sincerity in his eyes, and felt a profound shift within her. The intellectual debate had dissolved, replaced by a shared understanding, a nascent bond forged in the quiet confession of their deepest fears. She saw not an adversary of opposing viewpoints, but a kindred spirit, wrestling with the same fundamental questions about the future of their existence.

"It's a daunting thought," she said, her voice barely above a whisper, "to intentionally introduce elements of uncertainty into a system I've worked so hard to stabilize. It feels... counterintuitive to my very nature."

"And I understand that," Eli replied gently. "But sometimes, the greatest strength comes from embracing what we fear most. It's in facing our vulnerabilities, both personal and systemic, that we truly discover our capacity for resilience. Perhaps it's time, Mara, to move beyond simply preventing failure and to start cultivating the art of adaptation. Not just for the plants in your arboretum, but for us, here, in Havenridge."

The stillness of the winter night outside seemed to press in, a vast, silent canvas against which their fragile existence played out. But here, in the warm glow of the hearth, in the quiet space of shared vulnerability, a different kind of stillness settled – one of understanding, of shared hope, and of a deepening connection that promised to weather whatever storms, known or unknown, lay ahead. The fear was still present, a low hum beneath the surface, but it was no longer a solitary burden. It was a shared weight, and in its sharing, it felt a little lighter, a little more manageable, a little more like a challenge to be met, rather than a disaster to be avoided. The roots of their connection, though still young, were beginning to deepen in the fertile soil of their shared humanity.

CHAPTER EIGHT

The Thaw and New Growth

The slow retreat of winter's grip was a phenomenon Mara had observed countless times. The sterile, monochromatic landscape, once dominated by the stark geometry of snowdrifts and skeletal trees, began to soften. The air, crisp and biting for so long, now carried a subtle hint of moisture, a promise whispered on the wind. This year, however, her perception had shifted, imbued with a resonance that went beyond the predictable patterns of atmospheric change. It was more than just the melting of ice; it was the thawing of something within her, a subtle awakening that mirrored the burgeoning life outside Havenridge.

She stood by the reinforced viewport of her personal quarters, gazing out at the slow transformation. The stark white plains were yielding to muddy patches, revealing the dark, rich soil beneath, eager to receive the sun's renewed attention. The snow, once a symbol of Havenridge's isolation and the harshness of the world beyond its protective dome, was now transforming into a life-giving elixir. Rivulets of water snaked across the landscape, their gentle murmur a stark contrast to the oppressive silence of winter. It was a symphony of subtle sounds, a crescendo of quiet anticipation.

This annual rebirth was a meticulously planned event within Havenridge. The agricultural domes, the heart of their sustenance, hummed with an anticipatory energy. Automated systems were recalibrated, nutrient delivery schedules adjusted, and the vast hydroponic arrays prepared for their seasonal surge. Mara, as Head of Bio-Systems, was intrinsically involved in every step, her days a whirlwind of data analysis, resource allocation, and protocol refinement. Yet, this year, beneath the veneer of her professional duties, a deeper current flowed – one of genuine wonder.

She found herself lingering by the viewport long after her morning diagnostics were complete, her gaze drawn to the first, almost imperceptible signs of life. A cluster of hardy, winter-tolerant mosses, clinging to the sheltered side of a utility conduit, seemed to deepen in hue, their verdant life defying the lingering chill. Then, the truly remarkable occurred. A tiny, almost impossibly fragile shoot, no thicker than a strand of hair, pushed its way through the thawing earth near the edge of the cultivated perimeter. It was a speck of vibrant green against the still-somber browns and grays, a defiant declaration of existence.

Mara's breath hitched. She had seen countless such sprouts over the years, cataloged them, ensured their propagation within the controlled environments of the arboretum and the domes. But this, emerging unaided in the raw, unscripted landscape beyond their immediate confines, felt different. It was a testament to an unyielding vitality, a primal urge that transcended human intervention. It was, she realized with a sudden clarity, a mirror to the very resilience Eli had spoken of – not the resilience of endurance, but the resilience of renewal.

Her father, a botanist whose passion had ignited her own, had often spoken of plants as nature's eternal optimists. "They always reach for the light, Mara," he would say, his eyes crinkling at the corners. "Even when the shadows seem absolute, they will find a way to bend, to grow, to seek out the warmth." At the time, she had understood this in the context of optimal growth conditions, of light spectrum analysis and nutrient optimization. But now, observing that lone shoot, she saw it with a new, more profound understanding. It wasn't just about seeking light; it was about an intrinsic drive to *live*, to *grow*, to *become*.

The transition to spring wasn't merely a change in temperature or a shift in light cycles; it was a tangible manifestation of hope. The carefully managed ecosystems within Havenridge, while essential for their survival, had always felt, to Mara, like a testament to their ability to *preserve* life. But the world outside, in its untamed, unpredictable beauty, was a testament to life's inherent capacity to *reclaim* and *renew*. This distinction, subtle yet significant, began to reshape her perspective.

She found herself revisiting the arboretum with a fresh lens. The meticulously arranged specimens, each labeled and cataloged, the climate-controlled environments designed for perfection, suddenly seemed to possess a certain stillness. While they thrived, they did so within meticulously defined boundaries. The plants here were healthy, vibrant, and productive, but were they truly experiencing the full spectrum of adaptation, of proactive growth that the world outside demanded?

Eli's words echoed in her mind: "My fear is that in our relentless pursuit of order, in our desperate attempt to control every variable, we might inadvertently extinguish the very spark of what makes us human. The spark of curiosity, of spontaneity, of the messy, beautiful, unpredictable essence of life." She had initially compartmentalized his concerns, viewing them as abstract philosophical musings that threatened the tangible security she had worked so hard to build. But as spring began its slow, undeniable advance, she started to see the wisdom in his perspective.

The first signs of spring were not just external; they were internal. The thawing of the permafrost outside Havenridge was, in a way, a thawing of her own ingrained resistance to uncertainty. The emergence of that tiny green shoot was a quiet but potent reminder that life, even in its most fragile form, possessed an indomitable will to persist and to grow. It was a lesson in adaptation, a silent sermon preached by the earth itself.

She walked through the agricultural domes, observing the burgeoning rows of hydroponically grown vegetables. The lettuce leaves unfurled with a satisfying uniformity, the tomato plants reached towards the carefully calibrated grow lights, their nascent blossoms promising future bounty. It was a display of efficiency, of perfected cultivation. Yet, she found her thoughts drifting back to the single, defiant shoot outside. There was a wildness to its existence, an inherent strength that came not from protection, but from a deep, innate connection to the fundamental forces of nature.

"The most enduring ecosystems are not those that are perfectly static, but those that are dynamic, that are constantly adapting, integrating new elements, evolving," Eli had said. She had nodded, intellectually agreeing, but the emotional weight of his words was only now beginning to settle. Her life's work had been dedicated to creating a static, perfectly controlled environment, a bulwark against the chaos of the outside world. But perhaps, in doing so, she had inadvertently created a different kind of fragility – a fragility born of an inability to adapt, to integrate the unexpected, to embrace the dynamic nature of life itself.

The community of Havenridge was also stirring. The long, introspective months of winter had fostered a sense of quiet contemplation, a period of internal reflection. But with the arrival of spring, a palpable shift occurred. Conversations in the communal areas turned from abstract anxieties to practical plans. Teams began to organize for the exterior maintenance cycles, for the limited, carefully supervised excursions that would be necessary as the growing season commenced. There was a renewed sense of purpose, a collective focusing of energies towards the tasks ahead.

Mara found herself participating in these discussions with a newfound openness. Previously, her approach had been dictated by rigid protocols and risk-aversion. Now, she found herself listening more intently to the ideas of others, particularly those who, like Eli, spoke of innovation and the exploration of new approaches. The idea of managed experimentation, of controlled deviations from established norms, no longer felt like a direct threat to her life's work, but rather a necessary evolution.

She imagined the arboretum not just as a sanctuary, but as a living laboratory, a space where they could gently introduce elements of controlled unpredictability. What if, for instance, they allowed a small section of the arboretum to experience more natural, fluctuating light cycles, mimicking the subtle shifts of the exterior world? What if they introduced a wider variety of native flora, plants that had evolved in more challenging conditions, to see how they interacted with the established specimens? The thought was both exhilarating and terrifying. It represented a deliberate step away from the absolute control she had so long championed.

The thaw was more than just a physical process; it was a psychological one. It was the breaking down of barriers, both literal and metaphorical. The melting snow was eroding the sharp edges of winter, softening the landscape, and in doing so, it was also softening the rigid lines of her own thinking. The resilience she had always understood as the ability to withstand and recover was now being redefined in her mind as the capacity to actively seek out new growth, to adapt proactively, to embrace the inherent dynamism of existence.

One afternoon, while supervising the recalibration of the nutrient delivery system in Dome Gamma, she paused. A stray beam of sunlight, not from the artificial grow lamps, but from a small, transient opening in the dome's outer shell – a minor imperfection she had noted for repair – was hitting a patch of soil. Within that small circle of natural light, a few tiny wildflowers, seemingly dormant for months, had begun to unfurl delicate petals of vibrant purple. They were not part of the planned cultivation, not cataloged or accounted for. They were an anomaly, a beautiful, unexpected intrusion.

Mara knelt, her gloved fingers hovering inches above the tiny blossoms. They were a stark contrast to the orderly rows of genetically optimized crops surrounding them. These were wild, untamed, their beauty arising not from careful design, but from the sheer tenacity of their being. They were living proof that life found a way, that even within the most controlled environments, the inherent drive to grow, to flourish, to bloom, would persist.

She felt a profound sense of connection to those small, determined flowers. They were, in their own quiet way, embodying the very spirit of spring that was beginning to unfurl within Havenridge, and within herself. It was a spirit of renewal, of hope, of an unyielding belief in the possibility of new beginnings. The thaw had begun, and with it, a new season of growth, both for the world outside and for the hearts and minds within. The carefully constructed walls of Havenridge, while still vital for their survival, no longer felt like a complete containment of possibility. They felt, instead, like a nurturing ground, a place where the lessons learned from the wild, untamed world outside could be slowly, thoughtfully, and courageously integrated. The first signs of spring were not just a visual spectacle; they were a profound, internal awakening, a quiet revolution of perspective, hinting at a future where resilience was not just about survival, but about the vibrant, unpredictable, and beautiful art of thriving.

The scent of damp earth and awakening chlorophyll filled Mara's senses the moment she stepped through the pressurized airlock into the arboretum. It was a familiar perfume, usually associated with the meticulous restocking and recalibration that followed the winter's dormancy, a sterile choreography of preparation. But this year, it felt different. The air, even within the controlled environment, hummed with an echo of the thaw happening beyond the reinforced walls of Havenridge. Beside her, Eli's presence was a quiet warmth, a complementary rhythm to her own measured steps.

"It feels... expectant, doesn't it?" Eli murmured, his gaze sweeping over the rows of hushed greenery. His hands, usually restless, were clasped behind his back, a rare stillness that spoke volumes.

Mara nodded, a small smile playing on her lips. "Expectant and, dare I say, eager." She traced a finger along the cool, smooth surface of a dormant fern frond. Its tightly coiled fiddlehead held the promise of unfurling, a miniature universe waiting for the right cue. "The winter defenses held, as expected. Minimal breaches, easily contained. The thermal regulators performed admirably, and the atmospheric scrubbers kept the particulate count within acceptable parameters even during the worst of the storms." Her voice, though professional, carried a new lilt, a reflection of the shift in her perspective. She was no longer just reporting on systems; she was acknowledging the resilience woven into the very fabric of their survival, a resilience that extended beyond the engineered solutions.

Eli leaned closer, his eyes sparkling with a shared understanding. "The data is always reassuring, Mara, but it's the feel of it, the *spirit* of the place, that truly tells the story." He gestured towards a section where the light filters mimicked the soft, diffused glow of early spring. "Look at the *Phalaenopsis* hybrids. They've been through worse. See that slight blush of color in the leaves? That's not just nutrient uptake; that's their way of saying, 'We're ready.'"

Their collaboration had always been efficient, a seamless merging of Mara's data-driven precision and Eli's intuitive understanding of biological needs. But this year, a new layer had been added, a synergy born from shared introspection and a mutual acknowledgment of the limitations of absolute control. Their movements around the arboretum were less about separate tasks and more about a flowing dance. When Mara calibrated the humidity levels, Eli would adjust the nutrient feed, his hand movements anticipating her need for a slightly different mineral balance based on the subtle visual cues he detected. There were no lengthy explanations, no need for explicit directives. A shared glance, a subtle nod, a gestured indication – their communication had become as organic as the life they nurtured.

"The Venus flytraps are showing good tonus," Mara observed, peering into a terrarium where the iconic traps remained closed, a testament to their dormant state. "No signs of fungal infection, and the substrate moisture is optimal for their spring awakening." She was detailing the metrics, the quantifiable markers of success, but her focus was drawn to the way Eli was gently misting the air around them, a gesture that seemed to coax rather than simply moisten.

Eli smiled, catching her eye. "It's not just about the moisture, Mara. It's about the *feeling* of that first gentle rain after a long, dry spell. It's the signal that change is coming. They respond to that promise, not just the water itself." He paused, running a hand over the glass. "Think of them as tiny sentinels, each one waiting for the world outside to signal its readiness to re-engage. Our job is to provide that signal, but also to trust that they will know when to fully respond."

This was the essence of their renewed approach. Mara had spent years building the most robust, most failsafe systems imaginable, designed to insulate their precious flora from the harsh realities of the post-Collapse world. Her focus had been on preventing loss, on maintaining the status quo of survival. Eli, on the other hand, had always spoken of growth, of adaptation, of allowing life to express its inherent resilience. The thaw, the return of the growing season, had somehow bridged that divide, allowing them to see that true resilience wasn't just about withstanding, but about actively embracing change.

They moved to the section housing the delicate orchids, their blooms having been carefully preserved through the winter through a complex process of controlled dormancy. Mara checked the light spectrum readings, ensuring the gradual increase in intensity mimicked the lengthening days outside. Eli, meanwhile, was whispering to a particularly stubborn *Cypripedium* that seemed hesitant to stir.

"Come on now, little lady," he crooned, his voice a low rumble. "The world's waking up. The air's got that sweet tang again. Don't you want to show off your velvet lips?" He gently touched a leaf, his touch incredibly light, almost reverent. "It's safe now. The frost has retreated. The pollinators, even our little synthetic ones, are starting to get restless."

Mara watched him, a genuine warmth spreading through her. It was easy to get lost in the data, in the protocols, in the sterile perfection of it all. Eli's ability to connect with the plants on such a fundamental, almost emotional level was something she had always admired, and now, in a way, she felt she was beginning to understand it. It wasn't sentimentality; it was an acute awareness of the subtle energies, the unspoken language of life.

"The root system of the *Phalaenopsis* looks exceptionally healthy," Mara reported, her eyes scanning the translucent pots. "Excellent vascular development. We can begin to introduce a slightly higher nitrogen content in the nutrient solution, as per protocol."

"And perhaps a touch more warmth around the base," Eli added, already reaching for a small, handheld device that emitted a gentle, controlled heat. "Just a whisper of warmth, to remind them of the sun's embrace. They need to feel that promise deep within their roots, not just see it in the light." He looked at Mara, a question in his eyes. "What do you think? A subtle increase, enough to encourage new root hair growth without stressing the system?"

Mara didn't hesitate. The old Mara might have demanded more data, more simulations. But this new Mara, the one who had watched the tiny green shoot push through the thawing earth, the one who felt the promise of spring in her bones, simply nodded. "A subtle increase. Let's monitor the osmotic pressure closely, but I think you're right. A whisper of warmth. It's time to let them know the winter is truly over."

Their hands brushed as they both reached for a watering can, a silent acknowledgment of their shared purpose. It was a small gesture, but it encapsulated the shift in their dynamic. They were no longer two separate entities working towards a common goal; they were a unified force, their individual strengths interwoven, their approaches complementary.

"Remember the winter of '77?" Eli asked, his voice distant, as he meticulously checked the soil pH for a bed of sensitive alpine flowers. "The blizzard that seemed to last for months? We thought we'd lost half the specimens. The power grid flickered for days. We were so focused on just keeping the generators running, on maintaining the bare minimum temperature. We almost forgot to think about what the plants needed to *recover* after it was over."

Mara's brow furrowed slightly as she recalled the incident. It was a dark period in Havenridge's history, a stark reminder of their vulnerability. "That was a different time, Eli. Our systems were far less advanced then. We were reactive, not proactive."

"And yet," Eli countered gently, not with criticism, but with observation, "even then, some of them... they just refused to give up. They found a way. That little patch of forget-me-nots by the north wall, practically buried under snow for weeks, they bloomed the first week of spring as if nothing had happened. It was a stubborn, beautiful defiance." He smiled, a hint of wistfulness in his eyes. "I think we've learned to build better defenses, Mara, and that's crucial. But perhaps we've also learned, or are learning, to better understand that defiance, that inherent will to live."

He was right. The arboretum, once a symbol of their meticulously controlled survival, was becoming a testament to their evolving understanding of life itself. They weren't just preserving; they were nurturing, coaxing, encouraging. They were working *with* the plants, not just *on* them.

As they moved through the sections, the process of "awakening" began in earnest. It wasn't a sudden flip of a switch, but a gradual unfurling, a gentle coaxing. For some plants, it was a slow increase in light and warmth. For others, it involved carefully reintroducing specific humidity levels or adjusting the nutrient composition to simulate the spring rains and the richer soil.

Mara found herself entrusting more and more of the finer adjustments to Eli. She would set the parameters, the overarching guidelines, but she would watch as he instinctively knew when to slightly deviate, when to add a touch more warmth to a particular plant's enclosure, or when to mist a cluster of delicate blossoms with a solution that mimicked the first dewfall. He would then report back to her, not with a detailed justification, but with a description of what he felt, what he saw, what he intuitively understood the plant was responding to.

"This *Drosera*," he'd say, referring to a sundew, its sticky tentacles still retracted, "it's not just about the moisture. It's about the *idea* of insects returning. I added a tiny amount of a pheromone compound – synthesized, of course – to the mist. Just a trace. It's like a whisper of a promise that food is coming."

Mara, initially hesitant about such unconventional methods, found herself trusting his instincts. She would review the readings, and invariably, the subtle shifts he described would be reflected in the plant's physiological responses. The tentacles would begin to unfurl, the tiny droplets of adhesive glistening in the artificial light, ready to trap their first unsuspecting prey.

Their movements had become so synchronized that they often anticipated each other's needs before they were even spoken. Mara would reach for a data pad, and Eli would already be preparing the necessary tools. He would adjust a light panel, and she would be inputting the corresponding changes into the central system. It was a silent conversation, a testament to the deep roots their shared experience had laid.

"The Nepenthes pitcher plants are looking particularly promising," Mara observed, pointing to a cluster of developing pitchers, their vibrant colors muted by their dormant state. "The development suggests we can increase the nutrient solution by 5% within the next cycle."

Eli nodded, his fingers tracing the smooth, waxy surface of a pitcher. "And a gentle increase in CO_2. Just enough to give them that initial burst of energy, like the air getting fresher after a storm. They'll need it to start manufacturing those digestive enzymes." He met her gaze, a warmth in his eyes that mirrored the burgeoning life around them. "It feels good, doesn't it? Seeing them stir. Knowing we're helping them wake up."

Mara returned his gaze, a genuine smile finally breaking through her professional demeanor. "It does, Eli. It really does." The arboretum, once a sanctuary of control, was transforming into a vibrant testament to the power of collaboration, of understanding, and of the unyielding, beautiful spirit of life itself. The thaw had reached even here, not just in temperature, but in their hearts and minds, allowing for a new season of growth, both for the plants and for their own shared journey. The meticulous systems she had built were still vital, but now, they were infused with a new dimension – the intuitive, empathetic touch that Eli brought, a touch that Mara was finally beginning to fully appreciate and embrace. The arboretum was no longer just a meticulously maintained collection; it was a living, breathing entity, responding to their combined care, a microcosm of the hope that was slowly, surely, unfurling across the world outside.

The gentle hum of the atmospheric regulators, a sound Mara had once associated solely with the sterile preservation of life, now seemed to carry a deeper resonance. It was the steady heartbeat of a system that was not just maintaining, but nurturing. As the last of the winter's chill receded from the air, and the vibrant greens of the awakening plants intensified under the tailored light, a new energy began to stir within Eli. It was a palpable shift, a restless yearning for more. He watched Mara meticulously adjust the nutrient levels for a batch of newly sprouted ferns, her brow furrowed in concentration, and a thought, fully formed and brimming with possibility, took root.

"Mara," he began, his voice a low murmur that cut through the quiet hum, "I've been thinking." He paused, letting his gaze drift from her focused profile to the burgeoning life around them. The arboretum, a marvel of controlled bio-engineering, had proven its worth through the harsh winter. Its carefully curated ecosystem had weathered the storms, both literal and metaphorical, with remarkable grace. But Eli saw beyond its current success. He saw its potential, a potential that felt as vast and untamed as the world slowly beginning to reawaken outside.

Mara looked up, her eyes, usually sharp and analytical, softened by the ambient glow of the grow lights. "About what, Eli? The new irrigation cycles? I think we've finally optimized the flow for the *Nepenthes*."

He offered a gentle smile, a knowing glint in his eyes. "That, too, is going well. But it's more than just keeping things running smoothly, isn't it? It's about what we *can* do, not just what we *have* to do." He gestured broadly, encompassing the entire arboretum, from the towering cycads to the delicate mosses carpeting the shaded rocks. "This place, Mara, it's more than just a vault of surviving species. It's a testament to resilience. And I think... I think we can push that resilience further."

Mara's expression shifted from focused efficiency to intrigued curiosity. She put down her datapad, turning her full attention to him. "Push it how, Eli? We've worked so hard to ensure these species have the optimal conditions for recovery and propagation. What more could we offer?"

"Diversity," Eli said, his voice gaining a passionate edge. "And purpose." He walked towards a section where the light spectrum was deliberately varied, mimicking the dappled sunlight of a forest canopy. "We've focused on the species that could tolerate our conditions, those that we knew, with careful manipulation, could survive. But what about those that *thrive* in more challenging environments? Those that have unique adaptations, that require more than just controlled humidity and balanced nutrients? Imagine introducing species that are naturally more drought-resistant, or those that can tolerate a wider range of soil pH, or even those that have evolved symbiotic relationships with microbes that can enrich even the most depleted soil."

His eyes were alight with an almost childlike wonder, the kind that had always drawn Mara to him. He moved with a renewed vigor, his hands sketching imagined landscapes in the air. "We could create micro-environments within the arboretum itself. Small, distinct zones that mimic different biomes. A xeric garden for succulents and desert flora, a bog garden for carnivorous plants and amphibians, even a section designed to replicate the challenging conditions of the high altitudes. It would be a living laboratory, Mara, a place to truly understand adaptation, not just preservation."

Mara listened intently, her initial surprise giving way to a thoughtful consideration. Her mind, trained to assess risks and quantify outcomes, began to run scenarios, but they were different scenarios than she was used to. These were not about preventing failure, but about fostering innovation. "Introducing species with such varied requirements would necessitate a significant re-configuration of our environmental controls, Eli. The energy expenditure alone...."

"But think of the knowledge we'd gain!" Eli interjected, his enthusiasm undimmed. "We're not just trying to survive anymore, Mara. We're trying to *rebuild*. And to rebuild, we need to understand how life *persists* and *flourishes* in less-than-ideal conditions. This knowledge isn't just for the arboretum; it's for *everywhere*. Imagine being able to cultivate hardy crops in areas that were once considered barren. Imagine reintroducing plant life to landscapes scarred by pollution or desiccation. This isn't just about growing plants; it's about reclaiming the world."

He stopped, facing her directly, his gaze earnest. "And it's not just about 'wild' species, either. What about food? We've managed to maintain our hydroponic systems, of course, but they're sterile, efficient, yes, but... they lack something. What if we cultivated small, resilient food gardens within the arboretum? Not just for our own consumption, but as a demonstration. Hardy vegetables, nutrient-dense legumes, even some of the forgotten fruits and berries that have the genetic hardiness to withstand a wider range of environmental stressors. We could showcase how to grow food in a way that's integrated with the environment, not imposed upon it."

Mara felt a spark of something akin to excitement flicker within her. It was a dangerous sensation, a departure from the carefully guarded emotional neutrality she had cultivated for so long. But Eli's vision was infectious, a vibrant counterpoint to the quiet vigilance of their daily lives. She looked around the arboretum, seeing it with new eyes. The controlled environment, which had always represented a triumph of human ingenuity over a broken world, now seemed... limited.

"A living laboratory," she repeated softly, testing the words. "Demonstrating sustainable practices." The concept resonated with a part of her she had long suppressed, a part that yearned for more than just the meticulous maintenance of what remained. "You're not just talking about expanding the collection, Eli. You're talking about creating a blueprint for a future where life can thrive, not just survive."

"Exactly!" Eli exclaimed, clapping his hands together softly. "That's precisely it. Havenridge is a sanctuary, yes, but it can also be a seedbed for hope. We have the expertise, the technology, and now, with this thaw, we have the perfect opportunity to demonstrate what's possible." He walked over to a section of the arboretum that housed a small, experimental hydroponic setup, designed for research rather than large-scale production. "Think of this space, Mara, not just as a collection of specimens, but as an educational hub. We could invite others, when the time is right, to learn from us. To see how we've managed to coax life back, how we've learned to work *with* nature, not against it."

He picked up a small, perfectly formed tomato, its skin a deep, vibrant red. "This," he said, holding it out to her, "is more than just sustenance. It's a symbol. A symbol of what we can achieve when we combine our knowledge with an understanding of natural processes. It's a symbol of... of abundance, even in scarcity."

Mara took the tomato, its weight surprisingly substantial in her palm. It was a stark contrast to the nutrient pastes and synthesized rations they sometimes relied on. The scent, faint but distinct, was earthy and sweet, a promise of real flavor, real nourishment. She turned it over in her fingers, a profound realization dawning. Eli wasn't just proposing an expansion of the arboretum's biological scope; he was proposing an expansion of its very purpose.

"You envision this place becoming a center for learning, for sharing our techniques," she mused aloud, her mind racing. "Not just for horticulturalists, but for anyone who wants to understand how to cultivate life in this new world."

"Precisely," Eli affirmed, his gaze unwavering. "We have the most advanced bio-dome in this sector, perhaps in the entire region. We have the resources, the personnel... and a growing understanding of what it truly means to be resilient. Why hoard that knowledge? Why keep this beautiful, vibrant ecosystem confined within these walls without sharing its lessons? The thaw outside is happening, Mara. The world is slowly, tentatively, reawakening. We have a responsibility, I think, to be a part of that reawakening, not just a witness to it."

He paused, letting his words settle. The idea was bold, perhaps even audacious, given their precarious existence. But it was also deeply, profoundly hopeful. He could see the gears turning in Mara's mind, the analytical part of her grappling with the practicalities, but the other part, the part that had been subtly shifting with the changing seasons, was beginning to embrace the vision.

"We would need to conduct extensive surveys of potential new species," Mara stated, her voice regaining some of its professional tone, but now tinged with a newfound excitement. "Assess their compatibility, their resource demands, their potential impact on our existing ecosystem. We'd also need to rigorously evaluate the feasibility of incorporating food cultivation. It would require careful planning to avoid any cross-contamination or introduction of unwanted pathogens."

"Of course," Eli agreed readily. "I'm not suggesting we just throw open the doors and start planting anything. This would be a phased approach, meticulously researched and implemented. We start small. We test. We learn. But the potential payoff... think of the message it would send, Mara. That even after everything, life finds a way. That we can not only survive, but thrive. That we can rebuild a world that is not just functional, but beautiful and abundant."

He walked over to a section of the arboretum dedicated to various types of flowering plants, their blooms a riot of color even in the controlled environment. He gently touched the petal of a vibrant orchid, its intricate patterns a testament to millions of years of evolution. "These plants, Mara, they've been through so much. They've adapted, they've persevered. And now, we have the chance to nurture that spirit of adaptation, to learn from it, and to help it spread beyond these walls. Imagine small communities, struggling to grow food, being able to implement techniques we've perfected right here. Imagine reclaimed lands blooming with life once more because of the knowledge we've cultivated."

Mara looked at Eli, truly looked at him, and saw not just the pragmatic botanist, but a visionary. His passion was a powerful force, a beacon of optimism in a world often shrouded in the shadows of its past. The arboretum, for all its technological marvels, had always felt like a sanctuary, a place to hunker down and wait for the storm to pass. Eli's vision was to transform it into a launching pad, a place from which to actively engage with the rebuilding of the world.

"It would require a significant investment of resources," she admitted, her voice thoughtful. "But... the potential benefits, both scientifically and for the broader community... it's compelling. We could re-design certain sections, create distinct biomes that not only showcase diversity but also allow us to study the intricate relationships between species in varied conditions. It would be a more dynamic, more interactive research facility."

"And more inspiring," Eli added, his eyes shining. "Imagine young minds, coming here and seeing that it's not just about surviving in a bunker, but about actively participating in the restoration of life. It's about hope, Mara. Tangible, living, breathing hope." He reached out, his hand hovering near hers, a silent invitation for her to share in this burgeoning idea. "We've spent so long focused on defense, on containment. It's time to shift our focus to growth, to propagation, to dissemination. It's time to let the arboretum bloom, not just in color, but in purpose."

Mara met his gaze, and for the first time, she felt a complete alignment of her own desires with Eli's infectious enthusiasm. Her meticulous nature found a new outlet in the challenge of designing these diverse micro-environments, of calculating the precise needs of species she had previously deemed too risky to introduce. His vision of the arboretum as a living laboratory, a demonstration of sustainable practices, resonated deeply with her own underlying desire for a more meaningful impact.

"We could begin by cataloging species that exhibit remarkable resilience," she began, her mind already sketching out protocols. "Identifying those with genetic traits that allow them to thrive in challenging environments – drought tolerance, salinity resistance, adaptability to poor soil conditions. We could then conduct controlled trials, simulating those conditions within isolated sections of the arboretum."

Eli beamed. "And for the food gardens, we focus on staple crops that have proven hardy through history, but perhaps have been overlooked in our modern agricultural past. Root vegetables, hardy greens, nutrient-rich legumes. We could experiment with companion planting, natural pest deterrents, and soil enrichment techniques that don't rely on synthetic fertilizers. Imagine, Mara, a small patch of earth, carefully tended, yielding a harvest that is not only nourishing but also regenerative."

The vision expanded, encompassing more than just plants. It was about a philosophy of co-existence, of understanding and working with the natural world. It was about moving from a posture of defense to one of proactive restoration. Mara, who had always prided herself on her logical approach, found herself swept up in the sheer, unadulterated optimism of Eli's dream. It was a dream that felt not only achievable but necessary.

"This is... this is more than just expanding our collection, Eli," she said, her voice filled with a quiet awe. "This is about re-imagining what the arboretum can be. It's about turning a sanctuary into a school, a vault into a vibrant engine of recovery."

"Exactly," Eli confirmed, his hand finding hers, their fingers intertwining. His touch was warm, grounding. "It's about letting the lessons we've learned here, the resilience we've cultivated, spread beyond these walls. It's about actively participating in the thaw, not just waiting for it." He squeezed her hand, his smile reaching his eyes. "It's about planting seeds of hope, Mara. And watching them grow."

Mara listened to Eli's impassioned words, her mind a whirlwind of data, projections, and the undeniable, quiet tug of hope. His vision of a dynamic, living laboratory, a seedbed for a world slowly stirring back to life, was both exhilarating and terrifying. Her immediate instinct, honed by years of meticulous risk assessment and stringent protocol adherence, was to catalogue the myriad potential pitfalls. Expanding the arboretum's scope beyond its carefully defined parameters meant uncharted territory, and uncharted territory, in Mara's experience, was a breeding ground for unforeseen complications. The logistical hurdles alone seemed immense. Introducing species with vastly different environmental needs would necessitate a complete overhaul of the climate control systems, a monumental undertaking that would strain their already tight resources.

"Eli," she began, her voice measured, betraying none of the internal debate raging within her, "your ideas are... ambitious. And I admit, they are compelling. But the reality of implementing such a comprehensive diversification is... significant. The energy requirements for maintaining multiple, distinct microclimates within a single bio-dome would be astronomical. We'd need to reconfigure the entire power grid, and frankly, our current capacity is already stretched to its limits managing the existing ecosystem. And then there's the risk of invasive species, of unintended cross-pollination, of introducing pathogens that could devastate our existing, hard-won biodiversity." She paused, gathering her thoughts, her gaze sweeping over the verdant expanse around them, a testament to their careful, controlled efforts. "We've spent years perfecting the conditions for these survivors, ensuring their stability. To introduce a significant number of new variables... it requires a level of precision and foresight that even our advanced systems might struggle to maintain."

Her words, precise and grounded in practicality, hung in the air, a stark counterpoint to the vibrant life unfolding around them. Eli, however, met her concern with an understanding smile, his eyes reflecting the gentle glow of the grow lights. He didn't dismiss her reservations; he acknowledged them, but he also saw beyond them.

"I understand your concerns, Mara, I truly do," he said, his tone gentle. "And you're right. It's not a simple undertaking. But think about what we've already achieved. We've adapted. We've learned to coax life from seemingly barren soil, to manage unpredictable shifts in atmospheric composition. Remember the fungal bloom incident last cycle? We thought it was a disaster, a potential extinction-level event for the *Solenostemon*. But we innovated. We developed a targeted microbial treatment, a solution that was entirely novel, and it not only saved the *Solenostemon* but also, as we discovered later, seemed to have a beneficial effect on the nearby *Drosera* species. We adapted, Mara, and we succeeded."

He moved closer, his gaze earnest. "That's what I'm proposing, in essence. A controlled, intelligent adaptation. We don't just throw open the doors. We identify species with proven resilience, species that have, in their own evolutionary journey, demonstrated an ability to thrive in challenging conditions. We study them, we understand their needs, and then, and only then, do we begin to integrate them. We start small. We create a single, distinct biome first – perhaps a xeric zone, or a small bog garden. We monitor it intensely. We learn from its successes and its failures. And as we gain confidence and refine our techniques, we expand."

Mara felt a tremor of acknowledgment run through her. He was right. The fungal bloom incident had been a turning point, a stark reminder that even their meticulously controlled environment was not immutable, and that their ability to adapt had been crucial. She recalled the panic, quickly followed by the focused energy of problem-solving, the collaborative effort that had ultimately saved the

Solenostemon. It had been a moment of profound learning, a testament to the fact that sometimes, the greatest innovations arise from necessity, from the unexpected challenges that life throws at them.

She looked at the *Solenostemon*, its velvety leaves a deep, rich purple, thriving as if the fungal threat had never existed. Beside it, the sundews, *Drosera*, glistened with their tiny, sticky tentacles, looking more vigorous than ever. Eli was right. They had already proven their capacity for adaptation, for pushing the boundaries of what they thought was possible. His plan wasn't just a leap of faith; it was a logical extension of their ongoing efforts to understand and nurture life in its most tenacious forms.

"A phased approach," she murmured, the words a balm to her cautious nature. "That I can work with. We could begin by identifying species that have a high degree of genetic overlap with our current collection, thus potentially minimizing incompatibility issues. Or, conversely, species that exhibit strong symbiotic relationships with known organisms. For example, drought-resistant plants that have a proven affinity for nitrogen-fixing bacteria in their root systems. This would not only enhance their survival but also contribute to soil enrichment in a new micro-environment, reducing our reliance on synthetic nutrient solutions."

Eli's smile widened, the spark of shared vision igniting further. "Exactly! And the food gardens. We could start with a small, enclosed plot, perhaps using a hydroponic-aquaponic hybrid system that incorporates a closed-loop nutrient cycle. We could experiment with hardy, nutrient-dense crops – quinoa, amaranth, certain varieties of kale and spinach that are known for their resilience. Imagine the psychological impact, Mara, of seeing actual food, grown not in sterile vats, but in a living, breathing garden, right here within the arboretum. It would be a tangible symbol of abundance, a testament to our ability to cultivate sustenance not just for survival, but for well-being."

Mara's mind, once fixated on the 'why not,' was now actively engaged with the 'how.' She began to sketch out mental flowcharts, detailing the steps required for a pilot project. First, a comprehensive survey of resilient food crops. Second, the selection of a suitable, self-contained space within the arboretum. Third, the design and implementation of a closed-loop cultivation system, incorporating natural fertilization methods. Fourth, a rigorous monitoring program to track growth, nutrient uptake, and any potential issues.

"We could integrate educational components from the outset," she mused, her voice gaining a steady rhythm. "Designate a small viewing area for the food garden, perhaps with interactive displays explaining the cultivation techniques. This would serve not only as a demonstration but also as a subtle form of community outreach, a way to plant seeds of knowledge even before we harvest the first crop."

The idea of 'planting seeds of knowledge' resonated deeply. It was a concept that had always appealed to her, the quiet satisfaction of sharing hard-won expertise. For so long, their knowledge had been a matter of survival, a closely guarded secret to ensure their own continued existence. But Eli's vision was about more than just their own survival; it was about fostering a broader ecosystem of life and learning.

"And the biomes," she continued, her analytical mind already mapping out potential zones. "We could dedicate a section to simulating arid conditions, focusing on succulents and hardy desert flora. Another, perhaps, to a wetland environment, showcasing plants adapted to waterlogged soils and high humidity. We'd need to be meticulous with water management, of course, ensuring no cross-contamination, but the scientific value of studying these distinct ecosystems side-by-side... it's immense."

She recalled the long, arduous winter, the constant vigilance required to maintain the delicate balance within the arboretum. There had been moments of despair, moments when the sheer effort of keeping life alive felt overwhelming. But there had also been moments of quiet wonder, observing the tenacious growth of a new shoot, the unfolding of a delicate bloom, the silent, relentless pursuit of life against all odds. Those moments, she realized, were what Eli's vision was truly about. It wasn't just about expanding their collection; it was about amplifying the inherent beauty and resilience of the natural world, about creating a space where that resilience could be studied, celebrated, and ultimately, shared.

"The challenge will be in ensuring complete environmental isolation between these zones," Mara stated, her brow furrowing slightly as she considered the engineering implications. "We would need advanced air filtration systems, specialized barrier materials, and a sophisticated monitoring network to detect even the slightest atmospheric bleed. It's a significant undertaking from an infrastructure perspective."

"But one we are capable of," Eli countered, his voice firm with conviction. "We have the engineering expertise, Mara. We've designed and built this entire bio-dome, after all. We can adapt, we can innovate. We can create the necessary safeguards. Think of it as a new frontier of bio-engineering, pushing the boundaries of what's possible in controlled ecological environments. And the knowledge we gain from this... it's not just for the arboretum. It's for the world outside, when it's ready."

Mara felt a subtle shift within her, a loosening of the rigid framework of her usual approach. Her meticulous nature, once a source of hesitation, was now finding a new, expansive purpose. The sheer complexity of Eli's plan, which had initially threatened to overwhelm her, now seemed like an intricate puzzle, a grand design waiting to be solved. She saw the potential for elegant solutions, for innovative engineering, for a new era of scientific discovery born from their enclosed sanctuary.

"We would need to establish clear metrics for success for each new biome and for the food cultivation project," she said, her voice gaining momentum. "Not just survival rates, but indicators of healthy growth, reproductive success, and successful integration into the micro-environment. And for the food gardens, we'd need to track yields, nutritional content, and the efficiency of the cultivation system."

"Absolutely," Eli agreed, his hand reaching out to gently touch hers. The warmth of his skin against hers was a familiar comfort, a grounding presence that always seemed to anchor her when her thoughts threatened to spiral. "And beyond the scientific data, there's the qualitative aspect. The beauty. The inspiration. Imagine walking through a section that mimics a dense rainforest, the air thick with the scent of damp earth and exotic blooms, and then stepping into a sun-drenched desert landscape, with its stark, sculptural forms and surprising bursts of color. It would be a journey, Mara, a living testament to the astonishing diversity of life on this planet."

He paused, his gaze steady. "We've spent so long as custodians, ensuring the survival of what remains. It's time to become cultivators, nurturers of new growth. It's time to move beyond preservation and embrace creation. Your caution, Mara, is invaluable. It's what has kept us safe, what has ensured our success. But your adaptability, your quiet strength, your willingness to learn and to grow... that is what will make this vision a reality. You see the challenges, but you also see the potential for elegant solutions. That's a rare and powerful combination."

Mara looked at him, her heart swelling with a quiet understanding. He saw her, not just as the meticulous scientist, but as someone capable of more, someone who could embrace a future beyond the carefully constructed confines of their present. The lessons of the past few seasons, the unexpected triumphs born from adaptive strategies, the quiet beauty of life's persistent unfurling – they all converged in this moment, urging her to shed the last vestiges of her ingrained hesitance.

She took a deep breath, the recycled air filling her lungs, a familiar sensation that now carried a hint of something new, something akin to possibility. Her mind, which had always gravitated towards the solid ground of established protocols, now felt ready to explore the uncharted territories of Eli's ambitious dream. It was a significant step, a departure from the careful, predictable path she had always followed. But as she met Eli's hopeful gaze, she knew, with a certainty that settled deep within her, that this was a step worth taking.

"Alright, Eli," she said, her voice softer now, imbued with a newfound resolve. "Let's start by cataloging those resilient food crops. And let's identify a suitable location for a pilot biome. We'll begin with a small, contained system, and we will document every single variable, every single outcome. This will be... an experiment in growth, in every sense of the word."

The hum of the arboretum's life support systems, usually a constant, reassuring thrum, seemed to deepen its resonance as Mara and Eli meticulously mapped out the future. The preliminary plans for the arboretum's expansion, once a daunting collection of spreadsheets and schematics, were beginning to coalesce into a tangible vision. It was in these late-night planning sessions, illuminated by the soft glow of their holographic displays, that Mara felt the foundations of something far more significant than a collaborative project being laid.

"If we reroute a secondary conduit from the main atmospheric processor to the proposed arid biome," Mara murmured, her stylus dancing across the projected blueprints, "we can maintain a stable humidity differential of less than five percent with minimal energy expenditure. The key will be in the micro-sealing of the enclosure walls. I've been reviewing some of the old nanotech fabrication manuals from the pre-Collapse era. There were some remarkable advancements in self-healing polymers that could be ideal for this."

Eli, leaning over her shoulder, his presence a steady warmth beside her, nodded thoughtfully. "Self-healing polymers. That's ingenious, Mara. It would minimize maintenance and drastically reduce the risk of micro-leaks, which, as you know, could be catastrophic for a delicate desert ecosystem. I was thinking about the substrate for the arid zone. We'll need to replicate the mineral composition of a natural desert floor as closely as possible. I remember studying some archival data on the Gobi Desert's soil structure – extremely low organic content, high silicate levels, and a surprisingly robust microbial community adapted to extreme desiccation."

Mara's fingers paused, hovering over a section of the display. "Gobi Desert. That's fascinating. The microbial aspect is crucial. Our current nutrient solutions are designed for our existing flora. Introducing a new soil biome will require a completely new approach to nutrient cycling. We might need to cultivate specific extremophiles to break down organic matter and make nutrients bioavailable in such a low-moisture environment. It's... complex, but I can see a pathway." She looked up at Eli, a flicker of genuine excitement in her eyes, a sensation that was becoming increasingly familiar in his company. "Your understanding of these ecological intricacies, Eli, it's... profound. You can visualize the needs of these organisms in a way that goes beyond data points. It's almost intuitive."

A slow smile spread across Eli's face, warming his gaze. "And you, Mara," he said, his voice soft, "can take that intuition and build the impossible. You translate the whisper of a need into the solid framework of reality. Without your analytical rigor, my visions would remain just that – fleeting dreams. The fact that you can look at a challenge like self-healing polymers and immediately see its application, that you can conceptualize the creation of entirely new microbial communities... that's where the true magic lies. You make the impossible, possible."

The compliment, delivered with such sincerity, settled in Mara's chest like a gentle hand. It was more than just professional acknowledgment; it was a recognition of her essence, of the core of who she was. She often felt her meticulous nature, her adherence to protocol, was a necessary shield, a way to navigate a world that had taught her the sharp sting of vulnerability. But Eli saw it not as a limitation, but as a strength, as the very tool that would forge their shared future.

"It's the collaboration, Eli," she replied, her voice a little quieter. "Your connection to the natural world, my ability to translate that into quantifiable parameters and engineering solutions. We're creating something new, not just within the arboretum, but between us, too. A shared language, built on trust."

He reached out, his fingers brushing against hers as they both hovered over the holographic display. The brief contact sent a ripple of warmth through her, a sensation that had nothing to do with the climate-controlled air of the arboretum. "A shared language," he echoed, his thumb gently stroking the back of her hand. "And a shared understanding. I trust your judgment implicitly, Mara. When you say something is achievable, I know you've already run a thousand simulations in your head. And when I speak of the needs of a plant, of the subtle cues it gives when it's thriving or struggling, I know you're listening, not just with your ears, but with your mind, ready to find the practical solution."

Mara met his gaze, her heart thrumming a little faster. The fear that had once been her constant companion – the fear of failure, of loss, of the world's inherent fragility – seemed to recede in the face of his unwavering faith. He saw her potential, not just for meticulous scientific work, but for daring, for expansion, for a future that was brighter than the sterile, controlled present they had so carefully maintained.

"And I," she said, her voice laced with a newfound confidence, "trust your vision, Eli. Your ability to see the inherent resilience in life, to understand its intricate dance. It's a gift. It's what allows us to dream beyond mere survival, to aspire to something more vibrant, more alive." She allowed herself a small, genuine smile. "You remind me that even in the most controlled environments, there is always room for wildness, for beauty, for the unexpected bloom."

He squeezed her hand gently, his eyes reflecting the soft glow of the displays, and in that moment, the sterile efficiency of the arboretum seemed to fade, replaced by a burgeoning warmth that had nothing to do with engineered climates. It was the first bloom of trust, not just in their professional capabilities, but in each other, a quiet promise of growth in the fertile ground they were now cultivating together. The arboretum, once a sanctuary of survival, was slowly transforming into a testament to their shared resilience, and to the tender, burgeoning connection that was taking root between them, as tenacious and beautiful as the plants they so carefully nurtured. It was an ecosystem of hope, and they were its first, most precious seeds. The logistical hurdles, the potential setbacks, the sheer audacity of their ambition – they were all still present, looming on the horizon. But now, they felt less like insurmountable obstacles and more like challenges to be met, together. The thought brought a surprising sense of peace, a quiet joy that settled deep within her, warming her from the inside out. It was a feeling that had been absent for a very long time, and she found herself holding onto it, cherishing its nascent glow.

CHAPTER NINE

Seeds of Doubt

The sterile luminescence of the Council chamber cast long, sharp shadows that did little to soften the stern visages of its members. Elder Thorne, his face a roadmap of aging austerity, tapped a slender finger against the polished obsidian of the council table. Beside him, Elder Anya, her expression perpetually placid but her eyes sharp as flint, observed the holographic projection flickering before them. It depicted the burgeoning arboretum, a vibrant anomaly of greens and blues against the muted, utilitarian palette of Havenridge.

"Councilwoman Mara's recent proposals regarding the arid biome," Thorne began, his voice a low rumble that echoed the chamber's hushed reverence for order, "and her... unconventional methods for achieving them, warrant our attention." He gestured towards a section of the display showing complex schematics for atmospheric regulators and nutrient dispersal systems. "While the preliminary yield reports are, I concede, impressive, the departure from established protocols is... significant."

Anya inclined her head, her gaze remaining fixed on the projection. "The introduction of 'self-healing polymers' and the cultivation of 'extremophile microbial communities' are certainly novel. The rationale presented by Councilwoman Mara cites efficiency and ecological integrity. However," she paused, a subtle inflection in her tone that conveyed measured caution, "efficiency at what cost? Stability is the cornerstone of Havenridge. We have engineered every facet of our existence to mitigate chaos. These new elements, while perhaps beneficial in isolation, introduce variables we have spent generations eradicating."

Another Council member, a stoic man named Silas, whose domain was resource allocation, chimed in. "My projections indicate a marginal increase in energy expenditure, even with Councilwoman Mara's innovative energy conduit rerouting. Furthermore, the procurement of materials for these 'self-healing polymers' requires tapping into reserves designated for critical infrastructure maintenance. This is not a minor adjustment; it is a significant deviation, and the long-term implications are, as yet, unknown."

Thorne's gaze shifted to Anya. "Unknown variables are precisely what we must guard against, Elder Anya. The Collapse was not a singular event, but a cascade of unforeseen consequences stemming from unchecked innovation and a disregard for established order. We cannot afford to repeat those mistakes, however well-intentioned the deviations may seem." He turned his attention back to the arboretum projection, his lips thinning. "The arboretum, under Councilwoman Mara's stewardship, has become... exuberant. While the sustenance it provides is vital, its expansion, particularly into such radically different biomes, introduces a level of biological diversity that could prove challenging to manage. What happens when these new organisms interact with our established systems? What happens when the 'extremophiles' are no longer content to remain within their designated enclosure?"

Anya steepled her fingers. "Councilwoman Mara has provided assurances that containment protocols are robust, and the simulations supporting her proposals are extensive. She asserts that the unique properties of the self-healing polymers will actually *enhance* containment, adapting to minor breaches before they become significant issues. Her approach to the microbial ecosystem is designed to be self-regulating, creating a closed loop of nutrient exchange that theoretically minimizes external contamination."

"Theoretically," Thorne echoed, his voice dripping with skepticism. "Theory is a fragile construct, Elder Anya. It crumbles in the face of unforeseen pressure. We have established a delicate equilibrium. The introduction of such radically different life forms, even under the guise of innovation, risks disrupting that equilibrium. We have seen plants, even within the established zones, exhibit unexpected mutations or disease resistance when exposed to novel genetic material. The introduction of entirely new ecosystems, with their own microbial agents, is a leap into the unknown."

Silas added, "And the personnel. Councilwoman Mara has, with Councilman Eli's full support, brought in additional technicians, training them on these new fabrication techniques and bio-cultivation methods. This diverts specialized personnel from other critical sectors, a drain on our most valuable asset: our human capital. While their dedication is admirable, their focus is singular, and the Council must consider the broader implications for Havenridge's overall operational capacity."

"Councilman Eli's involvement is also... noteworthy," Thorne continued, a hint of something that might have been suspicion, or perhaps simply ingrained caution, coloring his tone. "His background is in xenobotany, a field historically associated with... speculative research. While his current role is vital, his enthusiasm for these more ambitious, less predictable projects is evident. Does his vision align with the Council's mandate for stability, or is it driven by a more personal, perhaps romantic, ideal of ecological diversity for its own sake?"

Anya's gaze remained steady. "Councilman Eli's contributions to understanding the intricate needs of our existing flora have been invaluable. He possesses a profound empathy for the life he cultivates, which, I believe, fuels his desire to expand and diversify the arboretum's capacity. As for Councilwoman Mara, her meticulous planning and rigorous adherence to scientific principles have always been her hallmark. It is precisely this blend of her analytical prowess and his... ecological intuition that appears to be driving these advancements. We should not dismiss the potential benefits out of hand, Elder Thorne."

"Potential benefits," Thorne repeated, a sharp edge to his voice. "And potential risks. The Council's primary responsibility is the safeguarding of Havenridge and its inhabitants. We have a duty to maintain the order that has allowed us to survive. Every deviation, no matter how small, must be weighed against the possibility of unintended consequences. These 'seeds of doubt,' as it were, are not born of an unwillingness to progress, but of a deep-seated understanding of what is at stake."

He leaned forward, his eyes locking with Anya's. "The arboretum is a vital resource, yes. But it is a *managed* resource. Introducing elements that are inherently less predictable, that require constant, perhaps even intrusive, monitoring and intervention, is a departure from the principles of sustainable, controlled growth. My concern is that in our pursuit of greater abundance, we are inadvertently creating new vulnerabilities. This is not simply about efficient resource management; it is about maintaining the very fabric of our controlled existence."

Anya nodded slowly. "I understand your concerns, Elder Thorne. The Council must always exercise prudence. Perhaps a more stringent oversight committee, dedicated to monitoring the arboretum's expansion and its potential impact on Havenridge's infrastructure and social stability, would be prudent. We could assign specific Council members to liaise directly with Councilwoman Mara and Councilman Eli, to ensure that all developments remain within acceptable parameters and that any emergent issues are addressed promptly and decisively."

Silas adjusted his posture. "Such a committee would, of course, require resources. Time, personnel, access to data. It would add to the administrative burden, but the justification, given the scale of the proposed changes, is undeniable. We would need clear protocols for reporting, for escalation of issues, and for... intervention, should the need arise."

Thorne's gaze swept across the other Council members, gauging their reactions. Most seemed to echo his sentiment, a quiet unease rippling through the chamber. The arboretum's success was undeniable, but its newfound dynamism felt like a stray current in the carefully regulated flow of Havenridge life.

"This is not about stifling innovation," Thorne declared, his voice regaining its measured cadence. "It is about responsible stewardship. The arboretum, under Councilwoman Mara, has exceeded expectations in its current capacity. The desire to expand, to introduce new life, is understandable. But we must ensure that this expansion does not come at the expense of our hard-won stability. The Council needs to be assured that these advancements are not introducing unforeseen risks that could jeopardize our long-term survival. We need to understand the full scope of these new technologies, the potential failure points, and the contingency plans in place. 'Self-healing polymers' sound reassuring, but what happens when the healing mechanism fails? What are the consequences of an unchecked microbial bloom? These are questions that require definitive answers, not optimistic projections."

He looked back at the projection, his gaze lingering on the vibrant green canopy that seemed to reach towards the chamber's sterile ceiling. "Councilwoman Mara and Councilman Eli are dedicated, I do not doubt it. But dedication without absolute adherence to the principles that have kept us safe can be a dangerous thing. We must proceed with caution. The Council will require detailed reports, ongoing data streams, and perhaps even periodic on-site inspections to ensure that these 'seeds of progress' do not become 'seeds of doubt' that threaten the very foundations of our civilization."

Anya added, "We will also need to understand the ethical considerations, Elder Thorne. As we introduce new life forms, and potentially new ecosystems, we must consider their intrinsic value, their place within the larger framework of Havenridge's purpose. While efficiency is paramount, we cannot afford to become purely utilitarian in our approach to life itself. There is a delicate balance to be struck between pragmatic necessity and a broader respect for the diversity of existence, even within our controlled environment."

Thorne acknowledged her point with a curt nod. "Indeed. But that respect must not supersede our primary mandate: survival. The Council will convene again in one cycle to review the proposed oversight committee structure and to receive a more comprehensive risk assessment from the relevant departments. Until then, Councilwoman Mara and Councilman Eli will be made aware that their ambitious endeavors are now under closer scrutiny. The future of the arboretum, and indeed, the very definition of growth within Havenridge, will be carefully considered. We will not allow the pursuit of novelty to blind us to the enduring value of order and stability." The hum of the Council chamber, usually a subtle undertone, seemed to deepen, carrying the weight of unspoken concerns and the quiet rustle of emerging apprehension.

The sterile hum of Havenridge, a constant, almost imperceptible thrum of life support and environmental control, had long been the defining soundtrack to existence. It was the sound of survival, of meticulously engineered order, a lullaby sung by a civilization that had learned to fear the silence that followed chaos. Yet, in the periphery of this controlled symphony, subtler melodies began to emerge, quiet arpeggios of individuality played on instruments long thought to be solely for utilitarian purposes. Eli's quiet revolution wasn't one of grand pronouncements or overt defiance; it was a gentle unfolding, like the slow, deliberate unfurling of a new leaf in the arboretum.

It started small, almost imperceptibly. Anya, a meticulous archivist whose life had been dedicated to the precise categorization of historical data, found herself lingering in the communal hydroponic gardens after her designated work cycles. She wasn't observing the nutrient levels or calibrating the light spectrum; she was watching the way the sunlight, filtered through the canopy of the arboretum's newly introduced bioluminescent flora, dappled the worn metal of the cultivation beds. One cycle, without conscious thought, she picked up a discarded sliver of nutrient-rich algae paste and began to sketch a pattern on the smooth, grey surface of a planter. It wasn't a schematic, or a data point. It was a spiral, reminiscent of the unfurling fronds of a fern she'd seen in one of Eli's less-documented excursions. A young technician, tasked with nutrient delivery, paused, his usual hurried gait slowing. He didn't report it as an anomaly, a deviation from protocol. Instead, he found himself humming a tune, a fragmented melody he'd overheard Eli whistling near the outer cultivation domes. He even added a swirl of vibrant blue algae paste to the edge of Anya's spiral, a subtle, unplanned collaboration.

Across the residential sectors, the communal dining halls, once models of efficient, silent consumption, began to see minor shifts. Instead of the usual staggered entry and departure, small groups started to linger, sharing their replicated nutrient paste and discussing not just work quotas or energy efficiency, but the strange beauty of the new 'sunpetal' flowers that bloomed in Sector Gamma, their petals shifting through a spectrum of hues. A discussion started, a tentative exploration of why these flowers evoked such a feeling of... warmth. It was a concept alien to Havenridge, where 'warmth' was a regulated environmental setting, not an emotional resonance. A maintenance worker, Jarek, whose hands were calloused from years of repairing conduits, brought a small, intricately carved piece of recycled plasti-steel to the table. He'd spent his off-cycle hours shaping it, inspired by the organic, flowing lines of the new bioluminescent fungi Eli had introduced into the lower levels. He'd never considered himself artistic, but Eli's relentless pursuit of life, of beauty in unexpected places, had chipped away at his ingrained pragmatism. He spoke hesitantly about the texture, the way light caught the carved ridges, and for the first time, his colleagues saw not just a worker, but a creator.

The children, too, were not immune. The mandated learning modules, designed for maximum knowledge assimilation with minimal emotional engagement, began to feel... insufficient. In one creche, a small group of youngsters, instead of assembling the standard geometric building blocks, started arranging them to mimic the branching patterns of the sky-vine Eli had so carefully cultivated. They weren't building structures for shelter or utility; they were building representations of life. Their instructor, a woman named Lena who had always prided herself on her adherence to curriculum, found herself improvising, guiding their play, asking them *why* they chose to arrange the blocks that way, encouraging their nascent imaginations to bloom beyond the confines of pre-programmed learning. She even found herself sharing a story Eli had told her, a fable about a tiny seed that yearned for the sky, a story that had no practical application but resonated deeply with the children's budding curiosity.

Eli, with his quiet demeanor and his almost reverent approach to the natural world, had become a silent catalyst. He never preached, never exhorted. His influence was in his actions, in the way he spoke to the plants as if they were sentient beings, in the meticulous care he gave to even the smallest microbial culture, in his unwavering belief that life, in all its forms, possessed an intrinsic value beyond its utility. He saw the arboretum not just as a food source, but as a testament to resilience, a vibrant ecosystem that was slowly, surely, reclaiming a piece of a broken world. He saw the potential for life to not just survive, but to *thrive*, to find beauty and purpose even in the most desolate of circumstances. This was the seed he planted, not in the soil of the arboretum, but in the hearts and minds of Havenridge's inhabitants.

The Council, of course, noticed. They had sensors for everything: atmospheric composition, energy consumption, population movement, even vocal stress levels. They could detect the subtle shifts in the communal nutrient paste consumption, the slight increase in non-essential fabrication materials, the infinitesimal deviations from scheduled routines. Elder Thorne, his gaze perpetually fixed on the monitors that displayed Havenridge's vital signs, felt a prickle of unease. He saw the data, fragmented and anonymized as it was, hinting at a growing decentralization of thought, a subtle erosion of the absolute conformity that had been the bedrock of their survival.

"The deviations are minor, Elder Anya," Thorne stated, his voice smooth but laced with a deep-seated concern. "A few extra minutes spent in communal areas, a slight increase in artisanal fabrication materials – that self-taught technician, Jarek, has been requisitioning more plasti-steel than his allocation suggests. And Councilwoman Mara's arboretum reports indicate a higher-than-anticipated energy draw in Sector

Gamma, attributed to 'aesthetic illumination enhancements'." He paused, letting the implications settle. "Aesthetic. It's a word that has no place in our lexicon of survival."

Anya, ever the pragmatist, reviewed the data streams. "The energy expenditure for the illumination is indeed higher, Thorne. However, the data also shows a corresponding decrease in the use of mood-regulating atmospheric supplements in that sector. It suggests a... self-generated sense of well-being, perhaps triggered by the visual stimuli. As for Jarek, his fabrication output on essential maintenance components has not decreased. His additional projects appear to be... personal. Non-disruptive, but... outside of his designated parameters."

"Non-disruptive *yet*," Thorne countered, his fingers tapping a restless rhythm on the polished surface of the council table. "This isn't about a single technician or a few extra lumens. It's about a pattern. A subtle, insidious shift away from the rigid logic that has kept us alive. Look at the creche reports. Lena, usually so by-the-book, is engaging the children in what is being logged as 'imaginative play' rather than directed learning. And the communal dining halls... the average dwell time has increased by nearly five percent. They are... socializing. Sharing. Not about resource optimization, but about... what? The color of a flower?"

Silas, the head of resource allocation, chimed in, his brow furrowed. "The increase in plasti-steel requisition by Jarek is an issue, albeit a minor one. My department has flagged it, but it doesn't impact critical supplies. What *is* concerning is the anecdotal evidence I've received from sector supervisors. They report a decline in... urgency. A softening of the drive for absolute efficiency. People are taking longer breaks, engaging in conversations that have no discernible purpose. It's a trickle, Thorne, but if it continues, it could become a flood."

"And Councilman Eli," Thorne continued, his gaze hardening as he looked at a holographic feed of Eli tending to a delicate, bioluminescent moss, his face a picture of serene concentration. "He is the nucleus of this... divergence. His philosophy, his insistence on the 'intrinsic value of life,' is permeating the lower sectors. He speaks of living, not just surviving, to his technicians, to the botanists, even to the children who visit the arboretum. It's a dangerous notion, Anya. Survival is our mandate. Anything that deviates from that singular focus is a threat."

Anya adjusted her optical implants, her expression thoughtful. "He speaks of life's inherent worth, Thorne, but not at the expense of survival. The arboretum's increased yield, the improved air quality in the sectors where these 'aesthetic enhancements' are present... these are tangible benefits. And the children's engagement... their cognitive development scores haven't decreased; in some cases, they've even shown a slight improvement in creative problem-solving. Perhaps Eli's perspective, while unconventional, isn't entirely detrimental."

"Unconventional is a polite word for it, Anya," Thorne retorted, his voice tight. "It's a deviation from the established order. Havenridge was built on the principle of absolute control, of predictable outcomes. This... this burgeoning individuality, this pursuit of... beauty for its own sake... it introduces variables. And variables, as we learned during the Collapse, are the harbingers of chaos. This isn't merely about personal expression; it's about the potential unraveling of the social fabric we've so carefully woven. What happens when this 'living' philosophy leads people to question directives? To prioritize personal fulfillment over collective necessity?"

He gestured towards a magnified image of Jarek's carved plasti-steel creation, a delicate, abstract bird-like form. "This object. It serves no function. It consumes resources. It takes a skilled technician away from vital maintenance tasks for... what? A fleeting sense of accomplishment? A connection to a lost artistic past? This is not what Havenridge was designed for."

"But it doesn't *harm* Havenridge, Thorne," Anya insisted, her voice calm but firm. "Jarek is still meeting his quotas. His work is exemplary. His... hobby... seems to be a stress-relief mechanism, something that contributes to his overall well-being, which in turn, can improve his performance. And the children... their 'imaginative play' is leading to a deeper understanding of spatial relationships and abstract thought. These are skills that could prove valuable in unforeseen ways."

"Or they could lead to complacency," Thorne countered, his gaze unwavering. "To a generation that values individual whim over the collective good. We have spent centuries instilling the discipline required for survival. Every action, every thought, has been geared towards efficiency and adherence. To allow these... seeds of dissent to sprout, even in the most benign forms, is to risk the very foundation of our civilization. Eli's influence is spreading like a benign infection, Anya. It's charming, it's alluring, but it's a threat to the sterile, predictable order that is our only safeguard."

He leaned forward, his voice dropping to a near whisper, yet carrying the weight of absolute authority. "We need to reinforce the protocols. Remind personnel of the absolute necessity of adhering to designated tasks and schedules. Councilwoman Mara's arboretum project, while providing essential sustenance, must remain strictly within its operational parameters. No more 'aesthetic enhancements,' no more unauthorized atmospheric adjustments. And Councilman Eli... his role is vital, but his extracurricular philosophies need to be... curtailed. We cannot afford to have the very architects of our survival subtly undermining the principles that have kept us alive."

Anya sighed softly, the sound almost lost in the hum of the chamber. "I understand your concerns, Elder Thorne. The Council's primary duty is to ensure the continued survival of Havenridge. But I also believe that true resilience lies not just in rigid adherence, but in adaptability. Perhaps there is a way to integrate some of these... new perspectives... without compromising our core principles. Eli's approach to fostering life has demonstrably improved the arboretum's productivity and ecological balance. And the sense of well-being he seems to inspire in others... that is a resource, too, Thorne. A human resource that we have long neglected in our pursuit of pure efficiency."

Thorne shook his head, his expression one of grim determination. "Well-being is a luxury we can only afford once survival is guaranteed, Anya. And survival, in this fragile world, is a constant, precarious battle. We cannot afford to be distracted by the ephemeral allure of individuality. The order, the discipline, the unwavering focus on function – these are our weapons. Any force that erodes them, no matter how well-intentioned, is an enemy. We will monitor this trend. We will issue directives. And if necessary, we will implement stricter controls. The arboretum is a tool, nothing more. And tools are to be used, not admired for their inherent beauty." His gaze drifted towards the live feed of Eli, a faint frown creasing his brow. "Councilman Eli's influence, while subtle, is measurable. And it is spreading. We will not allow it to compromise the integrity of Havenridge." The weight of his words hung in the air, a silent promise of increased scrutiny, a quiet assertion of control over the burgeoning sparks of individuality that threatened to disrupt the carefully orchestrated hum of their existence. The seeds Eli had sown were beginning to sprout, and the Council, vigilant as ever, was already preparing to weed them out.

Mara stood at the edge of the hydroponic bay, the cool, recycled air carrying the faint, earthy scent of growth. Elder Thorne's words, sharp and unyielding, echoed in her mind, a familiar refrain of caution and control. *"Survival is our mandate. Anything that deviates from that singular focus is a threat."* He saw Eli's influence as a virus, a threat to the sterile, predictable order that had been Havenridge's shield against the chaos of the outside world. But as Mara's gaze swept over the vibrant greens and subtle bioluminescence, she couldn't shake the feeling that Thorne was looking at the wrong thing entirely. He saw deviations, potential weaknesses; she saw... resilience.

Her own position within Havenridge was one of careful balance. As a Council member, she was entrusted with the oversight of vital resource allocation, a role that demanded a sharp, analytical mind and an unwavering adherence to established protocols. She had always prided herself on her pragmatism, her ability to see the most efficient path, the most logical solution. Her world was one of data streams, resource projections, and risk assessments. Yet, Eli's arboretum, her own domain, was slowly, subtly, rewriting her understanding of those very principles. Thorne viewed it as a utilitarian necessity, a biological engine for sustenance. But Mara had witnessed its transformation firsthand, from a strictly functional cultivation bay into something... more.

She remembered the early days, the stark efficiency, the rows of nutrient-rich algae and protein synthesizers. It had been a testament to their ingenuity, a triumph of engineering over scarcity. But Eli had arrived, not with grand pronouncements or demands for change, but with a quiet reverence for the life he cultivated. He spoke to the plants, not as data points or production units, but as living entities. He introduced new species, not for increased yield, but for their unique properties, their delicate beauty, their intricate symbiotic relationships. He'd nurtured the bioluminescent flora, initially dismissed as frivolous energy expenditure, into a network of soft, ambient light that transformed the very atmosphere of the sector. And the reports Thorne cited, the ones detailing increased energy draw for "aesthetic illumination enhancements," were the very same reports that noted a simultaneous decrease in the use of mood-regulating atmospheric supplements. People weren't seeking artificial happiness; they were finding it in the gentle glow of the petal-like fungi, in the soft pulse of the glowing mosses that Eli had cultivated in the lower access tunnels.

Mara walked deeper into the bay, the air growing warmer, more humid. She stopped beside a cluster of 'sunpetal' flowers, their petals shifting through a mesmerizing spectrum of soft blues and purples. A small group of children, their laughter like a chime in the controlled environment, were gathered nearby, sketching the flowers in worn synth-pads. Their instructor, Lena, usually so focused on rote memorization and logic puzzles, was kneeling beside them, her expression one of gentle encouragement. She wasn't correcting their drawings; she was asking them about the colors, about how the flowers made them *feel*. Mara remembered her own childhood, a sterile regimen of learning modules designed to forge efficient workers, not curious individuals. These children, bathed in the soft light of the arboretum, were learning something beyond mere facts. They were learning to observe, to appreciate, to connect.

The evidence was irrefutable, even to her own rigorously trained mind. Eli's approach, his belief in the inherent value of life and the power of adaptation, wasn't a threat; it was a vital component of a more robust form of survival. Thorne spoke of variables, of chaos. But Mara saw these "variables" as the very adaptability that allowed life to persist and evolve. The rigid, unchanging system Thorne championed was, in itself, a form of stagnation, a vulnerability. It was like a meticulously maintained machine, perfectly calibrated for a single, predictable environment, but utterly incapable of responding to unforeseen changes. Eli, on the other hand, was cultivating an ecosystem, a dynamic, interconnected web that could bend, adapt, and even thrive in the face of disruption.

She recalled a conversation with Jarek, the technician Thorne had singled out. He'd been painstakingly sanding a piece of recycled plasti-steel, his brow furrowed in concentration. Mara had initially approached him with a query about fabrication quotas, expecting the usual direct, efficient response. Instead, she found him lost in the creation of a small, intricate sculpture – a delicate, almost impossibly fragile bird. He'd explained, his voice hesitant at first, how the repetitive motion of sanding and shaping helped him process the stresses of his work, how the act of creation, of bringing something beautiful into existence from discarded material, offered him a sense of purpose beyond his daily tasks. He hadn't been neglecting his duties; he'd found a way to integrate his need for creative expression into his life, a way to maintain his own internal equilibrium. This, Mara realized, was not a deviation; it was a human need, one that Havenridge, in its relentless pursuit of efficiency, had systematically suppressed.

Thorne's fear stemmed from a place of trauma, a deeply ingrained memory of the Collapse, of the catastrophic consequences of unchecked variables. His worldview was a fortress, built brick by painstaking brick from the ruins of the past, designed to keep the world out and chaos at bay. But Mara was beginning to understand that the world wasn't something to be kept out. It was something to be understood, to be integrated with, to learn from. Eli's philosophy was not about abandoning the lessons of the past, but about building upon them, about recognizing that true strength lay not in rigid control, but in fluid adaptability.

Her loyalty to Havenridge's principles was deeply ingrained, a core tenet of her identity. She believed in order, in structure, in the collective good. But what was the collective good if it meant suppressing the very aspects of humanity that allowed individuals to thrive? What was survival if it came at the cost of one's soul? Eli's unwavering faith in the inherent goodness of life, his conviction that allowing life to flourish, in all its messy, unpredictable glory, was the most potent form of resilience, resonated with a part of her that had long been dormant.

It challenged the foundations of her carefully constructed worldview, forcing her to confront the limitations of her own rigid thinking.

She observed the interactions between Eli and his team – the botanists, the technicians, even the maintenance crew who now often sought him out with questions or simply to share a moment of quiet observation. There was a palpable sense of camaraderie, a shared purpose that transcended mere job functions. They weren't just following orders; they were invested, engaged, their work infused with a sense of meaning. Eli fostered this by treating them not as interchangeable components of a larger machine, but as individuals with unique perspectives and contributions. He listened to their ideas, no matter how unconventional, and encouraged them to see the larger picture, the interconnectedness of their efforts. He had, in essence, built a community, not just a workforce.

Mara found herself questioning her own role, her own allegiances. Thorne saw her as a pragmatic pillar of the Council, a reliable voice of reason. But what if reason, in its purest form, was insufficient? What if it lacked the crucial element of empathy, of understanding the human need for connection and meaning? Her place within the community's rigid hierarchy felt suddenly precarious, as if the ground beneath her feet was shifting. She was a guardian of the established order, yet she was witnessing, firsthand, the limitations of that order.

She approached Eli, who was meticulously tending to a delicate vine that spiraled up a support structure, its leaves shimmering with a soft, internal light. He looked up, his eyes, the color of deep earth, holding a gentle curiosity.

"Councilwoman Mara," he said, his voice calm and even. "I hope your visit to the arboretum is proving... illuminating."

Mara managed a small smile. "It always is, Eli. Elder Thorne believes your approach is... unorthodox."

Eli chuckled softly, a sound that was more like the rustling of leaves than a human laugh. "Unorthodox is simply a label for what is not yet understood, or perhaps, what is inconvenient for those who prefer the familiar. The arboretum thrives because it is allowed to be itself. It adapts. It seeks out the light, it draws sustenance from the soil, it forms symbiotic relationships with the microorganisms that inhabit it. It is not a machine, Councilwoman. It is a living entity, and it requires a different kind of stewardship."

He gestured to the sunpetal flowers. "These blooms, dismissed as frivolous, are now a significant source of serotonin production in the nearby residential sectors. The energy expenditure for their illumination is offset by a reduction in the need for mood regulators, which themselves require energy and resources to produce and distribute. The data, I believe, supports the efficacy of this... unconventional approach."

Mara nodded, her gaze sweeping over the vibrant display. "Thorne sees only the energy expenditure, Eli. He fears the unpredictability."

"And yet," Eli countered, his gaze meeting hers directly, "is not unpredictability the very essence of life? Did we not survive the Collapse not by clinging to rigid plans, but by adapting, by innovating, by finding new ways to live when the old ones failed? The greatest strength of Havenridge is not its sterile order, but its inherent capacity for life. And life, by its nature, is adaptable. It finds a way."

He ran a gentle finger along the smooth surface of a bioluminescent fungus clinging to a nearby support beam, its soft glow pulsing rhythmically. "This fungus, for example. It breaks down certain waste products that would otherwise require energy-intensive processing. It also releases a natural airborne purifier. Its introduction was not about aesthetics, but about creating a more efficient, a more sustainable, internal ecosystem. The beauty is a fortunate byproduct."

Mara found herself wanting to believe him, wanting to embrace the hope he offered. He spoke of resilience not as a shield against external threats, but as an internal strength, a capacity for growth and adaptation. He saw the individual sparks of creativity, the small acts of defiance against the tide of conformity, not as a threat, but as evidence of a vibrant, irrepressible spirit that was essential for their long-term survival. Her loyalty to Havenridge was absolute, but her understanding of what that loyalty truly entailed was beginning to shift. Perhaps protecting Havenridge meant not just preserving its structure, but nurturing its soul, allowing the seeds of life and individuality to bloom, even if it meant embracing a little more of the unpredictable, a little more of the beauty that Thorne so readily dismissed. The evidence of her own eyes, the quiet hum of well-being emanating from this vibrant sanctuary, was a powerful counterpoint to Thorne's rigid pronouncements. Her allegiance, once so firmly rooted in the sterile soil of protocol, was beginning to lean towards the fertile ground where life, in all its glorious unpredictability, was allowed to flourish. She was a guardian of Havenridge, yes, but perhaps, she was also becoming a guardian of its nascent, budding soul.

The air in Elder Thorne's study was always a few degrees cooler than the rest of Havenridge, a deliberate choice, Mara suspected, to evoke a sense of sterile efficiency. The polished chrome surfaces of his desk gleamed under the cool, recessed lighting, reflecting the stark lines of the room. Thorne himself sat behind it, a figure of unyielding discipline, his gaze fixed on Mara as she entered. There was no preamble, no polite inquiry about her well-being; his approach was always direct, like the sharp edge of a well-honed tool.

"Councilwoman Mara," Thorne began, his voice a low rumble that seemed to vibrate with an unspoken intensity. "I have been observing your recent... engagements. Specifically, your increasing proximity to the arboretum and its architect, Eli."

He paused, letting the implication settle. "And the data streams associated with your oversight have become... irregular."

Mara felt a familiar tightness in her chest, the subtle constriction that Thorne's scrutinizing gaze always invoked. She had anticipated this, of course. Her visits to the arboretum were no longer clandestine, and Eli's quiet subversions of the established order were becoming increasingly difficult to mask. She stood straighter, meeting his gaze with a practiced composure. "Elder Thorne, my oversight of resource allocation for the arboretum falls within my Council duties. The project is, after all, a vital component of Havenridge's sustainability."

Thorne's lips thinned. "Vital, yes. But its current trajectory is far from sustainable in the terms we understand. Eli's methods introduce variables. Unforeseen... divergences. You, of all people, understand the importance of predictability. The sacrifices we made to establish this haven were predicated on control, on the eradication of the very chaos that threatened to consume us." He leaned forward, his hands clasped on the desk, the knuckles stark white. "We built Havenridge from the ashes of a world that embraced every passing whim, every untested notion. We learned, at a terrible cost, that survival demands unwavering adherence to proven principles, not a flirtation with the unknown."

He gestured to a muted display screen on his desk, which flickered to life, showing a complex network of interconnected lines and data points. "This represents our resource grid. Stable, efficient, predictable. Every kilowatt, every liter of recycled water, accounted for. Then there is *this*," he tapped a different section of the screen, where the lines were more erratic, interspersed with bursts of vibrant color and seemingly random fluctuations. "The arboretum. Or rather, Eli's garden. The energy spikes for 'aesthetic illumination,' the 'experimental nutrient blends' that defy standard composition, the increased biological diversity that strains our containment protocols. These are not signs of progress, Councilwoman. They are symptoms of instability."

Mara took a steadying breath. "Elder Thorne, the 'aesthetic illumination,' as you call it, has demonstrably reduced the need for mood-regulating supplements. The increased biological diversity fosters a more resilient ecosystem within the bay, one that is proving more effective at waste reclamation and air purification than our purely mechanical systems. Eli's 'untested ideas' are yielding tangible, beneficial results."

"Tangible, perhaps, in the short term," Thorne conceded, his tone dry as dust. "But at what risk? You speak of reduced dependency on artificial mood regulators. I see a populace becoming accustomed to frivolous comforts, their emotional resilience eroded by these... bioluminescent distractions. You speak of a 'resilient ecosystem.' I see a breeding ground for unknown pathogens, a potential vector for contamination. We escaped the blight, Councilwoman. We built walls against the wild, untamed world. Are you suggesting we now invite its chaos back in, disguised as 'beauty' and 'adaptation'?"

He stood, moving from behind his desk to the large viewport that offered a panoramic view of Havenridge's central hub. The ordered, functional architecture stretched out below them, a testament to meticulous planning. "Every single structure, every ration pack, every breath of recycled air in this sanctuary was hard-won. It was forged in the fires of necessity, paid for with the currency of unimaginable loss. And you, Mara, as a member of the Council, are sworn to protect that legacy. Not to gamble with it."

He turned back to her, his eyes sharp and unwavering. "Eli's influence is seductive. He speaks of life, of growth, of inherent value. These are fine words, but they are dangerous in the context of our reality. Our reality is survival. Our mandate is security. Deviation from the established path, any deviation that introduces uncertainty, is a threat. And I am telling you, Mara, that Eli's vision, however well-intentioned, is leading us down a path of unacceptable risk. His charm, his 'unorthodox' approach – it's a siren song, luring us back to the very rocks upon which the old world shattered."

Thorne's words hung in the air, heavy with the weight of his conviction. He wasn't just expressing an opinion; he was issuing a directive, cloaked in the language of warning. He saw Eli's work not as innovation, but as a betrayal of the principles that had allowed them to endure. He saw Mara's engagement with it as a lapse in her duty, a dangerous susceptibility to sentimentality.

"The Council has always prioritized pragmatism over poetry, Mara," Thorne continued, his voice regaining a measure of its former coolness. "Eli's arboretum, while providing certain biological functions, has become a symbol of... indulgence. Of straying from our core purpose. We are not here to cultivate beauty for its own sake, nor to experiment with life forms that fall outside our carefully controlled parameters. We are here to survive. To ensure that future generations have a safe, stable existence. And that requires vigilance. It requires a commitment to what we know works, not to what might, perhaps, be prettier."

He returned to his desk, his movements precise. "I understand you have a certain... affinity for Eli's project. He has a way of making the intangible seem... vital. But remember, Councilwoman, that the foundations of Havenridge were not laid with sentiment. They were laid with necessity, with grim determination, with the understanding that sentimentality is a luxury we could not afford. The sacrifices made to bring this community into being were immense. To risk that carefully constructed order, to introduce the potential for instability, based on the persuasive arguments of one man who prioritizes aesthetics over security... that is a gamble we cannot take."

Thorne picked up a stylus, tapping it lightly against his desk calendar. "I am not asking for your agreement, Mara. I am informing you of my concerns. Concerns that will be brought before the full Council. Eli's influence is growing, and it is introducing elements of unpredictability that I, and many others, find deeply troubling. This 'resilience' you speak of, this 'adaptation' – it is merely a euphemism for chaos when it is not rigorously controlled. And Eli, by his very nature, seems incapable of the rigorous control we require."

He fixed her with a final, penetrating look. "The path we are on is the only path that guarantees our continued existence. Any deviation, however appealing, however superficially beneficial, is a step towards the abyss. Do not be swayed by the gardener's prose, Councilwoman. Remember the architect's blueprint. Remember the sacrifices. Remember what it took to build this sanctuary. And remember your duty to preserve it." The implicit warning was clear: align yourself with the Council's established order, or be considered part of the deviation. The seeds of doubt Thorne had sown were not merely about Eli's project, but about Mara's own judgment and loyalty.

The cool, sterile air of Elder Thorne's study seemed to cling to Mara, a tangible manifestation of the chilling pronouncements that had just filled the space. His words, precise and delivered with the unyielding logic of a meticulously crafted algorithm, had painted Eli's arboretum not as a vibrant sanctuary of burgeoning life, but as a dangerous anomaly, a crack in the carefully constructed edifice of Havenridge. Thorne saw it as a deviation, a potential vector for the chaos they had so painstakingly escaped. And Mara, by her association with it, her quiet advocacy for its unorthodox methods, was being framed as a deviation herself.

Stepping out of Thorne's imposing domicile and back into the regulated hum of Havenridge's central hub felt like emerging from a deep, cold immersion. The polished duracrete pathways, the uniform, utilitarian architecture, the softly glowing efficiency lights – it was all a testament to the order Thorne championed. This was the world she had sought, the antithesis of the fractured, unpredictable society that had birthed the blight. She had chosen Havenridge for its safety, its predictability, its unwavering commitment to survival through control. And now, the very system she had embraced was presenting her with a choice that felt like a betrayal of that fundamental decision.

The weight of Thorne's words settled upon her shoulders, a physical burden. He had spoken of sacrifices, of unimaginable loss, of the grim determination that had forged their sanctuary. He had reminded her of her sworn duty to protect that legacy. And in his stark pronouncements, he had drawn a clear line: adherence to the proven principles of Havenridge, or a dangerous flirtation with the unknown. Eli, with his talk of growth and adaptation, his belief in the inherent resilience of life, represented that unknown. His vision, Thorne had warned, was a siren song, luring them back to the precipice.

Mara found herself walking, her steps carrying her not towards her usual quarters, but instinctively towards the edge of Havenridge, where the bio-dome of the arboretum shimmered like an alien jewel against the muted palette of the settlement. The regulated atmosphere within Havenridge felt stifling, a cage built of security protocols and unwavering dogma. Outside its immediate perimeter, beyond the carefully monitored environmental seals, lay... something else. And within the arboretum, that 'something else' was being actively cultivated, nurtured, given a voice.

As she approached the arboretum's entrance, the air shifted, growing warmer, richer, perfumed with the earthy scent of damp soil and blooming flora. The familiar, gentle hum of the climate control systems was now overlaid with a subtle chorus of chirps, rustles, and the faint, rhythmic pulse of water circulating through the irrigation network. It was a symphony of life, an organic counterpoint to the sterile silence of Thorne's study.

Eli was there, of course, his hands stained with soil, his brow furrowed in concentration as he tended to a climbing vine that seemed to defy gravity, its tendrils reaching towards the apex of the dome. He looked up as she entered, a flicker of surprise followed by a warm, genuine smile that reached his eyes. It was a smile that held no calculation, no hidden agenda, only a simple joy in the work he was doing.

"Mara," he said, his voice a low, steady cadence that always seemed to soothe her. "I didn't expect you today. Thorne finally cornered you?"

The casual, almost irreverent question, coupled with the genuine concern in his eyes, pricked at the carefully constructed composure Mara had maintained. She nodded, finding it difficult to articulate the turmoil that churned within her. "He... expressed his concerns. About the arboretum. About... you."

Eli wiped his hands on a rough linen cloth, his gaze steady. He didn't flinch, didn't become defensive. He simply waited.

"He sees it as a risk," Mara continued, the words feeling inadequate to convey the depth of Thorne's apprehension. "He believes your methods introduce instability. That your focus on... adaptability... is a dangerous departure from the principles Havenridge was built upon."

Eli leaned against a sturdy wooden trellis, observing her. "And what do *you* believe, Mara? After all our conversations, all the hours you've spent here, observing, learning?"

The question hung in the air, demanding an honest answer. Mara looked around the arboretum, her gaze sweeping over the vibrant, interconnected ecosystem. She saw the bioluminescent mosses casting a soft, ethereal glow, reducing the need for artificial lighting. She saw the insect species, carefully introduced and monitored, diligently pollinating the plants and breaking down organic waste. She saw the carefully managed fungi networks enriching the soil, creating a living, breathing substrate that far surpassed the sterile, inert nutrient blocks of the central settlement.

"I see... potential," she began, choosing her words carefully. "I see a different kind of resilience, Eli. One that doesn't rely on absolute control, but on the ability to adapt. To integrate. To thrive *because* of its complexity, not in spite of it."

Eli's smile widened. "That's what I've been trying to show you. Thorne's world is a fortress, Mara. A testament to the fact that we *can* survive by building walls, by eradicating the unknown. But it's a finite survival. It's a life lived in perpetual defense. This," he gestured around them, "is an attempt at a different kind of survival. One that acknowledges that life, true life, is inherently messy, unpredictable, and yet, incredibly robust. It finds strength in diversity, in interdependency."

He walked over to a small, bubbling pool where iridescent dragonflies flitted. "Thorne fears the unknown pathogens, the potential for contamination. And he's right to be cautious. We *are* dealing with complex biological systems. But we are also learning to understand them, to guide them, to find the balance. Is it a risk? Yes. Every new seed planted is a risk. Every child born is a risk. But stagnation, Mara, is the ultimate risk. To refuse to grow, to refuse to adapt, is to ensure eventual obsolescence."

Mara traced the intricate patterns on a broad, emerald leaf. "The Council... they rely on predictability. On data streams that are clean, unambiguous. Your project... it generates variables. It defies easy categorization."

"Because life defies easy categorization," Eli replied gently. "We're not dealing with inert components; we're dealing with a dynamic, evolving tapestry. Thorne sees the unpredictable fluctuations in energy consumption, the unusual nutrient signatures, as threats. I see them as the pulse of a system working as it should. The bioluminescence isn't just pretty; it's a biological response to energy availability, a way the plants are communicating their needs and optimizing their growth. The nutrient blends aren't 'untested'; they're tailored to specific microbial communities that are, in turn, enhancing nutrient uptake and waste processing."

He picked up a smooth, grey stone from the edge of the pool. "Thorne wants to control every variable, to eliminate all uncertainty. But true resilience isn't about eliminating uncertainty; it's about building the capacity to *respond* to it. It's about having systems that can bend without breaking, that can learn and evolve when faced with unforeseen challenges. That's what this arboretum represents. It's a living laboratory for that kind of resilience."

He held the stone out to her. It was surprisingly warm, radiating a faint heat. "This stone was part of the original geothermal pipe system, dormant for decades. I found it, cleaned it, and placed it here. It's not 'part of the arboretum' in the way a plant is. It doesn't photosynthesize or respire. But it contributes to the thermal regulation of this microclimate, slowly releasing stored heat. It's a small thing, but it's an example of how we can integrate and repurpose, how we can find value in what was once discarded."

Mara turned the stone over in her hands, its warmth seeping into her skin. It was a simple object, yet it held a profound significance. It was a symbol of adaptation, of finding new purpose, of integrating the old with the new. Thorne's argument was rooted in the past, in the fear of repeating past mistakes. But Eli's vision, and the reality of the arboretum, pointed towards a future that was not a mere replication of the past, but a bold, courageous evolution.

"Thorne believes sentimentality is a luxury we cannot afford," Mara murmured, the echo of his words still resonating. "He believes your work is a form of indulgence."Eli met her gaze, his expression serious. "Is it indulgence to seek beauty? Is it indulgence to foster a connection with the living world that sustains us? Is it indulgence to believe that we can be more than just survivors, that we can also be cultivators, creators, integral parts of a thriving ecosystem?" He paused, letting his words sink in. "Thorne is afraid of losing what he has, and I understand that fear. But I believe that by clinging too tightly to the present, by refusing to look beyond the walls, we risk losing the very future we are trying to protect. We risk becoming as brittle as the old world, unable to bend and adapt when the next inevitable storm rolls in."

He walked with her towards a section of the dome where delicate, sapphire-blue flowers bloomed, their petals unfurling in a slow, deliberate rhythm. "The choice you face, Mara, is not just about the arboretum. It's about the kind of future Havenridge will have. Will it be a future of perpetual vigilance, a life lived under the shadow of fear, always defending against the perceived threat of the unknown? Or will it be a future that embraces the complexity of life, that learns to dance with uncertainty, that finds strength in diversity and adaptation?"

Mara looked at the flowers, their fragile beauty a testament to the power of life to persist and flourish. She thought of Thorne's stark, unyielding vision of survival, a survival that felt more like a slow, controlled demise. And she looked at Eli, his hands stained with earth, his eyes filled with a quiet hope, a belief in the possibility of a richer, more vibrant existence.

The weight of choice pressed down on her, not as a burden, but as a responsibility. To continue down Thorne's path was to remain safe, predictable, and ultimately, limited. To embrace Eli's vision, however, meant stepping into uncertainty, challenging the very foundations of Havenridge, and potentially facing the wrath of those who clung to the old ways. It meant trusting not just in logic and data, but in the often-unseen currents of life itself.

"You're asking me to trust what I cannot fully quantify," she said, her voice barely a whisper. "To believe in growth when everything around me tells me to prioritize control."

"I'm asking you to believe in possibility, Mara," Eli replied, his voice soft but firm. "To believe that Havenridge can be more than just a sanctuary. It can be a testament to what humanity can achieve when it learns to live *with* life, not just *apart* from it. The seeds of doubt Thorne planted were about Eli's project, about my methods. But perhaps the real seeds of doubt he planted were in your own heart, about the limitations of the path you chose. And perhaps, those are the seeds that need to be nurtured, to see what they might grow into."

Mara looked at her hands, the same hands that signed resource allocation directives and debated policy with Thorne. They felt capable, but also hesitant. Hesitant to embrace the unknown, yet increasingly unwilling to deny the profound beauty and potential she saw unfolding around her. The choice was no longer simply about Eli's arboretum; it was about her own definition of safety, her own vision for humanity's future. It was the daunting, terrifying, and undeniably hopeful realization that true safety might not lie in the sterile perfection of absolute predictability, but in the courageous embrace of life's inherent, beautiful, and boundless capacity for change. The weight of that choice was immense, but for the first time, it felt less like a burden and more like the fertile ground from which something new, something vital, could finally begin to grow.

CHAPTER TEN

Facing the Storm

The hum of Havenridge, usually a comforting lullaby of controlled existence, began to fray at the edges. It started subtly, a discordant note in the symphony of efficiency. A low growl that vibrated not just through the duracrete pathways but through the very bones of the settlement. Mara, still reeling from the pronouncements of Elder Thorne and the quiet revolution brewing within Eli's arboretum, felt the shift acutely. It was a primal disturbance, a raw power that the meticulously engineered environment of Havenridge seemed ill-equipped to absorb.

She had been halfway between the arboretum and her quarters, her mind still a battlefield of conflicting loyalties and burgeoning hopes, when the first true gust of wind tore through the central plaza. It wasn't the gentle breeze that occasionally wafted through the filtered air vents; this was a violent exhalation, a celestial rage that slammed against the transparent dome overhead. Dust, fine and insidious, swirled upwards, defying the sophisticated atmospheric regulators.

The soft glow of the efficiency lights flickered, momentarily plunging sections of the plaza into an unsettling dimness.

Panic, a sensation Havenridge had largely purged from its collective consciousness, began to manifest as a ripple of unease. Residents paused in their routines, their faces, usually placid and composed, now etched with a dawning apprehension. Children, their games momentarily forgotten, clutched at their parents' tunics, their wide eyes reflecting the agitated dance of the lights. The controlled order was being challenged, not by any internal dissent or ideological debate, but by an elemental fury that cared nothing for algorithms or protocols.

The low growl intensified, morphing into a sustained roar. The dome, designed to withstand atmospheric fluctuations and minor debris, groaned under the relentless assault. It was a sound that spoke of immense pressure, of forces far exceeding its engineered limits. Mara instinctively looked up, her gaze tracing the impossibly strong yet undeniably strained seams of the dome. She saw faint, almost imperceptible shimmers where the reinforced polymers were being pushed to their absolute breaking point. This was not a minor inconvenience; this was a direct threat to the very structure that sheltered them.

Then came the rain. Not the gentle, measured hydration cycles that nourished Havenridge's hydroponic farms, but a deluge. It struck the dome with the percussive force of a thousand tiny hammers, each drop a miniature missile. Water began to stream down the interior surfaces, blurring the already distorted view of the outside world. Worse, the intricate drainage systems, designed for predictable precipitation, were overwhelmed. Rivulets formed, then streams, snaking across pathways, pooling in depressions, threatening to inundate vital infrastructure. The controlled environment was rapidly devolving into chaos.

Eli emerged from the arboretum, his usual calm replaced by a focused intensity. His hands, still bearing the faint scent of damp earth and chlorophyll, were clenched at his sides. He had been preparing for a different kind of storm, one of adaptation and growth, not this sudden, violent onslaught. "Mara," he called out, his voice barely audible above the din, "The moisture levels in the arboretum are spiking. The systems are struggling to compensate. Some of the more delicate flora... they're not accustomed to this level of humidity."

Mara nodded, her own anxieties mirroring his. Thorne's words echoed in her mind: "Sacrifices will be necessary." Had she dismissed them too readily? Had the pursuit of controlled perfection blinded her to the possibility of a more primal, unpredictable threat? The arboretum, with its emphasis on natural processes and interconnectedness, was perhaps more vulnerable to such raw elemental forces than the sterile, hardened shell of Havenridge proper.

As if on cue, a particularly violent gust buffeted the dome, causing the lights to flicker wildly and a distant alarm to blare. It was a low, urgent tone, different from the usual efficiency alerts. This was a security breach, a structural integrity warning. A section of the dome, further out from the central habitation zones, began to sag inward. It was a horrifying sight, a visible manifestation of their vulnerability. The carefully constructed walls that had promised eternal safety were proving to be fragile in the face of nature's raw power.

"The outer perimeter dome," Eli said, his voice tight with concern. "Sector Gamma. It's... it's not holding."

Mara felt a cold dread seep into her. Sector Gamma. That was where Thorne had his primary atmospheric processing units, the heart of Havenridge's climate control. If that section failed, the very air they breathed would be compromised. The storm wasn't just battering their shelter; it was threatening to dismantle it piece by piece, starting with its most critical components.

The orderly flow of residents into designated safe zones turned into a desperate scramble. The calm, measured movements were replaced by a surge of fear. People who had never known true hardship, who had been raised in the predictable embrace of Havenridge, were now confronted with a reality that defied all their programming. The carefully curated narrative of absolute safety was shattering around them.

Mara found herself drawn back towards the arboretum, an instinct she couldn't explain. While the main dome groaned, the arboretum's smaller, more specialized structure seemed to be weathering the initial onslaught with a surprising degree of resilience. Its unique construction, a blend of reinforced polymers and bio-integrated materials, seemed to absorb some of the wind's fury rather than simply resist it. Eli, a flicker of grim determination in his eyes, was already working with his small team, his movements precise and urgent.

"The primary irrigation lines are under immense pressure," Eli explained, his voice strained as he adjusted a valve. "The storm runoff is far exceeding capacity. If we don't reroute, we risk rupturing the main conduits. That would flood the lower levels, and worse, it could destabilize the entire nutrient reservoir system."

Mara watched him, a new appreciation dawning for the meticulous, often overlooked work that went into maintaining this "anomaly." Thorne saw it as a drain, a risky experiment. But here, in the face of a crisis that threatened to overwhelm Havenridge's robust, but ultimately rigid, infrastructure, Eli's systems were proving remarkably adaptable. The arboretum's intricate network of interconnected pipes, sensors, and bio-filters, designed for a delicate balance, was now working overtime to manage an overwhelming influx.

"The auxiliary pumps are failing," one of Eli's assistants called out, his voice tinged with panic. "The surge is too great. They're overheating."

Eli didn't hesitate. "Mara, I need you to access the central environmental controls. Override the standard protocols for Sector Gamma's drainage. Divert everything – I mean *everything* – to the overflow reservoirs. It's designed for excess, but it can handle more if we force it. And see if you can isolate the failing pumps from the main grid. We don't want a cascade failure."

The request was fraught with peril. Accessing central controls, especially overriding protocols for a compromised sector, required clearance that was typically only held by Thorne and his inner circle. But Eli's urgency was palpable, and Mara knew he wouldn't ask if it wasn't critical. Steeling herself, she nodded. "I'll try. But Thorne will know."

"Let him," Eli said, his gaze locked on a monitor displaying rapidly fluctuating water levels. "Survival isn't about protocol right now, Mara. It's about adaptation."

The journey back to the central hub was treacherous. The corridors, usually brightly lit and bustling, were now dimly lit by emergency lighting, casting long, dancing shadows. Water seeped from ceiling panels and pooled around alcoves. The air was thick with the scent of ozone from sparking conduits and the damp, earthy smell that had begun to permeate even the sterile heart of Havenridge. The storm's fury was not confined to the dome; it was seeping into the very marrow of their sanctuary.

She reached the control nexus, a sterile room usually humming with the silent activity of technicians. Now, it was eerily quiet, save for the klaxons and the disembodied voice of the automated system issuing increasingly dire warnings. She found the console

Thorne often used, her fingers hovering over the interface. Her training had been rigorous, but this was beyond anything she had encountered in simulations. The storm was an uncharted variable.

With trembling fingers, she began to input the commands, her heart pounding against her ribs. The system resisted at first, red error messages flashing across the screen. Thorne's security protocols were formidable. But Eli had taught her about finding the seams, about understanding the underlying logic, about coaxing rather than demanding. She remembered his lessons about bio-feedback loops, about the interconnectedness of systems, and she began to apply those principles to the digital architecture.

"Accessing tertiary overflow protocols," she murmured, her voice a low chant against the storm's roar. "Diverting Sector Gamma excess flow to Reservoir Delta. Isolating pump units G-7 through G-12 from main grid. Engaging emergency coolant flush for auxiliary systems."

Each command was a gamble. The system was designed for equilibrium, for predictable inputs. She was forcing it into a state of controlled disarray, hoping to buy them time. The screen flickered, and a hesitant green confirmation appeared. It was working. A small victory, but in the face of the overwhelming chaos, it felt monumental.

She felt a surge of adrenaline, a clarity born of necessity. Thorne's fear of the unknown, his rigid adherence to control

– it was precisely what made Havenridge so vulnerable to an *unforeseen* crisis like this. His systems were designed to prevent deviation, not to manage it. Eli's arboretum, chaotic and unpredictable as it seemed, was built on the very principles of resilience and adaptation that were now desperately needed.

As she worked, a new alarm shrieked, more piercing than the others. "Structural integrity compromised. Outer dome breach detected. Sector Gamma emergency containment protocols initiated." A holographic map of Havenridge appeared on the main display, a section in Sector Gamma flashing a violent crimson. The containment field, a last resort, was struggling against the sheer force of the wind and rain.

Mara's blood ran cold. Containment meant sealing off the damaged sector, cutting it off entirely, including any personnel who might have been stationed there. It was a grim confirmation of Thorne's earlier pronouncements about sacrifices.

She had to tell Eli. The fate of his arboretum, his vision of a more adaptable future, was now inextricably linked to the survival of Havenridge itself. The storm had become a crucible, forging a new reality, and Mara found herself at its heart, no longer a passive observer, but an active participant in the desperate fight for survival. The carefully constructed order of Havenridge had been shattered, and in its place, a raw, terrifying, and perhaps, ultimately, hopeful fight for existence had begun. The resilience Thorne preached was about enduring the predictable; the resilience Eli championed was about evolving through the unpredictable. And the storm, in its terrible, magnificent fury, was forcing Havenridge to learn the latter, or risk perishing. The integrity of the dome was not just a structural concern; it was a metaphor for the integrity of their entire way of life. And that integrity was now being tested as never before. The wind howled like a banshee, and the rain hammered down, each drop a reminder that their sanctuary was not an impenetrable fortress, but a delicate bubble against the vast, indifferent power of the natural world. The fight for Havenridge had begun, not against an external enemy, but against the storm that threatened to tear it apart from within.

The immediate reaction from the Council was a wave of amplified directives, a digital chorus of reassurance that felt increasingly hollow against the gnawing roar of the storm. Every comm-panel, every personal audio implant, broadcast the same message: "Remain in your designated habitation zones. Trust the established safety protocols. The Council is managing the situation." It was the language of control, of order, of an unwavering faith in the systems they had so meticulously constructed. Elder Thorne, his holographic projection flickering into existence on the main plaza screens, his face a mask of stern resolve, was the loudest voice in this symphony of control. "This is an unforeseen atmospheric anomaly," he declared, his voice amplified to cut through the wind's lament. "Our crisis management plan has been activated. We have contingency measures for every foreseeable eventuality. Adherence to these protocols is paramount. Any deviation, any attempt at unauthorized intervention, will be met with severe consequences. We will weather this storm through discipline and unity, not through reckless experimentation."

His words, meant to inspire confidence, instead landed like stones in Mara's gut. "Foreseeable eventuality?" she muttered, watching as water now cascaded down the interior of the main corridor, bypassing the struggling drainage systems. Thorne's vision of safety was built on the foundation of predictability, on the assumption that the future would unfold along lines they had already drawn. But this storm was a testament to the chaos that lay beyond their carefully manicured horizon. His "crisis management plan" felt less like a lifeboat and more like a meticulously organized set of instructions for sinking. He was demanding rigid adherence to a framework that was clearly buckling under the strain, a refusal to acknowledge that the very rigidity he championed was now a liability.

Eli, his face streaked with grime and sweat, his eyes darting between the readings on his portable data slate, scoffed beside her. "Discipline and unity," he echoed dryly. "While his 'contingency measures' are busy short-circuiting and his 'established safety protocols' are drowning. Thorne sees this as a test of our obedience, Mara, not a crisis that demands innovation." He gestured to a series of flashing red lights near a failing pump. "Those auxiliary pumps are still connected to the main grid, despite my attempts to isolate them. If they overload entirely, it could draw power from critical life support systems in the residential sectors. Thorne's plan doesn't account for cascade failure. It only accounts for predictable failures, one at a time, neatly filed away in his protocols."

The Council's response was a frustrating echo chamber of Thorne's pronouncements. Messages filtered down through the network, reinforcing the order to shelter in place, to conserve resources, to await further instructions. There was no mention of exploring alternative solutions, no acknowledgement of the arboretum's unique capabilities, no hint of willingness to deviate from the pre-approved crisis playbook. The sheer volume of the storm, its relentless onslaught, seemed to be lost on them, or perhaps, worse, they were unwilling to acknowledge its power for fear of admitting the inadequacy of their own control. They were a ship's captain refusing to change course, convinced that their charted path, however treacherous the waters, was the only valid one.

Mara watched as a section of the plaza ceiling, weakened by the constant battering of rain and wind, began to sag. A collective gasp went through the huddled residents nearby. This wasn't just a minor inconvenience; it was a visible surrender of their sanctuary. The reinforced duracrete, designed to withstand meteorite impacts and seismic shifts, was yielding to the sheer, sustained pressure of the storm. The Council's directives, broadcast with unwavering certainty, seemed to be speaking to a Havenridge that no longer existed, a Havenridge of predictable stability, not the storm-ravaged reality that was rapidly unfolding around them.

"They're reinforcing the primary conduits in Sector Beta," a voice crackled over the local comms, its tone strained. "Thorne ordered a complete lockdown of that sector to divert all available energy to structural reinforcement. Anyone caught outside designated zones in Beta will be considered a security risk."

"Sector Beta," Eli said, his voice tight with alarm. "That's where the children's creche is. And the hydroponic farms that supply half our nutrient paste. A lockdown? He's sacrificing essential sectors for... what? To make a point about control?" He ran a hand through his already dishevelled hair. "This is madness. We need to be moving people, not locking them down. We need to be opening up access to alternative power sources, not hoarding energy for futile structural repairs."

The Council's rigid adherence to Thorne's directives was creating new dangers. The crisis wasn't just the storm; it was the Council's inability to adapt to it. Their focus was on preserving the *idea* of Havenridge, the perfectly controlled environment, rather than the lives of its inhabitants. Thorne's pronouncements about "necessary sacrifices" now felt chillingly literal, and they were being made not by the storm, but by the very people who were supposed to protect them. The crisis management plan, designed to maintain order in the face of disruption, was now actively exacerbating the disruption by preventing any form of proactive, adaptive response.

Mara felt a surge of frustration so potent it was almost a physical ache. She saw the fear on the faces around her, the dawning realization that the promised safety was an illusion. They were trapped, not just by the storm, but by the Council's intransigence. Thorne's obsession with protocol was a dangerous form of denial. He was so committed to the established order that he refused to see the new, terrifying reality that had emerged. The storm had rewritten the rules, and the Council, led by Thorne, was stubbornly trying to play by the old ones.

"The pressure on the arboretum's containment dome is increasing," Eli reported, his eyes glued to a rapidly scrolling graph on his slate. "It's designed for environmental regulation, not direct atmospheric assault. The bio-integrated materials are helping, absorbing some of the impact, but they're not invincible. If the primary dome fails, the arboretum will be exposed. The delicate ecosystems... they'll be destroyed in minutes. And if the nutrient reservoir is compromised, well, that's the end of our food supply."

He looked at Mara, his gaze earnest. "Thorne's plan is to reinforce the outer perimeter. That's where the breach is in Sector Gamma, and he's decided that's the priority. But that's like trying to patch a leak in a bathtub by reinforcing the faucet. The real problem is the uncontrolled influx, the systems failing to adapt. We need to reroute, to create new channels, to ease the pressure. The arboretum's water management system, if we can give it more leeway, if we can bypass some of Thorne's 'efficiency' limitations..."

He trailed off, the unspoken plea hanging in the air. Mara understood. Eli wasn't asking for permission; he was presenting a desperate necessity. Thorne's Council was a wall of rigid directives, a fortress of bureaucracy. They were so focused on maintaining their own authority, on proving the efficacy of their pre-ordained plans, that they were blind to the immediate, life-threatening consequences of their inaction. Their "rigid response" wasn't just insufficient; it was actively harmful, a testament to the danger of unchecked dogma in the face of unpredictable reality.

"They're not even listening," Mara said, her voice low and tight. She had tried sending a priority alert to the Council's command centre, detailing the critical situation in the arboretum and proposing a temporary diversion of power to bolster its defenses. The response had been a curt, automated reply: "Your request has been logged and will be reviewed in accordance with Protocol 7B: Non-Essential Resource Allocation During Environmental Crisis." Protocol 7B. It was a bureaucratic dead end, a polite way of saying no.

"Protocol," Eli spat, the word tasting like ash. "We don't have time for protocols, Mara. We have a storm that's tearing our home apart, and they're debating the finer points of paper-pushing. Thorne is so afraid of losing control, he's willing to let the storm take it from him entirely." He tapped his slate furiously. "I've managed to reroute some of the secondary irrigation lines, bypassing the main junction that Thorne's engineers are reinforcing. It's a temporary fix, but it's buying us a little breathing room. But it's not enough. The main pressure is still building."

He looked towards the central nexus, a flicker of defiance in his eyes. "I'm going to try and access the climate control core directly. Override Thorne's directives. Force a system-wide diversion to the overflow reservoirs. It's risky. If I trip his primary security alarms, they'll have grounds to shut down the entire arboretum. But if I don't..." He didn't need to finish the sentence. The arboretum, and with it, a significant portion of Havenridge's future, would be lost.

Mara felt a surge of renewed determination. Thorne's rigid response, his unwavering faith in his flawed plan, was a luxury they could no longer afford. The storm had stripped away the veneer of control, revealing the fragile, adaptable nature of true survival. "I'll go with you," she said, her voice firm. "I can help navigate the system. I know its... blind spots." It was a gamble, a direct defiance of Thorne's orders, but in the face of the raging storm, clinging to protocol felt like a surrender. The Council's rigid response was a testament to their fear, but fear, Mara was learning, was a poor navigator in a crisis. True survival lay not in rigid adherence, but in the courage to adapt, to innovate, and to fight for the resilience that Thorne so carelessly dismissed. The storm outside was a brutal, elemental force, but the storm brewing within Havenridge, fueled by the Council's inflexibility, was proving to be just as dangerous. The fight for Havenridge was no longer just about surviving the weather; it was about overcoming the inertia of its own leadership.

The cacophony of the storm was a constant, oppressive presence, a wild, untamed force battering against Havenridge's manufactured serenity. Inside, however, a different kind of storm was brewing – a tempest of frustration and dawning defiance. Eli, his face illuminated by the frantic glow of his data slate, turned from the flickering screens and met Mara's gaze, his eyes burning with a fierce conviction that cut through the ambient despair. The Council's pronouncements, once the bedrock of their security, now felt like the hollow echoes of a system that had lost its way, adrift in a sea of its own rigid protocols.

"They're still talking about 'containment' and 'protocol adherence'," Eli said, his voice tight with incredulity. "Thorne's 'crisis management plan' is a meticulously crafted document designed for a crisis that doesn't exist. This storm isn't a predictable ripple; it's a tsunami, and they're trying to stop it with a sieve." He gestured around them, to the growing dampness seeping through the walls, the frantic scramble of residents trying to shore up weak points with whatever they could find. "Look around, Mara. This isn't a drill. This is reality. And reality doesn't care about Thorne's spreadsheets."

His words resonated with a truth that was becoming increasingly undeniable. The Council's approach was one of control, of ensuring that every variable was accounted for, every action pre-approved. But the storm had introduced variables they hadn't anticipated, complexities that their neatly ordered world couldn't accommodate. Eli, on the other hand, saw not just the chaos, but the potential for emergent order, for a survival forged not from directives, but from collaboration.

"We can't wait for them to figure it out," Eli continued, his voice gaining momentum, drawing the attention of those nearest to them. "Their 'solutions' involve reinforcing structures that are already failing, diverting resources to areas that are already lost. It's like trying to bail out a sinking ship by bailing out the water that's already outside the hull." He looked out at the gathered residents, their faces etched with worry and uncertainty. "We need to do more than just survive this storm; we need to *adapt* to it. And that means working together, not waiting for orders."

A ripple of murmurs went through the crowd. The Council's message had been clear: shelter in place, conserve, obey. But Eli's words offered a different path, one that acknowledged their own agency, their own capacity for action.

"Thorne believes that unity comes from adherence to a single, imposed will," Eli explained, his tone passionate. "But true unity, the kind that can weather a storm like this, comes from shared purpose. It comes from recognizing that each of us has something to contribute. The engineers who know the grid's vulnerabilities, the botanists who understand the arboretum's delicate balance, the builders who can reinforce weak points, even those who can simply share their rations or offer comfort to a frightened child. All of us."

He scanned the faces, making eye contact with as many as he could. "The Council's plan is about isolating us, keeping us in our designated zones, so they can manage us. My proposal is the opposite. I'm proposing we open up. We share what we have – knowledge, skills, resources. If someone needs power, and you have a surplus, share it. If someone needs to reinforce a failing seal, and you have the tools, lend a hand. If you know how to bypass a faulty system or jury-rig a temporary solution, step forward."

His voice grew louder, projecting over the persistent rumble of the wind. "We need to create our own network, a network of mutual aid. The Council's communication channels are clogged with Thorne's pronouncements and status reports that are already obsolete. We need our own lines of communication, not for receiving orders, but for coordinating our efforts." He tapped his data slate. "I've managed to bypass some of the stricter network protocols. It's not official, it's not sanctioned, but it will allow us to share real-time information, to coordinate our efforts across different sectors. Anyone with a functioning personal comm unit, anyone who can help spread the word, I need you."

The idea was audacious, bordering on rebellion, but it resonated deeply. The Council's authority, built on order and control, was crumbling under the sheer force of the storm. Eli was offering not just a practical alternative, but a psychological one: a chance to reclaim a sense of control, to act rather than to be acted upon.

"Think about it," Eli urged, his gaze sweeping across the assembled residents. "The arboretum is facing critical pressure.

Its environmental systems are designed for regulation, not for this kind of direct assault. Thorne wants to reinforce the outer perimeter, but that's a losing battle. The real vulnerability is the internal balance. The bio-integrated materials are designed to absorb and regulate, but they can only take so much. If the primary dome fails, the delicate ecosystems will be gone in minutes. And if the nutrient reservoir is compromised... then what? Thorne's plan doesn't account for that cascade failure, does it? It only accounts for the predictable."

He paused, letting the gravity of his words sink in. "But we can help. The arboretum's water management system, with a few modifications, with some rerouting that bypasses Thorne's 'efficiency' protocols, could help alleviate some of that pressure. It can act as an overflow, a buffer. But it needs more than just a few rerouted irrigation lines. It needs a coordinated effort to manage the flow, to divert excess water from failing sectors, to use the arboretum's capacity to its fullest. That's something Thorne's command centre, buried in their protocols, will never consider."

He gestured to a group of individuals who had gathered nearby, their faces a mixture of apprehension and resolve. Among them were engineers, their hands calloused and their eyes sharp, who had been watching the failing power grids with grim fascination. There were botanists, their expressions pained as they considered the arboretum's plight. And there were simply ordinary citizens, people who had worked with their hands, who understood the practicalities of fixing what was broken.

"We need people who know how to work with the infrastructure," Eli continued, his voice ringing with purpose. "People who can help us reroute power, bypass failing systems, and reinforce critical points. We need people who can manage the flow of resources, ensuring that those who are most vulnerable are not forgotten. And we need people who can communicate, who can be our eyes and ears on the ground, reporting on the storm's progress and the effectiveness of our efforts."

He extended his hand, palm up, a gesture of invitation. "I'm not asking you to disobey the Council. I'm asking you to act with intelligence and compassion. The storm doesn't discriminate. Thorne's protocols do. We have the power to make our own decisions, to prioritize our own survival, and to do it together. This isn't about rebellion; it's about resilience. It's about recognizing that when the established systems fail, we, the people, are the ultimate resource."

He looked towards the increasingly strained containment dome of the arboretum, a vital organ of Havenridge, now under siege. "The Council is focused on the walls. We need to focus on the heart. We need to keep the core systems functioning, to manage the flow, to adapt. If the arboretum's systems are overwhelmed, it's not just a loss of plants and biodiversity; it's the loss of our food supply, our breathable air, our future. Thorne's plan might save a few structures, but it will condemn our future. We have to act."

The urgency in his voice was palpable. It was the urgency of someone who understood the precipice they were standing on, and who refused to accept the inevitability of the fall. He began to pull up schematics on his data slate, intricate diagrams of Havenridge's interconnected systems. "Look here," he said, pointing to a section of the arboretum's environmental controls. "These regulators are designed for micro-adjustments, for precise atmospheric manipulation. But they can be overloaded, temporarily, to handle surges. If we can reroute power from less critical sectors – and Thorne's definition of 'critical' is laughably out of date – we can use these regulators to buffer the storm's impact on the dome. It's risky, yes, but the alternative is certain failure."

He continued to explain, his words a rapid-fire torrent of technical details and strategic thinking. He spoke of creating temporary energy conduits, of diverting water flow through emergency channels that had been neglected for years, of using the arboretum's bio-luminescent plants as emergency lighting in sectors where power had failed. Each idea was a testament to his ingenuity, his deep understanding of Havenridge's systems, and his unwavering belief in the power of human ingenuity.

"This is not about Thorne's authority," Eli reiterated, his voice steady. "This is about our survival. We have the knowledge, we have the skills, and we have the collective will. The Council wants us to be passive recipients of their failing plans. I am asking you to be active participants in your own survival. I am asking you to collaborate, to innovate, to trust each other.

Because when the storm is over, it won't be Thorne's protocols that saved us, it will be our own courage, our own ingenuity, and our own willingness to stand together."

He looked around, a hopeful spark in his eyes as he saw the shift in the crowd. The initial apprehension was giving way to a hesitant but growing sense of determination. The fear was still present, a heavy blanket of dread, but now it was mingled with a burgeoning sense of purpose. People began to exchange glances, to nod in agreement, to whisper to each other with renewed vigour. Eli's call to action was not just a plea for help; it was an invitation to reclaim agency, to become architects of their own resilience in the face of overwhelming adversity. The storm raged outside, but within Havenridge, a quiet revolution of collaboration was beginning to take root, nurtured by the conviction that their collective action, not their blind obedience, was their only true hope.

Mara watched the unfolding scene with a growing unease that had little to do with the storm's external fury. The air inside Havenridge, once thick with the predictable hum of controlled existence, now crackled with a new kind of energy, a volatile mix of fear and burgeoning rebellion. Eli's words, broadcast not through official channels but through a makeshift network he'd conjured from ingenuity and sheer will, had spread like wildfire. They resonated in the hushed conversations between sheltered residents, in the determined glances exchanged by those seeking practical solutions, and in the increasingly anxious faces of the Council's appointed overseers. Thorne's pronouncements, delivered with chillingly detached calm, seemed to belong to a different reality altogether, a sterile, theoretical world where storms were quantifiable variables and human beings were merely data points to be managed.

Her entire life had been a testament to order, to the elegant precision of Havenridge's meticulously designed systems. She understood the Council's rationale, their unwavering commitment to protocol and hierarchy. It was the foundation upon which their society had been built, the bedrock of their security and survival in a world that had long since forgotten the meaning of such stability. To question it, to suggest that it might be failing, felt akin to questioning gravity itself. Yet, as the wind howled like a banshee and the structural integrity of their sanctuary came under unprecedented assault, the Council's rigid adherence to outdated doctrine began to feel less like wisdom and more like a dangerous delusion.

Eli's voice, amplified by the very network he'd created to bypass Thorne's suffocating control, echoed in her mind. He spoke of adaptation, of collaboration, of harnessing the collective intelligence of Havenridge's citizens. He saw not just the encroaching chaos, but the resilience that could emerge from it, the strength found not in obedience but in shared purpose. Mara, a woman who thrived on structure and defined roles, found herself unexpectedly drawn to his vision. Her innate respect for authority warred with the undeniable evidence of its current inadequacy. She saw the fear in the eyes of her neighbours, the desperate scrabble for resources, the dawning realization that their carefully constructed world was crumbling around them.

The arboretum, a jewel of biological diversity and a vital component of Havenridge's life support, was a particular source of anxiety. Mara knew its systems intimately, understood the delicate balance of its climate controls, the intricate network of nutrient delivery, the symbiotic relationship between its flora and the very air they breathed. Thorne's plan, as Eli had so accurately dissected, was a superficial attempt to reinforce the outer shell, a futile gesture against a force that threatened the very heart of the ecosystem. Eli's proposal, however, was different. It was a deep dive, a commitment to fortifying the internal resilience, to leveraging the arboretum's own adaptive capacity to mitigate the storm's destructive potential.

She recalled a conversation with a senior botanist, Dr. Aris Thorne – no relation to the Council head, thankfully – who had expressed grave concerns about the strain on the arboretum's atmospheric processors. "They're designed for regulation, Mara," Aris had explained, his voice strained, his hands tracing invisible lines on a data pad depicting the arboretum's complex circulatory system. "They manage fluctuations, maintain equilibrium. But this... this is a sustained, overwhelming pressure. We're pushing them beyond their designed parameters. If they fail, if the primary containment dome ruptures under the strain, it's not just a loss of beauty. It's a cascade of failures. The bio-filters, the nutrient synthesizers...

the very air we breathe is intricately linked to the health of this place."

Mara had listened, her mind already whirring with potential solutions, with ways to reroute auxiliary power, to implement emergency backup systems. But she had been bound by protocol, by the Council's unwavering directive to await further instructions. Now, those instructions were proving to be woefully insufficient, bordering on negligent. Eli's call for proactive, decentralized action had given her permission, not just to think outside the box, but to dismantle the box entirely.

A surge of adrenaline, a feeling entirely alien to her usual calm demeanour, coursed through her. She looked at Eli, his face alight with a fierce, almost desperate hope, as he continued to rally the growing crowd. He wasn't just talking about survival; he was talking about thriving, about finding strength in unity and innovation. He was offering a vision of resilience that was rooted in human agency, not in blind faith. And in that moment, Mara made a choice. It was a choice that went against years of ingrained deference, a choice that felt both terrifying and exhilarating. She would align herself with this nascent movement, not as a follower, but as a contributor.

Her own skills, honed by years of meticulous planning and system analysis within Havenridge's administrative sectors, were precisely what Eli's grassroots initiative needed. She understood the intricate web of resource allocation, the flow of energy and water, the interconnectedness of every system within their habitat. While Eli possessed the visionary spark and the technical prowess to identify solutions, Mara had the knack for translating those solutions into actionable plans, for organizing the chaos into effective action. She could be the bridge between Eli's radical ideas and the practical reality of execution.

She stepped forward, her voice, though not as loud as Eli's, carried a new resonance, a quiet authority that drew attention. "Eli," she began, her gaze meeting his, a silent understanding passing between them. "He's right. The Council's approach is too slow, too rigid. We can't wait for them to authorize every step. We need to move now." She turned to the assembled residents, her eyes scanning their anxious faces, seeking out those who looked ready to act. "I've spent years analyzing Havenridge's infrastructure. I know where the redundancies are, where the bottlenecks lie, and more importantly, where the critical vulnerabilities are that Thorne's plan completely overlooks."

She gestured towards a group of individuals who had been listening intently, their faces a mixture of apprehension and burgeoning resolve. Among them, she recognized a few skilled technicians from the environmental control division, engineers who had privately grumbled about the limitations imposed by the Council's 'efficiency' protocols, and even some of the logistics coordinators who understood the delicate dance of resource management. "We need to coordinate our efforts," Mara continued, her voice gaining confidence with each word. "Eli can identify the technical solutions, but we need people who can implement them. We need to map out where the greatest immediate needs are – structural reinforcement, emergency power rerouting, water management. And we need to do it systematically, not just reactively."

Her mind was already racing, cataloguing potential strategies. She envisioned a decentralized command structure, a network of team leaders, each responsible for a specific sector or task. She saw herself as an orchestrator, a weaver of disparate efforts into a cohesive whole. "I can help establish communication nodes," she proposed, her gaze sweeping across the crowd. "Not just for sharing information, but for assigning tasks, for tracking progress, for ensuring that no one is working in isolation or duplicating efforts. We can use the personal comm units, even simple visual signals if the network becomes unstable. We need a way to share real-time status reports on structural integrity, on power levels, on the storm's impact on key systems."

She spoke of the arboretum's water purification system, a marvel of recycling and purification technology. Thorne had planned to use it primarily for internal consumption, a predictable allocation of resources. But Mara saw its potential as a crucial buffer. "If we can reroute excess water from the storm's impact zones into the purification system's overflow reservoirs," she explained, her voice now firm and clear, addressing not just Eli but the growing throng, "we can alleviate pressure on the primary containment and prevent catastrophic breaches in lower sectors. It's a complex rerouting, one that bypasses Thorne's 'optimized flow' directives, but it's achievable. I can work with the water management technicians to map out the necessary valve adjustments and conduit reconfigurations."

Her evolving perspective was most keenly felt when she spoke of the residents themselves. For years, she had viewed them as inhabitants, as individuals to be managed and provided for. Now, she saw them as a resource, a vibrant, untapped reservoir of skill, courage, and resilience. "Everyone has something to contribute," she stated, her voice imbued with a newfound conviction. "Those with engineering skills can help reinforce our structures. Those with medical training can establish emergency aid stations. Those who know the residential sectors can identify vulnerable individuals and ensure they have what they need. And those who can simply offer comfort, who can calm a frightened child or share a ration, they are just as vital."

She remembered Thorne's rigid categorization of roles, the strict adherence to designated functions. It was a system designed for predictable stability, not for a crisis of this magnitude. Eli's call to arms was an invitation to dismantle those artificial boundaries, to recognize the inherent value and capability within each individual. "We need to empower people," Mara declared, her voice rising with passion. "We need to give them the tools and the information they need to act, to make decisions that affect their own survival and the survival of their community. The Council's fear of chaos is understandable, but their solution – enforced passivity – is the true threat."

She envisioned a dynamic, responsive organization, one that could adapt to the storm's ever-changing nature. Her organizational prowess, once applied to administrative spreadsheets and logistical matrices, would now be directed towards the immediate, life-or-death needs of Havenridge. She could foresee the challenges: conflicting priorities, communication breakdowns, the sheer exhaustion that would inevitably set in. But she also saw the potential for profound connection, for a sense of shared purpose that transcended the usual divisions and hierarchies.

"This isn't about undermining authority," Mara clarified, anticipating the inevitable accusations. "It's about *augmenting* it. It's about recognizing that when the established systems are insufficient, we have a moral imperative to create our own. We have the knowledge, we have the capability, and we have the collective will to overcome this. Eli's vision is about survival through ingenuity; mine is about survival through organization and empowerment. Together, we can build something that can withstand this storm, and perhaps, emerge stronger from it."

She looked at the faces around her, some still etched with doubt, but many now reflecting a flicker of hope, a spark of determination. They were looking to her, to Eli, for direction, for a path forward. The storm outside was a tangible threat, a force of nature unleashed. But the internal storm, the one brewing within the hearts and minds of Havenridge's residents, was a force that could be harnessed, redirected, and ultimately, overcome. Mara, the woman who had always found solace in order, was embracing a new kind of order, one born of chaos, resilience, and the unyielding power of human connection. It was a defining moment, a personal revolution that would reshape her understanding of leadership, community, and the true meaning of survival. She was no longer just an administrator; she was a catalyst, a strategist, a beacon of organized hope in the heart of the tempest.

The wind battered the arboretum's outer shell with a relentless fury, a symphony of groans and shrieks that echoed through the once-serene biodomes. Yet, amidst the cacophony, a subtle counterpoint began to emerge – a testament to the foresight of its designers and the inherent strength of living systems. Mara, having joined Eli's burgeoning network of action and now actively coordinating efforts to reinforce critical infrastructure, found her gaze drawn to the arboretum's shimmering, geodesic domes. Thorne's pronouncements had painted a grim picture, focusing on the fragility of such a biologically complex environment, a perceived weakness that his brute-force, external reinforcement strategy aimed to "shore up." But Eli, and now Mara herself, had begun to see it differently.

She remembered the conversations with Dr. Aris Thorne, the botanist whose passion for the arboretum's intricate ecosystems bordered on reverence. He had spoken not of rigid defenses, but of dynamic adaptations, of plants engineered for resilience, of a design philosophy that embraced the natural world's inherent ability to flex and endure. He had explained the layered defenses, the carefully curated microclimates designed not just for aesthetic beauty or scientific study, but for survival. The dense, interwoven canopy of specialized trees, chosen for their deep root systems and flexible, wind-resistant structures, acted as a natural buffer against the fiercest gales. The smaller, more vulnerable flora were nestled beneath this protective embrace, shielded from the direct onslaught. It was a living, breathing fortress, built on principles of symbiosis and interconnectedness, principles that Thorne, with his rigid, mechanical worldview, seemed incapable of comprehending.

As Mara watched, data streams from the arboretum's internal sensors began to flicker onto her portable display, fed through Eli's increasingly robust decentralized network. The readings were concerning, certainly. Stress fractures were appearing in some of the older glass panels, and the atmospheric processors were indeed struggling to maintain optimal humidity and oxygen levels against the relentless pressure differentials. Alarms, once a source of panic, now served as precise indicators, mapping the extent of the strain. But the catastrophic failure Thorne had predicted, the swift and total collapse of the arboretum's life-sustaining systems, was not materializing. Instead, a pattern of localized damage, a testament to the inherent resilience of the design, was emerging.

The reinforced outer layer, where Thorne's teams had been frantically applying sealant and bracing, showed signs of buckling. But deeper within, the arboretum's core was holding. The dense foliage, far from being a hindrance, was absorbing and deflecting much of the wind's kinetic energy. The deep, interconnected root systems of the ancient 'Ironwoods' and the flexible 'Wind-Willow' saplings were anchoring the soil, preventing the kind of widespread erosion that could destabilize the entire structure. The smaller, more delicate specimens, often dismissed by Thorne as decorative, were proving to be incredibly adaptable, their flexible stems bending and swaying, absorbing the shockwaves without snapping. It was a stark contrast to the rigid, unyielding architecture of some of Havenridge's older residential sectors, which were experiencing more severe structural damage, their unyielding angles becoming focal points of stress.

Mara felt a surge of vindication, a quiet thrill that resonated deep within her. This was it. This was the tangible proof of Eli's philosophy, the living embodiment of the principles he had been preaching. It wasn't just theoretical. It wasn't just an abstract idea about embracing flexibility. The arboretum, a jewel of Havenridge's existence, was actively demonstrating the power of adaptive resilience. It was a beacon of hope, not through sterile, technological intervention, but through the intelligent application of natural principles.

She directed a team of technicians, their faces grim but determined, towards the arboretum's auxiliary power conduits, rerouting energy to reinforce the less-damaged sections and to bolster the internal climate control systems that were still functioning. "We need to support what's working," she instructed, her voice calm but firm over the comms. "Don't focus on the breaches Thorne is so worried about. Focus on fortifying the core. Amplify the power to the atmospheric regulators in sectors four and seven. They're showing the greatest strain, but the system is still responding. We need to give them every available watt."

She was delegating tasks with a newfound confidence, her years of administrative experience now a powerful tool for organizing chaos. She saw the arboretum not as a single, fragile entity, but as a complex, interconnected network of living systems, each contributing to the overall survival. She understood the delicate dance between the towering trees, the understory plants, the soil microbiome, and the artificial systems that supported them. The storm, while destructive, was also a catalyst, forcing these systems into a more dynamic, and ultimately, more resilient state.

She recalled Aris's explanation of the arboretum's 'self-healing' properties. Not a true biological regeneration in the face of such immediate trauma, but an engineered capacity to redistribute resources, to reroute nutrient flow, to compensate for localized failures. The very design, he had explained, was meant to mimic the resilience of natural ecosystems, to weather periods of stress and emerge, if not unscathed, then intact. And it was working.

The data flowing in painted a picture of a structure under immense pressure, but not one that was buckling under the strain. It was bending, adapting, absorbing. The wind's impact was being diffused, its energy dissipated through the dense foliage and the flexible structures. Even the localized breaches, while concerning, were contained within specific zones, and the internal atmospheric controls were working overtime to isolate them and prevent them from spreading. It was a testament to the layered defenses, the natural windbreaks that acted as sacrificial shields, protecting the more delicate interior.

Mara felt a profound connection to this living testament of resilience. It mirrored the burgeoning spirit she saw rising within Havenridge itself. Eli's message, once a whisper of dissent, was now a chorus of determined voices. The people, too, were finding their own adaptive strategies, supporting each other, sharing resources, forging new connections in the face of adversity. The arboretum, in its silent, stoic endurance, was a powerful symbol of this collective strength. It was a reminder that true resilience wasn't about rigid fortifications and unwavering control, but about the capacity to adapt, to flex, and to find strength in interconnectedness.

She sent a priority message to Eli, her fingers flying across the interface. "Arboretum's holding better than expected," she typed. "Natural defenses are proving crucial. Thorne's brute-force approach is a distraction. We need to focus our reinforcement efforts on supporting its internal systems, not just patching external damage. It's a living demonstration of what we're trying to achieve – strength through adaptability." She knew Eli would understand immediately. He had always seen the interconnectedness of things, the organic nature of true resilience.

As the storm raged on, the arboretum stood as a silent, green heart within Havenridge's metallic shell. It was a stark reminder that survival wasn't always about the strongest armor, but about the most flexible roots. The wind howled, the rain lashed down, and the structures groaned, but within the arboretum, life, in its myriad forms, clung on with an unyielding tenacity. It was a victory, small yet profound, a tangible demonstration that even in the face of overwhelming forces, resilience could not only endure, but thrive. And in that enduring green heart, Mara saw not just the survival of the arboretum, but the nascent survival of Havenridge itself, a community learning to bend, not break, under the storm's relentless pressure. It was a powerful, living argument for their new way forward, a testament to the wisdom of working with nature, rather than against it. The arboretum, in its quiet strength, had become more than just a sanctuary of plants; it had become a sanctuary of hope.

CHAPTER ELEVEN

Rebuilding and Rediscovery

The wind, which had roared like a vengeful god for days, finally began to recede, its fury subsiding into a mournful sigh. The relentless downpour eased, transforming from a blinding curtain of water into a persistent drizzle that slicked the ravaged landscape of Havenridge. As the first tentative rays of dawn pierced through the bruised, lingering clouds, they illuminated a scene of widespread devastation. Yet, amidst the wreckage, a fragile, nascent hope began to stir. The immediate aftermath of the storm wasn't a tableau of despair, but a testament to human resilience, a chaotic canvas waiting for the first strokes of communal effort.

Mara, still buzzing with the adrenaline of her efforts at the arboretum, stepped out of the reinforced command center, her boots crunching on a mixture of shattered glass, twisted metal, and sodden organic matter. The air, scrubbed clean by the tempest, held a damp, earthy scent, overlaid with the acrid tang of ozone and the faint, unsettling aroma of ruptured fuel lines. The sheer scale of the damage was overwhelming. Buildings that had once stood as proud testaments to Havenridge's architectural ingenuity now bore gaping wounds. Facades were ripped away, revealing the skeletal remains of interiors. Entire sections of the residential sectors were reduced to rubble, a stark reminder of the unpredictable, destructive power of nature unleashed. It was a scene that would have shattered her spirit only months ago, but now, it spurred a quiet determination.

Eli emerged from the command center, his face etched with exhaustion but his eyes alight with purpose. He surveyed the wreckage with a familiar, measured gaze. "It's worse than we feared in some sectors," he said, his voice raspy from a lack of sleep. "But not everywhere. The reinforced infrastructure, especially where we managed to implement those adaptive bracing systems, held up remarkably well. The arboretum, as you saw, is a testament to Eli's philosophy. It's a beacon of what we can achieve when we work with natural principles, not against them." He gestured broadly at the surrounding devastation. "But this... this is the reality we have to face now. The immediate challenge is assessment and recovery."

Mara nodded, pulling up a holographic map on her wrist-mounted interface. "I've already routed teams to establish initial damage reports in the sectors bordering the arboretum. Sector Gamma and Delta took a significant hit. The hydroponic farms on the western rim are... well, they're mostly gone. The atmospheric processors there were exposed." She grimaced. "But sectors Alpha and Beta seem to have fared better, likely due to the natural windbreaks we established and the denser urban planning that provided some shelter." She tapped a section of the map. "The primary power conduits in Gamma are down, and the water reclamation system is showing critical breaches. We need to prioritize getting those back online. Without them, the long-term recovery is impossible."

Eli's gaze sharpened as he studied the map. "Focus on the immediate needs first. Water and basic power. We can set up temporary atmospheric generators from the emergency reserves. What about communication lines? Thorne's network was surprisingly resilient in some areas, but we need to establish our own independent channels."

"The decentralized network is holding," Mara confirmed. "Eli's been working non-stop to expand its reach and reinforce its nodes. Most of the core communication hubs are operational, albeit at reduced capacity. We're using them to coordinate rescue efforts and to send out initial damage assessments. The older, centralized systems are faring poorly. Many of them have been physically destroyed." She paused, her eyes scanning the debris-strewn ground. "The most pressing issue right now is ensuring the safety of the residents. We need to establish safe zones, account for everyone, and begin clearing the debris that poses immediate hazards."

As they spoke, the first wave of residents began to emerge from their battered shelters. Faces, streaked with dirt and exhaustion, were etched with a mixture of shock and relief. Neighbors, who in the pre-storm days had exchanged polite nods and fleeting greetings, now converged with a shared urgency. A woman with a soot-stained face was helping an elderly man from a collapsed dwelling, her movements surprisingly strong. A group of young adults, their clothes torn and muddied, were already forming a human chain, passing salvaged materials from a partially demolished store to a makeshift aid station. The storm, in its indiscriminate fury, had stripped away the superficial layers of their lives, exposing a raw, undeniable interdependence.

Eli watched them, a faint smile touching his lips. "See, Mara? This is the true strength. Not in the reinforced concrete or the advanced technology, but in the willingness to reach out, to help, to simply *be there* for one another. Thorne's approach was about fortifying the external, about building walls. Our approach is about building bridges."

Mara felt a warmth spread through her chest, a feeling that had nothing to do with the dissipating storm. She saw it in the determined set of the shoulders of a man clearing rubble with a salvaged piece of metal, in the gentle touch of a hand helping a child over a pile of debris, in the shared glances of reassurance between strangers. This wasn't the ordered efficiency of pre-storm Havenridge, but something far more profound. It was a messy, unvarnished, yet potent display of shared humanity.

"We need to organize this," Mara said, her voice firm. "Eli, I can start coordinating the debris clearing and structural assessment teams. We'll need to map out the safest routes for movement and establish priority areas for repair. I've already tasked a few of our technical teams with assessing the auxiliary power grid and the water purification systems. We can use the decentralized network to broadcast instructions and gather information from residents directly."

"Good," Eli replied. "I'll focus on ensuring our communication infrastructure remains robust and on organizing the distribution of essential supplies. We've got a good cache of emergency rations and medical supplies, but it won't last forever. We'll need to start assessing the damage to the agricultural sectors and begin planning for immediate resupply, even if it means venturing further afield." He looked at her, his expression serious. "This is where your skills in logistics and resource management will be invaluable, Mara. You can see the interconnectedness of it all, the flow of resources, the critical path to recovery."

The task ahead was immense, a mountain of broken pieces that needed to be painstakingly reassembled. But for the first time, Mara felt a genuine sense of optimism. The storm had tested Havenridge to its core, and while the scars were undeniable, the foundation had not crumbled. Instead, it had been revealed, stripped bare, and in that raw exposure, a new strength had emerged. The shared experience, the collective vulnerability, had forged an undeniable bond. The people of Havenridge were not just survivors; they were builders, united by a common purpose, ready to face the dawn and begin the arduous, yet hopeful, process of rebuilding.

As the day progressed, the true extent of the storm's impact became clearer. Entire blocks of residential units in the lower sectors were flattened, resembling dollhouses smashed by a giant hand. The vital agricultural domes, crucial for Havenridge's food supply, were in ruins, their transparent shells shattered, their carefully cultivated crops exposed to the elements. The central power grid, a complex web of energy conduits, was severely compromised, with multiple sections collapsed or severed. The hum of activity, however, began to pulse through the devastation. People emerged from their temporary shelters, not with despair, but with a steely resolve. The initial shock had given way to a pragmatic assessment of the situation, a collective understanding that the only way forward was together.

Mara, working from a temporary command post set up in the less damaged section of the old municipal building, directed teams with an efficiency that belied her recent immersion in the chaos. Her interface displayed a constantly updating map of Havenridge, color-coded to indicate levels of damage and the status of essential services. Red zones marked areas of complete structural collapse, where rescue operations were paramount. Amber zones indicated significant damage requiring immediate attention for structural integrity and the restoration of basic utilities. Green zones, though few and far between, represented areas that had largely escaped the storm's direct fury, and were now designated as staging areas for relief efforts and temporary shelter.

"Sector Gamma, sub-section four," Mara dictated into her comms unit, her voice steady despite the fatigue beginning to set in. "Structural integrity is at thirty percent. Reports of trapped residents. Prioritize extraction and immediate medical attention. Deploy the drone scanners to map any internal voids and assess potential collapse points. We cannot afford to lose any more lives." She glanced at the incoming data streams, her brow furrowed. "Water purification Unit C is offline. We need a rapid assessment team to determine the extent of the damage. If it's beyond immediate repair, we'll have to reroute all available resources to Unit B and implement emergency rationing protocols."

Eli, overseeing the distribution of salvaged supplies, joined her at the command post, his face grim. "The communal stores in the western quadrant are completely inaccessible," he reported. "The storm surge breached the lower levels. We're relying on what we managed to secure in the central reserves and the emergency caches. We'll need to start rationing food and clean water immediately. This is going to be a long haul."

"I understand," Mara replied, her gaze fixed on the holographic map. "But the people are resourceful, Eli. They're already organizing themselves. Look at this feed from Sector Alpha. They've formed a collective, clearing debris from the residential blocks and establishing a communal kitchen using salvaged equipment. They're not waiting for orders; they're acting." She pointed to a blinking icon on the map. "And the arboretum, despite its damage, is proving to be a vital source of clean air and even some filtered water. Dr. Thorne's foresight, combined with Eli's adaptive approach, has saved a crucial part of our infrastructure. It's a microcosm of what we need to achieve across Havenridge."

The spirit of self-reliance was indeed palpable. Small groups of residents, armed with salvaged tools and an unwavering determination, were working to clear pathways, secure damaged structures, and rescue those still trapped. The storm had stripped away the veneer of comfort and convenience, but it had also unearthed a deep-seated reservoir of courage and cooperation. Children, their usual boisterous energy subdued, were helping where they could, carrying water, assisting the elderly, their innocence a poignant contrast to the surrounding devastation. The shared experience, the common threat, had dissolved many of the social barriers that had once defined their interactions. Now, they were simply survivors, bound by a shared struggle and a collective hope for a better future.

"Thorne's teams are reporting extensive damage to the outer perimeter of the city's defensive shield," Eli mentioned, his voice tinged with a familiar weariness of Thorne's rigid approach. "They're advocating for immediate, large-scale repairs using conventional methods. It's going to consume a significant portion of our resources and manpower."

Mara sighed, a gust of frustration escaping her lips. "And Thorne will argue that it's the only way to guarantee our safety. He still doesn't grasp the concept of adaptive resilience, does he?

While his teams are focused on rebuilding a rigid barrier that the next storm will simply batter down again, we need to be investing in strengthening our internal systems, improving our response mechanisms, and fostering that spirit of community you just saw. The arboretum's survival is a testament to that. It adapted, it bent, it absorbed. That's the kind of resilience we need to cultivate, not just in our structures, but in ourselves."

She zoomed in on a section of the map showing the agricultural domes. "The loss of the hydroponic farms is critical. We'll need to divert resources to salvage what we can from the more robust sections of the food production infrastructure and begin planning for immediate, albeit limited, food procurement from external sources. This will require careful negotiation and likely involve bartering some of our salvaged technology."

"And the communication lines," Eli added. "Thorne's network is experiencing significant disruptions, as is to be expected with its centralized architecture. Our decentralized system is proving far more robust. We need to focus on reinforcing its nodes and expanding its reach. Information is our most valuable currency right now – coordinating rescue efforts, sharing vital resources, and maintaining morale."

As the day wore on, the initial chaos began to coalesce into a more organized effort. The shared experience of the storm had stripped away the pretenses and superficialities of their former lives, revealing a core of resilience and mutual dependence. The debris was still formidable, the damage extensive, but the people of Havenridge were not broken. They were battered, yes, but united by a common purpose and a newfound appreciation for the strength that lay not in individual fortitude, but in collective action. The path ahead was arduous, fraught with challenges, but for the first time in a long time, Mara felt a profound sense of hope. The storm had revealed their vulnerabilities, but it had also illuminated their greatest strength: each other.

The initial shockwaves of the storm had settled, leaving behind a landscape scarred but not broken. In the days that followed, as the dust, or rather, the sodden debris, began to clear, a different kind of reckoning began to take place. The rigid structures of Havenridge's governance, so meticulously designed for order and control, had been shown to be as vulnerable as any other edifice. The Council, a body that had prided itself on its foresight and its ability to maintain stability, found itself humbled. Their carefully orchestrated plans, their pre-storm protocols, had been rendered largely obsolete by the sheer, unbridled force of nature. It was a stark, and for many, a deeply uncomfortable realization.

In the sterile, reinforced chambers of the Council headquarters, the usual air of confident authority was replaced by a palpable sense of introspection. The storm had been a brutal, impartial judge, and its verdict was clear: Havenridge, for all its technological prowess and administrative rigor, had been caught unprepared for the scale of the unexpected. The limitations of their top-down approach, their reliance on pre-programmed responses, had been exposed. They had built a city designed to withstand predictable stresses, but they had not fully accounted for the chaotic, improvisational nature of a truly catastrophic event.

It was within this atmosphere of forced re-evaluation that Mara and Eli found their voices amplified. Their pleas for more decentralized decision-making, for a greater emphasis on adaptive infrastructure, and for fostering a more organic, community-driven response, which had once been met with polite skepticism or outright dismissal, now carried a newfound weight. The Council members, their faces etched with the fatigue of sleepless nights spent coordinating rescue efforts and assessing damage, were finally ready to listen. The data spoke for itself: the sections of the city that had incorporated elements of Eli's adaptive design principles, the areas where Mara's logistical networks had been allowed to function with a degree of autonomy, had fared demonstrably better.

The council sessions that followed were unlike any in Havenridge's history. Gone were the polished presentations and the lengthy debates over policy minutiae. Instead, the discussions were raw, urgent, and driven by a shared understanding that the old ways were no longer sufficient. Elder Thorne, a staunch advocate of centralized control and the architect of many of Havenridge's rigid systems, found his arguments increasingly falling on deaf ears. His focus remained on rebuilding the damaged infrastructure with the same robust, inflexible materials and methods, a strategy that Mara and Eli argued would only make Havenridge susceptible to the next inevitable challenge.

"We cannot simply rebuild what was," Mara stated, her voice resonating with a conviction born from witnessing the resilience of the people firsthand. "We must build what *can be*. The storm taught us that resilience isn't about being impenetrable; it's about being adaptable. It's about having the capacity to bend, to absorb, and to recover. Our current infrastructure, our governance model, all of it needs to reflect that understanding."

Eli, standing beside her, elaborated on the technical aspects. "The reinforced atmospheric processors, while robust, were also brittle in the face of extreme lateral forces. The adaptive bracing systems, on the other hand, allowed for controlled flex and energy dissipation. This principle needs to be applied across the board, not just in our buildings, but in our systems, our networks, and even our decision-making processes. We need to create redundancies that aren't just about backup power, but about backup *strategies*. We need to empower smaller, more agile units to make critical decisions at the ground level when the central command is compromised."

The Council, composed of individuals who had spent years meticulously crafting a city of predictable efficiency, struggled to grasp the concept of embracing such inherent flexibility. The idea of relinquishing a degree of control, of allowing for emergent solutions, was anathema to their ingrained belief in the superiority of pre-planned order. Yet, the evidence was undeniable. The images of residents spontaneously organizing to clear debris, to share dwindling resources, to comfort one another, painted a powerful picture of a different kind of strength – one that flowed from the bottom up, not the top down.

A consensus began to form, not through a formal vote, but through a gradual, almost reluctant, acceptance of reality. The rigid lines of authority were beginning to blur. The Council, humbled by the storm's indiscriminate fury, recognized that their authority needed to be tempered with a deeper understanding of the community's needs and capabilities. They began to actively solicit input from sectors and individuals who had previously been on the fringes of decision-making. Mara's expertise in logistics and Eli's innovative engineering insights were no longer seen as disruptive forces, but as essential components of the rebuilding process.

"We need to establish a more integrated approach," Councilwoman Anya Petrova, a pragmatist who had always championed a more balanced perspective, stated during one of the heated discussions. "Thorne's focus on defensibility is important, but it cannot come at the expense of our ability to adapt and to thrive. We need to find a way to integrate the strength of our established systems with the agility that the storm has proven to be so vital. It's not a choice between order and chaos; it's about finding a dynamic equilibrium."

This sentiment resonated deeply. The idea of "dynamic equilibrium" became a touchstone. It acknowledged the necessity of structure and safety – the fundamental requirements for any society – but it also recognized the unpredictable nature of the future and the need for a governance model that could respond to unforeseen challenges with grace and efficiency. It meant a shift in philosophy, from dictating solutions to fostering an environment where solutions could emerge.

Mara saw this shift reflected in the daily operations of the recovery. The ad-hoc committees that had sprung up in the wake of the storm, composed of residents from diverse backgrounds and skill sets, were proving remarkably effective. A group of former engineers, artists, and even educators had come together to design and implement a network of temporary shelters using salvaged materials and Eli's flexible design principles. Another collective of farmers and botanists, devastated by the loss of the hydroponic domes, were already experimenting with hardy, soil-based crops in sheltered areas, drawing on pre-storm ecological knowledge that had been largely sidelined in favor of controlled environments.

"These are the seeds of our new governance," Mara observed to Eli, watching a group of residents collaboratively reinforcing a damaged community center with a patchwork of salvaged metal and sturdy timbers. "They are self-organizing, identifying needs, and pooling resources. Our role now is not to direct every action, but to facilitate, to provide support, and to ensure that these emergent structures are recognized and integrated into the broader recovery effort."

Eli nodded, his gaze following the determined movements of the workers. "It's about creating the conditions for innovation, not just dictating the outcomes. We need to provide the framework – the essential resources, the communication channels, the safety guidelines – and then trust the ingenuity of the people to build within that framework. Thorne's approach was like building a fortress, but a fortress that, by its very nature, resists change. We need to build a thriving ecosystem, one that can evolve and adapt to the changing environment."

The Council began to implement tangible changes. The rigid zoning laws that had dictated every aspect of Havenridge's development were relaxed in certain areas, allowing for more spontaneous rebuilding and the repurposing of damaged structures. A new "Community Innovation Fund" was established, designed to provide resources and support for resident-led projects that demonstrated the principles of adaptive resilience. Communication protocols were overhauled, with a greater emphasis on decentralized information sharing and the establishment of local communication hubs that could function independently if the central network was disrupted.

Even Elder Thorne, though visibly pained, began to acknowledge the necessity of these shifts. He had witnessed the bravery of ordinary citizens, the quick thinking of individuals who had improvised solutions under extreme duress. His belief in the infallibility of centralized authority had been shaken. He saw that the true strength of Havenridge lay not just in its advanced technology or its carefully planned infrastructure, but in the spirit and ingenuity of its people.

"We have been too focused on control," Thorne admitted during a Council meeting, his voice hoarse with a weariness that went beyond physical exhaustion. "We believed that by meticulously planning for every eventuality, we could eliminate risk. But the storm has shown us that true security lies not in eliminating risk, but in building the capacity to manage it, to adapt to it, and to emerge stronger from it. The people have demonstrated a resilience that we, in our structured environment, had perhaps underestimated. We must learn from them."

This admission, coming from Thorne, was a significant turning point. It signaled a genuine willingness to evolve. The Council, once a monolithic entity, was becoming more dynamic, more responsive. The voices of Mara and Eli, once those of dissenting opinion, were now seen as integral to shaping Havenridge's future. The consensus was not about abandoning all structure, but about finding a new, more resilient balance. It was a recognition that the future of Havenridge depended on a collaborative approach, one that embraced both the wisdom of experience and the power of emergent innovation, a model where safety and adaptability were not mutually exclusive, but were instead inextricably intertwined. The storm had been a devastating blow, but it had also been a catalyst, forcing

Havenridge to confront its limitations and to embrace a path of rediscovery, one that promised a more robust and adaptable future. The governance was changing, not by decree, but by necessity, forged in the crucible of shared hardship and a collective yearning for a future that could withstand whatever trials lay ahead. The fear of the unknown was still present, but it was now tempered by a growing confidence in their shared ability to face it, together.

The days following the storm were a blur of organized chaos, a testament to the raw, unyielding spirit of Havenridge's citizens. Amidst the swirling dust and the scent of damp earth, a new rhythm began to emerge, one dictated not by the sterile pronouncements of the Council, but by the urgent needs of the community itself. It was in this emergent structure that the partnership between Mara and Eli truly began to crystallize, not as a formal alliance, but as a natural, vital extension of their shared vision.

Mara, ever the pragmatist, found herself at the nexus of countless logistical challenges. The storm had not just damaged buildings; it had fractured supply chains, disrupted communication networks, and displaced thousands. Her mind, already adept at dissecting complex problems into manageable components, worked tirelessly to reroute resources, coordinate rescue teams, and establish temporary shelters. She moved through the damaged sectors with an almost uncanny ability to anticipate needs, her presence a steadying force in the whirlwind of destruction. She saw the ingenuity of the people—a farmer repurposing an old atmospheric condenser to desalument water, a group of displaced engineers sketching out plans for modular temporary housing on salvaged data pads. Her role, as she saw it, was to amplify these grassroots efforts, to ensure that their spontaneous acts of resilience were not lost in the broader recovery. She began establishing decentralized distribution hubs, trusting local leaders to manage them, providing them with the necessary supplies and information, and then stepping back to let them execute. This was a far cry from the Council's top-down directives; this was about empowerment.

Eli, on the other hand, found his unique skills in demand in ways he had only theorized about. His designs for adaptive structures, once dismissed as overly complex or perhaps even unnecessary, were now being studied with a newfound urgency. He moved through the ruined landscape not just assessing damage, but identifying opportunities for innovation. He worked with construction crews, many of them hastily assembled from former office workers and retail staff, to implement his principles of flexible bracing and energy absorption. He didn't just offer blueprints; he offered a philosophy. He would explain, with infectious enthusiasm, how a slight deviation in structural angle could redirect lateral forces, how a carefully designed series of flexible joints could prevent catastrophic collapse. He saw the fear in people's eyes, but he also saw their determination, their willingness to learn and adapt. He spent hours in makeshift workshops, sketching designs on salvaged boards, demonstrating principles with salvaged materials, and igniting a spark of inventive confidence in those who had previously felt overwhelmed. He encouraged improvisation, celebrating the "beautifully imperfect" solutions that emerged from necessity. He knew that rebuilding wasn't just about replicating the past, but about creating something stronger, something more responsive.

Their collaboration was a dance of complementary strengths. Mara would identify a critical shortage of clean water in Sector Gamma, for example. Eli would then, with his understanding of the local environment and available salvaged technology, devise a series of ingenious, decentralized water purification units that could be quickly deployed and maintained by local residents. Mara would then orchestrate the distribution of these units, along with the necessary training and spare parts, ensuring that the solution reached those in need efficiently and effectively. Eli's ability to conceptualize and rapidly prototype innovative solutions was perfectly complemented by Mara's mastery of large-scale logistical implementation. They became a familiar sight together, Mara, her brow furrowed in concentration as she reviewed a supply manifest, Eli, his face alight with an idea as he pointed to a damaged structure, discussing how it could be reinforced with salvaged conduits and flexible polymers.

The Council, initially hesitant to relinquish direct control, soon recognized the unparalleled effectiveness of their joint approach. Elder Thorne, his usual stern demeanor softened by the shared hardship, would often observe their work with a quiet intensity. He saw Mara's meticulous planning and Eli's inspired improvisation not as separate entities, but as two sides of the same crucial coin. He began to understand that true governance in a post-storm world required not just foresight, but the ability to foster emergent solutions, to provide the scaffolding upon which the community could build its own resilience. He saw the way Mara's calm authority inspired trust and confidence, and the way Eli's passion ignited hope and a sense of agency.

"They are a living embodiment of what we need," Anya Petrova, a Councilwoman known for her pragmatism, observed to Thorne one evening, watching Mara and Eli address a crowd of residents gathered around a damaged communal hall. Mara was outlining a phased plan for rebuilding, emphasizing community involvement and resource sharing. Eli was illustrating, with a few well-chosen words and gestures, how the hall's weakened roof could be temporarily reinforced using salvaged weather balloons and a network of tensioned cables, a solution that was both structurally sound and aesthetically unique. "Mara provides the structure, the certainty. Eli provides the spark, the innovation. Together, they are building not just buildings, but a new way of thinking."

The impact of their partnership rippled outwards, influencing the nascent governance structures that were emerging from the ashes. They actively mentored and supported other emerging community leaders, encouraging them to identify their own unique strengths and to collaborate with others who possessed complementary skills. They facilitated workshops where residents could share knowledge and skills, fostering an environment of mutual learning and support. A group of former archivists, inspired by Mara's organizational prowess, began establishing a centralized repository of salvaged materials and blueprints. A collective of musicians and artists, seeing Eli's creative problem-solving, started organizing communal art projects to boost morale and foster a sense of shared identity.

Their conversations, often late into the night amidst the hum of emergency generators and the distant sounds of rebuilding, were a blend of strategic planning and nascent personal connection. They discussed the future of Havenridge, not just in terms of infrastructure and governance, but in terms of its soul. Mara spoke of the importance of preserving the human element, of ensuring that the pursuit of efficiency never overshadowed the need for compassion and community. Eli spoke of the potential for technology to enhance human connection, rather than isolate it, of building a future where innovation served the well-being of all.

"We've seen how fragile our systems can be," Mara said, tracing the condensation ring left by her nutrient paste on a salvaged table. "But we've also seen how strong people can be when they work together. My focus has always been on making sure the 'how' works. But you, Eli... you remind me that the 'why' is just as important. Why are we rebuilding? To create a community that is not just safe, but thriving. A community that remembers what it's lost, but is inspired by what it can become."

Eli reached across the table, his hand gently covering hers. His touch was warm, grounding. "And you, Mara, remind me that even the most inspired vision needs a solid foundation, a clear path to execution. You bring order to my chaos, purpose to my creativity. I used to think resilience was about building stronger walls. Now I know it's about building stronger connections. And our connection... that's becoming the strongest thing of all."

Their shared experiences, the gravity of the rebuilding, and the quiet intimacy of their shared purpose had woven a bond between them that was deeper than mere professional respect. It was a profound understanding, a shared language of hope and resilience. They had faced the abyss together, and in the process, had discovered a profound strength within themselves and within each other. Their partnership was no longer just about rebuilding Havenridge; it was about building a future, together, a future where their combined strengths could create something beautiful and enduring, a testament to the power of collaboration and the unwavering human spirit. The storm had tested them, broken them down, but in the crucible of that destruction, they had forged something new, something stronger, both in their community and in their hearts. Their shared vision for Havenridge was no longer just a professional aspiration; it was a promise, whispered in the quiet moments between the relentless demands of recovery, a promise of a future built on trust, ingenuity, and an unwavering belief in the power of two.

The days following the storm had stripped away the illusion of absolute control that had once defined Havenridge. The rigid structures of preparedness, meticulously crafted to preempt every conceivable threat, had crumbled with the winds and rain. Safety, Mara realized with a dawning clarity that was both humbling and exhilarating, was not a fortress to be built against the world, but a spirit to be cultivated within it. Her previous worldview, one that meticulously cataloged risks and sought to neutralize them through foresight and stringent protocols, now felt like an inadequate lens through which to view the complex reality of their present. She had always associated safety with predictability, with the absence of the unexpected. But the storm had demonstrated, with brutal efficiency, that the unexpected was not a deviation from the norm, but an intrinsic part of existence. True safety, therefore, could not be achieved by eliminating risk, but by building the capacity to absorb, adapt, and recover from it.

This redefinition had begun subtly, in the quiet conversations with Eli, amidst the cacophony of rebuilding. He spoke of adaptive structures, not just in terms of materials and engineering, but as a philosophy of living. His designs weren't meant to withstand every possible force, but to flex, to absorb, to reroute energy in ways that prevented catastrophic failure. He had a way of explaining these concepts that resonated deeply with Mara, a man who had always sought order and efficiency. He didn't just talk about structural integrity; he spoke of the resilience of nature, of how a forest, though battered by a storm, would regrow, its very ecosystem designed for flux. He showed her how the community, in its immediate response to the disaster, had embodied this very principle. The farmer's makeshift desalination unit, the engineers' rapid design of temporary housing – these weren't just acts of survival; they were acts of adaptive resilience. They were improvisations born from necessity, yet infused with an inherent understanding of how to persist and even thrive in the face of adversity.

Mara found herself shifting her perspective, moving from a top-down model of imposed security to a more organic, community-driven understanding. The decentralized distribution hubs she had established, entrusting local leaders with resources and decision-making, were a perfect example of this burgeoning philosophy. Initially, she had worried about the potential for inefficiency or error, the very things her previous protocols were designed to prevent. But instead, she witnessed an outpouring of ingenuity and shared responsibility. People who had always been on the periphery of decision-making were now stepping into leadership roles, their local knowledge invaluable, their commitment fierce. They weren't just following instructions; they were actively participating in their own recovery, their collective efforts creating a far more robust and responsive safety net than any centralized system could have provided. The 'why' behind their actions, Eli had reminded her, was not merely to survive, but to rebuild a better, more connected existence. This was the essence of a new kind of safety – one that was woven into the very fabric of the community.

She began to see how the physical rebuilding efforts mirrored this conceptual shift. Eli's work on reinforcing damaged structures wasn't just about making them stronger in a conventional sense. He was incorporating elements of flexibility, of shock absorption, inspired by natural forms and advanced biomimicry. He would explain, with animated gestures and salvaged diagrams, how a building designed to sway slightly with seismic activity or high winds was ultimately more durable than one rigidly resisting the forces. This, he argued, was akin to human resilience. A person, or a community, that rigidly adhered to a singular way of being, that refused to bend, was more likely to shatter when faced with life's inevitable storms. True strength, he believed, lay in the capacity for adaptation, in the ability to absorb the shock and then spring back, perhaps even stronger for the experience. Mara found herself nodding along, her own experiences validating his insights. She had seen individuals, clinging desperately to their pre-storm routines and expectations, struggle more than those who had embraced the necessity of change.

The concept of communal spaces, too, took on a new dimension. Before the storm, these were places of organized recreation or planned civic engagement. Now, they were becoming vital hubs of mutual aid and emotional support. The damaged communal hall, which Eli had proposed reinforcing with salvaged weather balloons and tensioned cables, wasn't just a structure being repaired; it was being reimagined as a testament to shared ingenuity and collective will. The fact that residents were actively involved in its restoration, learning new skills and contributing their labor, fostered a profound sense of ownership and belonging. This shared investment, Mara realized, was a powerful form of safety. It meant that people looked out for one another, that the well-being of the group was intrinsically linked to the well-being of the individual.

Anya Petrova, the pragmatic Councilwoman, had voiced this evolving understanding during a debriefing session. "We've been so focused on fortifying our external defenses, on creating protocols to prevent disaster," she had mused, her gaze thoughtful. "But Mara, Eli, what you're demonstrating is that true safety isn't about building higher walls. It's about weaving a stronger social fabric. It's about empowering people to be resilient, to trust each other, to know that even if something breaks, they have the collective capacity to mend it."

Mara found herself re-evaluating her own anxieties. Her inherent inclination towards caution, towards anticipating and mitigating every potential negative outcome, had always served her well in a stable environment. But in this new reality, that same tendency could become a paralyzing force. She had to consciously push herself to embrace the inherent uncertainty, to trust in the community's emergent strength, and to view potential setbacks not as failures, but as opportunities for further learning and adaptation. It was a continuous process of recalibrating her internal compass, of learning to navigate by the stars of hope and collaboration rather than by the rigid grid of control.

The storm had, in a sense, liberated her from the tyranny of perfection. She began to celebrate the "beautifully imperfect" solutions that Eli championed – the jury-rigged repairs, the creatively repurposed materials, the spontaneous acts of kindness that arose from the immediate need. These were not signs of inadequacy, but indicators of a dynamic, living system, capable of self-correction and innovation. Safety, she understood now, was not the absence of flaws, but the presence of the capacity to address them, collectively and with compassion. This was a far more potent and sustainable form of security than anything built on the false premise of absolute predictability.

This shift in perspective extended to how she approached her own role and her interactions with Eli. Their partnership, initially forged in the crucible of crisis, had evolved into something far deeper. It was built on a shared understanding of this redefined safety, a mutual respect for each other's strengths, and a growing personal affection. Mara, who had always prided herself on her self-sufficiency, found herself increasingly reliant on Eli's optimistic vision and creative problem-solving. He, in turn, found a grounding force in her meticulous planning and unwavering commitment to seeing things through. They complemented each other not just in their professional capacities, but in their fundamental approaches to life, creating a synergy that was greater than the sum of its parts.

The quiet moments they shared, often late into the night as they reviewed plans or simply sought solace in each other's company, became crucial. It was in these hushed intervals, away from the relentless demands of rebuilding, that the deeper implications of their work truly sank in. Mara would watch Eli, his face illuminated by the flickering light of a salvaged projector, as he explained a new design for water purification, his passion infectious. She saw not just an engineer, but a visionary, someone who believed in the inherent goodness and ingenuity of people. And he, she knew, saw in her not just a capable administrator, but a steady hand, a voice of reason, and a heart that, despite its inherent caution, was capable of immense warmth and resilience.

"We used to think safety meant having all the answers before anything happened," Mara confessed one evening, tracing patterns in the condensation on her nutrient paste container. "But the storm showed us that sometimes, the most important thing is to trust that we'll find the answers together, when we need them. It's about building the courage to face the unknown, knowing we have each other."

Eli's hand covered hers, a familiar, comforting warmth. "And that courage, Mara," he replied, his voice soft, "is contagious. You've shown me that even the most audacious dreams need a solid, compassionate foundation. You've taught me that resilience isn't just about building stronger structures; it's about building stronger connections, stronger communities. And you," he squeezed her hand gently, "are the heart of the strongest connection I've ever known."

Their shared journey had transformed the very meaning of safety for them. It was no longer a passive state of being, but an active, ongoing process of creation, of nurturing, and of unwavering belief. It was about cultivating a community where individuals felt secure not because disaster was impossible, but because they knew, with absolute certainty, that they could weather any storm, together. This was the new safety they were building – a safety forged in resilience, sustained by community, and illuminated by the enduring light of hope. It was a promise whispered in the quiet hum of generators, a tangible manifestation of their shared vision, and a testament to the enduring power of the human spirit to not just survive, but to thrive, even in the face of overwhelming adversity. The storm had been a destructive force, but in its wake, it had revealed a profound truth: that true safety lay not in the absence of challenges, but in the strength and unity required to meet them, and to emerge from them, transformed and renewed.

This was the essence of their rediscovery, a redefinition of what it meant to be truly secure in a world that would always hold surprises. It was a safety that resonated in the shared laughter, in the collaborative problem-solving, and in the quiet, unwavering trust they had cultivated, both within themselves and within each other, and in the Havenridge they were actively, lovingly rebuilding.

The skeletal remains of the storm's fury still clung to the edges of the Arboreum, a stark contrast to the burgeoning life that was already reclaiming its territory. Twisted metal girders, once part of the geodesic dome's protective canopy, lay scattered like fallen giants, testament to the brutal force that had swept through. Yet, amidst the wreckage, vibrant green shoots were pushing through the scarred earth, and the resilient, salt-crusted leaves of the native flora unfurled defiantly towards the sun. It was a scene that perfectly encapsulated the spirit of Havenridge: battered, bruised, but undeniably alive and, in its own way, even more beautiful for its survival.

For Mara, the Arboreum had always been a place of quiet contemplation, a meticulously curated sanctuary of botanical wonders. Now, in the aftermath of the tempest, it was transforming into something more profound. It was becoming a living monument to their collective resilience, a tangible representation of the 'beautifully imperfect' future Eli had so eloquently described. The grand vision, once a distant aspiration, now felt immediate, vital, a necessary next step in their arduous journey of rebuilding.

"It's a symbol, isn't it?" Eli said, his voice carrying a note of quiet awe as they stood on the main promenade, surveying the scene. His arm was around Mara's shoulders, a comforting weight that anchored her amidst the whirlwind of change. "A symbol of what we've overcome, and what we can become."

Mara leaned into him, the familiar scent of his work-worn clothes a grounding presence. "It was always meant to be a place of growth," she murmured, her gaze sweeping across the damage. "But now... it's about growth in a way we never anticipated. It's not just about preserving what was here, but about creating something new, something even more enduring."

The original plans for the Arboreum had focused on showcasing the botanical diversity of their region, a scientific endeavor intertwined with a desire to connect people with nature. There were carefully labeled specimens, controlled environments, and educational displays designed to foster an appreciation for the delicate balance of ecosystems. It was a beautiful concept, but one that had been built on the implicit assumption of stability, of predictable weather patterns. The storm had shattered that assumption, forcing a radical re-evaluation.

Eli's input had been instrumental in this shift. He didn't see the damaged dome as a failure, but as an opportunity to reimagine its purpose. His proposals, which had initially seemed audacious, now felt inspired, even essential. He spoke of a living, breathing structure, one that worked in harmony with the environment rather than against it. This wasn't just about reinforcing the existing framework; it was about a complete paradigm shift, integrating the Arboreum into the very fabric of Havenridge's renewed ethos.

"We're not just rebuilding a garden, Mara," Eli explained, his eyes alight with his characteristic enthusiasm as he unfurled a salvaged schematic, its edges singed but its lines still clear. "We're creating a living laboratory, a demonstration of how life can not only survive but thrive in a dynamic environment. Think of it as an adaptive ecosystem, mimicking the very resilience we've discovered within ourselves."

His vision for the Arboreum was far more than just aesthetic. It was about creating a biodiverse and sustainable living space that would serve as a vital resource for the entire community. Instead of rigid, enclosed sections, he proposed a series of interconnected microclimates, each designed to nurture specific plant communities while also contributing to the overall health and stability of the environment. These would be more forgiving of external influences, able to absorb and dissipate the impact of unpredictable weather patterns, much like a dense forest canopy.

"Imagine," he continued, his voice resonating with the passion that always captivated Mara, "each section acting as a buffer. The hardy, salt-tolerant species on the periphery can absorb the brunt of any future wind or salt spray, protecting the more delicate interior environments. The canopy itself won't be a solid barrier, but a permeable, adaptable structure, allowing for controlled airflow and light penetration, but also designed to flex and yield rather than shatter."

This concept of 'flex and yield' echoed so deeply with Mara's own recent epiphanies. The storm had taught her that rigid defenses, while seemingly strong, were ultimately brittle. True strength lay in adaptability, in the capacity to absorb and recover. Eli's architectural philosophy mirrored this perfectly. He wasn't proposing to recreate the old dome, but to build something entirely new, something that understood and embraced the inherent dynamism of their world.

One of his most innovative ideas was the integration of advanced hydroponic and aeroponic systems, not just for food production, but for water management and air purification. He envisioned a closed-loop system where water collected from rainfall and any residual atmospheric moisture would be filtered and recirculated through the plant systems, effectively acting as a natural dehumidifier and purifier. This would not only reduce their reliance on external water sources but also create a more stable and pleasant microclimate within the Arboreum, even during periods of extreme heat or humidity.

"We can even incorporate solar-powered atmospheric water generators into the structure," Eli elaborated, pointing to a series of small circles on the schematic. "And the filtration systems, powered by the same solar arrays, will ensure the water is clean enough for both irrigation and, eventually, for community use. It's about creating a self-sustaining, regenerative system."

Mara's mind, once trained to analyze risks and optimize for predictability, was now embracing this new language of integration and adaptation. She saw how Eli's designs were not just about engineering marvels, but about fostering a deeper connection between humanity and nature. The Arboreum would no longer be a static exhibit, but a dynamic, living entity, constantly interacting with and adapting to its surroundings.

"And the food production aspect," Mara interjected, her voice filled with a newfound excitement, "we can expand the community garden plots within the more sheltered zones. Imagine fresh produce, grown right here, year-round, supported by the Arboreum's own water and nutrient cycles. It's not just about beautification; it's about bolstering our food security, about making us more self-sufficient."

Eli beamed, a genuine smile that crinkled the corners of his eyes. "Exactly! It's about creating a holistic system. The Arboreum becomes a lynchpin, connecting our botanical heritage with our future needs. It's a place where we can learn to live in sync with nature's rhythms, not just observe them from a distance."

The plans also included expanded communal spaces. The existing amphitheater, partially damaged, would be reinforced and modernized, becoming an open-air venue for performances, gatherings, and educational workshops. Smaller, more intimate seating areas would be carved out amongst the flourishing foliage, offering quiet nooks for reflection and conversation. The idea was to create a space that encouraged interaction, fostering the very community bonds that had proven so vital in their recovery.

"We need places where people can connect, can share their experiences and their hopes," Mara said, her gaze drifting towards a section of the schematic that depicted a winding path leading to a secluded clearing. "The Arboreum can become a sanctuary, not just for plants, but for people too. A place where we can heal, and where we can celebrate our renewed sense of purpose."

The expansion wasn't just about physical space; it was about infusing the Arboreum with a new philosophy. Eli envisioned incorporating interactive exhibits that demonstrated the principles of sustainable living, waste reduction, and renewable energy. These would be hands-on, engaging displays designed to educate and inspire visitors of all ages, reinforcing the community's commitment to a more sustainable and resilient future.

"We can have demonstrations on composting, on water harvesting, on building with salvaged materials," Eli suggested, sketching a small icon of a sprouting seed. "And perhaps a section dedicated to the plants that have medicinal properties, showcasing the natural remedies that have been used for generations. It's about rediscovering ancient wisdom and integrating it with our modern innovations."

Mara found herself captivated by the sheer potential. The Arboreum, once a symbol of careful preservation, was now poised to become a vibrant hub of innovation and community engagement. It was a testament to their collective journey – moving from a reactive state of survival to a proactive embrace of a more hopeful, interconnected existence.

The funding for this ambitious expansion, which had been a pipe dream before the storm, was now being fast-tracked. The crisis had, paradoxically, created a sense of urgency and a renewed appreciation for the vital role of such a space. The community council, galvanized by the shared experience of loss and the subsequent outpouring of support and ingenuity, readily allocated resources. There was a collective understanding that investing in the Arboreum was an investment in their future, a tangible manifestation of their commitment to rebuilding not just structures, but a way of life.

"People want to contribute," Anya Petrova had stated during a recent planning meeting, her usual pragmatism softened by a newfound optimism. "They want to be part of something positive, something that represents hope and growth. The Arboreum, in its new form, can be that focal point. It's a project that unites us, that gives us a shared vision to work towards."

Mara agreed wholeheartedly. The Arboreum, scarred but standing, was more than just a garden. It was a living testament to Havenridge's renewed ethos. It symbolized their ability to adapt, to innovate, and to find beauty and purpose even in the face of devastation. It was a commitment to integrating life's natural rhythms into the community's design, a place where the lessons of survival would be woven into the tapestry of a more vibrant, hopeful existence. It was, in essence, the heart of their rediscovery, a promise of a future cultivated with resilience, nurtured by community, and inspired by the enduring power of life itself.

The physical reconstruction of the Arboreum's central dome was a complex undertaking. Eli's team, working alongside skilled artisans and volunteers, was employing a combination of salvaged materials and advanced composite fabrics. The new canopy would not be a monolithic structure but a series of overlapping, modular panels, designed to be easily repaired or replaced if damaged. These panels would be made from a bio-engineered polymer, lightweight yet incredibly strong, capable of withstanding extreme weather conditions. Interspersed within these panels would be translucent sections, allowing for natural light penetration, and integrated photovoltaic cells, harvesting solar energy to power the Arboreum's internal systems.

"It's about modularity and adaptability," Eli explained to a group of curious onlookers, his hands gesturing animatedly. "If one section is compromised, it doesn't jeopardize the entire structure. We can simply detach the damaged panel and replace it with a new one. It's a system designed for resilience, not just resistance."

The grounds themselves were being meticulously replanted, not with the rigid, formal arrangements of the past, but with a focus on native, drought-resistant species and plants known for their ability to thrive in diverse soil conditions. Zones were being created to mimic various local microclimates – coastal scrub, woodland edges, and wetland areas – each designed to be self-sustaining and require minimal intervention. This wasn't just about aesthetics; it was about creating an ecosystem that could naturally regulate itself, reducing the need for intensive maintenance and making it more forgiving of environmental fluctuations.

"We're choosing plants that have proven their mettle," Mara observed as she knelt to examine a hardy sea grass being carefully planted near a newly constructed water feature. "Species that can withstand salt spray, high winds, and fluctuating temperatures. It's a conscious effort to align our efforts with the natural resilience of our environment."

The former research labs were being repurposed into community workshops and educational spaces. These areas would host a variety of programs, from botanical illustration and sustainable gardening techniques to the practical skills of water conservation and renewable energy maintenance. The goal was to empower residents with the knowledge and tools to not only appreciate the Arboreum but to actively participate in its upkeep and to apply its principles in their own lives.

Eli was particularly excited about the potential for the Arboreum to become a living archive of the community's journey. He proposed installing interactive displays that would document the storm, the recovery efforts, and the evolution of Havenridge's philosophy of resilience. These displays would incorporate salvaged artifacts, personal testimonies, and data visualizations, creating a powerful and engaging narrative that would serve as a constant reminder of their shared experience and their collective strength.

"We want future generations to understand what we went through, and more importantly, what we learned," Eli emphasized. "The Arboreum will be a testament to our capacity for adaptation, for innovation, and for the enduring power of community. It's a place where history is not just remembered, but lived."

The expansion also included a dedicated section for a seed bank, a vital component for ensuring the long-term survival of the region's botanical heritage. This facility, equipped with state-of-the-art climate control and preservation technology, would safeguard a diverse collection of seeds, ensuring that even if disaster struck again, the genetic diversity of their local flora would be preserved for future restoration efforts.

Mara saw the seed bank as a powerful symbol of hope. It represented a commitment to the future, a belief in the ability of life to endure and to flourish. It was a tangible manifestation of their renewed ethos, a quiet promise whispered in the rustle of carefully stored seeds.

The development of the Arboreum was proceeding with a sense of urgency, yet also with a deliberate, mindful pace.

There was a collective understanding that this was not just a construction project, but a cultural transformation. Every decision, from the choice of materials to the design of the pathways, was being made with the overarching goal of creating a space that embodied the community's newfound appreciation for interconnectedness, sustainability, and resilience.

As the sun began to set, casting long shadows across the partially reconstructed dome, Mara and Eli stood hand-in-hand, watching the vibrant activity of the construction crews. The air was filled with the hum of machinery, the calls of workers, and the distant chirping of birds already finding refuge in the emerging greenery. It was a symphony of renewal, a testament to the indomitable spirit of Havenridge.

"It's more than we ever dreamed of," Mara whispered, her voice thick with emotion. "It's a living, breathing embodiment of everything we've learned."

Eli squeezed her hand, his gaze fixed on the evolving landscape. "It's a promise, Mara. A promise that even after the harshest storms, life finds a way. And we," he turned to her, his eyes shining with a love that had deepened in the crucible of their shared journey, "we are a part of that life. We are the architects of its future."

The Arboreum, in its reimagined form, was no longer just a sanctuary for plants; it was a sanctuary for the human spirit. It was a place where the scars of the past would be transformed into a canvas for a brighter future, a living testament to the enduring power of hope, community, and the unyielding resilience of life itself. It was the beating heart of Havenridge's rebirth, a vibrant, green promise blooming in the aftermath of devastation.

Chapter Twelve

Living After the Quiet

The air in Havenridge itself felt different. It was a subtle shift, like the atmosphere after a cleansing rain, carrying a new clarity and a lightness that had been absent for too long. The brutal efficiency that had once defined their community, a necessity born of scarcity and external threats, had undeniably served its purpose. It had allowed them to survive, to endure the harsh realities of their world. But survival, Mara had come to understand, was only the first step. True thriving, a flourishing existence, demanded something more.

The storm, in its indiscriminate fury, had swept away not only structures but also the rigid, calcified protocols that had become embedded in their way of life. These weren't just rules; they were mental frameworks, built to insulate and protect, to ensure predictability in an unpredictable world. But as Eli had so often observed, the very rigidity that offered protection also made one vulnerable to the sudden, violent shifts in the wind. The storm had been that violent shift, and Havenridge, in its battered but unbroken state, had been forced to adapt.

The change was most palpable in the interactions between people. Gone were the clipped, purposeful exchanges, the careful adherence to designated roles. In their place, a new fluidity had emerged. Neighbors who had once exchanged polite nods now found themselves engaged in spontaneous conversations, sharing not just practical concerns but also their hopes and fears. The lines between work and life, between individual tasks and collective endeavors, had blurred. A shared sense of purpose, forged in the crucible of crisis, had given rise to an organic sense of interdependence.

Mara witnessed this firsthand during a visit to the communal refectory. What had once been a precisely timed meal service, designed for maximum efficiency and minimal waste, was now a more relaxed affair. Tables were occupied by a mixture of individuals and small groups, their conversations weaving a tapestry of shared experiences. A grizzled elder, whose hands bore the permanent marks of a lifetime of labor, was patiently explaining a new method of water purification to a young woman barely out of her teens, her eyes wide with eager comprehension. Nearby, a group of children, their faces smudged with dirt from playing amongst the newly planted saplings, were being taught a traditional song by one of the community's musicians, their voices blending in a joyful, if somewhat off-key, harmony.

This wasn't a breakdown of order; it was a redefinition of it. The rigid hierarchy had softened, replaced by a more organic network of knowledge and support. Initiative was no longer something to be cautiously vetted through layers of bureaucracy; it was encouraged, celebrated. If someone saw a need – a patch of soil that needed tending, a community member who needed assistance, a new idea that could improve their collective well-being – they were empowered to act. And crucially, they were met not with suspicion, but with collaboration.

Eli's influence was undeniable in this shift. He had always championed a philosophy of adaptable systems, whether in architecture or in social structures. He believed that true strength lay not in impenetrable defenses, but in the ability to absorb and redirect, to learn and evolve. His constant refrain, particularly in the early days of rebuilding, had been about the importance of listening – truly listening – to the needs and ideas of everyone in the community. "When we're all looking at the same problem from slightly different angles," he'd said during one of their many late-night planning sessions, his brow furrowed in concentration, "we see the whole picture. And the whole picture is always more resilient than any single piece."

The weekly community council meetings, once formal affairs where decisions were announced rather than debated, had also transformed. Now, they were vibrant forums for discussion. Everyone, from the youngest to the oldest, who had something to contribute, had a voice. Resolutions were reached through consensus, or at least through a genuine effort to understand opposing viewpoints. The focus had shifted from enforcing compliance to fostering understanding and finding common ground.

Mara found herself increasingly drawn to these meetings, not just as an observer, but as an active participant. Her analytical mind, honed by years of managing complex systems, was now being applied in new ways. She wasn't just identifying potential problems; she was helping to brainstorm solutions, to weave together disparate ideas into coherent plans. She noticed, with a quiet satisfaction, how often her initial reservations, born from a habit of anticipating every possible pitfall, were being met with thoughtful counterpoints and innovative adaptations, rather than outright dismissal. The fear of failure, a constant companion in the past, was gradually receding, replaced by a growing confidence in their collective ability to navigate challenges.

One of the most significant developments was the open sharing of resources. The days of strict rationing and carefully guarded individual stores were slowly fading. While prudence was still a virtue, a new spirit of generosity had taken root. If a family had a surplus of vegetables from their garden, they were more likely to share it with a neighbor who had had a less bountiful harvest. If someone had a particular skill – be it mending, carpentry, or even storytelling – they were readily offering their time and expertise to others. This wasn't charity; it was a reciprocal exchange, a recognition that their individual well-being was inextricably linked to the well-being of the community as a whole.

This interconnectedness was also fostering a deeper sense of belonging. For years, Havenridge had been a community defined by its shared adversity and its collective efforts to survive. Now, it was evolving into a community defined by its shared aspirations and its collective commitment to creating a life of meaning and purpose. The storm had stripped away many of the superficial distractions, forcing them to confront what truly mattered. And what mattered, they were discovering, was each other.

The children, in particular, seemed to embody this newfound spirit. They played together with an ease and camaraderie that transcended age or previous social divisions. Their games were less about competition and more about collaboration. They built elaborate forts from salvaged materials, their imaginations transforming discarded debris into grand castles and hidden lairs. They learned from each other, sharing knowledge about the natural world, about the stars, about the songs their grandparents used to sing. They were growing up in an environment that, while still bearing the marks of hardship, was suffused with a palpable sense of hope and mutual respect.

Mara often watched them from her window, a soft smile playing on her lips. She saw in their uninhibited joy a reflection of the future they were actively building. Their innocence was not a lack of awareness of the world's challenges, but a testament to the resilience of the human spirit, a spirit that, when nurtured by community and hope, could find beauty and joy even in the shadow of past storms.

The physical reconstruction was ongoing, of course, but it was no longer the sole focus of their collective energy. While essential structures were being repaired and reinforced, there was an equal emphasis being placed on building spaces that fostered connection and well-being. The Arboreum, as Eli had envisioned, was becoming more than just a botanical garden; it was a central hub for community life. The open-air amphitheater, once a place for formal presentations, was now a venue for impromptu music sessions, storytelling circles, and lively debates. The smaller, more intimate seating areas, nestled amongst the burgeoning foliage, had become natural gathering spots for friends and families, places where conversations flowed easily and laughter echoed through the air.

Even the daily tasks of living had taken on a new rhythm. Meal preparation, once a solitary or narrowly familial undertaking, was often a communal effort. Families would bring their ingredients to the communal kitchens, working together to prepare dishes, sharing recipes and techniques. This not only made the task more enjoyable but also fostered a sense of shared responsibility and camaraderie. The act of breaking bread, once a simple necessity, had become a profound ritual of connection.

The spirit of innovation that had been unleashed by the storm was also continuing to flourish. People were no longer afraid to experiment, to try new things. Small workshops had sprung up, dedicated to various crafts and skills – from weaving and pottery to the repair of essential tools and equipment. These weren't officially sanctioned enterprises; they were organic endeavors, born from individual passions and a desire to contribute to the collective good. The community council, rather than dictating what should be made or how, was actively supporting these initiatives, providing access to materials and offering encouragement.

Mara found herself drawn into one such initiative, a small group dedicated to developing more efficient and sustainable methods for water collection and purification. Her expertise in systems analysis proved invaluable, helping them to identify bottlenecks in their current processes and to devise innovative solutions. She worked alongside a retired engineer, a former artisan, and a young woman who possessed an uncanny understanding of natural filtration methods. Their collaboration, a seamless blend of experience and fresh perspective, was a microcosm of Havenridge's renewed spirit. They shared ideas freely, challenged each other respectfully, and celebrated each small victory together.

The concept of "risk" itself had been redefined. It was no longer about avoiding all potential dangers, but about understanding and managing them, about embracing the calculated risks that were necessary for growth and progress. They were learning to navigate the unpredictable currents of their environment not by building higher walls, but by becoming more agile, more responsive, and more deeply connected to one another.

This newfound openness had also extended to their understanding of themselves. The storm had forced a collective introspection, a re-examination of their values and their place in the world. They had learned that true strength was not found in rigid self-reliance, but in the courage to be vulnerable, to ask for help, and to offer support without reservation. This emotional resilience, built on a foundation of trust and open communication, was perhaps the most significant and enduring legacy of the storm.

As Mara walked through the bustling marketplace, the scent of freshly baked bread mingling with the aroma of herbs from the community gardens, she felt a profound sense of peace. The scars of the storm were still visible, etched into the landscape and into the memories of its inhabitants. But they were no longer symbols of defeat. They were reminders of their strength, of their capacity for renewal, and of the beautiful, imperfect future they were bravely building, together. The air was alive with the hum of conversation, the murmur of children's laughter, and the quiet, steady beat of a community that had learned to not just survive, but to truly live. It was a Havenridge renewed, not by erasing the past, but by weaving its lessons into the vibrant tapestry of a hopeful, interconnected future. The rigid protocols of the past had given way to the flexible, flowing wisdom of the present, and in that transformation, they had found a resilience deeper and more enduring than any they had ever known.

Mara moved through the newly established community hub with a lightness that still surprised her. The central plaza, once a utilitarian space for mandatory gatherings, now pulsed with life. Children chased each other around the repurposed solar charging stations, their laughter a bright counterpoint to the gentle hum of the hydroponic gardens that lined the perimeter. She paused by the information kiosk, its screen displaying not just work schedules and resource allocations, but also community announcements: a call for volunteers to help with the spring planting, an invitation to a storytelling evening in the Arboreum, a notice about a nascent pottery collective seeking apprentices. It was a far cry from the stark, efficiency-driven directives of the past.

She recognized Elara, one of the younger members of the council, animatedly discussing an idea with an older man whose face was creased with wisdom and years of sun exposure. Elara, who had once been painfully shy, now spoke with a quiet confidence, her hands gesturing to emphasize her points. Mara felt a pang of pride, not just for Elara, but for the entire community that had fostered such growth. She remembered the early days after the Quiet, the pervasive fear that had clung to everyone, the desperate need for structure and control. Her own role then had been about reinforcing those structures, about ensuring every cog in the machine turned as it should. Survival had been the only metric.

But survival, as she had learned, was a finite goal. It was a foundation, not a dwelling. The storm, in its destructive chaos, had inadvertently cleared the ground for something more. It had exposed the fragility of their rigid systems and, in doing so, had made them open to new possibilities. Eli had been instrumental in guiding this transition, his calm, forward-thinking perspective a steadying force. He had never pushed for radical change, but rather for measured adaptation, for the embrace of a learning mindset. He had always said that true resilience wasn't about resisting the storm, but about learning to dance in the rain.

Mara's own journey had mirrored Havenridge's transformation. The paralyzing fear that had once dictated her every decision had receded, replaced by a quiet determination. She no longer saw potential threats lurking behind every shadowed corner. Instead, she saw opportunities for connection, for collaboration, for the creation of something beautiful and lasting. Her analytical mind, once a tool for anticipating disaster, was now dedicated to nurturing growth. She still served on the community council, her voice carrying weight, but her approach had softened. She no longer advocated for the strictest adherence to protocol for its own sake. Instead, she championed a balance, a thoughtful integration of order and flexibility. She understood that too much rigidity could lead to fragility, while too much freedom could lead to chaos. Finding that sweet spot, that dynamic equilibrium, had become her new purpose.

She found Eli by the edge of the Arboreum, his back to her as he studied a cluster of new bioluminescent fungi that had begun to bloom. The soft, ethereal glow cast a gentle light on his face, highlighting the lines of thought etched around his eyes. He turned as she approached, a warm smile spreading across his lips.

"Lost in the glow again?" Mara asked, her voice soft.

Eli chuckled, the sound a low rumble. "Just admiring the persistence of life, Mara. Even in the dark, it finds a way to shine." He gestured to the fungi. "These weren't here last week. A new species, perhaps, thriving in the dampness after the recent rains."

Mara stood beside him, taking in the vibrant, living ecosystem. It was a far cry from the sterile, highly controlled environments of their past. The Arboreum was a testament to Eli's vision, a space designed not just for scientific study, but for human connection and well-being. Families picnicked on the mossy clearings, children explored hidden pathways, and artists found inspiration in the riot of colors and textures.

"It's beautiful, Eli," she said, her gaze sweeping over the lush foliage. "It feels... alive. Truly alive."

He met her eyes, his expression one of profound contentment. "That's the goal, isn't it? Not just to survive, but to truly live. To create a space where life can flourish, in all its forms." He reached out, his hand gently covering hers. His touch, once a source of hesitant comfort, now felt like an anchor, a constant reminder of the depth of their shared journey.

"I used to think survival was the ultimate achievement," Mara confessed, her voice tinged with a hint of her former self. "That safety was the only thing worth striving for. I built walls, both literally and figuratively, to keep the world out."

"And look at you now," Eli said, his thumb stroking the back of her hand. "You're the one opening the gates, inviting the world in. Not the chaotic, dangerous world of before, but a world remade, a world we're building together."

Mara smiled, a genuine, unburdened smile. She remembered the gnawing anxiety that had been her constant companion, the sleepless nights spent meticulously planning for every conceivable catastrophe. That fear had been a heavy cloak, suffocating her spirit. The storm had ripped it away, leaving her exposed, yes, but also strangely liberated. She had learned to trust, not just Eli, but the collective wisdom of Havenridge. She had learned to embrace vulnerability, not as a weakness, but as a pathway to deeper connection.

"It wasn't easy," she admitted. "Letting go of that control. Trusting that things would be okay, even without every variable accounted for."

"But you did it," Eli said, his gaze steady and full of admiration. "You saw that true strength wasn't in rigid defenses, but in adaptability. You embraced the idea that we could learn and grow, even from disruption." He squeezed her hand. "And you found something more valuable than safety, didn't you?"

Mara looked out at the vibrant scene before them, the laughter of the children, the gentle murmur of conversation, the rich scent of blooming flowers. She thought of the collaborative projects, the shared meals, the spontaneous acts of kindness that were now woven into the fabric of their daily lives. She thought of her own role, no longer that of a gatekeeper, but of a builder, a facilitator, a nurturer.

"Fulfillment," she said, the word feeling both foreign and deeply familiar on her tongue. "Purpose. And... love." Her eyes met Eli's, and in their depths, she saw a reflection of her own transformed heart. The fear of loss, of vulnerability, had been replaced by a profound appreciation for what they had built, for what they were.

She still contributed to the council, her insights valued, her voice respected. She championed initiatives that fostered innovation and sustainability, always advocating for a measured approach that respected the lessons of the past while embracing the possibilities of the future. She worked with the education committee to ensure that the children were taught not only practical skills but also the importance of empathy and collaboration. She found joy in the small things – in the taste of freshly picked berries, in the warmth of the sun on her skin, in the quiet comfort of Eli's presence beside her.

The scars of the storm were still present, a reminder of the hardships they had endured. But they were no longer a source of pain or fear. They were markers of resilience, testaments to their collective strength. Havenridge was not a place that had erased its past, but one that had learned from it, weaving its hard-won lessons into the vibrant tapestry of a hopeful, interconnected future. Mara, once a prisoner of her own fear, had found her true freedom in embracing that future, in building it, and in loving it, with all her heart. She had stepped onto a new path, one paved not with caution and control, but with trust, connection, and the quiet, radiant glow of a life truly lived.

Eli's influence had become less about overt guidance and more about a pervasive, gentle encouragement, like the persistent sun coaxing new life from the soil after a long winter. His presence, his quiet conviction, had become a cornerstone of Havenridge's identity. He didn't just speak of resilience; he embodied it, demonstrating through his actions how one could not only endure but truly thrive. He continued to foster an environment where new ideas could blossom, where experimentation was not only tolerated but actively encouraged. This was most evident in the nascent workshops that were springing up across the community.

One such initiative was the 'Echoes of Earth' project, a collective dedicated to rediscovering and reinterpreting traditional crafts. Eli, with his deep appreciation for history and humanity's enduring creative spirit, had been a catalyst for its formation. He had unearthed old, almost forgotten journals from pre-Quiet archives, filled with detailed instructions for weaving, pottery, and woodworking. He presented these not as relics of a lost age, but as blueprints for the future, opportunities to reconnect with ancestral skills and imbue them with a new, modern relevance.

Mara found herself drawn to these workshops, initially out of a sense of civic duty, but soon, out of genuine fascination. She observed a group of young adults, their hands stained with clay, laboring over spinning wheels. Their initial attempts were clumsy, the pottery lopsided and fragile, yet their faces were alight with concentration and a shared sense of purpose. Eli was often among them, not directing, but observing, offering a word of encouragement, or a gentle suggestion on how to balance the centrifugal force. He had a remarkable ability to see the potential in imperfection, to find the beauty in the struggle.

"Look at this, Mara," he'd said one afternoon, holding up a small, misshapen bowl. "It's not perfectly symmetrical, but feel the weight of it. Feel the imprint of the maker's hands. There's a story here, a connection that a mass-produced item can never replicate."

Mara had taken the bowl, turning it over in her hands. She could feel the slight unevenness, the subtle ripples in the glaze. And he was right. It possessed a warmth, a tangible sense of humanity that was more compelling than any flawless object. It was a testament to Eli's philosophy: that the process, the act of creation, held as much value as the final product. This was a radical departure from the efficiency-driven mindset that had once permeated their society, where only the perfect outcome mattered.

Another area where Eli's inspiration flourished was in the community's engagement with the natural world. He had spearheaded the "Living Library" initiative, an ambitious project to catalog and cultivate the diverse flora and fauna that had begun to reclaim the land surrounding Havenridge. This wasn't just a scientific endeavor; it was a deeply philosophical one. Eli believed that understanding and respecting the natural world was crucial for their own long-term survival and well-being.

He organized guided walks through the rewilded areas, his explanations a fascinating blend of scientific fact and poetic observation. He pointed out the symbiotic relationships between plants, the intricate patterns of insect life, the subtle signs of changing seasons. He encouraged residents to record their own observations, creating a communal journal of discoveries. Children, in particular, were captivated by these excursions. Eli had a way of sparking their curiosity, of making the complex world of ecology accessible and wondrous. He taught them to identify bird calls, to track animal prints, to understand the delicate balance of the ecosystem.

"Every living thing," he'd once told a group of wide-eyed children gathered around him, "has a purpose, a role to play. Just like you do. When we learn to appreciate that, when we learn to work with nature, not against it, we become stronger, healthier, and happier."

These lessons extended beyond the educational sphere. Eli actively promoted activities that fostered this connection, from communal gardening projects to stargazing evenings. He believed that reconnecting with the rhythms of nature – the rising and setting of the sun, the cycles of the moon, the changing of the seasons – helped to ground people, to remind them of their place in the larger tapestry of existence. It was a counterpoint to the artificiality that had once defined their lives, a grounding force in a world that had become increasingly detached from its natural origins.

The impact of Eli's continued inspiration was palpable in the overall atmosphere of Havenridge. The fear that had once been a constant undertone had largely dissipated, replaced by a sense of shared purpose and a quiet optimism. People were no longer simply surviving; they were actively *living*. They were engaging with each other, with their environment, and with their own creative potential. This shift was not a result of grand pronouncements or strict mandates, but of a sustained, gentle cultivation of a different way of being.

Eli's philosophy of "dancing in the rain" had, in many ways, become the community's unofficial motto. They had weathered the storm, they had learned from its fury, and now, they were finding joy in the aftermath, in the unexpected beauty that had emerged from the chaos. He had encouraged them to see challenges not as insurmountable obstacles, but as opportunities for growth and innovation. This was evident in how they approached problems now. Instead of seeking to eliminate all risk, they sought to mitigate it, to learn from potential failures, and to adapt with agility.

Mara often found herself reflecting on this transformation. She had been one of the most resistant to change in the early days, her ingrained instinct for control making it difficult for her to let go. But Eli's unwavering belief in the inherent goodness and adaptability of people had slowly chipped away at her defenses. He had never dismissed her concerns, but rather, he had gently challenged her assumptions, guiding her towards a new understanding.

"Control," he had said to her once, during a particularly difficult council meeting where Mara was advocating for stricter regulations on resource allocation, "is often an illusion. True security comes from understanding, from adaptation, and from the strength of our connections. When we are truly connected, we are more resilient than any set of rules can make us."

His words had resonated deeply, and she had begun to see the limitations of her former approach. She started to embrace the idea of emergent order, of allowing systems to develop organically rather than being rigidly imposed. This had led to a more fluid and adaptable community structure, one that was better equipped to handle the inevitable uncertainties of their existence.

The community's commitment to fostering creativity and connection was further exemplified by the 'Art for All' program, which Eli had enthusiastically supported. This program provided resources and space for anyone who wished to explore their artistic talents, regardless of their previous experience. It wasn't about producing masterpieces; it was about the joy of expression, the therapeutic benefits of creation, and the shared experience of artistic exploration.

Eli often visited these studios, his presence a quiet encouragement. He would pause by a canvas splattered with vibrant, abstract colors, or admire a block of wood being painstakingly carved into a whimsical creature. He saw the value in every attempt, recognizing that even a seemingly simple doodle could be a profound expression of the artist's inner world. He understood that art, in its myriad forms, was a vital outlet for the human spirit, a way to process emotions, to communicate complex ideas, and to find beauty in the everyday.

He also championed initiatives that focused on intergenerational learning. He believed that the wisdom of the elders and the fresh perspectives of the youth were invaluable resources that needed to be shared and celebrated. This led to the creation of mentorship programs, where experienced artisans worked alongside young apprentices, and storytelling sessions where elders recounted their memories and experiences, bridging the gaps between generations and preserving their collective history.

One particular success story that Eli often highlighted was the story of Anya, a young woman who had been deeply traumatized by the storm. She had withdrawn into herself, struggling to connect with others. Through the 'Art for All' program, Anya discovered a talent for sculpture. Working with clay, she began to express the turmoil she had internalized, slowly, painstakingly, transforming her pain into tangible forms. Eli provided her with the space and the quiet support she needed, never pushing, but always present. Eventually, Anya began to share her work, and through her art, she found a way to communicate her experiences, to heal, and to connect with others on a profound level. Her journey became an emblem of Havenridge's capacity for healing and transformation, a testament to the power of creativity and community support.

Eli's continued inspiration was also about reminding people of the simple joys of life. He would often initiate spontaneous gatherings – a shared meal in the central plaza, a music session under the starlit sky, a communal effort to tend the rooftop gardens. These weren't planned events with elaborate agendas; they were organic expressions of connection and camaraderie. He understood that true community wasn't just about shared goals and responsibilities, but about shared moments of joy, laughter, and simple human connection.

He had a particular fondness for the bioluminescent flora that Eli had helped cultivate in the Arboreum, and would often lead evening strolls through its softly glowing pathways. He would point out the delicate dance of the light, the way it pulsed and shifted, a living testament to nature's quiet magic. He would speak of how this beauty, often overlooked in the rush of daily life, was a source of wonder and solace, a reminder that even in the darkest of times, there was always light to be found.

"These plants," he once said, his voice a hushed murmur amidst the gentle glow, "they don't strive for attention. They simply bloom, in their own time, in their own way. And in their quiet radiance, they bring a unique beauty into the world. We can learn a great deal from their resilience, their patience, their inherent radiance."

This emphasis on appreciating the subtle beauty of the world, on finding joy in the present moment, had become a crucial part of Havenridge's ethos. It was a conscious counter-movement to the frantic pace and consumerist culture of the past. Eli's philosophy encouraged a mindful existence, a deeper appreciation for the simple, fundamental elements of life. He helped people to re-evaluate what truly mattered, shifting the focus from material accumulation to the richness of experience, connection, and personal growth.

His advocacy for sustainability was not just about resource management; it was about a profound respect for the planet that sustained them. He encouraged the development of closed-loop systems, the use of renewable energy, and the reduction of waste, not as an obligation, but as an act of stewardship. He saw Havenridge as a part of a larger ecosystem, and their survival depended on their ability to live in harmony with it. This perspective fostered a sense of responsibility and interconnectedness that extended beyond the human community.

Mara, observing Eli's enduring influence, felt a deep sense of gratitude. He had not only guided Havenridge through a period of immense upheaval but had also helped to shape its soul. He had shown them that true strength lay not in rigid control, but in adaptability, creativity, and compassion. He had reminded them that life, in all its messy, beautiful complexity, was a gift to be cherished, nurtured, and celebrated. His inspiration wasn't a fading echo of the past, but a vibrant, living force, continually shaping the future of Havenridge, ensuring that they not only survived the storm but learned to dance, truly dance, in the rain. He was the quiet conductor of their evolving symphony, his gentle baton guiding them towards a future filled with purpose, connection, and the enduring, radiant glow of a life fully lived.

The gentle hum of the hydroponic farm, a constant, reassuring presence in Havenridge, had become the soundtrack to Mara and Eli's deepening connection. It was a sound that spoke of life sustained, of innovation born from necessity, and now, it seemed to echo the quiet growth of their own relationship. Their shared journey, which had begun with the pragmatic concerns of rebuilding a fractured world, had seamlessly interwoven into the intimate fabric of their lives. The early days, a whirlwind of crisis management and strategic planning, had given way to a more profound understanding, a partnership that extended far beyond the communal projects they championed.

Mara found herself drawn to Eli's quiet strength, a steady anchor in the often-turbulent waters of their new existence. He possessed a remarkable ability to see the inherent goodness in people, to foster it, and to allow it to blossom. This wasn't a naive optimism, but a deeply ingrained belief in humanity's capacity for resilience and compassion, a belief that had proven time and again to be a guiding light for Havenridge. In his presence, Mara felt a sense of peace she hadn't thought possible, a shedding of the hyper-vigilance that had become a second skin after the Quiet. He saw her not just as a capable leader, but as a woman, with her own vulnerabilities and dreams, and he met them with an unwavering tenderness that was both surprising and deeply welcome.

Their conversations, once focused on crop yields and resource allocation, now meandered into the softer landscapes of personal history, of aspirations, and of the simple, everyday joys that had begun to reassert themselves in their lives. They would walk hand-in-hand through the rewilded orchards, the scent of newly bloomed fruit trees thick in the air, discussing not the challenges of the harvest, but the way the sunlight dappled through the leaves, or the memory of a particular bird's song. Eli, with his poet's soul, would point out the subtle shifts in the light, the way it painted the landscape in hues of gold and rose, and Mara, usually so grounded in the practical, found herself swept away by his observations, her senses awakened to a beauty she had previously overlooked.

One evening, after a particularly arduous day of mediating a minor dispute over water rights, they found themselves sitting on the rooftop garden, the city lights of Havenridge twinkling below like fallen stars. The air was cool, carrying the faint, earthy aroma of the herbs they had planted. Eli turned to Mara, his gaze soft and full of an emotion that made her heart swell. "You know, Mara," he began, his voice a low rumble, "I used to think that survival was the ultimate goal. To simply endure. But you've shown me that it's so much more than that."

Mara leaned her head on his shoulder, the familiar scent of his worn linen shirt a comfort. "And you, Eli," she replied, her voice catching slightly, "you've shown me that survival can be beautiful. That the space between enduring and truly living can be filled with... this." She gestured vaguely at the peaceful scene around them, at the quiet camaraderie that had settled over Havenridge like a soft blanket.

Their love was not a tempestuous, dramatic affair. It was a slow, steady burn, like embers glowing in the hearth, providing warmth and light without consuming everything in its path. It was built on shared understanding, on mutual respect, and on a profound recognition of each other's strengths and vulnerabilities. Eli's unwavering belief in the good that resided within people, a belief that had been instrumental in Havenridge's recovery, was something Mara found herself drawing strength from. He didn't just talk about hope; he embodied it, and in his eyes, she saw a reflection of that hope, amplified and made real.

He often spoke of their relationship as a testament to the possibility of finding profound connection, even in a world that had been so drastically reshaped. "We've learned to rebuild our homes, our systems," he'd said to her, holding her close one night, "but more importantly, we're learning to rebuild ourselves, and to do that together." For Mara, who had spent so long guarding her heart, his words were a revelation. He saw the scars left by the Quiet, not as marks of weakness, but as evidence of resilience, and he loved her all the more for them.

Their days were filled with the purposeful rhythm of community life, yet woven within that were moments of profound intimacy. A shared glance across a crowded town hall meeting, a hand brushing hers as they passed a tool in the workshop, a quiet walk under the bioluminescent flora of the Arboreum, their steps synchronized, their breathing in tune. These were the small, precious moments that stitched their lives together, creating a tapestry of shared experience that was richer and more vibrant than anything Mara had ever known.

Eli's influence on the community extended into their personal lives in subtle yet significant ways. He had a way of encouraging people to embrace the quiet moments, to find joy in the simple act of being present. This was something he actively fostered in his relationship with Mara. He didn't demand grand gestures; instead, he cultivated an environment where their love could unfold naturally, organically. He celebrated her triumphs, big and small, and offered quiet solace during her moments of doubt.

He remembered one particular afternoon, not long after they had begun to openly acknowledge their feelings for each other. Mara had been wrestling with a difficult decision regarding the allocation of resources for a new educational initiative. She was torn between a practical, cost-effective solution and a more ambitious, resource-intensive approach that she felt would offer greater long-term benefits. Eli found her in her study, the papers spread out before her, her brow furrowed in concentration. He didn't offer advice, at least not directly. Instead, he simply sat beside her, his presence a calming balm.

"Sometimes," he said softly, his voice barely disturbing the quiet, "the most important decisions are not about what is most efficient, but what resonates most deeply with our values. What does your heart tell you, Mara?"

His question, so simple yet so profound, cut through the noise of her anxieties. She looked at him, his eyes reflecting the gentle light filtering through the window, and she saw not just a partner, but a confidante, someone who understood the weight of leadership and the importance of leading with integrity. She spoke her thoughts aloud, articulating the intangible benefits of the more ambitious plan, the potential for inspiration and growth it held, even if the immediate return was less predictable. Eli listened, not just hearing her words, but sensing the conviction behind them. When she finally made her decision, he simply squeezed her hand. "I trust your heart, Mara," he said. And in that moment, she knew she had made the right choice.

Their shared journey was a living embodiment of the book's central theme. In the aftermath of devastation, in the quiet hum of a world slowly finding its voice again, love and hope had indeed found fertile ground. Their relationship was a quiet testament to this truth, a promise that survival was not an endpoint, but a beginning. It was the promise of togetherness, of building a future not just of resilience, but of profound connection and enduring love, a future where they would truly live, side-by-side, hand-in-hand, weathering whatever storms might come, and finding joy in the sunlight that always followed. The strength they found in each other wasn't a shield against the world's harsh realities, but a foundation upon which they could build something beautiful, something lasting, something that whispered of a future painted in hues of hope and shared dreams. They were two souls who had navigated the darkest of nights, and in finding each other, had discovered a dawn that promised not just survival, but the sweet, enduring miracle of a life fully lived, together.

The Arboreum, once a symbol of precarious survival, now pulsed with an almost effervescent life. It was more than just a collection of plants; it had become the beating heart of Havenridge, a living, breathing testament to their rediscovered philosophy of co-existence. The air within its geodesic domes hummed not just with the gentle whir of atmospheric regulators and nutrient delivery systems, but with a palpable sense of peace, a quiet joy that seemed to emanate from the very soil. Sunlight, meticulously filtered and amplified, bathed the verdant landscape in an ethereal glow, coaxing forth an astonishing array of flora. Towering bioluminescent fungi cast soft, otherworldly light in shaded alcoves, while delicate, jewel-toned orchids unfurled their petals in meticulously controlled microclimates. Cascading vines, heavy with fragrant blossoms, draped themselves artfully over reclaimed structural elements, blurring the lines between the organic and the engineered.

Mara often found herself drawn to the Arboreum in the quiet hours of the morning, before the community's daily rhythm truly began. She would walk the winding paths, her bare feet sinking slightly into the springy moss that carpeted the walkways, breathing in the complex, layered scents of damp earth, blooming flowers, and ripening fruits. It was here, amidst this vibrant tapestry of life, that the weight of leadership felt lightest. The Arboreum was a sanctuary, not just from the lingering anxieties of the past, but a space where the future felt not like a daunting unknown, but a promise nurtured into being. Eli had been the architect of this vision, his understanding of botany and his innate connection to the natural world proving to be an invaluable asset. But it was Mara's pragmatic implementation, her ability to translate his visionary ideas into tangible, sustainable systems, that had truly brought it to life. Their shared effort, born from necessity, had blossomed into something far more profound, a living monument to their partnership.

The Arboreum served multiple critical functions for Havenridge, extending far beyond its aesthetic appeal. It was their primary source for many of their most vital food crops, cultivated with an understanding of soil health and biodiversity that had been lost to previous generations. Varieties of nutrient-rich vegetables, adapted to thrive in their controlled environment, grew in abundance alongside experimental strains of grains and legumes. Beyond sustenance, it was a vital center for medicinal research. Elder botanists, their knowledge painstakingly resurrected from fragmented digital archives and oral traditions, worked alongside younger apprentices, identifying, cultivating, and processing plants with healing properties. There were remedies for common ailments, of course, but also promising research into treatments for lingering environmental toxins and the psychological scars left by the Quiet. The sheer variety of plant life ensured a constant stream of new discoveries, a testament to nature's boundless ingenuity.

The educational aspect of the Arboreum was equally significant. It was a living classroom, where children and adults alike could learn about the intricate web of life, the principles of sustainable agriculture, and the importance of ecological balance. Guided tours, led by knowledgeable community members, were a regular occurrence. Children would marvel at the gigantic pitcher plants, their mouths agape as they learned about carnivorous flora, or delight in the gentle glow of the 'starflower' mushrooms, their bioluminescence explained by Eli's simple, yet captivating, analogies. Adults, too, found renewed appreciation for the natural world. They learned about companion planting, natural pest control, and the art of seed saving, skills that were crucial for Havenridge's long-term self-sufficiency. The Arboreum had become a hub of knowledge transfer, a place where the wisdom of the past was being woven into the fabric of their future.

One of Mara's favorite aspects of the Arboreum was the 'Whispering Grove,' a section dedicated to species that had been on the brink of extinction before the Quiet. Here, under a specially designed canopy that mimicked the twilight of their original habitats, ancient trees stood sentinel, their gnarled branches reaching towards the filtered light. There were species of redwood, their immense trunks a reminder of a bygone era of giants, and delicate ferns that had once carpeted forgotten rainforests. Eli had a particular fondness for this grove, often speaking of the resilience of these ancient species. "They've endured millennia, Mara," he'd said, his voice hushed with reverence during one of their private visits. "They've weathered storms, droughts, ice ages. They are a testament to life's unwavering will to persist, to adapt, to simply *be*." His words resonated deeply with Mara, mirroring the journey of their own community, and of their own hearts.

The legacy of Mara and Eli's journey was woven into every leaf, every bloom, every thriving root within the Arboreum. It wasn't just about surviving the Quiet; it was about learning to live again, to live *better*. They had fostered a philosophy that acknowledged humanity's mistakes, its capacity for destruction, but also its profound ability to heal, to nurture, and to create beauty. The Arboreum was the physical manifestation of this philosophy. It was a place of deliberate growth, of patient cultivation, of interconnectedness. The plants thrived not just because of optimal conditions, but because they were tended with care, with respect, and with a deep understanding of their needs. This was the same philosophy that had guided Mara and Eli in rebuilding their community, in fostering trust, and in nurturing the fragile seeds of hope within its people.

Eli's contribution to the Arboreum was multifaceted. He had not only designed many of its intricate ecological systems, but he also possessed an almost intuitive understanding of the plants themselves. He could diagnose a wilting leaf with a glance, sensing the subtle imbalance in nutrients or the early signs of pest infestation. His hands, often calloused from working the soil, moved with a gentle precision as he pruned, grafted, or transplanted. He would often spend hours simply observing, sketching in his worn leather-bound notebook, his brow furrowed in concentration as he documented growth patterns or noted the complex interactions between different species. He saw the Arboreum as a symphony, each plant a unique instrument contributing to the overall harmony.

Mara, while not possessing Eli's innate botanical knowledge, brought a different, equally vital, set of skills to the project. Her understanding of logistics, resource management, and community organization was instrumental in ensuring the Arboreum's sustained success. She oversaw the distribution of produce, ensuring that everyone in Havenridge had access to fresh, nutritious food. She managed the allocation of resources for research and development, ensuring that the most promising projects received the support they needed. She also championed the educational programs, recognizing their crucial role in shaping the minds of future generations. She ensured that the Arboreum was not just a scientific marvel, but a community asset, accessible and beneficial to all.

The integration of the Arboreum into the daily life of Havenridge was seamless. Community work parties were a regular occurrence, not just for maintenance, but for the joy of shared creation. People from all walks of life would gather, their hands in the soil, their laughter echoing through the domes. These were not just work sessions; they were opportunities for connection, for shared purpose, for strengthening the bonds that held their society together. Elders shared stories of their youth, of gardens they had tended before the Quiet, while younger generations learned valuable skills and contributed their energy and fresh perspectives. The Arboreum had become a melting pot of generations, a place where the past informed the present, and the present was actively shaping the future.

One of the most visually striking features of the Arboreum was the 'Sunpetal Garden.' Here, under a vast, transparent dome, were cultivated a variety of plants that required intense sunlight. Towering sunflowers, their faces turned perpetually towards the simulated sun, stood alongside vibrant fields of medicinal herbs that flourished under direct light. In the center of the garden, a magnificent specimen of a 'Solara Lily,' a flower known for its remarkable ability to store and slowly release solar energy, bloomed with an almost incandescent radiance. Eli had spent years cultivating this particular species, carefully cross-breeding and nurturing it to enhance its bioluminescent properties. At dusk, as the simulated sunlight dimmed, the Sunpetal Garden would transform into a breathtaking spectacle of soft, golden light, bathing the entire area in a warm, inviting glow. It was a popular spot for quiet contemplation, for evening strolls, and for young couples to find a moment of romantic solitude.

The Arboreum's success was not without its challenges, of course. There were always unforeseen environmental shifts to manage, the occasional pest outbreak that required swift and precise intervention, and the ongoing need to innovate and adapt as new scientific knowledge emerged. But the community faced these challenges with a unified spirit, a testament to the resilience they had cultivated. They understood that growth, whether in a plant or in a society, was not always a smooth, linear progression. There were setbacks, periods of struggle, but the underlying commitment to nurturing life, to fostering connection, always prevailed.

Mara and Eli's enduring legacy was, in essence, the Arboreum itself. It was a living, breathing embodiment of their journey, a symbol of hope rekindled, of resilience affirmed. It represented the profound truth that even after the deepest darkness, even after the most profound silence, life, when given the space to adapt, to connect, and to be nurtured, would always find a way to bloom. The Arboreum stood as a constant reminder that survival was merely the first step; true living was about cultivating beauty, fostering connection, and embracing the boundless potential for growth that lay within both nature and humanity. It was a testament to their love, their partnership, and their unwavering belief in a future where life, in all its magnificent diversity, could not only endure but truly flourish. The gentle hum of the Arboreum's life support systems, once a sign of desperate ingenuity, was now a soothing lullaby, a constant affirmation of life's enduring power, a symphony of growth that echoed the profound peace Mara and Eli had found, and helped to create, in the heart of Havenridge. The legacy was not just in the plants, but in the people, who had learned to tend to each other with the same care and dedication they showed to the verdant world around them.

Appendix

The Arboreum, the central living sanctuary of Havenridge, was designed as a multi-biome geodesic structure. Its core functions included:

Hydroponic and Aeroponic Food Cultivation: Optimized for nutrient-rich vegetables, fruits, and grains adapted to controlled environments.

Medicinal Herb Cultivation and Research: Focused on resuscitating lost botanical knowledge for healing and developing remedies for environmental toxins and psychological trauma.

Biodiversity Preservation: Dedicated zones for endangered and extinct plant species, including the 'Whispering Grove' and the 'Sunpetal Garden.'

Environmental Regeneration: Research into soil remediation, atmospheric purification through specific flora, and sustainable water recycling systems.

Educational Hub: A living classroom for all ages, demonstrating ecological principles, sustainable agriculture, and intergenerational knowledge transfer.

Key species highlighted in the narrative include:

Solara Lily: A fictional species bred for its remarkable solar energy storage and release capabilities, contributing to the Arboreum's ambient lighting.

Bioluminescent Fungi: Used for natural, low-light illumination in shaded areas.

Adapted Grain and Legume Strains: Developed for high yield and nutritional value in controlled agricultural systems.

Resurrected Ancient Trees: Species like Redwood and various ferns, preserved in the 'Whispering Grove' as living links to Earth's past.

Arboreum: The central, meticulously cultivated botanical sanctuary and life-support system of Havenridge.

Havenridge: A community established in the post-Quiet era, dedicated to sustainable living and ecological balance.

The Quiet: The period of societal collapse and environmental degradation that preceded the establishment of Havenridge.

Geodesic Dome: The structural architecture of the Arboreum, providing a controlled and efficient environment.

Nutrient Delivery Systems: The integrated network for providing essential elements to the plants within the Arboreum.

Atmospheric Regulators: Systems that manage air quality, temperature, and humidity within the Arboreum.

Whispering Grove: A specific section within the Arboreum dedicated to the preservation of near-extinct plant species.

Sunpetal Garden: A sun-drenched zone within the Arboreum housing plants requiring intense light, featuring the Solara Lily.

Solara Lily: A fictional plant species known for its capacity to absorb and emit solar energy.

This work draws inspiration from a wide array of disciplines and real-world advancements. While fictionalized, the concepts explored in the Arboreum are informed by ongoing research in:

Sustainable Agriculture and Permaculture: Principles of ecological design, closed-loop systems, and biodiversity. (e.g., Works by Masanobu Fukuoka, Bill Mollison)

Vertical Farming and Controlled Environment Agriculture: Technologies for efficient food production in urban or challenging environments. (e.g., Research from agricultural science institutions)

Ethnobotany and Traditional Ecological Knowledge: The study of indigenous knowledge of plants and their uses, and the efforts to preserve this wisdom. (e.g., Research in anthropology and ethnobotany)

Biomimicry and Ecological Engineering: Design inspired by nature's solutions to environmental challenges. (e.g., Works by Janine Benyus)

Resilience Studies and Post-Collapse Societies: Theoretical frameworks for rebuilding societal structures after major disruptions. (e.g., Works in sociology, futurism)